THE WRANGLER

Lindsay McKenna

CHIVERS

British Library Cataloguing in Publication Data available

This Large Print edition published by AudioGO Ltd, Bath, 2013.

Published by arrangement with Harlequin Enterprises II B.V./S. à r.l.

U.K. Hardcover   ISBN   978 1 4713 2712 4
U.K. Softcover   ISBN   978 1 4713 2713 1

Printed and bound in Great Britain by
TJ International Limited

Dear Reader:

The Wrangler comes from my background of growing up in the rural West. Our neighbors were ranchers, sheepherders or farmers. At one time, we had a milk cow named Elizabeth. At six years old, I learned how to milk. Of course, our barn cats loved milking time, too. They would line up near my stool as I milked Elizabeth. I would take one teat and squirt the stream of warm milk toward the nearest cat. She would stand up on her hind legs, mouth open, gulping it down. Not a drop of milk ever hit the wooden floor. Or the time when a neighbor's milk cow had a calf and we got to watch it being birthed. I was lucky enough to have such experiences, and inevitably they end up in the pages of one of my books. I can only write what I know and share it with you. It's not always the big events of life that we remember, but the small, emotionally satisfying ones. Such as giving milk to the kitties at 5:00 a.m. on a chilly morning.

Ranching and farming are a hard way of life, but a worthy one in my opinion. My husband and I bred, raised and showed Arabian horses for a decade in Ohio. My love of horses has been around since I was a three-year-old, when I was put in the

5

saddle for the first time. Being close to the earth, working with it, not against it, brings a fondness to my heart. People raised in cities never know the joy of sitting in a saddle, mending a fence line, digging post holes, working on an old truck engine or repairing a hay baler. They've never seen real milk come from a cow. Or heard the bleat of a newborn lamb, or watched the struggling efforts of a tiny foal trying to get to her feet for the first time.

I hope to translate my rural life experiences to you in the Wyoming series. Griff McPherson is Slade's twin brother. You met Slade in *The Last Cowboy.* For Griff, born on a cattle ranch in Wyoming, his life is suddenly upended by tragedy. At only five years old, he lost his parents in a car accident. Luckily his uncle from New York City rescued him from a foster home and took him in. Griff went from rural to city life. And along the way he lost his Wyoming soul. This is a story of redemption. Many people are thrown brutal curves in life. Somehow their heart, their inner knowing can act like an unerring compass. It can help them turn around and head in the right direction. Griff is about to make a life-changing decision. Will his

Wyoming genes trump the call of rich city life or not?

Lindsay McKenna

Rosemarie Brown, astrologer extraordinaire, who has been a part of my life for more than twenty years and still counting . . . I'm very lucky to have walked at your side through the good times and the bad times. Above all, I cherish your wisdom, your heart and incredible vision. I hope the rest of your life is nothing but an ongoing rainbow of beauty, happiness and unfoldment. Longtime friends are like diamonds; they are dazzling, but in the case of friends, money can never buy them. Thanks for being there for me, and I'm glad I could be — and always will be — there for you when you need support. Unlike family, real friends stick with you through "thick 'n' thin." Friends, in my view, are a greater cosmic family and they love you, warts and all. Thank you.

CHAPTER ONE

Home . . . It was the *last* place that Val Hunter wanted to be. She stood in the coolness of the Wyoming morning facing her past. The taxi had just dropped her off at the main house of the Bar H ranch. She bitterly recalled when her father, Buck Hunter, had remodeled the old one-story log home. Now, the house rose two stories and looked like an iconic cedar palace. Val's mouth quirked as she heard the robins singing in the background. They sounded so happy in contrast to how she felt.

She had to enter the home and let her grandmother, Augusta Hunter, know that she'd arrived. Gus, as everyone called her, had been the only bright spot in Val's upbringing. And she owed it to Gus to come home even though her heart felt weighted. Hot tears jammed into her eyes and Val hung her head and fought them back. Compressing her lips once her eyes were cleared, she picked up her two suitcases and slowly trudged up the cedar stairs as if she were going to her death.

After knocking on the huge wooden door with the emblem for Bar H carved across it, Val waited. It didn't take long for a small woman with short silver hair to answer.

"Val!" she cried, her face lighting up.

"Hi, Gus. I made it home."

Throwing her arms around her grand-daughter, Gus held her for a long time. "Thank you for coming," Gus said in a wobbly voice. She released Val and stood back, a cane in her left hand. "Come in. I have coffee waitin' for us."

Giving her short, wiry grandmother a forced half smile, Val picked up her luggage. It was always chilly on Wyoming mornings in June. "Thanks," she murmured, setting down the bags and closing the door behind her. Gus hobbled on her cane as she limped down the hall. "I'll take these to my old bedroom?"

"Yep, it's waiting for you." Gus pointed toward the polished stairs. "You get settled in and then come down and join me in the kitchen. Have you eaten?"

"Yes, I got breakfast on the flight over to Jackson Hole," Val said. Gus halted at the opening on the right, which led to a huge kitchen. A kitchen that her father had built for her mother, Cheryl, many years earlier. Bitterness swept through Val. She passed her grandmother and headed up the stairs.

Her father had been violently drunk one night. He'd beat her mother so badly that she'd had to remain in the hospital for three days. After she got home, Buck had been apologetic and promised her that kitchen she'd always dreamed of having. He hadn't built it because he loved Cheryl. No, it was a kitchen created out of guilt, terror and pain.

The hollow echo of her feet on the stairs sounded like an invisible ball and chain from the past. Her old bedroom was to the right of the stairs. Everything looked the same, as if time hadn't touched it. Yet, as Val trudged unwillingly toward her room of terrible memories, she wondered how her grandmother managed to keep the house so clean. It was a large two-story home and Gus had broken her hip shortly after Cheryl died. Before that, Gus and Cheryl had lived here at the Bar H together, barely keeping it on life support. Val was ready to pull the plug on it.

Nudging the bedroom door open with the toe of her shoe, Val stepped into her hated past. On the bed, she saw the colorful flying geese quilt that Gus had made for her when she was ten years old. She set the bags on the floor, staring at the red, white and blue quilt. How many times had she wrapped herself up in it pretending that Gus was there, holding her? Holding her safe against her father? Of course, back then, Gus had lived with her husband, Pete, on a five-thousand-acre spread near Cheyenne, Wyoming. And Val knew her mother had worked hard not to let Gus know what was really going on at the Bar H.

Sighing, Val turned and studied the quiet room. There were frilly white curtains bracketing the large window, light pouring in and making it seem far more peaceful than she felt. Her childhood had returned. Only this time, her mother or father weren't present. It was an odd, uncomfortable feeling and Val didn't know how to deal with it. Why had she agreed to come home?

She went back downstairs. The only comfort in this life change she was making was being with her feisty eighty-four-year-old grandmother. Entering the warm kitchen, she saw Gus setting two mugs of steaming coffee on the rectangular cedar table.

"Ah, there you are. Come and sit down," Gus invited with a smile. "I've got your sugar and cream here." She noodled an arthritic finger toward the white porcelain containers sitting in the center of the table.

"Why don't you sit down, Gus? You're the one with a broken hip." Val pulled out a chair for her grandmother.

"Thanks, honey." Gus slowly lowered herself into it and propped the cane against the edge of the table. Smiling up at her, she murmured, "I can't tell you how good it is that you're home." Gus gestured to the other side of the table. "Come on, sit down, Val. Let's talk over coffee. That's always a soothing, positive activity." Gus chuckled indulgently.

Val couldn't help but smile. As she walked around the table and sat opposite her silver-haired grandmother with her sparkling, lively blue eyes, a tiny part of her felt happy. The burden of the years living at the Bar H had overwhelmed any optimistic feelings. Picking up the creamer, Val said, "This is nice. Thanks for having coffee ready for me."

"God's lifeline." Gus picked up her mug of black coffee. She raised it in a toast and then took a sip. "Westerners and their coffee are one and the same." Sliding her work-worn fingers around the white mug, Gus watched Val as she poured the cream and sugar into her coffee. "I'm really sorry that I had to ask you to leave your career in the

Air Force and come back home. I know what kind of courage it took to walk away from something you loved in order to help me."

Val tasted the strong coffee and set the mug down. She reached across the table and brushed her grandmother's hand. "I wouldn't have done it for anyone else," she said in a whisper, a catch in her tone. "You know that."

Gus puckered her thin lips and nodded gravely. "You know, honey, when your mama died last year and you came home for the funeral, I knew . . ."

"Knew what?"

Gus shrugged and smiled a little. "I had this feeling you were coming home for good. Oh, I know you swore never to return." Her silver brows fell and she scowled. "What I didn't know is three months after your ma's passin', I'd fall out there at the corral and bust my femur." She touched her right hip in memory of the accident.

"I know you're giving up your career as an intelligence officer for this ranch."

"I'm not doing it for the ranch. I'm doing it for *you.*"

Gus was truly a savior in Val's life. Shortly after Cheryl had been released from the hospital that time Buck had laid into her,

16

Gus had suddenly lost her husband to a massive stroke. After the funeral, Gus had sold her husband's ranch and moved into the Bar H house. Val soon discovered Buck wouldn't beat up her and her mother with Gus around. From that time forward, she remembered Gus as a guardian angel.

The tough woman rancher might have been only five foot tall and a weighed a mere hundred pounds, but Buck wasn't about to push the envelope on her fierce protectiveness. And that's exactly what Val and her mother had needed: protection from Buck. Gus had been a shield against her father for Val's last two years spent in this house and for that she was forever grateful to her grandmother.

Reaching out, Val took Gus's hand and squeezed it. "You saved us from harm and that's why I came back. I wanted to pay you back for what you did for Mom and me."

Gus sighed and her blue eyes teared up as she squeezed Val's fingers. She gave Val a trembling smile and released her hand. "I didn't know what Buck was doing until he landed your mother in the hospital. Cheryl never let on, not until I visited her in the hospital that time. Lord knows, I wished I'd known sooner."

"My father was so careful to bruise me

where no one would see it," Val muttered. "He knew what he was doing. But my mother didn't have the guts to call the sheriff. I still can't believe she'd let my father beat the hell out of me." Val shook her head, anger bubbling up within her as it always did when she thought about that time in her life. "Why didn't my mother ever protect us, Gus?"

"Honey," Gus said gently, "your ma was so beaten down by that bastard that she didn't know she could ask for help and get it."

"Why didn't you take that information to the sheriff, Gus? I could never understand."

"Because your ma pleaded with me not to. She wanted to go back to Buck. She said she loved him. And when Pete suddenly died, I knew I had to get over here. I felt Buck would leave you two alone if I was in the house, and I was right. So while I couldn't go to the authorities, I did the next best thing."

"You have no idea how grateful I was that you moved here, Gus." Val gave her a look of admiration. "You gave up your whole way of life in order to protect us. I'll never forget what you did."

Giving her a gentle look, Gus said, "Honey, I'd do it all over again. I have no

18

regrets about any of my decisions. My gut told me that Buck would stop if I was around. He was the kind of man who was so wounded, so scarred by life, that all he knew how to do was take his anger out on others. Truth be told, I had a baseball bat hidden in the closet and I swore to myself that if he *ever* lifted a pinkie against either of you, I was going to beat the hell outta him." Gus gave her a wicked smile.

Val knew she meant it. Even Buck knew it. "You're a force of nature, Gus. You always have been." Val managed a slight smile toward her plucky grandmother.

Val unconsciously rubbed her tightened stomach. Looking around the warm, bright kitchen, she uttered, "This place is nothing but a vat of lousy memories for me, Gus."

Gus reached out and patted her hand. "Honey, I know how much I was asking of you when I made that phone call to you in Bahrain. I knew you hated Buck and hated this house."

Val slipped her hands around the mug of hot coffee. Warmth against the iciness inhabiting her knotted gut. "Like I said, I'm here because of you, Gus. If you hadn't broken your hip, I couldn't have gotten out of the Air Force. Because of the situation, I was able to get what they call a hardship discharge."

"I'm so glad you're here. An elder like me with a cranky hip can't run this place alone."

"Gus, why save the Bar H at all?" Val drilled a look into her grandmother's wrinkled, darkly tanned features.

"Why not?" The elder perked up, feisty now. "This is your *home,* Val. It doesn't have to always be the terrible place it was for you as a child. You can create happy memories here, too. I had to sell our ranch in Cheyenne and it was the last thing I wanted to do. Pete's family started that ranch a hundred and twenty years ago. It broke my heart to have to leave it in order to come back here. But I did it. Sometimes, life puts huge demands on us we don't want to face. But we must sacrifice for a greater good."

Guiltily, Val said, "You gave up so much. I knew you were grieving for Grandpa Pete's passing. And I know you two spent your sixty years together building that spread into a profitable ranch. You walked away from all of it for us, Gus. Even at sixteen I realized the terrible sacrifice you made for us."

"I did it," Gus said, her voice firm, "because you two were far more important than our ranch. Family comes first. Always. You're my granddaughter and all I ever wanted for you was happiness."

"That didn't happen," Val said in a rasp, fighting back rising emotions. She held her grandmother's teary blue gaze.

"I just wanted to put this whole damn thing behind me, Gus. I never wanted to be here again."

"Then," Gus said gently, "maybe it's time to start healing up from it? Everyone deserves to have a home. A place where they came from. A place where they can come back to and call their own. Us Westerners believe in family, home and loyalty. Maybe between you and me some healing and good might come from this."

"You're such an optimist, Gus."

Perking up, she grinned. "Yes, I hold out hope for hopeless, that's for sure. Pete always called me a cockeyed idealist," and she chuckled.

Laughing a little with her grandmother, Val took a sip of the hearty coffee. She thought back on her life since she'd left this ranch. She'd gone to college at eighteen. From there, she went into the Air Force. She was twenty-eight now. She'd only spent six years in the military and had been counting on making it to twenty years so she'd have a pension. "This ranch's back is broken, Gus. The corrals are in terrible shape. The barn needs a new roof. I don't see any cattle. I see a few horses out in one pasture. This place is not a moneymaker, it's nothing but a money pit."

Nodding, Gus said, "After Buck died of a heart attack, your mother made a lot of poor choices insofar as hiring good wranglers. It wasn't her fault. She didn't know how to budget because Buck kept her out of the money and finances. He refused to let her know anything about the running of the ranch, and he took all his knowledge of keeping this ranch solvent to the grave with him. I tried to pick up the slack, figure out the accounting books, but there was only so much I could do."

Val recalled that time. "I celebrated when Mom told me Buck had died."

"No one can blame you, honey. But without Buck, this ranch went to hell in a handbasket. Your mom was depressed. No matter what kind of medication the doctors put her on, she spiraled deeper and deeper into a very dark place. I couldn't talk or reason with her. She just locked herself away in her room."

Val's heart wrung with pain over her mother's decline. She hadn't been there to help her. She'd run as far away as she could.

"When it came to finding the accounting books," Gus continued, "and then discovering all the places Buck squirreled money away, it took me a year to figure it all out. And your mother, by that time, had been diagnosed with the most virulent form of breast cancer and she died six months afterward."

Val recalled the phone calls, the fact her mother was drifting away from her. Val had felt abandoned and adrift. "I remember the funeral."

"Yes, and I remember telling you not to worry, that I could handle the Bar H. I felt at the time, I could bring it back bit by bit. But your mom chose wranglers like she chose Buck. They were young men who talked the talk but couldn't walk the walk. That series of wranglers did nothing but allow the ranch to slide further into destruction. Good wranglers are worth their weight in gold."

"And then, you fell and broke your hip," Val said. She saw what the Bar H meant to her grandmother because of the fierce look that sparked in her watery blue eyes. Her jaw was set. Val knew the bulldog feistiness she'd always possessed was there even at eighty-four. "But even if that hadn't happened, no one person could ever run this two-hundred-acre ranch by themselves."

"No, I couldn't. And then the hip replacement went wrong, and I'm stuck with this damned cane for the rest of my life. I can't ride a horse or go out and mend the fences. So much was taken away from me when I broke my hip, Val. I grieved over this situation a long time before calling and asking you to come home. I don't want to see this ranch sold, too. It broke my heart to sell ours. I cried for weeks over that decision. I was hurting so badly from Pete suddenly being torn away from me, too. We were a good team. The best of friends. And then, suddenly, in one moment, he was gone. . . ."

Val reached out and gripped her grandmother's hand, its knuckles slightly enlarged with arthritis. "You've had to go through so much, Gus. I'm sorry."

"Oh, honey, I know you are. We've all gone through our share, it seems. When Cheryl would bring you to visit our ranch in Cheyenne, I couldn't understand why you were such a shy shadow that hid from all of us. And every time Pete came near you, you were like a wild horse running in the other direction. Lord, how I wish I had picked up on your reactions properly. After the fact, I talked to a therapist about abused children. It was then I realized you were terribly wounded and wouldn't trust *any* man. Not even my Pete. And he was one of the most gentle, loving men you could ever meet."

Dragging in a huge breath of air, Val felt as if the weight of the world was bearing down on her shoulders. "Gus, you can't blame yourself for not knowing what was going on. I myself wish I'd done something. If only I'd called the sheriff. Or talked to one of my teachers."

"Don't go there," Gus warned her. "You were innocent in all of his, Val. You were a trusting, vulnerable child."

Hot tears wedged into Val's eyes. With an angry swipe, she wiped them away. "I just couldn't *ever* understand why my Mom lied to the doctors when she was taken to the hospital. She had a broken arm and collar bone, eyes blackened and both cheeks fractured. And she lied to them! She told them she'd been bucked off a horse, hit the pipe corral fence and then fell to the ground." Gulping, Val stared helplessly at Gus. "They *believed* her! When you came here and told me that, I just felt like I was going to implode with rage."

"You were raised in a toxic environment, so you thought love was being beat. You never knew any different as a child. How could you?"

"I've tried so hard to *forget* my past!" Val

choked, the tears flowing down her taut cheeks. "When you asked me to come here, I threw up. I couldn't hold back the fear, the memories avalanching me again."

Gus scraped the chair back, picked up her cane and hobbled around the table. Leaning down, she slipped one arm around Val's shoulders and kissed her red hair. "You've had nothing but pain from the time you were born," Gus agreed. "But you listen to me. You're a Hunter. You have the blood of my family running strong through you, Val. I know this is the hardest thing you've ever done, but really, it isn't."

Val lifted her head, the tears blurring her grandmother's deeply wrinkled face inches away from hers. "W-what do you mean?"

"Honey," Gus said in a whisper, placing a kiss on her wrinkled brow, "the worst was living in this house when Buck was alive. He's dead and gone now. I know you have the past to work through, but he ain't here any longer. That makes this easier than the first eighteen years of your life, doesn't it?" She gently held Val's tearful blue gaze.

"I — I don't know."

"I do. Besides," Gus said, gently wiping the tears from Val's pale cheeks, "you have *me*. Together, you and I are a force to behold. We can bring this ranch back to life, and make it even better than before. We can make it beautiful, successful and you'll have the money you need for when you want to retire." Giving her a soft smile, Gus added, "Family should be a team, Val. Oh, it's true, there's always a rotten apple in every family barrel, but don't walk away from it all just because of one person. Your ma put her heart and soul into the Bar H. Now, we'll do the same. Together . . ."

CHAPTER TWO

The sweet smell of alfalfa hay entered Griff McPherson's nostrils. He walked into the large, airy barn, carrying a huge baling hook in each of his hands. A ranch customer had backed his Chevy truck up against the lip of the wooden platform and was waiting for twenty bales to be placed onto its bed. Sweat trickled down the sides of Griff's temples as he approached the first bale and quickly sank the long, sharp hooks into it. With a grunt, he hefted the eighty-pound bale out of the building and dropped it into the truck. He reveled in his strength, feeling close to the earth and to all life of late. Working at Andy's Horse Emporium, a central place in the valley for ranchers to buy hay, feed and other supplies gave him deep and growing satisfaction.

Just having a job in this sputtering economy made Griff feel grateful as he walked quickly back into the barn. His well-worn boots thunked hollowly against the graying oak plank floor. Andy had taken pity on him when Griff's brother Slade had kicked him out of the family ranch house. Mouth tightening as he leaned down and hooked a second bale, Griff turned and walked it out to the truck.

There was another full-time young man working at the Emporium with him, and between the two of them, they were kept busy all day long. It was hard, physical work and Griff absorbed it with quiet joy. It was a far cry from his days as a banker on Wall Street. As he hefted another bale and carried it out of the barn, he glanced up at the blue morning sky. How could he ever have left Jackson Hole, the place he was born and raised? The Tetons Ranch had been in his family for a hundred years. His *soul* was here. How could he have not come home as soon as he'd turned eighteen?

The third bale was dropped into the pickup. Griff leaped down into the bed of the Chevy and expertly arranged the bales so he could make a solid foundation for the rest to come. Inhaling deeply, his white cowboy shirt clinging to his body, Griff smiled to himself. In one easy, fluid leap he was back on the platform. Grabbing the hooks with his sweat-stained leather gloves, he moved into the shade of the barn. His mind lingered on his past life, working in derivatives at his uncle's Wall Street firm. When the crash hit, he'd been out of a job. Coming home had been a rough landing.

The air was full of fine dust and bits of the alfalfa that had been trucked in for ranchers in need for their horses or cattle. The growing season in this part of Wyoming was only seventy days and not long enough to grow a crop of either alfalfa or grass hay. It all had to be brought in from nearby Idaho or from other surrounding states. And it made the price higher than usual.

Griff's nostrils flared as he sank the hooks into the next bale. In about twenty minutes, he'd have the order filled, the bales neatly stacked upon one another, tied in place with the rancher's stout nylon straps so they wouldn't fall off during transit. The work satisfied him. It was far better than sitting in a chair staring at a computer and translating graphs and analysis. He was born into a Wyoming ranch family. And God, it was good to be back home even if it meant living hand to mouth. If not for Andy hiring him to work five days a week, Griff knew he'd have to leave Jackson Hole for a soup kitchen in a major city.

"Hey," Andy hollered to him from the office across the way, "when you get done, I need you in here, Griff. There's a lady in here lookin' to hire a full-time wrangler."

Straightening, Griff pushed the tan Stetson cowboy hat off his brow. "Fifteen minutes," he called back. He saw Andy nod, raise his hand in acknowledgment and disappear back inside the main store. Lifting the hat off his head, Griff quickly wiped his brow. He could smell his sweat. It came from good, hard work. He now realized he'd been wasting away in New York City. Out west, he was once again hard-muscled, physically fit and ready to take on his newly evolving world.

Val watched Andy return to the front desk where she stood waiting. She had received a warm welcome from him when she'd first walked in the door. He'd recognized her right away. "Griff will be in here in about fifteen minutes," he told her.

Val felt leery. "Are you *sure* he's a good wrangler, Andy?"

"Yep, I am," the man said, ringing up her items at a cash register.

"But, you said he's only been here a couple of months."

"I know you've been gone a long time, Miss Val, but surely you know Slade

31

McPherson? Owner of the Tetons Ranch?"

"Yes, of course. Everyone thinks well of him."

"Griff is Slade's younger fraternal twin brother. Now, you recall that at six years old these two boys lost their parents?"

Scrunching her brow, Val tried to remember. "I was young at the time, Andy. Humor me?"

"That you were. And you're still young and beautiful, Miss Val," he said with a wink. "Slade and Griff's parents were killed in an auto accident. Red Downing, who owned the ranch next to them, was drunk when he struck them. All three of them died in that tragic event. The two boys were split up. Slade stayed with a local uncle and Griff got shipped out to New York City to the other uncle who owned a financial services firm. Griff went on to get an MBA from Harvard and became a banker at his uncle's company. That is, until the Wall Street crash. Griff came home hoping that his older brother would hire him, but he couldn't."

"I see," Val said. "He's a city slicker, then, Andy."

"Ah, well . . . sort of . . . but he's a darned hard worker, Miss Val. He isn't lazy. He likes what he's doing, and he's good at it."

Val found that hard to believe. "My

mother was really poor at picking good wranglers. I don't want to follow in her footsteps, Andy."

Andy gave her a sad look. "Your mom was really hurting, Miss Val. I tried to tell her the men she was hiring were lazy and no good, but she didn't listen."

"Did she come in here to ask for a referral?"

With a heavy shake of his head, Andy said, "You know Buck hated me and my store. He was always badmouthing me. It's no wonder your mom, after his death, didn't come in here for my help. I would gladly have offered it."

Reaching out, Val touched the man's arm. "I'm so sorry, Andy. I really am."

"Hey," he said, brightening, "it's not your fault. You're *not* your father's daughter, thank goodness. Give yourself credit — you came to me and asked for a good wrangler. Griff won't let you down. Now, he's green, that's true, but he's eager to learn and he makes things right."

"I don't know. When has a city slicker ever turned into a wrangler?"

Chuckling a little, Andy leaned his hands on the counter. "I know what you're saying, Miss Val. But Griff is changing *my* mind about that old saying, too. I didn't think he

33

could reinvent himself. But he has."

"Work is hard to find," Val agreed. "I'm just worried that he has too high-powered a résumé to want to stick it out as a wrangler. As soon as this economy turns around, he'll be gone. We really need someone long-term who will work with us to get the Bar H back on its feet."

"I know," Andy said in a soothing voice. "I hear you, Miss Val. I can't stand here and say Griff won't leave at some point. I really don't know. What I do know is he's been invaluable to us here at the Emporium. It'll be a shame to lose him but I know he'll do a great job for you. He's a good mechanic, fixing engines and other ranch equipment, and that's what you need."

McPherson sounded like the right man, but her gut warned her against getting her hopes up. She looked toward the back door where Val knew he would be coming in any minute now. "Can you give me fifteen minutes to talk with him? To see if he's really what we're looking for, Andy?"

"Sure." He pointed to the coffee station at the rear of the store. "You two help your-selves to coffee and then go out back to talk. You'll have privacy out there."

Val saw the door open. She wasn't pre-pared for her reaction to the person who entered the shop.

Griff McPherson was tall, about six feet three inches, a hundred and eighty pounds of lean, cougar muscle. When he took off his tan Stetson hat, she got a good look at his face. His short black hair was plastered against his skull with sweat. His face was square with a broad brow, clean-looking nose and a stubborn-looking jaw. It was his startling spring-colored green eyes, large and filled with intelligence, that snagged her beating heart. He was ruggedly handsome, Val thought.

In fact, he could easily pose as a model for a marketing ad. She saw him remove his stained leather gloves and tuck them into the belt of his Levi's. The dusty white shirt he wore clung to his upper body, outlining his broad shoulders and well-sprung chest. And when he lifted his head, his gaze settling on hers, Val quickly lowered her eyes. She felt shaky. And excited. And scared. What were all these crazy-quilt emotions about? Confused and taken off guard, she didn't have time to process them.

"Miss Val, meet Griff McPherson," Andy said, and gestured for the wrangler to come over and shake her hand.

"Miss Val, nice to meet you." Griff held his hat in his left hand and extended his right one toward Val Hunter as he took her in. She was beautiful. He searched his mind trying to remember her. Was she new to the area? Unsure, he managed a slight smile as she lifted her head and looked up at him. Val wasn't short. In fact, she was only about four inches shy of his height. And she was fit, her body long and reminding him of a supple young tree. It was her dark blue eyes that looked like deep pools of water from a nearby lake, that grabbed at his heart. Instantly, Griff felt heat move through him as their hands met and clasped. Val's face was oval, cheekbones high, eyes wide spaced and filled with intelligence. As his gaze dropped to her bow-shaped lips, he felt his entire lower body tighten with desire. Shocked at his response to her, he quickly released her hand.

"Andy said you were looking for a full-time wrangler?" he said.

Clearing her throat, her hand pleasantly tingling, Val said, "Yes, I'm here to interview candidates." She didn't want this eye candy of a cowboy to think this was a done deal.

"Of course," Griff said.

"Andy invited us to get a cup of coffee and go outside to talk." Val gestured toward the coffee station.

Griff gave his a boss a quick look. "My

break time?"

"Yep," Andy said with a grin.

Val couldn't get her heart to settle down. The man walked a respectful distance behind her. She strained to pour the hot coffee into an awaiting paper cup without spilling it. Mouth dry, she felt tongue-tied in front of this iconic-looking cowboy. She had to repeatedly warn herself he was a city slicker in disguise.

"I'll meet you outside." Val hastily opened the door. She saw him nod as he reached to pour himself a cup of coffee.

On the back porch, Val took a long, calming breath. The wrangler had rattled her. Her reaction wasn't something she'd expected. Val tried to steady her heart and breathing. How could a stranger take away her breath? She knew she'd been too long without a relationship. The last man she had been with, Dan Bradley, was a Marine major who had gone to Afghanistan and been killed two years ago. He'd stolen her heart, infused her dreams and she had been looking forward to marrying him once his tour was over. She had yet to fully recover from the loss. The next year, her mother had died. Most recently, she'd had to walk away from her career to save the Bar H. Pressing a hand to her chest, Val tried not to dwell on all the loss and sadness she carried within her. Funny enough, Griff made her forget all of the baggage and scars life had given her. It was an amazing and shocking moment. Val had no answer as to why he could have affected her so.

"Miss Val?" Griff murmured, meeting her out on the platform. He settled his hat on his head as he approached her. He noticed she looked distracted and nervous and he wondered why. Griff remained a respectful distance from the woman. He silently appreciated her rosy cheeks and sparkling blue eyes that spoke of such life in their depths. Why hadn't he seen her around Jackson Hole? Was she a stranger to the area? Had she just bought a ranch? Griff's curiosity was piqued.

"Yes, Mr. McPherson. My grandmother, Gus, would like me to find a wrangler who can help us around the Bar H ranch." She gulped inwardly and looked up to meet his narrowing green gaze. He had such large, black pupils and it made him look incredibly handsome. His mouth . . . oh, sweet Lord, his mouth was sinfully shaped, the lips neither too thin nor too thick. The corners were curved slightly upward. She wondered if he had a good sense of humor.

"The Bar H? Isn't that a two-hundred-acre spread south of Jackson Hole?"

"Yes, it is." Val moved uneasily and barely tolerated his interested gaze. Why did McPherson have to be so blatantly masculine? "Gus broke her hip recently. She can't do the work as she did before and we need help. Good help."

"I'm sorry to hear that." Griff sipped his coffee. He liked the way Val's slightly curled red hair lay across her shoulders. She stood with her back straight, her chin at an angle. She was a proud woman. "I've heard of Gus. My brother, Slade, said there were several matriarchs in the valley. Iris Mason is one and I've met her. And he also mentioned Gus. I don't suppose there would be another Gus?"

"No, just the one." She liked his low, mellow voice. It was the kind of voice that could soothe a fractious horse. Or a nervous female like herself. "I had to come home to help her. And even I can't do it all alone."

He bit back his questions. Val was tense, her shoulders locked. Was he affecting her that way? Griff hoped not, because if it was him he could kiss this job goodbye. "I see. You don't have any wranglers at the Bar H right now?"

"No." Val grimaced. "My mother didn't hire any good ones. They left the place a wreck, took her money and disappeared into the night."

Ouch. Griff nodded and frowned. She was probably tense because she wanted to hire someone with better morals and values. He hoped Andy had spoken well of him because his dream job was to become a full-time wrangler on a ranch. Andy knew working here was temporary until some rancher could hire him. "Wranglers are the grist that make a ranch work."

His modulated voice wafted through her like a feather gently settling upon her wildly beating heart. Val could tell Griff was sincere. "No question about that." Val cleared her throat. "I need to know what your skills are, Mr. McPherson."

"I'm a hard worker," he said, opening his hand to show her the palm, "but I think my calluses will attest to that." He smiled a little.

Val stared at his large, well-shaped hand. Indeed, there were thick calluses across his palm. What a beautiful hand. For a blinding instant, she wondered what it would be like to have those fingers graze her flesh. The thought was so startling, so out of the blue, that Val unexpectedly coughed. She stepped away from him, a hand pressed against her slender throat.

Griff allowed his hand to drop back to his side. Val Hunter looked absolutely confused. About him? Something was going on between them but he couldn't ferret out exactly what it was. One thing Griff knew for sure: Val was very athletic. She wore a set of Levi's that showed off her shapely hips and long, long legs. The pink blouse she wore had its long sleeves rolled up to her elbows, showing that she was ready to work. He liked the way the breeze played with some of the strands of her copper-colored hair. The freckles across her cheeks and nose seemed darker for a moment. She looked like a young teen, although Griff suspected she was probably in her late twenties.

"I can mend fence, fix trucks and other farm equipment, do any odd jobs you need done," he said after she seemed to have regained her composure.

"Have you done any cattle breeding? Vaccinating? Do you know the signs of a cow in distress?"

"No," he admitted slowly, "but I'm willing to learn if you're willing to show me." He wanted to lie and say he did, but Griff wouldn't do that. He had the integrity of a Westerner in his blood. He knew from his old job that young men and women would lie all the time about their skills and experience just to get a job. He wasn't going to lie to Val. Griff saw her brows dip over his admittance.

"Do you even ride a horse?" she demanded. Val saw his mouth curve faintly.

"Yes, ma'am, I do ride."

Looking down, Val studied his long, muscular legs. "Most wranglers I've met have bowed legs, from all the riding they do. You don't."

"I only got here a few months ago." Griff realized this interview wasn't going well. "I worked at my brother's ranch. I did a lot of riding, moving cattle, roping and branding there." He gave her a slight grin and pointed to his legs. "I haven't had enough saddle time to bow them properly — yet."

"Do you have your own horse?"

"No, I don't. I rent a room at the Mac-Murray house on the west side of town and there's no room there to own a dog or cat, much less a horse."

"Andy said you just came from back east?"

The question was hurled like a gauntlet at him. Griff didn't lose his slight smile. "New York City. Yes, I'm a city slicker, Miss Val." He saw surprise in her expression. A faint blush fanned across her cheeks and her freckles momentarily darkened.

"Andy said you were a good worker." She ignored his humor.

He glanced at the barn over his shoulder and hooked his thumb in the same direction. "I work six a.m. to three p.m. daily. I haul hay, feed and other items to the trucks."

"And what do you do when you get off work?" It was a personal question, but Val's curiosity got the better of her.

"I take odd jobs with any rancher that needs a little extra muscle or a mechanic."

Val knew it spoke of his work ethic and she nodded. "Gus wants a man who can do it all, Mr. McPherson. She's paying ten dollars an hour and we put in twelve-hour days. Not eight. Although you'll get paid for eight." Val thought for sure the poor pay would make him refuse the potential job on the spot.

"My brother works from dawn to dark. I would expect the same on any ranch."

"There's a lot of cleanup to be done. The property has been let go for years. The barn needs a new roof. The shed not only needs a roof, but new siding, as well. I have four wooden corrals and they all need post replacement. I've got piles of manure that need to be shoveled into a truck and then taken to the dump. The place is in ruins."

Val drilled him with a hard look, thinking that for sure he wouldn't want to do those jobs, which were expected of a wrangler. She was betting his Eastern upbringing would make him walk away.

"I've already worked at taking out posts, digging new post holes and putting in both wood and pipe fences."

"Most of the work we need is not done on a horse," Val warned. She just didn't think he could do it all. Yet, he looked easygoing and completely confident as she handed him the duty list.

Shrugging, he said, "That's what I found to be true, too. Getting to throw a leg over a horse is a real gift compared to the everyday work on the ground."

Frowning, Val sipped her coffee. She took a step back, making sure she didn't get too close to this cowboy. He didn't seem to be aware of his effect on her. She'd expected with his deadly good looks, he'd be arrogant. Instead, McPherson was quiet, thoughtful and seemed to listen. Those were all qualities Val knew many men did not have. "Well, whoever we hire," she muttered, "they're going to be busting their butt day in and day out."

"That's fine," Griff answered. "I'm looking for a long-haul kind of job."

44

Her eyes widened. "Really?"

Hearing the disbelief in her voice, Griff wondered if Andy had told her about his past life and career. "Yes, ma'am, I am." He looked around and added, "I was born in Wyoming and love it here. I like waking up in the morning and seeing a clear blue sky, smelling fresh air instead of gas pollution and hearing the robins singing instead of sirens and car horns blaring." Griff turned and met her lustrous blue gaze. "I'm sure Andy told you I grew up in New York City. The truth is, I hated it. I didn't know it then, but I do now." Gesturing toward the sky, he added, "I like the smell of the air after a rain. In the city, all you got was a dampening down of pollution. I spent a lot of time in Central Park, looking to reconnect with nature. I prefer grass under my feet to concrete."

Mesmerized by the wistfulness in his voice, Val gulped. "That's all fine and dandy, Mr. McPherson, but I don't have time to teach you the skills you're missing. We need a man who can do it all right now."

"I understand," Griff said, regret in his voice. "I admit I'm not fully qualified. But maybe if you let your grandmother know that I'm a fast learner and will make up for it, she might think about hiring me?"

"I'll tell her," Val promised.

"Great, let me give you my cell phone number. Could you let me know what her final decision is? I'd really like the job. It sounds like it's difficult but I like a challenge." Griff smiled a little and drew a business card out of his pocket. When their fingers met briefly, he felt a zigzag of heat move through his hand. He saw confusion and unsureness in Val's eyes as she hesitantly took the card. She placed it in the back pocket of her Levi's.

"We'll let you know shortly." She pulled the door open and disappeared into the Horse Emporium. Andy gave her a questioning look, as she approached the counter. Lifting her hand, she thanked Andy and left. As she climbed into the ranch's red Ford pickup truck, Val felt all the tension flow out of her. She wondered if Gus would want this greenhorn wrangler or not. Val sure didn't. He was powerfully male and it called to her dormant femininity in a way she'd never experienced. The truth, Val realized, was that she was drawn to McPherson. Woman to man. It was raw. Untamed. And it scared the hell out of her.

CHAPTER THREE

"What did you think of the wrangler?" Gus asked her granddaughter as they sat together in the kitchen. "You looked concerned when you came in."

Val sipped her coffee as she eyed Gus. "Nothing gets past you, does it?"

Mouth turning down, Gus said, "I wish that were true. If it were, I'd have seen what Buck was doing to you and my daughter out here."

Reaching over, Val touched her grandmother's wrinkled, brown-spotted hand. "You lived clear across the state and my mother wasn't telling you what was really going on here at the ranch."

"Doesn't matter. I should have been more nosey."

"Well," Val replied, "that's over."

"It is and it isn't," Gus pointed out. She studied Val and pursed her lips. "Beating an animal or human makes them scared."

Laughing, Val said, "I'm hardly the scared type, Gus."

"We'll see. . . ."

Val had no way to understand her grandmother's enigmatic statement. "Well, Andy said this man, Griff McPherson, was a good wrangler and was looking for steady work."

Her thin silver brows rising, Gus said, "McPherson? The Tetons Ranch folks?"

"Yes, one and the same. From what Andy said, his brother Slade owns and runs the family ranch now."

"But, Griff is here in Jackson Hole? And not working for Slade?" Wrinkling her brow, Gus muttered, "That sure don't make common sense. Families out here stick together like glue through thick and thin. I would expect him to be working with Slade. Not at the Horse Emporium."

Shrugging, Val said, "Andy didn't get into specifics." She shared with Gus her talk with the wrangler. Val left out the fact he was mouthwateringly handsome. She didn't want her grandmother to get the wrong idea.

"Okay, so he's not a polished-off wrangler." Gus rubbed her chin. "But it sounds like he wants to work. And that's the kind of spirit we need around here. He can be taught whatever he's missing."

"Gus, we have ten-percent unemployment in the U.S. There are a lot of people out of work and looking for anything in order to survive. He's just one of those poor people."

Gus considered the information. "Let me guess, you don't want to hire him because he's an ex-city slicker."

"Well . . . yes and no. But same as you, I wonder why he's not working with his brother."

"Slade just got married to Dr. Jordana Lawton," Gus informed her. "I imagine the ranch belongs to both of them now."

"You'd think that Slade would hire his brother part-time, though, if he could. Griff said he does odd jobs for other ranchers around the county on weekends."

"Maybe there's bad blood between them we don't know about. From the sounds of it, I like his work ethic. This guy is busting his hump seven days a week to make ends meet. And you know ranchers won't put up with a lazy wrangler. They get fired real fast."

"All except here at the Bar H." Val saw Gus quirk her thinned lips and nod her head.

"No disagreement there. Well, what should we do?"

"I want to pass on Griff McPherson," Val

said carefully. She wrapped her hands around the mug. "There's just so much work around here for me to do that I don't want to take the time out to teach him what he doesn't know."

Gus saw her point. "Before we make any decision, ask him to come out for coffee and cookies. I'll interview him."

Heart sinking, Val nodded. Her grandmother had the money, not the Bar H, which meant she could have the final say if she wanted it. "He's a city slicker, Gus."

"Yes, but his *soul* was born here." She jabbed her finger down at the floor. "He's got Wyoming blood movin' through his veins. I'd like to scope him out myself if you don't mind?"

"Sure," she agreed, finishing off her coffee. There was a lot of work to get to and Val knew every day counted before the snow started falling in early September.

"Good," Gus said. "You call the Horse Emporium. I'd like to see McPherson tomorrow afternoon if Andy will give him a couple hours off."

"I'll call Andy now," Val promised, moving into the formal dining room to use the the landline phone set on a hundred-year-old walnut sideboard.

■ ■ ■ ■

Griff tried not to feel anxious, but he did. Getting out of his dented blue Ford pickup, he shut the creaky door and looked up at the main ranch house on the Bar H. The day was sunny and warm, the sky clear. He had been told by Andy yesterday that he was going out for a second job interview with Gus Hunter, one of the three matriarchs in the valley. He knew Iris Mason very well and loved the straight-shooting woman who owned Elk Horn Ranch. He'd never met Gus but had heard plenty about her. She was a pistol-packing granny and had a gruff personality from what Andy had told him.

Removing his red bandanna, Griff felt his nerves. He'd taken a cleansing shower, put on his best clothes, polished his well-worn boots and made sure his Stetson was free of hay or straw. His boots sounded hollowly as he climbed the reddish-gold cedar steps. Quickly wiping his face, he retied the red bandanna around his neck. The screen door was open. Would Val be present? Griff wasn't sure. He knew she wasn't too enthused about him working here. Andy said Gus was the boss of the Bar H and Griff

51

wasn't sure if that was good or bad news.

Standing at the screen door, Griff knocked. He could see a long, gleaming hall through the screen. Val appeared from a side room and walked toward him. Instantly, Griff's heart pounded hard to underscore seeing her once more. Her shoulder-length red hair lay like a shining cloak around her shoulders. Today, she wore a mint-green short-sleeved blouse, Levi's and cowboy boots. Stuffed in her belt was a ragged pair of leather gloves. Clearly, she had been out working earlier.

"Hello," he murmured as she opened the screen door.

"Come in, Mr. McPherson. Gus is in the kitchen waiting to see you."

"Yes, ma'am," Griff said, nodding deferentially to Val as he removed his hat.

Val caught the faint scent of lime soap as he passed by her. Today, he looked spruced up and much cleaner. Her heart beat a little more quickly as she closed the screen door and gestured for him to go down the hall.

"Turn right," she called out to him.

Griff turned and found himself in a large kitchen. At the table sat a wiry woman with short silver hair, a cane leaning against the table next to her. He smiled and walked over to the table. "Mrs. Hunter?" he asked, holding out his hand toward her. "I'm Griff McPherson. It's nice to meet you."

"Call me Gus, young man," she said, and gripped his hand firmly. Feeling the calluses, she said, "My granddaughter, Val, will bring us coffee." She gestured to a cedar chair opposite her. "Have a seat. We can chat a spell."

"Thank you," Griff said in a respectful tone. Gus Hunter might be small, but she was like packed dynamite ready to go off. She, like Val, wore work clothes. The lavender blouse brought out the glint in Gus's blue eyes. Her hair was like a curly silver crown around her head.

"I made you chocolate-chip cookies," Gus said proudly, pointing to the large plate on the table.

Heartened, Griff smiled a little. "That was mighty kind of you, ma'am."

Snorting, Gus said, "Don't ma'am me! Call me Gus."

"Yes . . . Miss Gus," Griff murmured, trying to curb a smile over the elder's spunky personality. Andy had warned him Gus took no prisoners.

Val brought over the coffee and set it in front of them.

"Sit down, Val," Gus ordered, pointing to the chair next to the wrangler.

53

Val took a seat next to Griff. She could see her grandmother measuring and weighing the wrangler as he poured cream into his coffee. He was tall, muscular and relaxed.

"Take a couple of cookies, too," Gus ordered him. She pushed the plate directly in front of Griff.

"Thank you," he said, reaching for one. "I don't usually get home cooking and these look real good." He bit into the cookie, filled with chocolate chips and walnuts. It melted in his mouth. Griff couldn't speak but held up the remainder of the delicious dessert to Gus to show his appreciation.

Gus glowed. "Now, young man, this is an interview for a job as our wrangler here at the Bar H. You understand that?"

"Yes, ma— I mean, Miss Gus, I do."

"Val told me you're from back east."

Griff swallowed the cookie, nodded and told her the story of how he'd wound up in New York City, as well as how he landed back in Jackson Hole.

"So, you were filthy rich and lost it all in the crash on Wall Street?" Gus surmised. She saw the sunburned wrangler's brow dip.

"Yes, I lost everything."

"And did your brother Slade call you and invite you back to your family ranch?"

Her questions were sharp and painful for Griff. "No, he didn't call me. I wanted to come home because I had nowhere else to go. I thought I could stay with him and we could rebuild the Tetons Ranch together."

"Well," Gus said, brows knitting, "everyone in the valley knew Slade was a heartbeat away from losing his ranch. When the economy went south, he and a whole bunch of ranchers were walking the line on bank foreclosure. If it weren't for Dr. Jordana Lawton and his horse, Thor, winning that ten grand at the endurance race, the bank would own that ranch by now."

"I know. I helped them out during the endurance contest." Griff finished off the cookie. Gus was firing off questions almost faster than he could answer them. Just as Andy had warned him she would. . . .

"So how come you're not working for your brother now?"

Moving uncomfortably, Griff said, "We got split up at six years old, Miss Gus. I was bad about staying in touch with him over the years, and I guess it took its toll. The fault was mine. I was living in a rich, wealthy city and frankly, I looked down on him and the ranch. Half the ranch is legally mine, but it was Slade whose hard work, sweat and blood kept it going. Not mine."

"You're honest to a fault, aren't you?"

Griff gave her a twisted grin. "Is there any other way to be?"

"No, frankly, there isn't. But the generations ahead think it's okay to tell half-truths or no truth when it suits them. In my book a lie is a lie, pure and simple."

Nodding, Griff said, "Some do, that's true, but not all of them. I'm from the same generation you're talking about."

"Points scored," she said, respect clear in her voice. She glanced over at Val, who looked worried. Gus couldn't fathom why. So far, this gent was the real deal. "Okay, Mr. McPherson, you tell me why you think you'd be a good addition to the Bar H."

Griff wondered if Val had shared with Gus his answer to a similar question she'd asked him. Devoting his attention to Gus, he replied, "It's clear to me now that Wyoming is where I belong. I couldn't help that Slade and I were split up at six and sent to different uncles to be raised. I'm grateful they were there for us. Coming home after the stock market crash, at first, I hated it. Then, every day, it seemed as though Wyoming was working a little more of her magic on me. It was scrubbing off all those city years and I was rediscovering what I really loved to do. Working with my hands gives me a satisfaction that no Wall Street job ever did. Mending a fence and making sure it's stout and can withstand a bull makes me feel good."

Gus saw some redness appear in the wrangler's cheeks. He was struggling to put his feelings into words. She studied his hands. "You got work hands," she confirmed. Holding up her own, she added, "Hands to thrust into the rich soil of Wyoming. To help things grow. There's a feeling that comes with being one with the land. And if you weren't born here, you couldn't understand."

"Right." Griff studied the old woman's long, thin hands. Her knuckles were slightly enlarged due to arthritis. He saw the calluses across her palms. Her nails were short and jagged. Despite her cane, it was clear nothing could stop her from working on the ranch. He liked the sturdy, straight-talking elder. Griff wondered if his mother had lived, would she have turned out to be like Gus? He wanted to think so because the elder had a backbone of steel.

"I was missing something out in New York. I had the best of everything. My aunt and uncle loved me fiercely and I loved them. In my heart —" and Griff touched his chest "— I felt an emptiness and I never understood it until I arrived back here. When I worked with Slade at the Tetons Ranch, the ache started to go away. Later, I realized I was starving for my roots. My real home." He became serious, his voice low. "I want a job as a wrangler because I feel I can contribute. My heart is in my work, Miss Gus. It's true, I don't know everything about wrangling, but I'm hungry to learn."

Nodding, Gus shot a look across the table toward Val. She looked vulnerable, her eyes glinting with unshed tears. Gus knew she hadn't been yearning to come home the way Griff was describing. Pinching her lips, Gus swung her gaze back to Griff. "Young man, I like where you come from. It's true, you aren't a fully realized wrangler yet, but I feel over time it will happen. Now, I can't give you much money. Ten dollars an hour for eight hours a day. And you know you'll be workin' twelve hours a day, from dawn to dusk."

"That's more than fair," Griff answered, grateful. "I'll prove my worth to you."

"I expect that. Now we got a problem. The wrangler's bunkhouse was destroyed by a fire. One of the wranglers my daughter hired burned it down smoking in there one night. I ain't hirin' anyone who smokes. Too darned dangerous. Anyway, I hope to get that bunkhouse rebuilt next summer and you can move into it then. Meantime, we've got no bunkhouse for you. But, if you're okay with it, I have another bedroom upstairs with its own bathroom and shower. It's yours if you want it. I won't charge you rent."

Surprised, Griff looked over at Val. She looked displeased but refused to meet his gaze. Gus, on the other hand, looked like an excited child. He smiled a little hesitantly and said, "That's very decent of you, Miss Gus. I'll try not to get underfoot. And I've never smoked."

"I do the cookin' around here," Gus warned. "And I'm a darned good cook, too. But I do expect you to wash and dry dishes every other night. And you'll do vacuuming and dusting once a week in this house. You got a problem with that?"

Grinning, Griff said, "Miss Gus, if those cookies are any indication of your cooking ability, then I'm in hog heaven. And I don't mind cleaning up after myself or doing housework. It's all the same to me. Just tell me what you want, when you want it, and I'll be happy to do it."

Giving him a keen look, Gus asked, "You got any plans to leave Wyoming anytime soon, young man? Once this economy staggers back to its feet, are you going to leave and go make your millions again on Wall Street?"

"No, ma— I mean, no, Miss Gus, I won't." Griff looked around the warm, beautiful cedar kitchen. The cabinets shined red and gold in the afternoon sun that poured in through the large windows. "I'm home for good. I don't want to go back to Wall Street."

Gus slapped the table. "Okay. Good!

"You can move your gear in. Val will get the room ready for you. Tomorrow morning, you start your new job with the Bar H, Mr. McPherson."

Joy skittered through Griff. The old woman's blue eyes glinted with elfin exuberance. He was elated over the job opportunity. Finally, someone was going to give him a chance! "Thank you, Miss Gus. I will do everything in my power to never disappoint you."

Shaking his hand firmly, Gus grinned. "Sounds good to me. Val will be your everyday boss. We've written up a very long list of things that need to be done around here. She'll go over that with you this evening after dinner. You like pot roast with potatoes, onions, carrots and gravy?"

Griff got up and carefully pushed his chair

back into place. "Miss Gus, that sounds wonderful. I don't want to tell you what I tend to fix for myself if I'm left to my own devices."

"Just don't go gettin' fat on me," Gus warned, grinning.

Touching his hard, flat stomach, Griff said, "Oh, with all the work to be done around here, I don't think that will happen. I have a feeling I'll be putting in dawn to dusk days around here."

Val got up to show him to the door. "Those are the hours we'll both work." She tried to remain immune to the happiness dancing in his green eyes. He held the Stetson in his left hand as he followed her out of the kitchen.

As they stepped onto the porch, Val gazed around the broken ranch. Everywhere she looked, there was fence line begging to be fixed. She watched Griff settle the Stetson on his head and hoped his proud stance would work out for them and their ranch. Lowering her voice, she said, "I hope you meant every word you shared with my grandmother in there, Mr. McPherson. What she didn't tell you is that if you don't do the work and do it right, I'll fire you myself."

Griff stared over at Val's set face. She was

deadly serious. "I'll make every effort to prove my worth to you and your grandmother every day."

His deep voice moved through her like music. Val fought to ignore it. Why did Griff have to be this easy on her eyes? It would be so much easier to dislike him if he was unattractive. "Better get going, Mr. McPherson. Gus sets the table at six o'clock sharp. She *hates* when people are late."

Grinning a little, Griff said, "Fair enough. I'll be back as soon as I can. Thank you for the opportunity."

Standing on the porch, Val watched the tall wrangler walk down the slight slope to his beat-up Ford truck. It was painfully obvious that McPherson didn't own a dime. Her heart finally settled down after he drove away. Turning, she looked toward the dirt road that led to Long Lake. It was half a mile away. The green of the surrounding mountains made her feel suddenly hopeful. Maybe she was wrong and Gus was right about this city slicker. Time would tell. . . .

The sun shone across the mountains as Griff drove back toward Jackson Hole. The evergreens were dark and lush. He had rolled down his window, his arm resting on the door frame. Few people used air-conditioning in Wyoming. And his truck's compressor had died long ago. The fresh air filled his lungs and it felt good to be alive.

He had a job! His heart swelled with hope. The past few months had been hard. Griff was barely able to pay his room rent and grocery bills. Now he was going to live with a feisty grandmother who probably cooked like an angel — he had a real ranch job and a roof over his head.

His mind and, if he were honest, his heart, turned gently back to Val Hunter. She was a beautiful, accomplished woman. She wasn't happy that her grandmother had hired him, but Gus was in charge, that was clear. He looked forward to seeing that list of to-dos tonight after dinner. Hands on the steering wheel, Griff felt something flow through him like the river that paralleled the highway. Happiness. He was actually happy for the first time since returning to Wyoming!

At first, after the crash and losing his job, Griff had felt hopeless. Coming home was his only option. He'd thought Slade would welcome him with open arms, but he hadn't. His sibling had worked hard all his life to keep the family ranch from going under. And Slade had lost all respect for him because he was a city slicker.

Was Val seeing him through similar eyes?

His gut told him that she was. Mouth tightening, Griff slowed the truck as he entered the outskirts of Jackson Hole. It was a busy town during the summer months. Millions flocked here on their way to Yellowstone National Park, which lay fifty miles north of the cow town. A few tourists stopped first at the closer, magnificent Grand Teton National Park. It was his favorite place and Griff enjoyed hiking when he got the chance. Now he'd have no time for such activities.

As he continued into town, Griff's cell phone rang. He picked it up and saw it was Josh Gordon. Grimacing, Griff answered the FBI agent's call. "Hello, Josh."

"I'm checking in to see if you've gotten anything on Curt Downing yet."

Griff pulled off the road and put the truck in Park. "No, I haven't."

"I thought you might get something on him at the Horse Emporium. You said he picks up his feed supplies there."

"Yes, he does, but I haven't seen him. He sends a kid who works for him, Zach Mason, to fetch the supplies."

"Look, we need your full attention on this. I know we're not able to pay you anything for your help, but if we could prove Downing and his trucking company are moving drugs or guns, it would be of great help to our ongoing regional investigation. You know I can't get authorization to send an undercover FBI agent there until I can prove that there's good reason to do it."

"I understand," Griff said, his frustration bubbling up at the situation he was in.

The FBI had first approached him shortly after the Wall Street crash. They'd needed someone on the inside to help them understand the derivatives schemes. Griff felt guilty that he'd contributed to the economy's downfall, and had agreed to help them. When that assignment was over, the FBI had called him into their office in Washington, D.C. They knew he was going back home to Wyoming, and Josh had asked if he'd be a mole for them on Curt Downing. And, of course, they couldn't pay him a dime for his help. All the same, Griff readily agreed to the task because it was Downing's father who had killed his parents.

"You said you hear all kinds of gossip at the hay and feed store. Haven't you gleaned anything there?"

"Josh, I can't force information out of people. If I go around asking a bunch of questions, I'll blow my cover. And that's not what you want. I have to be patient and cultivate relationships over time. Wyoming people tend to distrust outsiders for a long time until they can prove themselves. I'm still trying to fit in." And then he told the FBI agent about being hired to work at the Bar H.

"But that takes you out of the Horse Emporium."

"Yes, it does. But I need to pay my bills, somehow. And I'll be in town several times a week running errands. Gus gets her hay and feed at the Horse Emporium, too."

"Damn, Griff, this is a real setback."

Raising his brows, Griff said nothing for a moment. Did Josh expect money to fall from the heavens? The agent was being ridiculous. "I know I'm out of the mainstream because of my new job, but I'll keep my eyes and ears open."

"All right, good. Because I'm positive Downing is behind the movement of drugs through Wyoming. We have agents in Idaho, Montana and Colorado, and they're picking up noise on the main hub that the drug dealer is located in Wyoming. It has to be Downing. We just can't prove it yet. We also suspect a Guatemalan drug cartel called Los Lobos is moving into your area. They're gunrunning from what we've been able to ascertain."

"Is Downing mixed up in both?"

"Not that we know of," Josh said. "Not yet, anyway. Guns and drugs don't usually mix. But I want you to see if you hear anything on either of them."

The exasperation was evident in the agent's voice. "Well, if that's so, then shouldn't these two separate reasons be enough to bring an undercover ATF and FBI agent in here to get the goods on Downing? Or the Los Lobos cartel?"

"You don't understand, Griff. Everyone's budget has been slashed. My boss is turning down all kinds of requests from his field agents. Until we can get proof of some kind, my hands are tied."

"I'll do what I can, Josh, but I have to eat and pay my bills first."

"Yeah, yeah, I understand. Okay, stay in touch."

Griff hung up and made his way to the MacMurray house, a turn-of-the-century home painted a turquoise-blue. It was a haven for people like him. He could rent a room, have a small hot plate and a bed. Apartments in Jackson Hole were way out of his reach, as they were for most people who worked in the town. Even the sheriff's deputies had to live in Star Valley fifty miles south of Jackson Hole because they couldn't afford the high-priced housing in the "Palm

Springs of the Rockies." And the ranchers, only a small handful of whom were rich, continued to lead hardscrabble lives.

Getting out of his truck and remembering what good today had brought, his tension from the phone call dissipated. He'd pack up his room here, pay his last rent and drive back to the Bar H. A real home. Griff liked the idea of staying in the main ranch house. The kitchen reminded him of the Tetons Ranch kitchen. It was almost like being home. Not quite, but close.

Feeling like crowing to the world, Griff quickly made his way up the carpeted stairs.

In his room, he threw two pieces of luggage from the closet onto the bed. He was a champion pistol shot and all his weapons were in a special wooden case, under lock and key. His uncle had recognized his interest in shooting. Griff had risen quickly in the world of pistol shooting in his twenties. As he placed it next to the door and began to pack his clothes, his heart centered back on Val. The coverlet of freckles across her high cheeks. Her blue eyes the color of the deep Wyoming sky. As he packed, he couldn't put his finger on why she appeared to feel so sad. Was it that she was unhappy Miss Gus had hired him? Or was it something else?

Griff made quick work of packing. Hefting both pieces of luggage and his weapons case to the downstairs door, he went in search of the owner so he could pay her. Getting free room and board at the Bar H was a huge leap in resolving Griff's money problems.

What lay ahead for him? Above all, Griff didn't want to disappoint or anger Miss Gus. She was clearly on his side. Val was another situation, however. Griff knew she'd be watching him critically for any mistake he made. And he knew that if he couldn't do the work, she'd get him fired in an instant.

Losing this job was the last thing Griff wanted. Somehow, he had to understand Val and make her a team player and not his enemy. Even if she disliked his New York roots, Griff knew that his hard work and attention to detail would prove to her once and for all he was the right person to be hired. Above all, he had to make sure no one ever found out he was eyes and ears for the FBI. Not only would it turn the people of Jackson Hole against him, he'd been sworn to total secrecy. And you didn't mess with the bureau. If he was going to find the goods on Downing, the FBI felt he was the perfect foil. After all, he had been born here and was now returning home. A lot of children came back to their parents' nest these days. Downing would never suspect him. Nor would anyone else. And if Griff had any hope of keeping his dream of life as a wrangler alive, he had to keep his secret safe.

CHAPTER FOUR

Sitting down to a home-cooked dinner felt like going to a five-star restaurant to Griff. He'd come down from his room at the Bar H promptly at six, as Gus had ordered. Inhaling, he could smell apples and cinnamon in the air. The rectangular cedar table had six chairs, one of them placed at the head of it. Gus and Val were bringing the steaming plates of food to the table. Griff had had enough time to take a shower and throw on some clean clothes. He stood uncertainly at the opening to the kitchen.

"Would you ladies like some help?"

Gus poured applesauce from a pan into a bright green ceramic bowl. "No, you go ahead and sit down. Take that chair to the left of the one at the end of the table."

"Yes, Miss Gus." Griff couldn't help but notice how beautiful Val looked. She'd put her thick red hair into a ponytail and tied it up with a bright green ribbon. She wore a faded apron of green and white checks across her slender waist, which reminded him more of the 1950s than present day. In fact, everything about the home shouted of that earlier era. Somehow, it was comforting to Griff.

As he sat at the table, Val brought over a bowl of mashed potatoes with a huge chunk of butter in the center. It was melting quickly, creating yellow rivers flowing down the mound of hand-whipped potatoes.

Gus hobbled over on her cane. "Now, young man, I hope you have an appreciation for organic, home-cooked food. These are apples off our trees out back. I have a root cellar and I store the potatoes, yams and apples down where it's dark and cool. That way, they last a long time without rotting."

Griff took the bowl of applesauce from her. "I have vague memories of doing something similar at our ranch when I was kid."

"Good, then you're not a complete loss."

Chuckling, Griff saw the old woman crack a grin.

He watched as Val brought over a huge platter that contained the beef roast.

"Will you slice it up?" she asked, setting it down in front of him. She walked to the counter, grabbed a carving knife and fork, and brought them over to Griff. As Val handed him the utensils, she tried to ignore his looks. His hands were rough with many small, white scars across the backs of them. He was darkly tanned, which spoke of the time he spent outside. Why did he have to look like dessert to her?

"I'm not the world's best at this," he said, "but I'll give it a go."

"That's the kind of attitude I like," Gus praised, setting down a bowl of streaming carrots that had been drizzled with butter and wildflower honey.

Griff quickly stood and pulled out the elder's chair for her.

"At least some of your Western protocols are still workin', Mr. McPherson," she teased, slowly sitting down. Hooking the cane over the edge of the table, Gus added, "Thank you."

Val carried the gravy boat over to the table. Griff walked around the table and pulled out her chair. She gave him a pained look, set the gravy down in the center of the table and sat down.

Griff sliced into the thick, well-done roast beef. "Everything smells so good."

Val smiled a little. Once he'd sliced the beef, she took Gus's plate and added a dollop of mashed potatoes to it. "Home-cooked food is the best." Avoiding Griff's gaze, she smiled over at her grandmother.

"Better than military food," Gus grumped, taking the plate. She set it down and reached for the gravy ladle. "I know you said you loved the Air Force, but I'll bet the chow-hall food paled in comparison."

Griff looked across the table at Val, raising his eyebrows. She wore a pale green blouse that showed off her slender figure. "You were in the Air Force?"

Unwilling to say much, Val filled her plate. "Yes, I was." She didn't feel comfortable confiding her life to a wrangler. He felt like an outsider in her kitchen, even though she knew McPherson wasn't to blame. She hadn't been home long enough to come to terms with her fate, much less deal with an attractive stranger now living among them.

Gazing at Val with newfound respect, Griff put a couple of slices of steaming beef on his plate along with heaps of mashed potatoes. He found he was starving, but it was as much for the company as the food. "How long were you in the Air Force?"

Val was hesitant. "I enlisted after college."

"What did you do?" Griff saw the blanket of freckles across her cheeks darken. Was he being too nosy?

Gus chuckled as she ate the carrots with relish. "Val won't say a peep. Not that it's a secret. She held a top-secret clearance and was an intelligence officer. She also did fieldwork, finding drug runners. Talk about an exciting life."

Griff couldn't help his surprise as he heard that Val had expertise in exactly the area the FBI had enlisted his help for. But somehow, he was glad she wasn't in such dangerous work anymore.

"Gus . . ." Val begged. "I don't really want to talk about it."

"I understand, honey." Gus patted her granddaughter's hand. She turned her focus on Griff. "What about you, Mr. McPherson? Do you miss Wall Street?"

Griff shrugged. "I'm finding I'm missing it a lot less than I thought I would."

"Did you really want to come back here?" Gus asked before she spooned some mashed potatoes with gravy into her mouth.

"At first, no. I was in shock, I guess. I thought with my credentials and knowledge, I could easily land another investment job. But that was fool's gold. When I was running out of money and options, I did what a lot of other people did — I went crawling home."

"Home isn't such a bad place." Gus gave

Val a warm look. "I'm very glad to have Val home. But like you, she's still getting used to it."

Griff curbed his tongue. He had a hundred questions for Val, but the look on her closed face warned him not to ask them. Her mouth was usually full and shapely. Now, it was thinned with displeasure. "We owe thanks to our troops, no matter what service they're in," he said. "You all put your lives on the line for the rest of us."

Heat nettled Val's skin. She could feel the warmth creeping up from her neck and flow across her face. She hated blushing, but that's exactly what she was doing. When she glanced up and saw the sincerity banked in Griff's green eyes, she nearly choked on a carrot. Coughing, she quickly took a sip of water. Wiping her mouth with the white linen napkin, she managed, "Don't paint a bigger picture of me than you have already."

Stung by her gruff response, Griff wondered inwardly how he was going to get along with this woman. Out of the corner of his eye he could see Gus shake her head. For a bit, the clink of silverware against the bright yellow plates was the only sound in the kitchen.

"Before you two go over the to-do list," Gus finally said, "I made us a special dessert for tonight. Apple pie."

Val couldn't help but smile over at her grandmother. "Thank goodness for your cooking. Otherwise, we'd both probably starve," and she managed a sour smile in Griff's direction. She saw him respond immediately. There was a sense of abandonment around this man. And she could feel him trying to fit into the awkward situation they were all caught up in at the moment. She felt sorry for him. Val tried to put herself in Griff's place: suddenly losing his job and all his money. Plus, he had no place to go. Val decided it would be hard. She finished off her carrots and mashed potatoes.

"My pies are famous in these parts," Gus confided to Griff. "Have you ever tried apple pie with a slice of sharp cheddar cheese melted on it?"

"No, Miss Gus, I haven't. But I'm willing to try it." Griff quickly finished off his food. He was like a starving mongrel who'd come upon an unexpected bounty.

"I have a hunch," Val said in a droll voice, "that you'd eat *anything* if it was home cooked."

He grinned sheepishly. "Guilty on all counts."

Chuckling, Gus said, "You aren't like most

77

gents I've met in my lifetime, Mr. McPherson. Seems you don't ride a horse named Pride. Although you're certainly a confident young man."

Griff warmed to the elder. "My uncle and aunt made sure any pride I had was ironed out of me a long time ago.

"They instilled morals, values and a hard work ethic in me. They opened up their lives to me after our parents died." His voice lowered with feeling. "And I'll always be grateful to them for that."

"They alive?" Gus wondered aloud.

Shaking his head, Griff said, "My aunt died two years ago of a heart attack. No one suspected it. She had complained about a week earlier about pain under her jaw, but we all thought it was a toothache. My uncle begged her to go to the dentist. She booked the appointment, but never made it. My uncle came home that evening and found her dead on the couch."

"Sorry to hear that." Gus gave him a sympathetic look. "What about your uncle?"

Griff smiled faintly and smoothed the linen napkin across his lap. "He died of heartbreak, Miss Gus. He loved my aunt in a way I've seen few people love another person. They were very happy together. And she was his world. He died three months after her, of an undetected brain aneurysm."

Val felt her heart open as she saw sadness in Griff's face. He'd lost his parents and then his guardians, and she felt deeply for him. "Your aunt and uncle sound like they were wonderful people."

Griff saw tears glistening in Val's eyes and was stunned by her response. In that moment, her guard was down. And his heart ached to explore her in every possible way. Swallowing a lump in his throat, Griff managed in a pained tone, "They were my world. They didn't have to take in a grieving six year old, but they did."

Gus blotted her lips with her napkin. "They might have lived in New York City, but they had solid Wyoming values. You can't take the country out of a person no matter where he or she lives. And they instilled those principles into you." She looked Griff up and down. His hair was short, recently washed and combed. Gus doubted he went anywhere without a red bandanna around his throat. His white cotton cowboy shirt with pearl buttons was pressed to perfection and clean. "I feel you'll blossom here over time. You're kinda like a tulip bulb — all covered with city-slicker soil. But once you shake off that city dirt, you'll rediscover your roots here."

Griff felt a deep warmth toward the women. They cared and it showed in their faces. "I'm already starting to bloom. I like waking up in the morning to clean, fresh air. And instead of skyscrapers outside my window, I have the Teton mountains."

Rubbing her hands, Gus cackled. "And it don't get any better than that!"

Val got up to clear the dishes, and instantly Griff was on his feet to help her.

Gus smiled. "That's what I like, a man who knows his way around a kitchen." She wagged her finger in Griff's face. "Remember, I cook, you wash dishes."

"It's a great trade-off." Griff filled his hands with plates. Val was collecting all the bowls from the table and setting them on the counter. For the next five minutes, Griff felt dizzy and as if in a dream. A slice of memory from his childhood flowed into his mind, stunning him, filling him with love and appreciation. He recalled his mother showing him how to clear a table after the family was finished with dinner. He'd been short and clumsy and had dropped a cup on the floor. Slade had chided him, but Griff remembered his mom leaning over to hug him and tell him not to worry. Carrying dishes simultaneously was all about balance and she was proud of him for learning.

His heart contracted with grief as he care-fully placed the plates into the sink to rinse them off before transferring them to the dishwasher. The kitchen was warm, the fra-grance of food a perfume for his lonely soul. The clink of dishes and silverware was pleasant music from the past. Griff wished he could confide in the women just how much this moment meant to him. They may have taken it for granted, but he never would. Dinner with family was something he'd pined for and rarely gotten when he'd come home to the Tetons Ranch. Slade had not wanted him around. He was angry with Griff for things that had transpired in the past, and saw him as a threat to his control over the ranch even though half of it was le-gally his. Griff understood his older frater-nal twin's reaction. Slade had put his whole life into keeping the family ranch solvent, and he'd nearly lost it. If not for Jordana Lawton, his new wife, winning the ten thou-sand dollars in the endurance race, Slade would have no ranch. Now, they were mar-ried and things were slowly improving. Griff felt an undeniable relief to know the Tetons Ranch would not only survive but, some-day, thrive. And he'd been here to see it.

"Time for apple pie and cheese!" Gus

crowed from her chair. "Val, you want to do the honors?"

Smiling, Val murmured, "Absolutely." She put on a set of oven mittens, opened the oven door and pulled out a warm apple pie. Griff was standing at the sink, looking to help. "You can take three bowls down from that cabinet to the right of the sink."

An incredibly warm feeling swept through Griff as he took out three red ceramic bowls from the cabinet. It felt so good to be part of a household again. Setting the bowls on the counter, he watched Val retrieve the cheddar cheese from the fridge. Her hands were beautiful, fingers long and movements fluid. Watching as she cut the pie and placed thick wedges into the awaiting bowls, Griff sliced the cheese.

He was a bit awkward with the knife.

"Cheese alert, ladies," he said. "These slices aren't going to be exactly even."

Picking two bowls up, Val accidentally brushed against his arm and tried to ignore his blatant masculinity. Griff was lean like a mountain lion. She controlled her voice as she responded. "Oh, don't worry about it. Where this dessert is going, it won't matter."

Chortling, Gus called, "The stomach don't care at all, Mr. McPherson. It's just going to sing with pleasure at getting filled, is all."

"You're right about that." Griff wrapped up the cheese and put it back into the fridge. Val took the bowls to the table and her eager grandmother. The pie smelled marvelous and Griff quickly moved to pull out Val's chair so she could sit down. Again, she said nothing. What did he expect? After all, he was a stranger who had suddenly fallen into her life.

Sitting down, he confided to Gus, "You really know how to make someone feel welcome. Thank you."

Grinning a little, Gus cut eagerly into her pie. "It's a Wyoming custom to welcome those who come through our door and to treat them like family."

Griff remembered that from so long ago. As he cut into the warm pie with cheddar cheese melting across its browned crust, more memories arose from his childhood. When Griff was five his aunt and uncle had come out from New York to Jackson Hole for a weeklong visit. It was something they did every year. He and his brother always looked forward to their arrival because they brought them gifts of toys. Their parents were dirt-poor and even though they never made the boys feel their economic status, the boys certainly never had much. But they were always extremely hospitable to any guests.

"Did your real mom cook and bake?" Gus asked.

"Yes, Miss Gus, she did," he said, savoring the warm tartness of the apples and cinnamon along with the tangy sharp cheddar melting in his mouth. "My dad worked the ranch and she sewed our clothes, did the washing and kept us and the ranch house together."

Val heard the far-off dreaminess in Griff's lowered voice, and found herself hungry to know more about him. He seemed attuned to helping out women in the kitchen, which surprised her. Looking up, she asked, "Did your mom make you boys work in the house? Dry dishes? Clean up the table up after dinner?"

"Yep, she did," Griff fondly recalled. "My brother and I were like wriggling puppies growing up. Mom harnessed all that energy. We learned to dry dishes standing on top of a stool at the kitchen sink as she washed them and handed them to us. Slade hated dish duty, but he liked dusting and sweeping. So we made an agreement to each do the chores we preferred."

"Did she teach you to cook?" Gus demanded.

"No, but I wish she had. Slade liked to cook, so he was always in there watching Mom. Sometimes, she'd let Slade make chocolate-chip cookies."

Val saw the gleam in his green eyes as he spoke. There was happiness lurking in the depths of them. And for whatever reason, it made Val feel good. To her utter surprise, an ache centered in her lower body. She couldn't help but stare at his strong mouth. Griff smiled often. He reacted to their questions and took them seriously. Part of her was relieved to realize Griff wasn't one of those proud cowboys. They were such a pain in the butt to deal with.

"I preferred being outside helping our father," he continued. "Slade was always mesmerized by recipes and mixing ingredients together to create new things. Mom swore he'd grow up to be a chemist." He chuckled fondly over those memories.

"What did you do?"

"I liked riding, Miss Gus. Our father gave us each a mustang gelding when we were three years old. I rode my horse as much as I could."

"That's good." Gus spooned into her dish. "Because you're going to get a lot of saddle time around here. We have one real nice

85

quarter horse and an Appaloosa left. I'm sure Val will assign you one of 'em tomorrow."

"I will," Val promised. Their black Appaloosa, Freckles, had a white blanket with black spots over its rump. Griff would be well matched with the gelding, as it stood sixteen hands tall.

"I think you're gonna be good for the Bar H, Mr. McPherson," Gus said.

"Could you call me Griff?" He knew ranchers were always respectful and would call a person by their surname, unless otherwise asked.

"Why sure I can." Gus smiled. "Griff's a good, strong name. Why'd your parents decide to call you that?"

"My dad got to name the firstborn, Slade, but the agreement was my mom would get to name the second twin. She loved King Arthur and the Knights of the Round Table. She was really into dragons and griffins in literature, so she called me Griff."

"Griffins were often found on the shields of royalty," Gus noted with pride. "They had the body of a lion, the head and wings of an eagle. In mythology, they were considered heroic, courageous, and represented strength."

Smiling faintly, Griff was impressed with

her knowledge of the ancient symbolic animal. "My mother shared many stories about griffins with me. She said that they would find gold in the mountains and make their nest out of the metal. I remember she told me that I'd grow up and be very rich someday." His heart filled with pain. "And she was right about that. When I worked at my uncle's company, I was worth millions. I wish she'd lived to see that."

Val frowned and said nothing. Seeing the anguish in his eyes, she felt badly for Griff. No one should have their parents torn away from them.

Gus sighed. "I can't even begin to know how it would feel to lose millions."

"I stupidly tied everything up in derivatives. My uncle was always chiding me to put a chunk of it into the blue-chip stocks, instead. I didn't listen." Griff shrugged. "If I had, I wouldn't be flat broke as I am today."

Val absorbed the pain and the frustration embedded in his deep voice. When she glanced up, Griff was frowning down at the half-eaten dessert in front of him. She could see he was thinking about the past, about the horrendous mistakes he'd made. But didn't everyone make mistakes? Oh, yes. Everyone made plenty. But to lose millions?

Val couldn't fathom that. She cleared her throat. "Maybe this is your chance to rebuild your life back here in Wyoming."

Griff caught and held her blue gaze. For once, the walls that kept him from reading Val's face weren't up. "That's exactly what I'm going to do. I'm hoping I can find the fabled gold of the griffin here, where I was born."

Chuckling indulgently, Gus said, "Oh, I think you have what it takes to be successful, Griff. Now, your focus is different. I don't know too many wranglers who get rich, but over time, you can build a nice nest egg."

"That's my plan." Finishing off the dessert, Griff sat back and rubbed his belly. "That was really good pie. Thanks, Miss Gus. It's almost like I'm home again . . ."

"Well, get used it, Griff."

Val rose. "Will you help me clear the table, Mr. McPherson?"

Inwardly, Griff's heart sank. He'd wanted Val to call him by his first name, too. The set look on her face and her tight jaw told him she was going to continue to keep him at arm's length, though. "Of course." He scooted the chair away from the table. "It's the least I can do for such a great five-star meal." When he aimed a smile over at Gus, she blushed like a teenager. Griff wanted to reach out and carefully hug the elder.

"Griff, you're a delight," Gus crowed. "I'm happy to see you here with us."

As Griff thanked her and carried the empty bowls over to the sink, he wondered if Val felt the same way.

CHAPTER FIVE

"Dammit, Zach, work faster!" Curt Downing's fine, thin nostrils flared as he stood on the wooden dock at the Horse Emporium. The twenty-year-old kid, still gawky and pathetically thin, wrestled with an eighty-pound bale of hay. The bale was winning. There was no use trying to make a cowboy out of this kid. Placing his hands on his hips as he watched his three wranglers working efficiently to transfer a hundred bales on the waiting flatbed, Curt fumed. If he didn't need Zach Mason, the grandson of Iris Mason, owner of the Elk Horn Ranch, he'd have fired his ass a long time ago. But the kid was useful to him in other ways.

With the two hooks, Zach hurled the bale onto the flatbed where another wrangler stood impatiently waiting for it. Releasing his heavy load, he saw Downing glare at him. Zach wiped the sweat out of his eyes. He hated what he was doing. Shuffling back inside the huge two-story barn to get another bale, he wished he was in his rented room in town, smoking a joint. Marijuana soothed and calmed him. His heart still ached, missing his mother, Allison. She was in a federal prison, serving out a twenty-five-year term for trying to kill Iris Mason, his grandmother, and Kam Trayhern. Kam, his stepfather Rudd's illegitimate daughter, had come home to claim her inheritance. Allison had seen her, as well as Iris with whom Kam was bonding, as a threat and tried to have them murdered to save the inheritance for her own kids: himself and his sister Regan. He still blamed all of them for his mother being torn from him.

Stopping at a table, Zach grabbed a bottle of water, opened it and slugged down its tepid contents. His large Adam's apple bobbed repeatedly. Tossing the empty container into a barrel next to the table, he pulled off his baseball cap and wiped his brow with the back of his arm. The prickly alfalfa hay nettled his sensitive skin, turning it a splotchy red.

Zach knew he wasn't cut out for ranch life, even though his stepfather and grandmother owned the largest and most prosperous ranch in the valley. But he wasn't from their bloodline. His mother had been a

Hollywood star. And his sister, Regan, who lived a block away from him in town, took after Allison. He tried to forget his promiscuous mother had had sex with an A-list Hollywood director. That was his real father. But Zacharius Blanchard refused to accept his illegitimate son. He refused to even talk to Zach. That hurt. Why did his Hollywood star mother have to screw with so many different men? His older sister, Regan, had a filthy rich film producer for a father. Patrick Dobson refused to acknowledge her as his daughter, too. What was wrong with these irresponsible bastards?

Until recently, Zach's mother had led him to believe that Rudd Mason was his real father, and in the end, Rudd had turned against Allison and helped send her to prison. Damn him. Damn the whole, stinking lot. Again, Zach wished he was back in his room smoking pot and zoning out of his godforsaken, miserable existence.

"Hurry up!" Downing shouted into the barn. "You're falling behind, Mason. Get a move on!"

"Screw you," Zach muttered. Several wranglers, plus the hired help at Horse Emporium, were bustling like busy bees all around him. Not for the first time, Zach wished his real father would acknowledge him, because he was rich and could pay for his drugs. Then, he wouldn't have to work for Downing, who was a son of a bitch to please.

Curt Downing stood on the dock but his attention turned from the lazy kid to notice his sister, Regan Mason, driving into the parking lot. Unlike her drugged-up brother, she was sharp and didn't touch drugs. Regan had red hair like Zach, only hers was a dull red in comparison to his carrottop color. The very sight of her annoyed Downing, although he did like her from one standpoint. Regan was in her late twenties and had a killer body like her mother. Allison had known how to use sex to get what she wanted. What did Regan want? Downing tried to figure it out as he watched her climb out of her dark blue Chevy pickup and head directly toward the loading platform.

She was tall with full breasts, wide hips and long legs. Even though she wore a white cotton blouse and Levi's, it did not detract from her sensual beauty. Downing saw the glinting look of a feral predator in her blue eyes as she quickly climbed the steps up to the bustling platform. Spotting him, Regan made a beeline for Curt.

"Is Zach here?" she demanded without

preamble.

Curt nodded. "Yeah, but he's busy earning his monthly paycheck."

Regan disliked the millionaire rancher and her voice didn't hide it. "I need to see him."

"He's working," Downing said in a growl, glaring down at her. He saw the petulant set of her full mouth. Her red hair was in a single braid and hung down her long, curved back.

"When does he get a break, then?" she demanded, meeting his narrowed brown eyes.

Downing snorted. "He's lucky to even have a break. Your candy-assed brother is weak and shuffles around like the pothead he is. For every bale of hay he manages to cart to the truck, my other wranglers have already put three of 'em in."

Regan shot Downing a dirty look. He might be a tall, good-looking red-haired man in his midthirties, but his arrogance rubbed her the wrong way. He stood with his hands on his hips like he was lord of all he surveyed. "I should be grateful to you, Curt. You gave my brother a job when no one else would." Before the ordeal with their mother, Zach had been holed up in his room smoking pot every day. He never took part in ranching. Even she knew he was lazy and spaced-out. But he was her half brother and she loved him.

Curt preened a little under Regan's husky voice. He'd been trying to bed this woman for ages, but she always evaded him. "He does his best," he said, giving her a slight smile. He knew from Regan's many visits during Zach's shifts that she was overly protective of her druggie stepbrother. When word got out in Jackson Hole about the Mason family's poisonous, dysfunctional relationships, the town reeled in shock. Now, Regan and Zach lived in town and their every move was scrutinized by the citizenry. "So, what's happening in your world?"

"I'm working on a Hollywood movie script."

Curt was sure that Regan would send it to her estranged father, even though he refused to acknowledge her as his daughter.

"Word on the street is that you've written four scripts and all of them have been turned down by everyone in Hollywood." Curt softened his tone a little. "Hollywood is the hardest place in the world to break into."

Wrapping her arms around her chest, Regan muttered, "I'm not giving up. Once I break in, I'm leaving this place."

Zach came staggering out with another bale between the hooks. He saw Regan, perked up and smiled a hello in her direction.

Regan lifted her hand. She watched her brother barely able to handle the bale. The other wranglers, all fit men in their twenties, were hustling back and forth with ease. Her heart sank as she watched her weak brother finally drop the bale onto the flatbed. "Mind if I take five minutes with him, Curt? I'm leaving unexpectedly for a job interview and he needs to know I'm leaving for a week."

Curt didn't want her hatred. And God knew, Regan hated with great ease. "Sure, go ahead."

"Thanks." She walked quickly toward Zach.

Standing there watching his minions work, Curt felt victorious. The world was literally in his hands. He felt strong and invincible. He had a damn good crew over at Ace Trucking who were very well paid to receive and help distribute the drugs he ran to six different states around Wyoming. Pride sizzled through Curt. He laughed to himself because he was the regional drug lord and not one bastard suspected him. Such was his stealth and cunning at keeping it a buried secret here in Jackson Hole. Everyone looked up to him. He was a successful rancher and an astute businessman. And he could have any woman he wanted. Except, perhaps, Regan Mason. Eyeing her, Curt promised himself to relentlessly pursue her until he got her into his bed.

Curt spotted another flatbed truck pulling into the gravel yard. The truck was at least fifteen years old, a beat-up red Ford that had certainly seen better days. Scowling, he recognized the driver: Griff McPherson. But who was the woman with him? Curt couldn't place her. His focus shifted to the flatbed now backed up next to his rig.

"Well, well," he said to himself as he saw Griff get out. "He's finally got a real job. . . ."

Val eased out of the truck. The door squealed as she shut it. Turning around and seeing Curt Downing on the platform, she frowned. Great. She recognized his features from many years ago, and since her return Gus had been warning her about him. He'd been the rebellious son of Red Downing who had taken over his parents' ranch after their deaths. Since then, Gus had told her, he'd become a local kingpin and made it known to everyone how filthy rich he was. With so many ranchers struggling just to make ends meet, Val couldn't stand to see the arrogant look on his face. It turned her stomach.

She walked around the front of the truck to Griff.

"You start putting bales on the truck. I'll pay Andy for them in the store."

Griff nodded. He knew the way things worked around here. "No problem," he said as he tugged on his elk-skin gloves and scooped up the two hooks from behind the seat. Val was all business. She hadn't talked much on their drive to the Emporium. While he wished she'd be a little warmer, Griff understood better why she continued to be standoffish.

Looking up at the platform that swirled with wranglers, Griff saw Curt standing off to one side. The red-haired cowboy stared belligerently back at him. In addition to the FBI fingering him as a suspect, Griff disliked Downing because he was a cheat and a liar. He'd heard from Slade's wife, Jordana, that he'd tried to hit Thor with a crop during the endurance contest. Downing had forced her off the trail and was well-known for such underhanded tricks. Word had it that other endurance riders had been at the end of his attacks, too. And Downing always did his dirty work out of the sight of judges so no one had proof. And in the world of endurance riding, it had to be seen to be believed by the judges.

Mounting the stairs, Griff saw Downing's brown eyes go steely. He was Slade's brother and there was automatic hate between them as a result. Griff had never done anything to Downing, but this man couldn't separate them. He was a McPherson therefore, to be distrusted. Griff met his hard gaze with one of his own as he stepped onto the busy platform. He wasn't going to make small talk with this bastard.

"Hey, McPherson, you finally get a gig?" Downing asked in a pleasant tone.

Griff halted about six feet away from the rancher. "Don't you have better things to do, Downing?" He saw Downing's mouth curve into a rueful smile.

"No, not really. Looks like you got a red-haired filly in that truck. Who is she?"

Anger moved through Griff. He saw the arrogant smile increase across Downing's full lips. "That's Val Hunter, owner of the Bar H."

Brows rising, Downing said, "What?"

Seeing shock register on the man's face, Griff moved past him and got on with the business of hauling fifty bales of grass hay to his flatbed. Griff figured few people knew

Val had returned home. Chuckling to himself, he hooked the first bale and wrestled it out to the flatbed. He was sure Gwen Garner, the owner of the quilt store, would know. That was the place to go if anyone wanted to find out what was going on in Jackson Hole. He wondered if Downing would take a drive over there to talk with her. Probably.

Val emerged from the Horse Emporium. The sun was warm upon her shoulders. She looked toward the hay platform, filled with hardworking, sweaty men. What she didn't like seeing was Curt Downing. He was such a pain in the ass.

Val retrieved her elk-skin gloves from the truck, intending to arrange the bales Griff had delivered to the truck.

"Hey!" Downing called, walking over to the edge of the platform.

Val looked up and frowned. "Yes?" she called, pulling on her gloves.

"I'm Curt Downing. You must be Val Hunter? Gus's granddaughter, right?"

She hated even making small talk with this bastard. Hauling herself up into the bed of the truck, Val said, "Yes, I am. Excuse me, I've got work to do."

Nostrils flaring, Downing watched as she turned her back to him. Despite his anger at her affront, he watched the woman with interest, perusing her long, lean body. She was in fine shape as she moved those bales around, lifting them without a problem. Not only that, she was damn good-looking. When did she get into town? And why was she suddenly back? Rubbing his chin, Downing decided he'd have to make a call on Gwen Garner. She'd know a lot more. And it was obvious that Val wasn't interested in talking to him. Too bad, Downing thought. He'd seen no ring on her left hand before she'd pulled on her work gloves. Maybe she came back because the Bar H was going belly-up? Curt had wanted to buy the two-hundred-acre ranch for a long time now. It was strategic to his valley-wide plans.

Moving down the stairs, he quickly walked to his red Chevy pickup and climbed in. While the mice were away, the cat could play. It was time he gave Gus Hunter a little visit.

Gus heard the pounding on the screen door. She was in the kitchen making cookies when the harsh sound echoed down the hall.

"Hold your horses!" she yelled, wiping off her hands and grabbing her cane. Who could it be? Val and Griff had left an hour ago to get supplies in town.

101

Hobbling down the hall, she saw a tall, broad-shouldered man standing at the door. Lifting her upper lip into a snarl, Gus quickly recognized him. She shoved the screen door open, making him leap back.

"What the hell you doin' here?"

Curt doffed his cowboy hat in deference to the small woman glaring up at him. "Why, Miss Gus, I thought I'd drop by and say hello." Downing held up a sack. "I brought us some lattes. I thought we might sit out here on your porch and chat a spell?" Curt saw the silver-haired woman sneer at him. Oh, he knew Gus was a red-hot pistol. She spoke her mind and didn't care at all about diplomacy. He added a hopeful smile and gave her a pleading look. "Please?"

Snorting softly, Gus let the screen door slam shut behind her. "You listen to me, you young whippersnapper, I'm not inter-ested in sellin' the Bar H! That's why you're here, isn't it?"

Curt ambled over to the small table near the swing at the end of the enclosed porch. "Why, Miss Gus, you misunderstand my intentions," he said in a soothing voice. Set-ting the sack down, Curt opened it up and placed two Starbucks coffee cups on the table. "I was at the Horse Emporium just now and I saw your truck. Griff McPherson was driving it." He walked over and offered one to Gus. "I was surprised. I wanted to make sure that he hadn't stolen it from you." Curt congratulated himself on planting seeds in her mind that McPherson was not to be trusted.

"Get that crappy coffee outta my face!" She raised her cane and threatened to strike the cup out of Downing's hand. "I like *real* coffee! Not that citified stuff!"

"Oh, I'm so sorry, Miss Gus." Curt feigned a hurt look. He quickly placed the cups back into the sack. "Might you invite me in for a real cup of coffee, then?" He added a warm smile along with a coaxing look he hoped would melt her anger.

Gus scowled. "I'd rather invite a pissed-off rattler in to dine with me, Downing."

He looked up and placed his hand over his heart. "Miss Gus, you hurt me to the quick."

"You can't hurt a rock."

Downing had always respected her spunk. Prodding Gus was like prodding a bull elk in heat: you knew he would get angry and charge. "Now, Miss Gus, I came out here with concern for you. That *was* your flatbed I saw at the Horse Emporium?"

"Of course it was! And what business is that of yours? You aren't Gwen Garner! I don't mind speaking to her, but you, I don't trust any further than I could throw you."

Curt smiled inwardly. The old woman's face was pinched, angry, and she looked like she was going to have a heart attack any moment. Not that he would mind. Then he could scoop up her ranch. "Miss Gus, I saw a lovely young red-haired woman with McPherson," he said, playing dumb. "She was in the truck with him. Who is that?"

Gus grinned savagely. "That, Downing, is my granddaughter, Val Hunter."

Downing pretended to be as shocked as he was at the Emporium earlier. "What? I thought she was in the Air Force? Is she on leave to visit you?"

"No, you fool, she's home for good!" Gus pointed to her hip. "And it's not gone past your nose to know I can't handle this ranch by myself any longer because of my broken hip. Everyone in town knows it never healed right. Val has come home to help get the ranch back up to an operational level."

"I see. . . ." Downing choked and nervously coughed. His mind spun with shock. He'd been expecting Gus to put up the For Sale sign any minute precisely because she was now crippled and no longer able to work. This was a definite setback. "But . . . what about McPherson? Yesterday, he worked at the Horse Emporium."

Giving him an irritated look, Gus barked, "Well, he's now our wrangler. With Val and Mr. McPherson's help, the Bar H is going to be just fine. How about that, Mr. Big Shot?" Gus waved her cane in his face. "I know your type. You're like a snake that slinks through the bushes just waiting for the right moment to lunge out and bite someone on the ankle. But you ain't gettin' our ranch. So don't even *think* you can!"

Standing there, Curt felt like the world had fallen out from beneath him. Damn! He desperately needed this ranch! Of course, he couldn't tell the angry old woman why. Even if he could, it'd only raise her hackles more. "I'm so glad to hear you got help once more, Miss Gus," he murmured in a placating tone, trying to ratchet down her anger toward him. Walking over to the table, Curt picked up the sack. Turning, he said, "I really hope that your granddaughter can stay."

"Oh, she'll stay. This is her home!" Gus said, jabbing her finger down at the porch. "You know ranch families stick together. And I know you're wantin' to buy up any ranch land you can get your filthy hands on. Well, it won't be our ranch. Git goin', Mister. I have cookies to bake and I don't like talkin' to the likes of you!"

Moving down the porch steps, Downing turned, doffed his hat again and said, "I wish you a good day, Miss Gus. I'm here for you in case you need any help. The Bar H has a wonderful history and I know with your granddaughter home, things will get better. Good day."

Gus snorted, breathing raggedly as she watched the bastard climb into his big gussied-up truck. The damned pickup held so much chrome it glittered like a Christmas ornament. But that was Downing. She'd watched him grow into a bully through the twelve grades of school. His father, Red, had been a bully, too. An abusive drunk always causing havoc for people in the valley. There were times when she'd hear that Curt had a black eye at school. And a small part of her felt sorry for the younger Downing. Well, minus the drunkard part, the kid had grown up to be just like his daddy.

Gus watched the truck pull out of the driveway. And then she saw that Val and Griff had returned. The two trucks passed one another on the road into the ranch. She watched Griff drive the truck around to the barn. Hobbling off the porch, Gus went to greet them.

Val climbed out of the truck as Gus approached. "Was that Curt Downing we just passed?"

"Sure as hell was." Gus looked up at the bales of hay tied down on the flatbed.

"What did he want?"

Griff came around the truck to hear the conversation. Gus was clearly upset, her eyes narrow along with her pursed lips. He saw Val was concerned because she tugged at her ponytail. It was a habit he'd seen before and finally recognized it for what it was.

Gus told them what had transpired. She patted Val's arm. "Now, get that worry wiped off your face. He's gone and out of our lives."

Griff pushed his hat up on his head. "Downing was surprised that we're here?"

Cackling, Gus said, "Oh, it looked for a moment like he was going to fall through the porch. He was *that* surprised!"

Griff grinned a little. Gus got pure pleasure out of meeting Downing head-on. He liked her backbone. She might be small but that didn't stop her from taking on the likes of Downing. Most of the town was afraid of him, but Gus was not. "Are you okay?"

"Ohhh," Gus said, reaching out and patting Griff's arm, "I'm fine, son. Not to worry. I'm not afraid of that bully!"

Val frowned. "He came out to ask about me?"

"Yep," Gus said. "He's a nosy son-of-a-gun."

Mouth quirking, Griff said, "I'm going to start moving this hay inside, ladies."

Val was pleased to see the wrangler move into action. She placed a hand on Gus's shoulder. "Why don't you go in? You look like you're in pain, Gus. Do you need some aspirin?"

Moving her hand over her hip, Gus muttered, "Yeah, Downing got my dander up for sure. I was waving my cane around instead of using it to support myself."

Smiling gently, Val said, "Come on, I'll walk you back into the house."

Nodding, Gus gripped her hand. "You're a good granddaughter. Do you know that? It's nice to be taken care of every once in a while."

Laughing a little, Val escorted Gus back toward the house. The morning sun was warm, the sky blue and there was a pine scented breeze. "Oh, Gus, I always worry about you. You're like a little banty rooster. I agree, Downing is dangerous and I don't trust him. But you don't need to get your blood pressure up because of him."

"He's a snake snoopin' around, Val. You

108

can't *ever* trust a snake!"

Gus was moving very slowly and in obvious pain. "You know, I heard a commercial for the Scooter Store on the radio this morning when we were driving into town, Gus. A power chair could get you around here much more easily, even outside."

"Oh, don't you start jawin' about a scooter for me. Cowgirls ride horses. What an embarrassing comedown."

Chuckling, Val knew it would take a while to get her grandmother to consider another type of transportation. She was a proud, tough, Wyoming rancher woman who was used to using her two legs to get where she was going. Helping her slowly negotiate the stairs to the porch, Val replied, "Maybe we can talk about it another time."

Gus snorted. She rested a moment at the top of the stairs. "I'll bet Downing's heading for Gwen Garner's quilt shop. He's gonna ply her with questions about you."

Unconcerned, Val opened the screen door for Gus. "Gwen is a trusted friend to our family. I'm not worried about her. Come on, I'll make us some coffee and you can sit down and give that hip of yours a rest."

"Might help me finish those cookies, too?"

Grinning, Val said, "Absolutely."

CHAPTER SIX

Gwen Garner stood at the rear of her quilting store next to a grocery cart filled with new fabrics that had to be placed out for sale. The store was busy and she had her head down, tucking a bright, colorful Hoffman batik fabric into place when someone tapped her smartly on the shoulder.

Looking up, Gwen scowled. "Mr. Downing." She continued placing the fabric into the end cap.

"Mrs. Garner, how are you today?" Curt tipped his tan Stetson hat in her direction. He saw her face turn sour. Curt didn't like having to come into the quilt shop and beg for information. And by the look in Gwen's narrowing eyes, he wondered if coming here was smart. He added a hopeful smile and settled his hat on his head. "I was just over at Andy's Horse Emporium getting hay for my horses when I saw Val Hunter." His voice dropped to a whisper. "Did you know she was in town?"

Gwen pushed her cart to the next island of fabrics. "Of course I did, Mr. Downing."

Curt followed her, keeping his voice low and always scanning the store. "Val was in the Air Force. She was making a career of it. Why would she return home?"

Raising an eyebrow at him, Gwen said, "It ought to be pretty obvious, Mr. Downing. After Gus broke her hip, she couldn't maintain the Bar H by herself. She asked her granddaughter to come home and help."

"Wow," Curt said, "that's asking a lot."

"Ranching families stick together," she retorted, iciness in her tone as she picked up another bolt of fabric and slid it into place.

Continuing to follow her, Curt asked, "Then, she's here for good?" That made him anxious. The old biddy wouldn't sell no matter what.

"As far as I know, yes."

"A shame to throw away her career like that."

"And an even bigger shame if a family ranch goes belly-up, don't you think?"

Curt tried to hide his irritation. Gwen obviously didn't want to talk to him, her voice sharp with rebuke over his questions. "I mean," he said, "why not hire a wrangler or two?"

"Enough of this, Mr. Downing." Gwen jammed her hands on her hips. "I don't pretend to know what's in the mind of anyone, but the facts are in front of your nose. Val Hunter has come home for good." She gave him a frosty smile. "Guess that sort of stops your plan to steal the Bar H out from under Gus, doesn't it?"

Curt felt heat sweeping up from his neck and into his cheeks. He clenched his teeth for a moment, his jaw becoming hard. This bitch of a woman was too powerful in Jackson Hole. He hated her, but he needed her. If she only knew what he could do to her and her family . . . Forcing a thin smile, he continued, "You have to admit, the Bar H is a very nice property. With Long Lake on half of it, I could see bringing in a realty development to build a lot of condos. It could be a great place for tourists and their families. And it would help the town's economy."

Nostrils flaring, Gwen said, "Gus knows you would never honor the ranch or its land. Frankly, I'm glad Val is home."

Curt watched as Gwen turned around and pushed the cart down another aisle. He didn't follow her this time. Hiding his anger toward the woman, he strolled out of the quilt shop. On the wooden porch, Curt looked around. He decided to go visit his Realtor, Bobby Fortner. It was a mere walk around the corner to Raven Realty.

Fortner was at his desk when Curt entered his office. Instantly, the short man was on his feet.

"Mr. Downing, an unexpected pleasure." Fortner scuttled around his massive oak desk and gestured to the chair in front of it. "Please, have a seat. May I get you some coffee?"

This was more like it. Curt secretly reveled in Fortner's beta wolf reaction to him. He should. Over the years, he'd made this plain man with squinty brown eyes and lifeless black hair very rich. "Thank you, Bobby. And no, I'll pass on the coffee."

Quickly running his short, thin fingers through his hair, Bobby sat down. "What can I do for you, Mr. Downing?"

"Well," Curt said, leaning back in the chair and crossing one leg over the other, "I need more in-depth information on the Bar H."

"Oh, yes sir." Bobby quickly typed the name into the computer in front of him. "What would you like to know?"

"First, is it completely paid off? Or is there a still a mortgage on it? Any liens?"

"No, it's paid in full and no liens, sir."

Fortner's brow scrunched. "They continue to be up-to-date with their property taxes, too." He peered around his computer. "Is this what you needed?"

Mouth thinning, Curt growled, "Yes, I suppose so. If that crusty old woman wasn't so damned stubborn, the Bar H would have been easy to snap up."

"I know you've wanted the property for a long time. You're looking for ways to get Miss Gus to hand it over." Fortner shrugged. "Realistically, unless she *wants* to sell it, there's nothing else that can be done."

Snarling out of frustration, Downing said, "She's eighty-four years old, for God's sake. You'd think she'd die. I need that ranch, dammit!" Curt clenched his fist. Fortner had no idea he moved drugs for a Mexican cartel, but he didn't seem suspicious of why Curt wanted the land so badly.

"Short of a forest fire or an earthquake taking the ranch down," Bobby said in jest, "I don't know what else could be done."

Curt thought about the Realtor's offhand remark but said nothing further about it to Fortner. The Bar H stood in a clearing and was surrounded by heavy forest. "I want you to go out and visit Miss Gus. Be nice to her. See if she'll bite on my offer again. Up the bid to one point five million dollars.

114

That should get her attention."

"I'll try, but she always turns me down," Bobby said, giving him a helpless look.

"Take a box of chocolates to the old dame. Just get her talking and see what her ideas are for the ranch. But call ahead and make an appointment. She hates someone showing up unannounced."

Flustered, Bobby wiped his perspiring brow with his handkerchief. "Er . . . you want me to just drop by, chat and find out what I can?"

Rising to his feet, Curt said, "Yes. She'll talk to you more easily than she did to me." He didn't add that Miss Gus had practically thrown him off the property, such was her hate for him. Settling his cowboy hat on his head, Curt walked to the door. "Call me after your visit."

"Yes, sir, I will."

Curt left the office. As he walked around the corner toward his bright red truck, his mind revolved around how to get Miss Gus out of that damned property so he could have it. He *needed* it. Now. Not later. Fortner's offhand comment about a forest fire consuming the ranch had given him a new idea.

Griff was in the barn with the parts from an

old automatic posthole digger spread across a canvas on the floor. The day was warm and he appreciated the breeze through the box stall area where he was repairing the cranky equipment. Working alone for long stretches of time had given him time to think. The honesty and goodness of Miss Gus and Val had shown him how important it was to have integrity. It made him really want to apologize to Slade for the way he had treated him when he was a big shot on Wall Street. His brother had needed his help and he hadn't offered it. He felt terrible about it now and realized the right thing was to apologize sincerely to his twin.

He heard footsteps approaching across the concrete. Lifting his head, he saw it was Val. Griff felt she was a secret pleasure to him. She was tall, lithe, her red hair in a ponytail swinging behind her shoulders. Even though she wore typical ranch clothing, Levi's and a white, short-sleeved tee, they lovingly outlined her body. He wondered as he had many times if she had a man in her life. He'd not heard it come up in table talk and wasn't about to broach the topic himself. That would have been out of line. He was the hired hand. Not a family member.

"How's it going?" Val asked, halting and studying the parts of the posthole digger.

She tried to quell her reaction to Griff's gaze. On his hands and knees, a wooden toolbox nearby, he was easy to look at. The light and dark in the barn accentuated the hard planes of his sun-darkened face.

Griff gave her a half smile and he wiped his hands off on a nearby rag. "It's going."

"That thing hasn't been used in years," Val said. "I'm sure the carburetor needs to be cleaned out or replaced."

"You're right," Griff agreed. He pointed to the engine piece. "I was just starting to pull it apart to see if it's gummed up. I'm sure it is." And that meant buying a rebuilt carburetor for the digger. If one could be found.

"Did you try starting it first?"

"I broke the rope trying to get it going. I'll have to buy a replacement rope in town." Griff had a tough time keeping his eyes on his work. Val was a powerful draw. Loneliness, having been without a woman for a long time, was part of the allure. Another, which Griff tucked away in his heart, was his appreciation of her as a woman who was not only attractive but had a lot of common sense. Val was nothing like the women he'd had relationships with in New York City. They were beautiful tropical birds in comparison and would never survive the harsh environment of ranch life. Val wore no jewelry, no makeup, not even lipstick. She didn't need cosmetics. Her lips were a natural pink color. Most of all, he liked her freckles. They made her look like a young girl instead of the mature woman she was.

Val picked up the frayed and broken rope. "Well, this auger is about thirty years old. It's DOA, dead on arrival." She squatted in front of him, elbows resting on her thighs, opposite of where he was working. Griff had strong-looking fingers and yet, he expertly opened the engine and delicately began checking it with expert ease. His head was bent and she had a chance to absorb his strong profile. His mouth, which she found delicious, was pursed as he focused on his inspection. Her curiosity got the better of her.

"Do you miss your home?"

"What?" Griff looked up briefly. He saw in Val's face that she was open to his answer, and she was almost approachable. It was the first time she'd talked to him in a voice other than that of a boss, and it took him by surprise. Recovering, he managed a twisted smile. "New York? No."

"Why not? You lived there most of your life."

"I didn't have a choice as a kid," he said,

his fingers getting oily and dirty as he studied the carburetor. "I do as an adult."

"Do you think you'd have come back here if you hadn't lost your job?"

Shrugging, Griff said, "Probably not. But that's how things happen. Life takes unexpected turns." He looked up to see her features grow pensive. Did Val know how beautiful her blue eyes were? He wished he could tell her their color reminded him of the deep blue sky after sunset, but Griff thought better of sharing the observation. After all, she was his boss.

"I'm sorry you lost your aunt and uncle. And then to have your business fail. That must have been hard on you."

"It was a tough time," Griff agreed. Although it had helped to work with the FBI to help clean up the mess left behind. He'd done it gratis because he felt he'd been partly responsible for the economic collapse. The least he could do was help the FBI understand the inner workings of his and other firms on Wall Street. It had eased his guilt.

"I wonder how anyone could deal with losing *all* their money at once. Especially millions of dollars." Val studied him intently and watched his mouth pull in at the corners. Griff was experiencing frustration or pain of some kind over her probing question.

Placing the carburetor into a pan that had some cleaning fluid in it, he said, "My parents didn't have much money. My Dad would hunt deer and elk to put meat on our table. We were pretty much raised on wild food. When I got taken back east by my uncle, it was a whole other life for me to adjust to." Griff glanced up at her. Val's eyes were readable and he saw so many emotions in them. Heartened that she cared, he decided to open up. "At first, I wasn't used to the rich foods they gave me. I remember eating too much one time and throwing it up afterward." Griff added, "I was a poor ranch kid who lived off the land, not off the fat of the land."

Heart twinging, Val heard the pain in his low voice. He'd laughed, but it wasn't happy laughter. "I'm sorry. I've seen how shock and trauma can change a person's life in an instant."

"Being in the Air Force and over in the Middle East, I imagine you saw a lot."

"Yes, sometimes I saw a lot," Val murmured. She found the tension utterly disappearing as they talked with one another. Mesmerized, Val realized Griff was a man of many talents and much knowledge. "I had a lot of friends in Iraq. I saw what war did to them. They came out completely changed people." She met and held his stare. "I was just wondering if, what happened to you at six . . . do you think it changed you forever?"

The question was incisive and personal. Griff didn't mind, though. "You know, you're the first person I've ever met to ask me something like that."

"If it's too personal," Val backtracked, "you don't have to answer it."

"No, not at all." Griff managed a partial smile. "It's kinda nice someone cares enough to ask." He drowned momentarily in her softened blue eyes. When his gaze dropped to Val's lips, they parted. Groaning inwardly, Griff felt his attraction to Val grow as he realized she was someone he could honestly talk to. "I changed," he admitted. "My life took a one-hundred-and-eighty-degree turn. My uncle decreed that I would someday own his Wall Street firm. He had big dreams for me. I went to Harvard because that was his alma mater."

"That's quite a plum university," Val said. "I'll bet thousands would die for a chance to go to Harvard."

"I know," Griff said, retrieving the carburetor from the solution and resting the piece on his knee. He continued to clean it out with a cloth.

"Did you like going to Harvard?"

"Yeah, it was okay."

Val saw the sudden wistfulness come to his expression. "It wasn't Wyoming, though?" she guessed.

He met her gaze. "You are uncanny. Do you also mind read?" he teased.

A grin tugged at her lips and Val said, "No, not really."

"You have a lot of insight. How did you come by that?"

"The details of our lives shape us. As an intelligence officer in the Air Force, we looked at the little details in order to create a larger and more complete picture."

"Intelligence as in spy work?"

Val said, "Sometimes. Part of my job was working with a drug task force and we would pull raids in Iraq. For the most part, I was safe and I read satellite and drone maps and photographs. I would assess them and then write up reports on what I saw."

"Then you were in the thick of the fighting?" Griff asked. This was the first time she'd opened up. Griff wondered why today was different. He had so many questions for her but he was gun-shy. He felt his heart open and a silent joy trickled through it.

Sitting in the center of a barn, tearing apart an auger and talking with Val was a delicious and unexpected dessert.

"Yes, I was. It gave me personal pleasure to stop drug trafficking in Iraq. I worked with a group of men who were absolute professionals. We took down a lot of dealers."

"Sounds dangerous. Does Miss Gus know what you were doing over there?"

"It got dicey sometimes, but I never felt in serious danger. And I signed papers to not reveal what I did or learned. I didn't want my grandmother to worry any more than she otherwise would."

"That makes sense," Griff agreed. He held up the engine part. "You know anything about mechanics?"

"What ranch kid doesn't?" She took the part from him and enjoyed the contact with his fingers more than she should have.

Grinning, he said, "I remember working on machinery with my dad. He took Slade and me out with him to the barn from the time we were four. He'd spread the machine parts out on the floor just like this and teach us about every one. And then, he'd challenge us to put the thing back together again."

Examining the part, Val handed it back to him. "Well, I'm glad, because I think this carburetor is DOA. We'll need a rebuilt one to replace it."

Their fingers accidentally grazed one another. Instantly, warmth flowed into Griff's hand and he was surprised by his reaction. Secretly, he wanted to hold Val's hand, explore her skin and trail his fingers slowly up her arm, shoulder, and . . . Griff abruptly stopped where his hunger was taking him. Clearing his throat, he said, "Yes, you're right."

"Brent's Machine Shop carries old engine parts," Val said. "He's your best resource for this digger. And if you can't find anything, we'll have to put out money to buy a new one."

Gathering up the parts, Griff said, "Do you want to come with me?" She had never spelled out who was to pay for such items. Sometimes a wrangler merely identified what was needed to be bought but was not entrusted with the checkbook. His question had an ulterior motive, though. Griff wanted more time with Val. She made him feel like a man, and that felt damn good to Griff.

"Sure," Val said, rising. "Let me tell Gus. She may well have a grocery list, too."

"Great." Griff placed the parts in a nearby bucket and wiped his hands on a rag. "I'll meet you out at the truck in twenty minutes?"

"Yep," Val said as she left.

Watching her hips sway gently as she walked down the concrete corridor between the empty box stalls, Griff found himself feeling light-headed. That woman had the ability to spin his heart around. Griff cleaned up his mess and put everything away. The late afternoon sun's slats were now flowing into the barn. He felt like he was walking on air. Would Val continue to be open with him? Or was this just a fluke? Trying to tamp down his burning curiosity about who she was and how she'd come by this ability to see deeply into him, he couldn't help wanting another chance to speak openly with her on a personal level.

Griff strode out of the barn and placed the bucket in the truck. He'd need these parts in order to buy replacements. Turning, he looked at the rough, natural beauty of the Bar H. The ranch house was huge. The cedar had long ago taken on a silvery patina from the hard, long winters in Wyoming. He climbed the steps, needing to clean up before he left for town.

Entering the foyer, Griff inhaled the fragrances wafting from the kitchen. Gus seemed delighted to be cooking for them and he was grateful. The odor of Middle Eastern spices filled the air. Tonight, Miss Gus was making lamb kebabs. His mouth watered as he quickly moved up the stairs to his room on the second floor. As he opened the door to his room, he heard Gus and Val's laughter drifting up from the kitchen. A sudden vision came to him, of himself at five years old with his parents in the kitchen at the Tetons Ranch. His father was sharing a joke with their mother. He and Slade were sitting at the table waiting to be served dinner. He recalled the lightness, the happiness that always exuded from their kitchen. His father possessed a deep, booming laughter that rolled out of his chest like thunder. His mother had a good sense of humor. Smiling sadly, Griff gently tucked away the warm memory, quietly closed the door and headed to the bathroom to wash up.

Val was sitting in the driver's seat of the truck when Griff walked out of the house a few minutes later. He climbed in and shut the squeaking door. He needed to get oil on those hinges.

Val started up the truck and drove slowly down the graveled driveway. Pulling a paper from her blouse pocket, she handed it to him. "Gus gave me a long grocery list."

Griff chuckled and read it. "Is she buying out half of Albertson's?" he asked, referring to the local grocery store.

Laughing a little, Val turned the truck onto the main highway leading into Jackson Hole. There were more cars on the road than usual because it was high tourist season. Millions drove through the town in order to reach Yellowstone National Park. "She said we're running low on everything. And cooking for three is different than cooking for one. Lots of adjustments for her right now."

Resting his arm on the window frame because the air-conditioning didn't work on the old truck, Griff said, "Miss Gus is a treasure. You're lucky to have a grandmother like her."

"She is," Val agreed. Giving him a quick glance, she asked, "Are your grandparents still living?"

"No, neither set, unfortunately."

"You and your brother Slade have really suffered serious family losses."

Again, Griff was truck by her compassion. "I guess I never looked at it that way," he admitted.

"Sorry to hear that," she said, and again Griff was struck by her compassion. "Family is everything. When Gus asked me to take a hardship discharge and come home, I couldn't refuse her."

"Miss Gus said you didn't want to come home." Griff cautioned himself, because he saw her fine, thin brows dip over his blurted statement. "I'm sorry, it's none of my business." And it wasn't. He wondered if he'd just slammed the door that had magically opened up between them earlier. Damn, why didn't he think before he spoke?

"That's okay." Val sighed. "There's something about you, Mr. McPherson, that makes it easy for me to talk to you." She slid him a glance. He looked surprised. The worry in his green eyes dissolved. Did he know how readable he was? Val had learned a long time ago in the military to hide her real feelings. All they wanted from her was her threat-assessment skills or her abilities on a drug raid. Not her insight. Not her personal feelings. Somehow, Griff was pulling them out of her whether she wanted to reveal them or not. What was it about this wrangler?

Giving him a quick smile, Val added, "I guess my years in the military are showing."

"Doing top secret work," Griff said, his anxiety reducing as he saw that she wasn't going to take his comment the wrong way.

"That's part of it," Val slowly admitted.

She followed the long, flowing curves of the highway. On her right was the river. On her left, a thousan-foot rocky cliff. Wyoming was a wild, beautiful country. Her fingers open and closed around the steering wheel. "The truth is, I didn't want to come home." Mouth compressed, she felt an old pain rising up in her again. "I really didn't. But when Gus broke her hip, I knew. . . ."

Griff watched Val retreat somewhere deep inside of herself. There was an ache in her husky tone. He waited. He needed to keep his curiosity in check and his mouth shut. Watching Val wrestle with something unknown, Griff could see anguish in her expression. And then, it disappeared. She straightened her back a little and gave him an apologetic look.

"I knew that my grandmother couldn't keep this place going by herself anymore. I guess, deep in my heart, I knew this would happen someday."

"Coming home?" Griff ventured.

"Yeah." The word came out hard. Flat.

"I guess, in a sense," Griff probed gently, "we've both been torn from the world we knew and plopped down here once more. For whatever the reason."

"That's a very good insight, too," Val praised. "You're right — we're both orphans of a sort who were forced to come home to an unknown situation."

"You nailed that one," Griff said. "When I showed up at Slade's ranch, he wasn't really happy to see me. And honestly, I couldn't blame him." Mouth turning downward, Griff added, "I need to apologize to him. A long time ago, he called asking me for a loan. The Tetons Ranch was going under. I turned him down, thinking he was a bad loan risk." Shaking his head, Griff uttered tiredly, "It was so stupid of me not to help him out. What was I thinking? I had millions. All he wanted was fifty thousand dollars to pay off the mortgage. Slade was struggling to keep our family ranch from being lost and a loan would have cured those problems. I was so arrogant then."

Val couldn't help her surprise. "You turned your own brother down for a loan?"

Griff said, "I did. It was the worst choice I've ever made. And then I was the one who came crawling back to our ranch asking for help." Griff knew he deserved whatever judgment she may have of the situation. Hearing the disbelief in her voice, he managed a twisted smile. "Just desserts, don't you think?"

"Karma in action, for sure," Val agreed.

"Wow, you didn't give him a loan? He is family."

"I know. I've got a lot to atone for," Griff quietly admitted. "One of the things I'm going to do very soon is go over and make amends. I need to make things right between Slade and me."

"It's the right thing to do," Val agreed. She slowed down as they drove into the outskirts of Jackson Hole. "I know it will help heal the wound between the two of you. Think of it as a burr under your collective family saddle. It will keep things raw between you until it's permanently removed."

Gazing over at her, Griff said, "It's up to me to remove it."

"You're lucky," Val growled, more to herself than to him. "Not everyone gets the chance to remove the burrs in their families."

CHAPTER SEVEN

It's time. . . . Griff dragged in an unsteady breath and pulled into the driveway of the Tetons Ranch. Turning into the graveled parking area between the ranch house and the big red barn, Griff spotted his brother out in an arena with his endurance mustang stallion, Thor, putting the stud through its paces.

Griff suddenly became anxious. The stupid decision years earlier weighed heavy on his shoulders as he emerged from the truck and saw Slade look in his direction. Griff couldn't read the expression on his face because he was too far away.

Girding himself internally, Griff looked around. He saw Shorty, the wrangler, walking a student's endurance mount toward the barn. Lifting his hand in greeting, Shorty waved and smiled. Griff wondered whether Jordana was home or at work. She was an emergency-room physician at the local hospital. He liked her. In so many ways, he'd seen Slade's rough demeanor tamed by her gentle smile and soft approach. Now, Griff wished she was here. In the past, Jordana had been the referee and ratcheted down the anger between the brothers.

Today we put an end to that anger, he thought, the gravel crunching loudly beneath his boots as he approached the pipe fence corral. The morning sun had just topped the mountains to the east, the golden slats flooding silently across the rich, green valley. He halted at the closed gate.

"I thought I'd stop over, Slade," he called. "Do you have a moment to talk?"

Slade called out a command to Thor. Instantly, the stallion, who was on a twenty-foot longe line, skidded to a stop. He snorted, tossed his head, his attention fully on his master.

"Yeah," Slade called. "Give me a minute."

Griff stood patiently. He hadn't called ahead. This wasn't something he wanted to tackle with Slade over the phone. No, this had to be done in person. His stomach twisted into a painful knot. Years earlier, the doctor had warned him that the stress of Wall Street would give him ulcers if he didn't take a step away from it. His stomach had always been his tension barometer in life. Griff knew this would be one of the hardest things he'd done in a long time. And he wasn't looking forward to it.

Slade led the endurance stallion to the gate.

"What brings you over?" he asked, opening it and leading the stallion out of the corral.

Griff fell in step beside Slade. "I wanted to find out how you and Jordana are doing." That wasn't a complete lie, but it was secondary. Slade gave him a questioning glance and a glare, as if sensing something else was up. His brother was very close to the earth and had his sixth sense well in place.

Slade nodded and took off his Stetson for a moment, wiped his brow and settled it back on his head. "Let me give Thor to Shorty. I don't really have a lot of time to spend with you."

Inwardly, Griff felt the gritty anger barely veiled in Slade's tone. "Do you have time for a cup of coffee?"

With a grimace, Slade muttered, "Barely."

Griff's anxiety soared. Slade was in a crusty mood, as always. Griff had hoped his recent marriage to Jordana would dissolve the vinegar in him. To be fair, Griff acknowledged, his twin had been struggling since the age of seventeen to hold on to their family ranch. The harsh lines in Slade's face attested to that. He was as rough and hardy as a Wyoming winter. Not much survived winters around here, but Slade had. He'd thrived in the harsh elements and challenges that life had constantly thrown at him. Maybe his apology would put them on a better footing with each other. Griff hoped so. He wanted his twin's approval and support. But would Slade forgive him?

Shorty took Thor, nodded to Griff and then turned the stud around and led him into the barn.

"Let's go inside," Slade ordered in a gruff tone.

Griff tried to keep his voice light. Maybe if he remained unruffled, his brother's behavior toward him would ease. "Things going well?"

"Couldn't be better. Jordana just got a promotion. She's now head of E.R. at the hospital. Got a big raise too, which helps us."

"Good," Griff said. He heard relief in his brother's voice. "Does it mean longer hours for Jordana at the hospital?"

"Actually," Slade replied, opening the back door to the house, "it doesn't. She's got a regular nine-to-five job now, five days a week."

Entering the ranch house that had once been his home, Griff waxed nostalgic. Slade had never redecorated the house since their parents' deaths. It was the same and he found it comforting. Griff knew Slade did too, or he'd have changed it a long time ago. Moving into the kitchen, Griff took off his hat and set it on the end of the rectangular pine table. Slade went to the counter and pulled down two mugs from the cabinet.

"Sit down," he said.

Taking a chair, Griff felt himself winding up internally. He wasn't sure of Slade's reaction to what he was going to say. Slade had a terrible temper and Griff didn't want to stir it up. His brother had a right to be angry but he hoped that anger wouldn't appear.

Boots thunking against the waxed pine flooring, Slade brought over two steaming cups of coffee and sat down.

"I don't have much time. What really brings you over here?" he demanded in a growl, sizing up Griff.

Guarded, Griff said, "I wanted to catch you up on what was going on."

Slade gave him a wary look. "I hear from Andy you just got a job out at the Bar H."

"Yes, I did and it's a good job."

"Miss Gus has probably got her whip in hand and you're working from dusk to dawn." Slade drank his coffee.

Managing a slight smile, Griff said, "I like Miss Gus. She's a typical Wyoming rancher. Too bad she broke her hip in her fall last year."

Frowning, Slade said, "Yes, when that happened, all the ranchers in the valley rallied around her. We all took time out to go over and help her keep the ranch going. Cheryl, her daughter, died just prior to that, so it was really hard on Miss Gus."

Moving the thick white ceramic mug between his hands, Griff felt a bit of Slade's defensiveness dissolve. Griff asked, "Did you know that Gus's granddaughter, Val Hunter, has returned? She took a hardship discharge out of the Air Force to come home and try to save the Bar H."

Brows rising, Slade said, "No . . . this must be recent."

"Last week."

"Hmm, I haven't spoken with Gwen Garner of late. I'll bet she knew about it. So, you're saddled with two women over there?"

"It's not hard," Griff admitted. Slade seemed less prickly. Maybe by starting out with small talk he could build up to why he had come for the visit. "They're good

137

people. They want to get the Bar H back on its feet."

Slade rocked back in the chair. "I never thought Val would *ever* come home again."

Griff gave his brother a quizzical look. "Why?"

"She didn't tell you?"

"No. I'm hired help, not family."

Smiling thinly, Slade said, "Of course. Buck Hunter, her father, was a drunken son of a bitch. And he was a mean drunk." Slade's mouth turned down and he eased the chair back down on four feet. Staring at his mug, he muttered, "He was abusive. One time, his wife ended up in the hospital. I found out from Gwen Garner she suspected he was beating up Val, too. But no one could prove it. Gwen wanted to intervene, but until Cheryl or Val pressed charges or asked for help, it was all conjecture. Cheryl lied to the paramedics who took her to the hospital. She told them a horse dumped her on a rail."

Alarmed, Griff sat up. "I didn't know any of this." His mind spun with shock. Now, it made more sense to him about Val's wariness. He was a man. Did she distrust him because of what her father had done to her? It left a lot of questions and a bad taste in Griff's mouth.

138

"Buck was as mean as Red Downing," Slade warned him. "Those two bastards had a lot in common, including no respect for anyone. As much as I dislike Curt Downing, you gotta feel for a kid whose father used to beat him black-and-blue. In those days, the law never did anything about it. The mind-set was it was your family and anything you did to them was none of anyone's business." His brows flattened.

"Downing is mean, though."

"If Val was abused, how come she's not mean, too?" Griff said, more to himself than to his brother.

"Not everyone carries abuse forward to the next generation," Slade replied. "Jordana told me when a child is abused, their cortisol levels remain high. Cortisol is similar to adrenaline, the flight-or-fight hormone. She said the abuse survivor can either get violent toward others or internalize it. There's a price to pay for that, too."

Rubbing his chin, Griff murmured, "Maybe, if I get an opening with Val, I'll share the information with her. Think she'd see Jordana for help?"

"I don't know," Slade said, sipping his coffee. "Bring it up to Val and see what she thinks."

"Well," Griff said, a grimace crossing his mouth, "Val doesn't exactly trust me."

"Maybe," Slade said, "she's seeing you through her abuse. It'll be hard for her to trust any man, since it was a man that abused her. Some part of her may see her father and not you. There are a lot of wounds to be healed between an abuse survivor and their world at large."

"That would explain a lot of Val's behavior toward me," Griff said. He gave Slade a grateful look. "This really helps me understand more about her."

"You should talk with Jordana. She can give you tips and pointers on how to deal positively with Val."

Griff held Slade's gray gaze. The small talk had made Slade less defensive. "I appreciate your help, but I should admit I came over here for a different reason." He took a deep breath. "Slade, I owe you an apology for my behavior toward you." Griff forced out the rest. "I was wrong not to give you that loan for the ranch."

Surprise flared in Slade's eyes. He stared for a long moment at Griff, sizing him up. His mouth hardened and he dug into his brother's eyes. "I never understood why you did it, Griff. You came from this ranch, yourself. And I'm your brother."

Griff sat back and absorbed his twin's anger. "At the time you called and asked me for the loan, I'd just been promoted to the head of the derivatives department at the financial services firm." He looked down at the table, shame flowing through him. Griff forced himself to meet Slade's angry gaze. "The truth is, I was full of myself. I thought I was king of the world. At just a snap of my fingers, I could do or have anything I wanted. I was arrogant and stupid. . . ."

Slade shook his head. "And you were so full of yourself that you didn't care what happened to our family ranch?"

Nodding, Griff swallowed against a dry throat. His heart was pounding hard and inwardly, he felt sad. "Yes, I screwed up. I'd been gone so long from the Tetons Ranch, it no longer meant what it should have to me."

Slade's eyes were a mixture of anger and grief. "You were cut off from this ranch and from me. Our aunt and uncle from New York weren't very family oriented. They conveniently forgot about the rest of us."

"You're right, they did," Griff admitted quietly, the charge paining him. "I grew up with a focus on making money."

"Money is a heartless bastard at best," Slade said in a low growl. He wrapped his hands around the mug and stared hard at Griff. "You got brainwashed. Our parents taught us better." Slade jammed a finger down at the floor. "The land is our *soul,* Griff, plain and simple. There aren't many people anymore who have a ranch, a family history and hope for the future. We were lucky and didn't even know it."

"No question. I wish . . . I wish I could do this all over again, Slade. I wish I'd have been more mature and had less of an ego. I should have loaned you the money out of my own pocket, simply because you were family. You are my brother." His eyes narrowed and he held Slade's stare. "I'm sorry. I was wrong and if I had to do it all over again, I'd loan you that money in a heartbeat."

Nostrils flaring, Slade absorbed Griff's sincere apology. He saw his twin was suffering badly from his choices. "It's a little too late for that," he ground out.

"I know it is, and I deserve your anger. I disappointed you, Slade." His voice rose with emotion. "I want to try and change the bad decision I made. I can't make it up by giving you that money because I'm flat broke. In a way, maybe God paid me back for what I did to you." Swallowing hard, Griff added in a hoarse tone, "My whole life went belly-up with the crash and the first place I thought to go was here."

Listening to Griff's emotional explanation, Slade scowled. He stared down at the cup of coffee between his hands. "That's how it always is — get in trouble and you run home for a roof over your head."

"Yes, I did, Slade. And thank God, you took me in even though you didn't want to. You had more maturity, more courage, than I did. I'm grateful for your compassion."

Sighing loudly, Slade shook his head. "In the end, you're my brother, Griff. I would never let you starve."

"I was willing to let you lose our family ranch," Griff reminded him in a grim voice. "I was riding a high of money, power and position. I chose it over family and home. That's something I can't forgive myself for." He looked down at his hands that now bore the calluses of hard work. "I wanted to stay here and reinvent myself as a Wyoming rancher." He placed his hands on the table and stared across at Slade. "This is something I have to do on my own and without your help. When I came here after losing everything, I began to realize just how much hard, consistent work you'd put into our ranch. And you were right — it didn't belong to me anymore. I know in Mom and

Dad's will, they gave each of us half of the ranch." He hung his head, the words being torn out of him. "But the truth is, Slade, I don't deserve any part of this ranch."

The silence became heavy in the kitchen. Slade shoved the chair back, the sound a screech. He unwound his tall body as he stood up. Hands on hips, he walked to the kitchen counter and stared sightlessly out the window.

Griff understood his brother's emotions. He'd helped cause them. Griff stood and walked over to him. "I'm prepared to go to an attorney of your choice and to turn over my half of this ranch to you."

Slade slowly turned his head and stared at Griff. "You'd do that?"

Heart pounding, Griff said in a steady voice, "Yes, I *want* to do this, Slade. It's the only way I can prove to you I *am* sorry. I can't change the past." He motioned out the window where he could see the parking area, the red barn and, in the background, the magnificent Teton that jutted toward the blue sky. "I lost my half of this ranch when I turned you down for that loan."

Slade stared at him for another long moment. Finally, he said, "I'm going to take you up on your offer, Griff. It's the right thing to do. I never thought you would give

144

me the ranch, but I was wrong."

Griff gave his brother a half smile. "Life has a funny way of rearranging us. At first, when I arrived, I hated Wyoming, but I had nowhere else to go. Now, I wake up in the morning knowing I'm the luckiest man on the planet." Griff gestured out the window. "There's fresh air out here instead of car pollution. Sunshine, not canyons of skyscrapers that blot it out. The only place I could go to see green grass in New York was in Central Park."

Slade relaxed, tension bleeding out of him. "Central Park cannot compare to Wyoming," he agreed, the edge off his tone. Again, he stared at Griff. "You really mean this? You're willing to sign over our ranch to me?"

"Yes, with my heart and soul." Griff stuck out his hand to his brother. "Out here in the West, a man's word and a handshake is all that's needed. Shake my hand, Slade, and the deal is done. All that's left is for me to sign the papers whenever you want me to do it."

Slade clasped Griff's proffered hand. "Okay," he rasped, suddenly emotional. "You got a deal."

Tears pricked the back of Griff's eyes. He saw tears in Slade's, too, but he wasn't about to point it out. His brother's grip was firm and strong. As they released each other's hands, Griff managed a slight smile. "This ranch is in good hands. You never wavered, Slade. You loved this place with your whole heart. You never lost sight of its importance like I did. I want to start over, Slade. I love ranching, I've discovered. I find a peace in doing everyday things out here in Nature. I guess I'm rediscovering myself."

"The prodigal son returns home."

"Yes, I am a prodigal son in every way," Griff agreed. "I got lost, Slade. And I lost the morals and values I was born and raised with."

"Losing all that, though, brought you home," Slade said. "And now, you're picking up the pieces of your life."

They headed back to the table where Griff sipped his cooled coffee. Now, there was relief and even some peace in Slade's expression. The wall between them had disappeared. Griff felt a tender thread of love in his heart for his estranged brother. "You're the rudder for our family," he told Slade. "Your moral compass, your knowing it was right to fight to keep our ranch in the family, deserve a good outcome."

"Well, you sure as hell have surprised me," Slade admitted, finishing off his coffee. He walked to the kitchen counter and put his cup in the sink. "I never expected an apology from you, Griff."

Walking over to his brother, Griff also placed his emptied cup in the sink. "It was time, Slade. I intend on staying here the rest of my life."

"Really? You aren't going back east when things pick up?"

"No. I'm home no matter what happens," Griff said, and he managed a smile. "I feel good handing the Tetons Ranch over to you. We need to celebrate in some way after I sign those papers."

Happiness flowed through Slade. It was a stunning, unexpected gift. The ranch he'd given his sweat, blood and life for, was finally going to be all his. "Jordana is going to be over the moon when she hears what you're doing for us."

"I'm sure," Griff said. "Maybe I can wrangle a dinner invitation out of it after we do the transfer of ownership?"

"You bet," Slade said. "I'll talk to Jordana and give you a call."

"You sure? I don't want to butt in where I'm not welcome." Griff knew he couldn't tell Slade how much he'd missed that unspoken but magical connection with his twin. Since he'd come home, Slade had

147

wanted as little as possible to do with him.

Slade self-consciously wiped his eyes. He gave Griff an embarrassed look. "You don't know how many years I wished you were here, Griff. I missed you, but I couldn't tell you that."

Griff moved forward and threw his arms around his brother. For a brief moment, they hugged one another. Stepping back, Griff wiped away tears forming in his eyes. No longer was there pain or anger in Slade's gray gaze. Instead, if Griff was reading his twin right, there was a lot of unspoken love for him. Something old and hard broke loose in Griff's chest. It was as if a lump of black coal that had lived in his heart all these years suddenly dissolved. And in its place was a joy so euphoric he felt like shouting to the heavens with happiness.

Slade slapped him on the shoulder. "Come on, let's go see what Shorty is up to. I just bought two new mares I'm going to breed to Thor. I want you to look at them and see what you think."

Just the simple act of being included by Slade sent a powerful shaft of hope through Griff. "Okay," he murmured, his voice unsteady, "I'd like that."

Griff breathed in deeply as they stepped into the warming summer air. Settling the

Stetson on his head, he quickly caught up with Slade on his way to the barn. He wasn't very experienced regarding a horse's conformation, but Slade was trying to reach out to him the only way he knew how and for Griff, the gesture was enough. Hurt and anger no longer separated them. They were family again.

CHAPTER EIGHT

"Good day, Miss Gus!" Bobby Fortner called cheerily through the screen door of the Bar H. He mustered a big smile and held up the gift in his hands. "I've brought you the *best* two-pound box of chocolates that Jackson Hole has to offer!"

Frowning, Gus pushed the screen door open and stepped out onto the porch. "Why do I get the feelin', Bobby, that you're a Trojan horse come avisitin'?"

Blushing to the roots of his receding black hair, Bobby said, "Why, I have no idea, Miss Gus. When I called you, you said it was okay to come over."

Gus peered about. The ten-o'clock sun was warming the land. Val was out in the barn working on repairing the box stalls. And Griff was visiting his brother. "You're about as welcome as a rattler under my porch," she told him, squinting up at the thin, sloppily dressed Realtor. Gus had no patience with this guy even though she had relented to his pleading request to come for a short visit. "I know you work for Downing, so let's just cut to the chase, shall we?" She poked him in the chest with her index finger.

Bobby jumped back, almost spilling the box of candy he held. "Now, Miss Gus, it's true I've done some land deals for Mr. Downing, but I've been a Realtor here in this county for fifteen years." He gave her a simpering smile and tried to cajole her out of her black mood. "Here, please take these."

Eyeballing the box, Gus muttered, "Set them over there, Bobby," and she waggled her finger in the direction of the small table near the porch swing.

Quickly, he did as she requested. He returned, brushed his sweaty palms against his brown slacks and smiled at her. Gus didn't smile back. Gulping, he said, "I like to drop by the ranches in the valley from time to time."

"The Bar H ain't for sale, Fortner."

"Yes, ma'am, that's fine. I just wanted to see how things were going. I heard your granddaughter Val was home and you hired a new wrangler. I figured you were gussying up the place?"

Gus sat down on a nearby wooden rocking chair. She never took her eyes off Fortner, whose brow was gleaming with perspiration. He nervously pulled out a white linen handkerchief and blotted his forehead. "Yes, we are makin' a lot of repairs," she told the Realtor. "But that don't mean it's for sale."

"Pity," Bobby said, and he looked around with appreciation. "This is a beautiful place, Miss Gus. And you have half of Long Lake on your property. You know, there's a lot of developers who would give their eyeteeth for your place. And pay darn good money for it to boot." He gave her a hopeful look.

Mouth twisting, Gus said, "The day I sell to a developer is the day I'm dead!" She jabbed her cane toward the unseen lake. "There's too many developments in this county already! Why on earth would I want one more tourist here in Jackson Hole? We're overrun every summer. It's gettin' so you can't drive in town because of bumper-to-bumper traffic."

Bobby assumed a soothing tone. "Well, Miss Gus, this is just progress. You have to agree with me that our county has two of the most beautiful national parks in the USA — Yellowstone and the Grand Teton. You can't blame folks for wanting to visit here, can you?"

Snorting, Gus glared up at him. "The problem is developers, Fortner. And you're part of that cow-manure pile of money-grubbing Realtors who lays in bed with 'em. You're part of the problem, Bobby. Thank you for the chocolates, but I'm done talkin' with you."

He managed a weak smile. "I'm sorry to have upset you, Miss Gus. That wasn't my intention. I do need to let you know that Mr. Downing has offered you one-point-five-million dollars for this beautiful ranch."

"That's the real reason you came," Gus gritted out, her lips lifting away from her teeth. "Last time I feel sorry for you when you call and beg to come over with a gift. Tell him to stop makin' offers. I don't care if he laid a trillion dollars on this porch, I'm not selling. Now, leave!"

Fortner rubbed his hands on his slacks, jerkily bobbed his head and aimed himself toward the stairs.

"You don't get it," Gus called, standing up and leaning on her cane.

"Pardon?" Fortner turned and gave her a confused look.

"All you see is dollar bills where I see green, rollin' hills and forests."

He chuckled a little and gave her a hopeful look. "They're both green, aren't they?"

Frowning, Gus snapped, "That's a poor joke, Fortner. Skedaddle!" and she waved her cane threateningly in his direction.

Smiling unevenly, he waved good-bye and headed down the incline toward his black Mercedes-Benz. "Enjoy the chocolates," he called over his shoulder.

Gus waited until he drove away before moving over and grabbing up the box of chocolates. Setting them on the kitchen table inside, she figured they'd make a nice addition to the coming ten-o'clock coffee break they all took. Setting her cane against the cedar table, she pulled her red-checked apron off a nearby hook and wrapped it around her thin waist. She heard the screen door open and close.

"Who was just here?" Val called, coming in and taking off her leather work gloves.

"Oh, just that pity party Realtor, Bobby Fortner," Gus griped, motioning for Val to sit down at the table. "He comes by at least once every six months to see if I'm ready to sell." She told Val about the latest offer to buy the Bar H. Pointing to the box on the table, she said, "He's upped his ante. Today at least he bought me a two-pound box of chocolates!"

Val touched the box. "That was nice of him."

"Just part of his game, Val. It means nothing. But —" and she brightened with a wolfish smile "— we got some real nice chocolates to munch on for the next week or two. Ready for a cup of coffee?"

"More than ready," she said, dropping the gloves over a hook on the wall. "I can get the coffee, Gus. . . ."

"No, sit, sit," she replied, and motioned her toward a chair.

"I needed this break." Val watched her grandmother move slowly from one end of the kitchen counter to the other.

"Those box stalls all need replacing. It's a hard, thankless job," Gus agreed. She poured the coffee and brought the pot over to Val. "How far have you gotten on dismantling them?"

Grimacing, Val poured two cups of coffee. "Not far enough. A lot of the wood is over sixty years old. At first I thought we could save it, but we can't." She sipped the coffee. "It's not only the work involved, but the money to buy replacement posts that's giving me sticker shock."

"Buck should have replaced all of it when he was alive." Gus gave a sigh of frustration and sat down opposite Val. "Your mom told

155

me even though your father worked hard, he avoided doing the big, important projects."

"Yeah," Val griped, "just look at the miles of fence post that need to be replaced. The corrals are practically falling down."

"Good thing we have Griff. From what I could see the other day, he's doing a good job of pulling out the rotted posts, enlarging the holes and replacing them the right way."

Nodding, Val chose a chocolate from the box. "He is."

"That young man has good ranching genes in his blood. He's a darned hard worker. You'd have thought after dinner, he'd quit for the day. But he didn't. He was out there with a floodlight off the tractor until ten last night. Now, that's devotion."

"The kind we need to get this place out of its crippled state," Val said.

Patting her hip, Gus said, "Well, let's not get rid of *this* cripple." She chuckled.

Val gave her a pleading look. "Why won't you let me call the Scooter Store for you? I remember you were like a tumbleweed, always on the move, before your hip broke. I feel badly that you're hamstrung and having to rely on a cane to limp around on. Wouldn't you like to be pain-free and be the gadfly you were before?"

"I don't like relying on anything but my own two legs," Gus remonstrated. "My body used to be strong and healthy. Everything went to hell in a handbag when I broke my hip. I just hate the idea of getting weak."

Reaching over, Val covered her hand for a moment. "I understand, Gus. You've always been outdoors and active."

"But the power chairs come in different colors. They even have a red one." Red was Gus's favorite color. She watched the elder's silver brows rise with interest.

"Really?"

"Over lunch, let me show you the scooter website on my iPad."

Sticking out her lower lip, Gus warned, "Now, just because I *look* at 'em don't mean I'm gettin' one!"

Val fought not to laugh and remained serious. "Of course." She felt such a fierce love for her feisty grandmother. Gus was vital, independent and had pride. A lot of it. And confidence in herself. Val could see how the broken hip had shattered her sense of independence and kept her housebound for nearly a year. There was interest in Gus's eyes but Val knew she couldn't push her into anything. Gus had to be led to the water trough but she wasn't sure she'd drink from it.

The screen door opened and closed.

"Howdy," Griff said, hanging his Stetson on a peg near the entrance. "I'm back and I'll be getting to work." There was a sense of peace that descended upon Griff as he stood in the entrance to the kitchen. Gus smiled in his direction.

"Whoa," Gus said. "Grab a cup of coffee and join us for a moment."

Griff hesitated, wanting to continue removing and resetting the posts in the corral. "Well . . ."

"Git over here, young man!"

"Yes, ma'am," he murmured, giving Miss Gus a slight grin. Griff poured himself a cup of coffee. Internally, he compared how he felt being at Slade's home to being here at the Bar H. It was the same feeling. That surprised Griff as he walked over and took a seat next to Gus, who always sat at the head of the table, a spot she'd earned.

Val couldn't keep her gaze off Griff. He had cleaned up, his red bandanna tied around his throat and looking ruggedly handsome in his pale blue cowboy shirt and Levi's. It was his well-shaped mouth, the corners tipped slightly upward, that made heat begin to awaken in her lower body. Did

158

Griff know how sexy he was? Val didn't think so. "How did your visit go with your brother this morning?" she asked as he sat down.

"It went well," Griff said, meeting her warm blue gaze. Strands of red hair curled at her temples and became a crimson frame for her beautiful face. Tearing his gaze from Val, he looked over at Gus. "I think we've buried the hatchet."

"Good," Gus said, slapping him heartily on the shoulder. "Family should get along, not fight."

Val said nothing and sipped her coffee. She wondered what her life would have been like if her father hadn't always instilled fear in them.

"I'm going to work on the corral the rest of the day," Griff told the elder.

"From what I can see, you did one heck of a job yesterday pullin' twenty posts."

"It's just a drop in the bucket. I counted two hundred posts."

"It needed to be done a long time ago," Gus said, her brows knitting. "But that son-in-law of mine was immune to the really hard work that was required to keep a ranch running in good condition."

Griff glanced over at Val. She looked introspective and felt withdrawn. Was she thinking about her father? Fighting his concern, he said to Gus, "I figure if I work hard, I can replace another twenty posts today."

"Val is dismantling those ten box stalls in the barn. You two young'uns are going to be dragging by the time dinner rolls around."

Val suddenly got up from the table. She couldn't handle being so close to Griff. He stirred things up in her and it left her feeling confused. "Hey, speaking of that, I'm off to the barn again." She took her cup over to the sink, rinsed it out and picked up her gloves. "What's for lunch, Gus?"

"Lessee . . ." she murmured, touching her sharply pointed chin. "I just made up some tuna for sandwiches, got some sweet pickles I canned last year from my greenhouse garden out of the pantry and I'll be puttin' in the bread to bake shortly. I got chocolate cake for dessert. Will that do?"

Val said, "Sounds delicious. Thanks for making it. I really appreciate it."

Gus snorted and muttered, "Well, I'd better be good for *something* around here!"

Griff laughed with Val. He watched her wave goodbye to her grandmother and disappear down the hall. Cupping his hands around his mug, he stole a look over at Gus. Should he ask? He heard the screen door open and close. His curiosity was eating him alive.

"My brother Slade said that Val's father, Buck, was abusive when he was drunk." He searched the elder's wrinkled face. "I hope I'm not overstepping my boundaries here. I just wanted to understand the truth of the situation."

Sighing, Gus raised her brows. "No, you're not oversteppin' your bounds, son." She liked this young man. He was a fine, hard worker and he was respectful. There weren't many men like him around anymore. Griff reminded her of her late husband, Pete, and she warmed to his question. "We're a small cow town so everyone knows everyone else's business. Buck Hunter married my daughter, Cheryl. Even when he was courtin' her, I could tell he was a mean son of a bitch. I could see it in his eyes and in the way he overreacted to the least little thing. I tried to get my daughter to see how dangerous he was."

"But she didn't see it?"

"Nope. There's all kinds of love, Griff. My husband cherished me. He thought I was a goddess walkin' this earth and he treated me as such." Her eyes narrowed and her voice dropped to a growl. "And then you have a man like Buck who abuses and disrespects women. Cheryl was sure she could cure Buck of his alcoholism. But the truth was, after they got married, she couldn't change him one bit."

"From what I know," Griff said gently, seeing the woman's pain, "an alcoholic won't get better until they want to, no matter what the family wants."

"Yep, bang on." Gus shook her head. "And then it got worse. When Cheryl was pregnant with Val, he began to use the smallest excuse to beat the tar out of my daughter."

"Didn't Cheryl call the sheriff?"

"That's what I asked her — why didn't you get help? For whatever reason, my daughter felt that she'd caused the situation. She was an enabler. She took on the guilt and said it was her fault that Buck was beating her up."

Sitting there, Griff digested the information. "What happened after Val was born?"

"For a while, Buck was good. But that's because we had Cheryl come over to our ranch in Cheyenne. Val was born there and for the first two months of her life, they stayed with us while Buck remained at the Bar H. At that time, I had no idea Buck was beating up on my daughter. I was just reacting on my gut hunch that something was terribly wrong.

"I tried to get Cheryl to see Buck for what he was. I warned her that when Buck was drunk, he might harm her or Val. I was so scared for the baby. Pete was so upset he talked to the county sheriff where we lived. But he said as long as Cheryl didn't press charges against Buck, there was nothing we could do legally."

"What did you do?" Griff knew Gus was not the type of person to let something like this slide, legal or not. Her family was at risk.

"I drove Cheryl and Val home. And when we got here, I cornered Buck in a back room and read him the riot act. I shoved my finger in his face and told him that if he *ever* laid a hand on them, I was calling the sheriff and charging him with assault."

"Did that work?"

"It worked for three years," Gus said. "You gotta understand, I was driving hundreds of miles once a week to check on them. Buck knew I was good for my word. When I'd arrive, I'd thoroughly check Val out. I didn't want to see any bruises on her little body. Cheryl promised that Buck had settled down. He'd yell at them, but he never lifted a hand toward them when drunk." Gus heaved a sigh.

"But that changed. When Val was four, she left the house one day in early June because she saw a butterfly on a flower in the front yard. Val loved butterflies. Buck caught her down in the garden area where she'd chased it to. He pulled off his leather belt and beat the tar outta her. Val wasn't supposed to leave the house on her own at that age."

Anger flowed through Griff. "She was only four years old. Little kids explore. They don't realize —"

Gus held up her hand. "I know what you're gonna say. And I agree with you. Buck brought Val back to the house screaming to the high heavens. He tossed her into her bedroom and locked the door. Cheryl, who was in the basement doin' washing, heard her daughter screaming. She ran up the stairs and confronted Buck. He told her she should have been watching Val. Cheryl was outraged that he'd struck Val with a leather belt. Buck went after her with his fists. She never told me or Pete about it. Then, when Val was sixteen, Buck beat Cheryl so badly she ended up in the hospital."

"God," Griff whispered. He saw Gus frown, her blue eyes squinting with pain. "I'm so sorry. . . ."

"Cheryl called me from the hospital. She had a busted jaw, fractured eye socket and a broken arm. I called the Teton County sheriff and slapped assault charges against Buck."

"Pete and I immediately drove over to the Bar H. Val was in terrible emotional shape. She was so broken by her father's latest, worst attack upon her mother. When we got here, Val sobbed and ran into my arms. She shook like a leaf in a storm." Gus wiped the tears from her eyes. "To this day, I'll *never* forget that moment. That girl clung to me like I was the last life preserver thrown off the Titanic."

Griff didn't know what to say. The anguish in Gus's face and voice was palpable. He wanted to help, but didn't know how. He reached out and touched her arm for a moment. "Are you okay?"

"Oh, don't never mind me!" She dug a tissue from her pocket and wiped her eyes. "I just get so angry over it all. Cheryl refused to press assault charges against Buck. He came home with a smirk on his face. I'll never forget the smug look he gave me. I'm convinced Cheryl died early because she was so beaten down in every way by Buck.

"Val went off to college because she

wanted to get away from this horrible place full of evil memories and experiences and never return." Gus sighed and stuffed the tissue back in her pocket. "I feel bad for cajoling her to come home. I know the memories that haunt her. But I'm *not* going to let Buck Hunter drive our family away from our homestead! Val has a lot on her table, Griff. She's wrestling with the past every minute of every day. She lived in a hell we can't *ever* imagine."

Shaking his head, Griff gave her a sympathetic look. "I'm really sorry, Gus. I wish I could do something to fix it."

"No one can. Val's carrying her family's collective wounds. I try to love her, support her, but she's got the past all bottled up inside of her just like her mother did. She's sitting on a keg of dynamite. I'm worried that it will manifest itself as a disease. Cheryl died of cancer. It's a proven medical fact that people who get this dreaded disease are often suppressing or repressing their bad feelings and terrible experiences. I'm trying with all my heart to get her to open up, but she's just as closed up as her mother was."

"I noticed," Griff said, "that she doesn't trust me. At first, I couldn't figure it out. I wondered if it was something I'd done or said."

Patting his hand, Gus said, "No, it's not you, son. I really think Val sees all men through the glass darkly of her father. He broke her trust in *all* men with what he did to her."

A cold, drenching feeling flowed through Griff. "She's beautiful and intelligent, Gus. I was wondering why she wasn't married."

Gus grabbed her cane and walked over to the kitchen sink. "She's avoided men most of her life. And then, when she went into the Air Force, I cried, thinking she'd gone from a war in her family to a different kind of war. I've done a lot of reading up on abused children. People like Val, who are wounded and haven't been able to discharge the terror and anger toward their abuser, often choose risky or dangerous careers."

"Sort of like carrying a psychic disease," Griff suggested.

"Yep." Gus rested her hips against the sink and looked toward him. "Abuse is like a toxic infection to a person's heart and soul. If they don't learn how to release it, clean themselves out, they live with this monster inside them forever.

"Val carries the family's skeletons within her. I'm confounded on how to help her."

"I don't know how I should act around

her, either. I don't want to cause her more stress."

"You know, I've worked with abused animals before and the best thing you can do is have a quiet voice, a gentle touch and don't press them. Over time, I've seen animals overcome their hurtful past and learn how to trust once more. But it all takes time. . . ."

His heart ached for Val. He had never had as powerful a reaction to any woman as he had to her. There was something mysterious and desirable about her. She beckoned to him and Griff knew it wasn't mutual. This all explained what he had seen in her, why every time Val looked at him, he saw wariness in her gaze. His heart lurched in his chest. Griff felt driven to help her escape the prison of her past. But how could he get her to trust him?

CHAPTER NINE

Val needed some help. It was late afternoon, the temperature in the high eighties and the barn sweltering with heat. Wiping her perspiring brow with the back of her glove, she walked outside and dragged in a deep breath of cooler air. Down below the gently sloping hill where the barn stood, she saw Griff at work pulling out old posts from the dismantled corral. He'd removed his shirt, his upper body gleaming with sweat. For a moment, she simply watched the powerful movements of his well-muscled arms, his broad shoulders bunching and deep chest expanding as he hauled the recalcitrant post out of the dry ground. He looked like a Greek god, Apollo, come to life. And it stirred her heart and lower body. The sensations were unexpected, but lush and gratifying.

This was the first time she'd seen Griff naked from the waist up. He was focused on his work, his Stetson shading his eyes from the harsh rays of the sun overhead. His flesh shone like bronze. In this part of the country, sun was at a premium and men would often shed their shirt during the summer just to absorb the rays. Winter came early to Wyoming and stayed late. With so many cloudy days ahead, Val understood why Griff was taking maximum advantage of the sunshine.

Griff crouched to pet their black-and-white barn cat, Tuxedo. The five-year-old male had a white vest, black body, four white paws and a blaze down his face. He kept the area free of mice, gophers and rats. A softened smile came to Val's lips as she watched Tuxedo rub himself across Griff's knees. Her heart lurched when Val realized he was smiling and talking to the cat as if it were a human.

A memory came smashing back to Val. She was eight years old and she watched her father shoot a stray cat walking through the pasture. Val had tried to give the cat warning, but it had been too late. Buck hated cats. Val remembered running away from her father and into the ranch house. She'd found her mother baking in the kitchen. Clinging to her, Val sobbed out the shocking event. Her mother had become agitated. She'd pulled her into a bedroom upstairs and told her to stop crying. She now understood that her mother was just scared that Buck would become enraged at her tears, but back then Val couldn't stop the tears streaming down her cheeks. She loved all animals and to see her father kill one for no good reason was just too much for her tender, young heart.

Sighing, Val dragged herself out of the unhappy memory. Just focusing on Griff as he talked to and petted the cat soothed some of the anguish she felt. What was it about this wrangler? He made her feel safe in an unsafe world. Something deep inside of her urged her to go down and ask Griff for the help she needed but was afraid to ask for. Val rarely trusted any man. She had found safety in her job as an intel specialist and working with a drug unit from time to time. Her day job was mostly comprised of women and she felt secure among them. Sometimes, she was out in the field in undercover operations. Men always made her feel threatened for no obvious reason. Her boss had been a man in his fifties, and was considered a wonderful boss by everyone. Yet, Val's alarms went off any time he walked by her desk or worked with her on interpretation of the photos taken by drones.

She was always relieved when he walked away from her desk.

But Griff inspired a different feeling from her entirely. Somehow feeling safe enough to ask this man for help, Val sauntered down the grassy slope toward the dismantled corral to the left of the ranch house. As she approached, she saw Griff glance up in her direction. At first, he looked surprised. And then he straightened up and reached out to grab his shirt from a nearby post. By the time she arrived, Griff had buttoned his shirt up. There was a curious code in the West, Val realized. Most men still treated women as special. They were like knights from the olden days. And a woman was treated like a princess.

"I need some help up in the barn," she told him without preamble, trying to remain immune to his perspiring face and those narrowing green eyes. "I've run into some trouble removing a corner four-by-four. Do you have a moment?"

"Sure." Griff leaned down, petted the cat one more time and then pulled the gloves from his belt. "Let's go."

As they walked side by side, Val made sure there was plenty of room between them. She liked his easy gait. Griff carried himself proudly, his shoulders back and head held high. A question tore out of her before she could stop it. "Were you ever in the military?"

"Me?" Griff smiled at her as they walked up the gravel driveway toward the barn. "No. I thought about it. My father had been in the Marine Corps. I remember a number of times him urging us boys to think about going in for an enlistment. He said the military was a real gift to him."

They entered the shade within the barn. "How was it a gift?" she wondered, walking down the main passageway. Val felt herself yearning to know more about Griff. He wasn't like a lot of other men she'd known. There was a sensitivity to him and it drew her whether she liked it or not.

Griff lifted his hat off his head and wiped the sweat from his brow. "Dad said it gave him a good work ethic. You finished what you started." Settling the hat on his head, Griff tried not to stare at Val. She was wearing a form-fitting dark blue tee that outlined her upper body to perfection. Her arms were firm and clearly well muscled. He watched as she pulled on her sweat-stained gloves and halted at the box stall she'd been dismantling earlier. His body stirred. There was nothing about Val that didn't beckon to him. Griff tucked those needs away. "Looks like you're doing a good job here," he said, gesturing to the box stall. All the wood had been removed and only two main corner supports were still in the ground.

"I was," Val groused as she patted the four-by-four in front of them. "I can't haul this thing out by myself." She pointed to the large hole she'd dug around the base of it. "I think when my grandfather built this barn, he used twelve-foot lengths of posts, not eight."

Crouching down, Griff studied the hole. Running his gloved hand down the length of what she'd dug up, he said, "I think you're right." Straightening, he grabbed a nearby shovel and began to widen the hole. "Your grandfather did it right. You want a box stall sturdy enough to hold the most cantankerous bull or a stallion."

Val stood back and watched. "He never shied away from doing the hard work," she said. Griff shoveled the dirt into a nearby wheelbarrow.

Another memory from the past flowed into Val's mind. When her father was forced to muck out the box stalls, he'd hurl the straw and horse poop out the door and onto the aisle floor. Later, Val was made to shovel it all into the wheelbarrow. She could never understand why her father hadn't put the stuff directly into the wheelbarrow. Buck hated cleaning out stalls and had his wranglers do it whenever they were available. Most of the wranglers quit the Bar H within three or four months because Buck did nothing but yell and curse at them.

For the next ten minutes, Griff widened the hole. He was acutely aware of Val standing there. She made him feel strong, and there was something warm and satisfying simply being near her. Finishing the chore, he straightened and rested the shovel against the wall. "Okay, I'm going to try and pull this post out."

"Good luck, I tried it a number of times," she said, pointing to the front of her dirty tee.

Griff positioned himself, feet on either side of the hole. He wrapped his arms around the thick oak post. Using his legs and knees, he tried to haul the post upward. It wouldn't budge. Grunting, he tried again, but was surprised by how stubborn the corner post was. Releasing it, he took a step back. "This is one ornery customer."

"Tell me about it."

Griff met and held her amused gaze. Wiping the sweat off his brow, he said, "Okay, time to rethink this."

Val pointed to the other wall opposite the stall. "How about we wrap that chain around it and use the tractor to pull it out?"

Brightening, he smiled at her. "Hey, that's a great idea. You're pretty good at problem solving."

Heat stung her neck and moved into her cheeks. Val groaned inwardly. Griff's sincere praise went straight through her defenses and touched her wildly beating heart. When he smiled, she felt like the sun itself was shining upon her. "Women have brains, too," she said a bit defensively, going over to retrieve the chains off a large wall hook.

Griff chuckled. "No need to convince me. I'll go get the tractor and be right back."

Dragging the chains across the aisle to the posthole, Val tried to ignore Griff walking out of the barn. But she couldn't. He moved with fluidity and confidence. What would it be like to feel strong and powerful? Scowling, Val set to work wrapping the chains several times around the post. She wished for the thousandth time Griff wasn't so easy on her eyes. Surely, he had a woman in his life! How could he not? Yet, Val thought as she placed the thick metal hook into the wrapped chains, she had never heard him speak about anyone. Somehow she felt it would be safer if she convinced herself he was attached.

Minutes later, Griff rode the green John Deere tractor into the barn. He backed it in slowly to where the chain hooks lay about three feet away from the post. Val secured the hooks to the large round metal hole at the rear of the tractor. "You want to do the honors?" Griff asked, gesturing to the machine.

Val was surprised at his invitation. Most men would never relinquish their position to let a woman do the work instead. But the look in his eyes was searching and sincere. "Yes, I'd like to." Val walked to the tractor, mounted it and turned the key. The tractor spit and sputtered, finally catching and coming alive. Val slowly eased the vehicle forward until the chains grew tight.

"Okay," Griff shouted above the sound of the engine, "go ahead." He gestured for her to begin to inch the tractor forward.

Val knew from long experience that one didn't roar and jerk on a post or chain. It could flip the tractor and potentially injure or kill her. This was not something attempted lightly or without thought. She slowly eased her foot down on the accelerator pedal and felt the tractor hunker down, the thick tires digging for purchase on the concrete. The roar of the engine echoed throughout the tall, high barn.

Suddenly, the chain snapped. The tractor lurched forward, nearly unseating Val. She slammed on the brakes and quickly twisted around in the seat. Her eyes widened in terror as she saw that the broken chain had struck Griff's left forearm. He had been standing too close to the post and was thrown backward by the powerful strike of the loose chain. His face was frozen with pain, his right glove over his bleeding arm.

Oh, God! Val quickly killed the engine and leaped off the tractor. Without thinking, she knelt near Griff. "Are you all right?" she gasped unsteadily, her fingers touching his gloved hand.

Grimacing, Griff rasped, "It's not broken, I know that much." He wriggled his fingers.

"This will hurt." Val gently pulled his hand away to look at the injury.

Griff was amazed as the pain momentarily went away. Val's touch was gentle, their heads nearly touching as she studied the damage done to his left arm.

"Oh, Griff, this is bad." The chain had struck his lower arm, ripped the shirt fabric and chewed up his flesh. It was bleeding heavily. "We have to get you to the hospital right away!"

"Get me a clean towel first," he told her

in a gruff tone. Pain drifted up his arm as he tried to get to his feet. Val slipped her hand around his waist and helped him stand. For a moment, Griff felt dizziness wash over him. Val's face held terror. Her lips were parted, her blue eyes huge with fear — for his injury. "I'll be okay," he whispered, forcing out the words. "I'll meet you at the truck. Just get me a towel to put over this thing so I don't bleed out."

Nodding, Val ran out of the barn and raced for the ranch house. She hit the porch at a run. Jerking open the screen door, she found Gus in the kitchen. She quickly explained what happened and pulled a clean, fresh hand towel from a drawer.

"I'll call you as soon as I can," she called breathlessly to Gus, racing out the door, the keys to the truck in hand. She saw Griff already in the passenger seat as she skipped down the stairs. Gasping for breath, Val pulled open the passenger-side door.

"Here . . ." Val gently wrapped the white towel around Griff's bloody forearm. Glancing up, she saw how much pain he was in. His strong mouth was nothing more than a pursed, thin grimace.

"I got it," Griff said in a rasp, his right hand moving over the towel.

Heart pounding with fear, Val pulled the

seat belt across his chest and snapped it into place. Shutting the door, she trotted around to the driver's side and hopped in and kicked the truck into gear. Remaining alert, she quickly drove to the highway, gunning the accelerator. The old truck protested, the engine whining. Val pushed it faster, going over the speed limit. She didn't care.

Hands clammy, Val kept glancing from time to time toward Griff's arm. Bright red blood was soaking through the towel. "How are you doing?" she asked in a fearful voice.

"Feeling pretty stupid, if you want the truth. I know better than to stand close to a chain. It was my fault, Val. I'm really sorry." And he was. The abject terror in her eyes shook him as little else could. Her touch had been tender. Even though his wound was bleeding profusely, Griff could feel the warmth of her fingers on his flesh. He laid his head back after taking off his hat and he closed his eyes.

"It's all right. Everyone makes mistakes." Val drove intently, passing slower moving cars.

"My brother will laugh his head off over my amateur mistake," Griff said. "He'll say something like, yep, that's a city-slicker move, all right." He chuckled weakly and then opened his eyes and glanced over at Val.

"I don't think Slade would laugh at all about this." Val gripped the steering wheel, knuckles white. As they approached the outskirts of Jackson Hole, she took the lesser-known roads that would be relatively free of tourist traffic. "No one is going to make fun of you, Griff. I just pray to God that your injury isn't serious."

Griff continued to fight the heightening pain. "You're a good person, Val. You give people a long rope to go hang themselves on." One corner of his mouth hitched upward. He felt blood oozing through the towel around his arm. Griff didn't need to be a medic to know he was losing a lot of blood. The chain must have hit an artery. That was the last thought he had before everything faded to blackness.

Val waited impatiently out in the visitors' area. It was crammed with people today and she paced up and down the hall, hating the antiseptic smells. When they'd arrived, she'd driven to the E.R. door, hopped out and yelled for help from the orderlies and nurses within. Instantly, two men and a gurney flew out of the E.R. doors. They collected an unconscious Griff and quickly got him inside for treatment. It was only when Val had seen Dr. Jordana Lawton-McPherson appear that she'd broken down and cried in relief. Because Griff was Jordana's brother-in-law, Val knew he'd get instant treatment. Just now, she spotted Jordana coming out of E.R.

"Val?" Jordana called, gesturing for her to come.

Instantly Val hurried toward Jordana, who was dressed in her white lab coat and green scrubs, with a stethoscope hanging around her slender neck. "Griff. Is he going to be okay?"

"Yes," Jordana said in a low voice. She placed her hand on Val's upper arm. "That chain chewed up a lot of tissue but he's going to be fine. No permanent muscle damage."

"He fainted in the truck."

Jordana patted her arm gently. "It was from shock, not loss of blood. I know his arm looked awful, but really, he's going to be okay."

Relief shot through Val. "Thank God. And thank you, Jordana. What would we have done if you hadn't been on duty?" Val looked at the busy visitors' lounge. Many people were still waiting to be seen.

"Griff's injury was enough to admit him immediately." Jordana led Val through the visitors' area. "Do you want to see him?"

"He's awake?"

"Yep. He's a little out of it. He probably lost about half a pint of blood, so his work-day is over." Pushing open the door, she led Val into the green-curtained cubicles of E.R.

Val was anxious to see Griff. "He's got full use of his arm? His hand and fingers?"

"Yes, no nerve damage." Jordana grinned a little. "He's got more hurt feelings over his greenhorn moment than anything else."

Val managed a slight smile. "Hey, we've all done things like that."

"Yes, we have." Jordana halted halfway down the row. "He's in cubical ten, at the end. I think he can use a kind smile and some nice words about now."

Relief shattered through Val. She gripped Jordana's hand. "Thanks so much. I was so scared. His arm looked like ground hamburger."

"It doesn't now," Jordana said. "I sewed him up after scrubbing the area clean. All you'll see is a nice six-inch incision and lots of shorter stitches."

Dragging in a shaky breath, Val closed her eyes for a moment. "He's such a nice guy, Jordana. He works so hard and he's honest . . ." The words tore out of her. "He's really special. . . ."

Patting her hand, Jordana said, "Griff is a work in progress, like all of us." She smiled gently. "And to tell you the truth, he was more worried about you than himself. He's concerned you're going to think him weak because he passed out."

"You're kidding me!" Val compressed her lips. "I'd have passed out just looking at that injury had it been mine."

"Go talk with him. I'm having the nurse at the desk get the discharge papers ready for him to sign. He's already received a tetanus booster shot. There will be a prescription for antibiotics and for a mild pain medication. You'll need to pick those up for him before you drive home.

"He shouldn't work until I see him in two days. I need those stitches to close properly."

"I promise."

Griff looked up as the curtain was pulled aside. "Val!" She looked pale, the freckles across her cheeks much darker than usual. He managed a sheepish smile of welcome and held up his bandaged arm. "I'm going to be okay. Jordana told me that it looks worse than it really is."

Val pulled the curtain closed and walked over to his side. She saw the shirt he'd worn hanging on a chair. Griff was wearing a green hospital gown. Without thinking, she touched his shoulder. "I'm just so glad you're okay. Are you in pain?"

"No." He added wryly, "I feel really stupid right now. I keep asking myself why I didn't step away when you started to pull out the post." Griff shook his head and gave her an apologetic look. "I'm sorry, Val. It was an amateur wrangler's mistake."

Her heart swelled for Griff. He was like a little boy who'd had the stuffing knocked out of him. She kept her hand on his broad shoulder and could feel the powerful movement of his muscles beneath the fabric. Contact with Griff sent a frisson of desire through her. She'd never found herself so drawn to a man before. Licking her lips, she said, "Don't be hard on yourself, Griff. Things like this happen. None of us are perfect."

Griff could see terror banked in her blue eyes. He could literally feel her anxiety and fear. It was written clearly across her tense features. "I feel bad for you."

"Don't worry about me." Val shifted uneasily at the side of the gurney. She told him about Jordana's prescriptions and her orders.

"I'm laid up for *two days?* No way."

"Way," Val growled. "Jordana said you

wouldn't take her orders well." She gently tapped him on the shoulder with her index finger. "We'll get you out of here and then we'll drive over to the drugstore and pick up the prescriptions, Griff. Then, we're going home and you are going to *rest*."

Wincing, Griff said, "My arm feels fine. No pain. It's as good as new."

"Jordana warned me that if you pull those stitches by working too soon after the injury, you're in bigger trouble."

Damn. Griff sat there feeling like the perfect fool. "Maybe I can find some odd jobs around the place while I'm recouperating?"

"Listen," Val said more firmly, "you scared the living daylights out of me, Griff. You will follow Jordana's orders and rest." Tears suddenly formed in her eyes, surprising her. Self-consciously, Val wiped them away. Her voice trembled. "I've had more than enough turmoil in my life. I — I can't handle any more trauma right now. Do you understand?"

The tears in her eyes tore at Griff. He felt badly and, in a raspy voice, said, "Yes, I'll rest. I promise you, I will." Val looked devastated. She was fighting back the tears and her lower lip trembled. All Griff wanted to do in that moment was hold her. That was what Val needed, he realized. Someone to just hold her. To keep her safe. Reaching out with his good hand, he tangled his fingers among hers for just a moment. "I'll be good. Maybe I can push a vacuum cleaner around or do some dusting for Miss Gus? She'd like that."

Sniffing, Val wiped the last of her tears away. Griff gently squeezed her hand, as if to reassure her. Her skin tingled pleasantly in the wake of his unexpected gesture. "We'll see," she said, her voice unsteady. "The ranch isn't going to die in two days if you rest."

Griff would do anything to see the terror leave her eyes. "Are you sure? When Miss Gus finds out I'm laid up for two days, she's liable to lay an egg or two."

Laughing, Val shook her head and drowned in his mirthful green gaze. "What is it with you guys? You get hurt and all you do is joke about it. Gus would *never* have a hissy fit over this." Val pulled her cell phone out of her pocket and said, "And I'm going to call her right now. I know she was worried. I'll meet you out front after they release you."

"Sounds good." Griff watched Val leave the cubicle. Despite his injury he felt a keen ache in his lower body. Val's tears had surprised him. Usually, she was remote with him. He remembered her hand resting lightly on his shoulder and how good it felt. Did Val realize the power she had over him? Griff didn't think so.

CHAPTER TEN

Val was busy scrambling eggs for breakfast when Griff stepped into the kitchen. He appeared well rested, if a bit pale. His left arm was still in the waterproof bandage and he'd rolled his shirtsleeves up to his elbows. She couldn't tear her gaze from him.

"Good morning. Anything I can do to help?"

Val shook her head. "No thanks. You're up earlier than usual."

He smiled a little as he poured himself some coffee. "So are you."

"Guilty." Val found herself melting beneath his warm gaze. "How's the arm this morning?"

"Testy," Griff admitted, raising the cup and savoring the hot coffee.

"Did you sleep?" Val knew she was getting personal but she couldn't help herself. Usually she was quiet and reserved when Griff would show up for breakfast, but things seemed to have changed within her after yesterday's accident.

"Off and on. Those pain meds do make a difference." He looked around. "Where's Miss Gus?"

"Still in bed. It's only five-thirty."

Grunting, Griff retrieved three plates from the cabinet and placed them on the counter. They had established an unspoken rhythm for breakfast. Either Miss Gus or Val cooked. He set the table and poured coffee. As he placed the salt-and-pepper shakers on the table, he said, "I have an idea."

"Uh-oh," Val teased, looking over her shoulder. She saw him grin a little. Unable to stop being personal with Griff, she wondered what was responsible for the change.

"Hey, even wranglers have a few good ideas every now and then." Griff smiled and walked to the drawer next to the stove where she was cooking and pulled it open. He began collecting the flatware. "Since I'm not allowed to do any serious work today, I thought I'd ride the fence line of the property. It's on the to-do list you wrote up. I know there's fence down along the line so I figured I'd make some notes about where it needs repair."

Nodding, Val said, "I don't think Jordana would object to you riding the fence." She carried the skillet over to the table. Dividing the mixture of eggs, bacon bits and cheese onto the three platters, she added, "I'd like to come with you."

Surprised but pleased, Griff said, "Sure, no problem." He took the plate Miss Gus would eat from and placed it in the micro-wave. When she got up, she'd know where to look for it. He popped slices of bread into the toaster on the counter. "We've got two horses so we can do it."

Wiping out the cast-iron skillet, Val set it on the stove. "Since arriving home, I haven't had time to ride the property lines to see what's going on. God only knows what all needs to be fixed or replaced." She sat down at the table trying to ignore the happiness threading through her. Opening the pink linen napkin and spreading it across her lap, Val wondered if her tears had opened up a door between them. She never cried. Yet, tears had sprung to her eyes with such sur-prising fierceness that it had taken her by complete surprise.

Griff waited for the toast to pop up and then carried the slices over to the table, di-viding them between their plates. "It's a good idea to ride together. We can both un-derstand the layout of the property." As he sat down, he realized he felt so much closer to her today than ever before. He tried to ignore the feeling and reached for the strawberry jam. This morning, unlike yesterday, she looked peaceful. He decided to speak up on another idea he had. "What do you think about packing a picnic lunch in the saddlebags and that way we don't have to starve to death if it takes us a while?"

Heart leaping unexpectedly, Val moved the fork through her eggs. For a moment, she wanted to jump up and shout yes! Caution won out, however. "I guess we could."

Sipping his coffee, Griff said, "We've got two hundred acres to ride. And there's going to be a lot of mounting and dismounting on my part. I want to test the strength of those posts about every hundred feet or so where they're sagging."

"I'm glad you're thorough," Val said, not tasting her eggs. Being around Griff was like inhaling cold, fresh air compared to being trapped inside a stale building. Val found herself confused by the array of emotions Griff triggered and brought to life in her. Her heart thumped every time he gazed at her. And when his strong mouth would lift into a smile, she felt herself starting to go weak inside.

"I like crunching numbers. I see fence

posts as numbers. One and the same, I guess."

"You can't run a ranch successfully and not be a number cruncher," Val agreed. She stole a glance over at Griff as they ate. He looked happy. There was a peacefulness mirrored in his ruggedly handsome face.

"Maybe this is none of my business," Griff began, as he cleaned up his plate, "but is the Bar H in any financial difficulty?"

"Miss Gus knows more about the books than I do right now," Val admitted. She watched his expression as he savored Gus's homemade jam. Not many men showed their real feelings, but apparently Griff wasn't one of them. Val wasn't sure what it meant, because most men in her life up to this point had been stoic, unreadable types. She never knew what lurked in their minds or hearts until it was too late. Griff was an open book in comparison. Maybe his unique demeanor was what made her feel safe around him. She could read him and know where she stood with him.

"You don't know?" Griff pressed gently. Usually, wranglers knew nothing of the inner workings of a ranch's financial health. They got paid twice a month and did their jobs.

Val finished off the eggs and set her plate

to one side. "I'm still going through the accounting books. Gus, bless her, did the best she could, but I'm finding a lot of mistakes."

"She's eighty-four. No one can expect her to be perfect on keeping a set of complex ranch books."

"Right." Val said, "Before bed every night, I try to read for an hour and understand the whole thing. If I find a mistake, I correct it, but I'm certainly not an accountant. I feel vulnerable because I'm afraid I'm not seeing some of the mistakes she's made."

"Do you want some help?"

Her heart raced for a moment over his offer. "Are you sure about this?" Val demanded, digging into his gaze. "Accounting isn't one of the things you're getting paid to do around here."

"Hey," Griff joked, "I gotta do *something* with that MBA of mine."

Val smiled. "I'll ask Gus. The ranch is in her name. My mother knew I never wanted to come back here, so in her will she named Gus as the owner."

Hearing the veiled pain in her suddenly husky voice, Griff nodded and shared a warm look that he hoped would make Val feel better. The urge to slip his arms around her ate into Griff. Any fool could see she needed an embrace. "That's fine. I don't

194

want to be sticking my nose in where it's not welcome."

"I appreciate your offer. I've got some things in the accounting books that I can't make sense of. I was thinking of asking Gus about the entries to try and figure out why she put them in there. I'll ask her if she minds if you help me out."

"Good approach." Griff placed his napkin on the table after wiping his mouth. Standing, he carried the dirty plates and flatware over to the sink. In no time, he had them washed, rinsed and in the drainer to dry. Wiping his hands on a towel, he turned and said, "Would you like me to get the horses saddled?"

"Yes, please." Val remained at the table drinking her coffee. "I'll make us lunch. Is there anything you don't like to eat?" she asked, turning and looking at him. Griff was leaning against the counter. Again, she felt gently suspended in his green gaze, her lower body hot wax melting beneath this very male stare.

"Okra?" Griff answered with a grin. "I hate the stuff."

"No problem there. I can't stand the slimy veggie, either. I was thinking of cutting up some of that roast beef we had last night, putting some horseradish sauce on it and slapping it between two pieces of bread."

"That sounds great."

"Fritos?"

"Count me in."

"Dessert?"

Raising his brows, Griff said, "Miss Gus made some apple dumplings last night. Are there any left?"

"Yes. I'll put a couple of them in plastic containers along with flatware and napkins."

"Sounds like a great lunch." He rubbed his hands together and smiled.

Warming beneath his little-boy grin, Val said, "You're so easy to please. . . ." She thought back to her father, who had been a control freak in comparison.

"Hey, I'm one lucky dude," Griff called over his shoulder as he sauntered toward the hall.

When he disappeared out of the kitchen, it felt as if the sunlight had left with him. Val was amazed at his energy, his thoughtfulness and intelligence. Griff was just too good to be true, Val decided, walking to the refrigerator. There had to be a flaw in him that would one day be exposed. He was too virile, too damnably good-looking and that smile of his was enough to melt ice. Even . . . the kind that encased her heart.

■ ■ ■ ■

Though his arm ached, happiness thrummed through Griff as he saddled the two geldings. The one Val had chosen was a red chestnut with four white socks and a wide blaze down his face. Socks, as he was known, was a quiet, common-sense ranch horse and Griff liked him a lot. After saddling and bridling the Quarter horse, Griff got to work on his horse, the ten-year-old Appaloosa named Freckles. This was an unexpected turn of events and he was looking forward to spending quality time with Val.

Griff stopped at the tack room for two saddlebags and tied them onto the back of each saddle cantle. He buckled the leather rifle sheath onto the right side of his saddle and pulled out a 30.06 rifle from the locked gun cabinet in the tack room. Griff was good with guns, having been a champion pistol shot, and this one was big enough and had enough firepower to stop a grizzly bear in its tracks should it charge them. He never rode anywhere on this ranch without a loaded rifle, in case of an emergency.

As he led the horses out of the barn and into the early-morning sunlight, Griff saw Val waiting for him on the porch. The sun was slowly raising the temperature. In the lower pastures, fog hung like white cotton, but was rapidly burning off as the sun lifted higher into the pale blue sky. Griff led the horses around to the front porch and tied them to a nearby hitching post. Val had tamed her shining red hair into a ponytail. She always wore a gray Stetson on her head. Those Levi's clearly outlined her long, beautiful legs and curved hips. She wore an orange tee with a light denim jacket over it. At seven a.m., the morning was cool.

Val walked to the where the horses were tied and packed the saddlebags with their lunches. Griff waited until she was done and untied the horses, placing the reins over their heads. They worked like a well-oiled team. After buckling down the flaps on the saddlebags, Val untied Socks's reins. Over her shoulder she said, "I brought my camera with me," and she patted the pocket on her jacket. "So we have visual references of what kind of work needs to be done and where."

"Good thinking." Griff gripped the saddle horn with his right hand and swung easily up on Freckles. The Appaloosa was sixteen hands high, heavily built and perfect for ranch work. He snorted and tossed his head, eager to stretch his legs. "That'll help us know what supplies to buy for the repairs instead of guessing at what we need." Val was nothing but grace as she swung her long leg over Socks's broad back and settled into the saddle. He saw her cheeks flush a pink color. Griff wondered what that meant. His gaze dropped to her soft, parted lips and he thought he saw a hint of a smile at the corners.

What would it be like to kiss Val? The thought drifted provocatively through him. He felt his body tighten over the meandering of his mind and foolish heart. Pushing all those sensations and needs deep down inside himself, he walked Freckles alongside Socks as they left the house and plodded down to the nearby dirt road.

"It's a beautiful day," Val said with a sigh, looking around. The hills were gentle and undulating, hiding pockets of white fog here and there. The forest was a blue-green color to her left and looked like a thick carpet across the taller hills that loomed above them. The call of robins filled the area as the horses moved spiritedly in the morning air. To her left was the first major cattle pen where Griff was replacing all the posts and rebuilding it from the ground up. Ahead was the dirt road filled with tire ruts from the rain a few days earlier. There were several other corrals hidden around the curved corner. The route rounded and would eventually lead them to the fence line.

"Have you ever ridden a fence line before?" Their boots occasionally brushed one another as the horses walked side by side down the narrow dirt road.

"Yes, I helped Shorty, who is Slade's head wrangler over at the Tetons Ranch." Griff laughed a little. "I'm afraid I was all thumbs at first. Shorty was real patient with me. He said I had McPherson blood, so he knew sooner or later I'd learn how to patch, stretch and fix a barbed-wire fence."

"Do you enjoy doing it, though?"

Shrugging, Griff glanced over at her. "Yes and no." He gestured to the five-strand fence that they were starting to ride parallel to as they turned and started up a grassy slope. "I like being outdoors. I like to feel my muscles working. What I don't like is getting bit by the barbed wire. Shorty showed me his hands and forearms. There were all kinds of scars he'd gotten from fixing fence over the years."

Val held up her left arm and pointed to her elbow. "See that? My father was teaching me from ten years old how to fix fence."

Griff saw the thin line of a one-inch white scar near her elbow and frowned. "You

200

couldn't have weighed enough to pull a fence tight," he said in a low, concerned tone. Wanting to reach out and touch the scar, to take away the pain he was sure she experienced from being snagged by the barbed wire, Griff forced his hands to remain where they were.

Val gave a derisive laugh. "He didn't care. When I cut myself and started to cry, he threatened to hit me. He said cowgirls didn't cry."

Unable to stop from staring at her, Griff was speechless. Finally, he forced out, "That's such bull."

"Know it now. Didn't know it then."

"What happened next? Did he take you home and get you first aid?"

"No. He threw his bandanna at me for me to wrap it with, and we kept on fixing fence line."

Disbelief exploded through Griff. "That's child abuse if you ask me."

"Back then no one recognized it as such.

"We'd get home after dark and my father would tell me to go upstairs and clean up before dinner. I knew where the medicine cabinet was and I scrubbed it out with soap and put Mercurochrome and a Band-Aid on it."

"And you were only ten?" he asked,

amazed. He saw the pain in Val's eyes. Her mouth was set, too, as if fighting the pain of that old memory.

The gentle back-and-forth sway of the horse soothed some of Val's tenseness. "I think that if you and Slade hadn't been torn away from your parents at six years old, you would be pretty independent by ten. A ranch kid is a little adult running around in a child's body."

Griff couldn't argue with that. "It's true, kids grow up fast on a farm or ranch."

"They have to. There's a lot of work on a ranch and there's no playtime. We learn responsibility at a very early age. Or at least, I did."

"Did your mom ever know about this?" He motioned to her left elbow.

"No."

Shaking his head, Griff said, "Even at six, I remember our mom checking us out, head to toe, every night during tick season. And if we got hurt, she was there to fix us up."

"You were lucky."

"Yeah, I guess I was." Still, he hurt for her. More and more, Griff was beginning to understand how tough and independent she had been forced to become. "I don't agree with what your father did. You could have caught tetanus. A cut like that needs immediate medical attention."

"Buck never liked children," Val said. "He hated them in general and barely tolerated me being around. I realize now it wasn't my fault. At that age, I would do anything to get his attention. And when I cut myself on the barbed wire, I wanted to be strong like him. I wanted him to like me . . . maybe love me, because I could tough it out and not cry or complain."

Nostrils flaring, Griff said, "I hope by now you realize how screwed up he really was? And that none of his behavior had anything to do with you. It was about him. What I can't understand is why your mother wasn't there to protect you, Val. You were a child. You were vulnerable and innocent."

Feeling the warmth of tears jamming into her eyes, Val tore her gaze away from Griff. His eyes were alive with anger and confusion. "When you don't grow up in an abusive or dysfunctional family, Griff, it's hard to understand the toxic family dynamic. You and Slade, even though you were torn apart and lived with different uncles, were not abused, nor were you placed in dysfunctional situations. I didn't know anything was wrong. When you grow up in such a poisonous environment, you accept as if that's the way it is in all families."

"I hear you," Griff said. He reached down and threaded his fingers through Freckles's short black mane. The gelding's ears moved back and forth. Griff glanced over at Val, saw her well-shaped mouth pursed. In a heavy voice, he said, "You're right. You would think it was normal."

Val pulled her horse to a halt after spotting some weak fence. "When I went to college, I talked to my roommate about her parents. They were a hundred-and-eighty degrees opposite from mine. That's when I realized that Buck was an abusive son of a bitch and my mother was a victim incapable of protecting herself or me."

Dismounting, Griff studied the fence line. "You're a survivor, Val. Of the first order. You have my admiration." He escorted her to the fence. Three of the five strands of barbed wire were sagging. Val critically studied the post. It was leaning, broken off at ground level. She pulled out her pocket camera and took a photo. Griff wanted to reach out, touch Val's shoulder, hold her and tell her everything was going to be all right. The sun was warm against him. A slight breezed stirred, carrying the scent of pine. The tendrils at her temples moved with a passing breeze. They glinted with red-and-gold highlights. The temptation to reach out and tuck those errant strands behind her ear was almost too much for him.

Griff forced himself to test the lower two barbed-wire strands instead. "If we had cattle, they'd push their way through this portion without a problem."

Straightening, Val pushed the tendrils away from her eyes. Griff stood so close. He was incredibly confident in a quiet, dangerous way. Her self-esteem on the other hand, had been gained through sheer, hard work. Gesturing across the wide, grassy pasture, she said, "Gus wants to buy some heifers, breed them to a local bull and get some beef on the ground come spring of next year. That's her plan."

"Does she have the money set aside to do it?"

Nodding, Val said, "Gus sold her ranch over in Cheyenne to come here to help my mother after Buck died. Whatever profit she made is in her savings account. When I got home, Gus and I went over her plans to get the ranch back on its feet. I think you'd enjoy looking at her ideas." She smiled into Griff's narrowing green gaze. He was so close . . . oh, God, why did she want to take that one step and find herself pressed against his hard, lean body? Kiss him senseless? Never, in all of Val's years, had she ever felt like this toward any man.

Watching Val's blue gaze soften for a moment, her lips slightly parted, Griff saw the signs. But was he reading her right? Did she want to be kissed by him? He knew enough about Val's background to hold back. The breeze loosened those tendrils again. Without thinking, he lifted his gloved hand and gently tucked them behind her ear.

Startled, Val took a step back, her ear tingling wildly in the wake of his unexpected move. Automatically, she touched her tingling ear, staring up at Griff. What had just happened? Suddenly, Val felt frightened. Taking another step back, she dropped her hand and said in an oddly husky voice, "Let's mount back up. We've got a lot of fence line to cover today."

Griff followed her without saying anything. Inwardly, his feelings were churning. What the hell had he just done? It wasn't like him to touch a woman without her consent. As he picked up Freckles's reins and mounted, he glanced worriedly over at Val. Once more, her face was expressionless and she had retreated. And it was his fault. Damn. Griff felt guilty. What had prompted him to do that? What was going on between them? He clucked to Freckles and took the lead. Griff was sure Val didn't want to ride beside him now. He'd just broken any trust he was building with her. Rubbing his chin, he scowled and focused on the fence line.

Val breathed a sigh of relief as Griff took the lead. Grazing her ear once more with her gloved fingers, she wished she hadn't reacted so powerfully to his unexpected touch. Val tried to shake off the surprise. Griff's touch had felt good. Warmth pooled deep within her body. The sensation was delicious. And for the first time, Val felt like a woman.

CHAPTER ELEVEN

Griff drew in a deep breath of appreciation as they rode around a lazy curve on the road. They had finished part of the fence check when Val suggested riding back to have lunch on the bank of Long Lake. He pulled his horse to a halt just to absorb the beauty of the sparkling cobalt-blue water. It was surrounded by thick stands of evergreens except at the end of it where there was a rocky, pebbled beach.

"Have you seen Long Lake yet?" Val asked, bringing her horse to a stop close to his. She saw wonder in his expression as he admired the body of water.

"No. Miss Gus talked about it, but I haven't had time to see it. Nice-looking lake. The color reminds me of Lake Tahoe."

"When I was a kid, I spent a lot of time on our side of the lake." She gestured toward the beach that was a good half mile away. "We're at our property line. Long

Lake is half ours and the other half belongs to the U.S. Forest Service. There's two dirt roads into it. One is on the forest service side and then there is our private ranch road."

Griff spotted a red kayak and a small aluminum fishing boat out on its smooth surface. "Must be good fishing?" He turned in his saddle and absorbed her expression. If Val was still upset over his stupid gesture, her expression didn't show it. Right now, she looked serene. Anxiety washed off Griff's shoulders. He had to apologize at some point for what he'd done. A wrangler just didn't touch his boss.

"Yes, trout. Although, truth be known, this lake completely freezes over in the winter and the fish die from lack of oxygen. The forest service replaces the different species of trout every spring for the tourists and the locals who like to fish here."

"So, it's not spring fed?" Griff asked, rising in his stirrups to get a better look at the lake. The noontime sky was reflected in the waters. He saw a great blue heron near the shore on its long stiltlike legs looking for a tasty meal of a frog or fish. A red-tailed hawk flew overhead in lazy circles near the pebble beach where he saw a boat ramp.

"It is, but the ice grows so thick it can't

209

supply the fish the necessary oxygen they need in order to survive."

"That's a shame," Griff answered, settling down in the saddle. He saw the fence line was about twenty feet away from the lake's bank. They had paralleled it for some distance. In front of him was an opened gate. He pointed to it. "Do you want your ranch gate left open?"

"No," Val said, dismounting. "This is an ongoing problem. No ranch wants any of their gates left open because it allows their livestock to escape." Leading Socks, she walked over to the gate and pushed it shut. The hinges squealed. Val locked the gate. "Locals and tourists who don't want to stay on the Forest Service land open this gate, come through to fish on our land."

"Without your permission?"

"Yep. It's usually the locals. They know better, but they don't want to have to fight through the forest and thick brush that surrounds that part of the lake. It's much easier just to follow our road, open our gate and have lots of elbow room to fish in peace. As you can see, we're bush-free on the banks. It's a strong call to fishermen."

"That's not good."

"No, it isn't. Gus has been on the phone with the Teton Forest Service supervisor,

Charley. He's sympathetic, but he can't put a ranger out here to watch our gate. And we can't afford to have a wrangler out here to watch it all the time, either." Her mouth turned down. "Gus wants cattle again, but I worry they'll wander through this opened gate onto forest service land only to get eaten by a grizzly."

Nodding, Griff eyed the gate. It was stout, made of lightweight steel and rust colored by time and weather. "That's a pretty hefty chain and padlock on it. You're telling me someone has a pair of bolt cutters, cuts through that chain and walks onto your private lake property?"

"That's exactly what I'm saying." Val shrugged. "It's been an ongoing hassle. I think I'm going to have to speak to Charley in person about it. Phone calls from Gus haven't done any good."

Griff recalled when he'd gone to see Charley about his brother's bid to provide horses for rangers. The older ranger was gruff. And when he'd suggested throwing in an extra horse if Charley would consider choosing Slade's bid, the man got furious with him. Only later did Griff find out from angry Slade that Charley had considered his visit a bribe. As a consequence, Slade had lost the contract he needed so desperately to keep up the monthly payment on his ranch. "It might be a good idea to approach him and see what resolution he might have up his sleeve."

"Gus and Charley are like oil and water. They don't get along at all. I think if I make an appointment with Charley and coax him into working as a team member to resolve this problem, we might get somewhere." Val managed a one-sided smile. "At least, I hope I will."

"You're a cool cucumber under fire," he said. "Not much ruffles your feathers."

Distracted, Val drank in the tenderness she saw glinting in Griff's eyes. Her ear still tingled in memory of his gloved fingers brushing those strands behind it. The gesture had been gentle. Intimate. "Oh, I can get my dander up, believe me."

"Ah, the military officer coming out?" he said in a teasing voice, warming as she smiled at him. The sunlight danced across Val and she was relaxed standing near Socks. Griff wasn't sure what was going on between them. One moment she was remote; the next, available. It made him anxious.

"I can bring out my military side if I have to."

"I hope you never bring it out against me.

Hey, it's noon. About time for lunch?"

She saw the little-boy eagerness in his expression. "Sure, let's eat," she agreed, leading Socks over to a shady area near the bank of the water.

As Griff dismounted Freckles, he saw a horse and rider in the distance on the forest-service side. "Hey, we have someone on horseback coming around the lake toward us," he called to Val, pointing in the general direction.

Val tied her horse's reins to a nearby tree limb and walked up to where Griff was standing. Squinting, she let out a harsh breath. "That's Curt Downing on his endurance stallion, Shah."

Hearing the rancor in her voice, Griff turned and looked over at her. He saw anger leap to her eyes. "What's he doing out here?"

Shrugging, Val muttered, "I don't know."

"He's coming our way."

"Yeah, and he probably thinks we should open the gate to let him ride through." Val walked over to Socks and detached the saddlebags. "He's got another think coming."

Griff tied up Freckles and walked up to the gate to meet the approaching rancher. Downing, on his Arabian black stallion, was dressed in a tan Stetson, Levi's and a short-sleeved white shirt. The animal shone like polished ebony as he trotted along the road parallel to the lake. The hair on the back of Griff's neck rose as Downing approached. His stallion was fighting the bit, wanting to run, but the man was keeping the animal at a steady trot.

"Afternoon," Griff called as the rider pulled up on the other side of the gate.

Downing scowled and nodded to Griff. He saw Val spreading out a red blanket beneath the shade of a huge old oak tree, completely ignoring him. The bitch. There was no love lost between them.

"Are you riding Shah to keep him in shape?" Griff rested his hands in a relaxed fashion on the top of the gate.

"Yeah, I use this particular trail once a week." Downing motioned to the gate. "Would you mind opening it?"

Val straightened, overhearing the conversation between the two men. She walked up to the gate and glared up at Downing. He sat on the pawing stallion looking like a conquering hero. The arrogance written across his face made her even more angry. Reining in her feelings, she said, "Mr. Downing, this is Bar H property. No one is allowed to come onto it without my permission."

Curt forced a smile. He lifted his cowboy hat and settled it back down on his head. "Why, Miss Hunter, I have no wish to upset you. It's just that for the last ten years I've ridden my stud here, down your road and back up it. We stay on the road. I don't wish to harm any of your property."

"Is that why our gate is always open?" Val demanded in a dark tone. Downing was a rancher. He knew damn well if you opened a gate, you shut it behind you.

"I know enough to keep gates closed," he told her amiably. Looking around, he pointed to the lake and the fishermen. "It's these local yahoos that do this, Miss Hunter. Not me."

Val didn't believe him for a moment. Downing was smug and treating her like a recalcitrant child. "It doesn't matter. This is Bar H property and our gate now has a solid lock on it. We really don't want anyone on our property from now on, Mr. Downing." She saw his eyes flash with anger for a moment and then he tamped it down and, instead, gave her a lazy smile.

"Perhaps we could strike a monetary deal, Miss Hunter? I would genuinely like to ride the four miles down your road and back once a week. It's a good road and easy on my stud's legs."

Val saw Griff frowning. He was staying out of the conversation but his hands resting on top of the steel pipe gate had tightened. "Mr. Downing, I'll ask my grandmother about your request." Val knew damn well she'd turn it down.

"Great," Curt said. He pulled a business card out of the pocket of his shirt and passed it over the rail to Griff. "I'm appreciative. If I remember correctly, you've just come home?"

"I have," Val gritted out. She really didn't want to talk to this jerk who thought he was king of the valley. Val knew he was worth millions and owned a local trucking company. He sat on his horse with his chin slightly lifted, imperious and condescending.

"Well," Curt said smoothly, adding a warm smile, "do come over for a visit. I'd like to show you my endurance training facility. I know you have a good eye for horseflesh and would appreciate Shah's offspring."

Downing was a smooth operator, Val decided. He was very good-looking, clean shaven and in top shape, his red hair trimmed military short. But when Val looked over at Griff, Downing was drab in comparison. She could literally feel the protective energy exuding around Griff toward her. Right now, he reminded her of a big, bad guard dog on alert. That made her feel safe and gave her the confidence to confront Downing. Otherwise, she probably wouldn't have been so bold and forthright.

"Thanks for your invite, but I really don't have time right now to do that, Mr. Downing."

"Perhaps a rain check?" he suggested. Curt appraised her with appreciation. Indeed, Val Hunter was one hell of a good-looking woman. She was curved in all the right places and the tee she wore beneath the denim jacket couldn't hide her breasts from his hungry gaze.

Shrugging, Val said, "We'll see."

Tipping his hat to her, he said, "I'll wait for that day, Miss Hunter. And I appreciate you talking with Miss Gus about allowing me to use your road once a week. Just call me and let me know. I'll be happy to pay her any sum she wants. It's important we remain good neighbors." Turning Shah around, he trotted off in the opposite direction.

"That dude is over-the-top," Val spit out as she walked over to the blanket. "I hated him just from what Gus told me about him. Now, meeting him in person, I can see why he angers her so much." She handed Griff a plastic container. When their fingertips met, she absorbed the contact. Whether Val wanted to or not, she enjoyed it.

Kneeling down opposite her, Griff set the sandwich on the blanket and took off his gloves. He tucked them into his belt. "He smirks a lot."

Snorting, Val sat crossed-legged and opened her container. "He's so sure of himself. And he treated me like some kind of child. I hate it when men talk down to me. Who does he think he is?" She bit into the beef sandwich as if she were taking a bite out of Downing.

Griff smiled a little as he pulled out his sandwich. "From what I've seen of Downing, he's an oily, scheming rich guy who thinks his money can buy anything he wants in the valley." Not only that, Griff thought, but if the FBI is after you, you can't be good news.

"Yeah, well, he's not getting our ranch!" Val rolled her eyes. "Sorry, I'm really upset. The guy raises my hackles. All I wanted to do was punch him in that smarmy mouth of his."

With a chuckle, Griff ate the sandwich. "Well, he didn't get on your property. It was an important boundary to erect."

"I'm just worried when Gus says no, he'll come riding up with a pair of metal cutters and use the road anyway."

"What about putting an alarm of some kind on that gate? That way, we would know if it was being opened."

"We don't have electricity out here."

"You could purchase a small solar panel. I could hook it up so an electronic radio alarm goes off in the house if the gate is opened."

"You could do that?" His ability to think outside the box and resolve serious problems impressed her.

"When I worked on Wall Street, we had a solar-panel company in our portfolio. I visited them in Arizona to check out their facility. I was really impressed."

"You have the electrical knowledge to do this?"

"I do."

"You are amazing."

Griff wasn't prepared for her praise. For one moment, Val's walls came down and he saw the real woman who hid behind them. Her blue eyes had grown soft, her lips slightly parted, as if breathless. His heart thudded in response to the gaze she shared with him. She admired and respected him. Two things Griff always desired from the people in his life, but coming from Val, it felt like the richest reward. "I spent a week out at their facility and the owner showed me all their products."

"This is a great idea, Griff. Yes, I'll talk to Gus about buying a solar panel. If you could put it out here, it should stop trespassers."

"I can install the alarm that will be powered by the panel. If it goes off, one of us can drive out here immediately and find out who cut the lock and broke in."

"I'm *sure* the only person we'd find is Downing. He thinks the valley is his and he owns everything and everyone."

Griff finished off his sandwich. Val handed him a container with an apple dumpling slathered with caramel sauce. "I can set up the gate so that it has a mild electrical shock?"

"I like the idea."

"We'd have to put a sign up to warn people, though. It will deter most of them, I would think."

"Of course. What I'd give to see Downing touch our gate not believing it's electrified."

"Well," Griff said, "if he thinks the sign is a bluff, he'll find out otherwise."

Her mouth pulled into a wide smile. "Gus said you were the right man to hire and now, I agree with her. You have a lot of different background skills you're bringing to the ranch. Thank you." Val saw his face go soft for a moment. The sincere compliment allowed her to see another side to this wrangler. And she liked what she saw. Maybe a little too much.

Griff finished the dumpling with relish. Val's compliment resonated in Griff's heart like nothing else ever had. He wanted her to like and admire him. And now, she definitely regarded him on a higher level than before. Pride and happiness flowed through him. Clearing his throat, Griff got serious and held her gaze.

"I owe you an apology, Val. I shouldn't have reached out and touched your hair earlier. I'm really sorry. It won't happen again."

Val saw how sad Griff looked. What to say? She wanted to say, *No, I loved it!* I was surprised, but not angry. Instead, she held back, as always. "Thanks for apologizing. I appreciate it."

Risking a glance over at Val, Griff realized her guard remained down. Her blue eyes had softened. Did he see longing in them? For him? Griff couldn't trust his assessment. His interpretation could be completely off the mark. "Thanks," he said, meaning it. Nervously, he got up and walked over to the gate. There was so much Griff wanted to say, but didn't dare. Val was his boss. She could have fired him for what he'd done earlier today, but she hadn't. And he needed this job too much to risk doing anything else like that again.

Despite that, Griff couldn't help wanting to do something other than sit with her on that blanket. She was simply too close, too beautiful, and the urge to tunnel his fingers through that red hair of hers was eating him alive. He made himself get up. Moving to the gate, Griff studied the best possible spot to hide a solar panel from approaching eyes.

Val ate in silence. She wanted Griff's company but understood he felt ashamed for touching her hair. Beyond wishing he didn't feel that way, there was little else she could say. After all, she was the owner. Val studied the lake, the noon breeze riffling its surface. A great blue heron took off from the bank and flew lengthwise down the center of it. For whatever reason, right now, Val felt serene. It wasn't something she felt often enough.

Glancing over at Griff, who was busy measuring and taking notes of the gate, Val wondered if it was because of his presence. Was it possible that a man could make her feel safe and secure? And that her constant anxiety could go away as a result of it? Only one other man had ever given her a sense of peace. And the only explanation Val had was that her reactions were due to Griff's calm and steady presence.

Val finished off her lunch, stuffed the containers into the saddlebags and stood up. She carried them over to Socks's saddle. The raucous call of a blue jay filled the air. She saw a red ground squirrel race near the bank of the lake. A trout jumped out of the water after a tasty bug treat. Val rested her hands on the saddle for a moment, absorbing nature and the beauty surrounding her. Maybe it wasn't so bad being home after all. Glancing over her shoulder, she saw Griff ambling toward Freckles, who was tied next to Socks. His brows were drawn and she could tell he was thinking about the solar panel and the gate. He was so easy to read and it amazed Val once more.

"Ready?" she called, mounting up.

"Yeah," Griff said, untying Freckles's reins from the tree branch. He looked down the long fence line. It stretched along a flat piece of land and then moved upward on a grassy slope and disappeared over the other side of it. "This is a beautiful property," he said, mounting his horse.

"The land is healing," Val agreed, gently nudging Socks forward with her heels.

Griff followed Val and Socks across the road and up the fence line. There was a serenity around her he'd never seen before. Looking over his shoulder, he took one more glance at Long Lake. Truly, it was a peaceful place. A place where a man or woman could let down, relax and just be. Appreciating Val as never before, Griff turned his attention forward.

As they climbed through the knee-high green grass, the sun strong and warming, Griff moved his horse beside Val's. He made sure there was plenty of room between them. The horses breathed heavily as they chugged up the steep slope. Once on top, Val pulled Socks to a stop. "Look," she said, gesturing to the vista before them.

Griff had never ridden this part of Bar H property. Now, he could see why Downing wanted to buy the place. The two hundred acres was comprised of hills and gently sloping valleys of green grass. "This area looks like green velvet," he said, impressed. Southward, he could see the ranch and the outbuildings. Everything sloped toward the ranch. It was perfectly situated, Griff thought.

"I know." Val sighed. She hooked her right leg up and around the saddle horn. Resting her elbow on her drawn-up leg, she said,

"This is where I always came as a kid. When things got too violent and threatening for me, I'd saddle my horse and ride out here." She pointed to the ground. "I used to dismount and sit or lay in the grass. It was like a soft, sweet-smelling blanket beneath me." Looking up, Val pointed to a few soft, white puffy clouds starting to drift across the sky. "I spent hours up here watching the clouds. I'd see shapes in them like fish, deer, bears or other animals. . . ."

Griff was grateful she was sharing something very private and personal with him. It was a gift, he realized, whatever her reason. "Funny, when I was a little kid, I'd do the same thing over at our Tetons Ranch. My dad would find me laying out in the pasture, hands behind my head, just watching the clouds take shapes."

Glancing over at him, Val appreciated the faraway look in his eyes. "Nowadays, kids don't do that anymore. They're hooked into the iPods, iPads or computer games. They're constantly looking down, not up. Pity."

Hearing the sadness in her voice, Griff nodded. "I know. They're missing a lot." He moved around and the saddle creaked.

"When I could escape out of the house," she said, gesturing to the large hill, "I could cry up here and not be worried my father would hear me."

Heart contracting with pain, Griff said, "No child should suffer like you have. I'm really sorry, Val."

His words were like salve to the open wounds she still carried within her. "Thanks . . . it means a lot."

"I wish . . . I wish I could help you, but I don't know how."

Unhooking her leg from around the horn, she said, "Coming home has brought up so much of the past once again. I don't know if there is any way to help. The memories are right there." She held her gloved hand up to her head.

Griff could say nothing. What he wanted to do was hold Val. Hold her until he saw all the sadness and terror leave her eyes forever. Somehow, Griff knew in his heart, he could help her. If only she would let him. . . .

CHAPTER TWELVE

Gus sat at the cleared table after dinner with a cup of coffee between her arthritic hands. She waited until Val and Griff were done with the dishes before saying, "Grab yourselves some coffee and join me."

Griff dried his hands on a towel and hung it up on a hook. Val was busy wiping down the counter until it sparkled. She wore a very old, thin red-checked apron around her waist. Her red hair was loose and damp tendrils stuck to her temples. They'd finished riding the fence line two hours earlier just as evening had begun to fall. Gus had a roast with mashed potatoes and gravy waiting for them as they returned to the house. Griff felt so much a part of their family already. It made him feel good. Wanted. And appreciated.

He walked over to the coffeemaker. "Want a cup?" he asked Val.

"Yes, please." She rinsed out the cloth and

folded it next to the double sinks. After hanging the apron on a nearby hook, Val sat down at her grandmother's right arm.

"I want to hear how the fences look," Gus told her.

Griff brought over two steaming cups of coffee. He set one in front of Val and then took a seat opposite Gus.

"Well," Val said, "it's good news." She glanced over at Griff. He had taken a shower and changed before dinner, but he hadn't shaved. Stubble shadowed his face and gave it a dangerous quality. "Do you want to share with Gus what we discovered?"

Pleased that Val would invite him into the conversation, Griff said, "Sure." He laid out the areas that needed work. When he was finished with his report, he saw Miss Gus's mouth was pursed and he knew when that happened, she was formulating a plan.

"In terms of replacing posts and buying barbed wire, what are we talking?" Gus asked.

Griff took out his notebook from his left pocket, opened it up. "We're looking at replacing fifty posts. In terms of wire, we'll need one large spool."

Satisfaction wreathed Gus's face. "That's not so bad, is it, Val?"

"No. I was really surprised as we rode the fence today," Val agreed. "I thought it would be in a lot worse condition."

"This is good news," Gus said, sipping her coffee. She looked across the table at Griff. "So, why don't you go to the Horse Emporium tomorrow morning, buy those items and get started? I figure it will take you about a week to complete it. Assuming your arm can handle it."

Nodding, Griff said, "Yes, my arm will be just fine. I can have it done in a week."

Gus gave her granddaughter a pleased look. "Now, that means we can buy those heifers. Once the fences are mended, we can release them into the pasture."

"So, are you sure we have the money for this, Gus?"

With a chuckle, Gus said, "Of course we do. I told you much about my ranch savings account. What I didn't share with you until now is I set up two accounts. One is connected with the books for the Bar H. The other has most of the money I received from the sale of our ranch. It's my personal stash. And that's the one I'll use to buy twenty heifers."

"Really?" Val saw Gus's eyes gleam. She was a shrewd rancher and businesswoman, there was no doubt.

"That's why when Downing and that darned Realtor come by wanting to buy the Bar H, thinking we're in dire straits, I let 'em think it." Her lips curved into a wily smile. "Our finances are no one's business."

"Of course not," Val agreed. She gave Griff a glance and saw the surprise in his expression. Turning back to Gus, she said, "But that's your personal money, Gus. You don't need to spend it on this ranch."

"Why not?" Gus demanded, petulant. "This is your *home*, Val. It's where you were *born*." She jabbed her finger down at the table. "It's important to have roots, child. And to have family. Without either, you're nothin' more than a tumbleweed flailin' and wanderin' all over the prairie of life. Whether you know it or not, you're very blessed to have this ranch. It's your heritage." Her mouth thinned and she narrowed her gaze on her granddaughter. "I know this place holds painful memories for you, but over time they will dissolve. The Bar H is a beautiful ranch. We have a creek and a lake. We have cleared pastures. Everything a rancher could want is right here. You just need time to realize it."

Reaching out, Val gripped Gus's wrinkled hand. "I do realize it. I hope you don't think

I'm not grateful for your help, because I am."

Patting her hand gently, Gus dropped her gravelly voice. "I know how hard this is for you, honey. I'm hopin' the longer you stay here, the more the Bar H will grow on you like a good friend. Your mom and dad were lousy parents to you. I'm so sorry I wasn't here earlier in your life to help protect you. But all we can do now is pick up the pieces, Val. And I'm here to make sure that happens. You have the money to make this place solid, business-wise, again. Okay?"

Hot tears scalded Val's eyes. She felt the warmth and strength of her grandmother's hand around hers. Gus had worked all her life. She still had calluses on her palms to prove it. "Okay," Val said in a wobbly voice. Embarrassed, she wiped away the tears in her eyes. "You're such a guardian angel, Gus. I love you so much." She lifted her grandmother's hand and pressed a kiss to the back of it.

Griff sat quietly watching their conversation. Although he was an interloper, his heart was solidly tied to this ranch. The strength of the two women at this table was responsible for that. The tears in Val's eyes tore at his heart. He wanted to get up, lean over and give her a hug of support. Tucking the need away, he said, "Miss Gus, have you decided on who to buy the cattle from?"

Releasing Val's hand, Gus focused on his question. "Yes, I have a ranching friend over in Cheyenne that raises the best Herefords in the state. I've already contracted with him to select twenty of his best two-year-old heifers. If you get that fence patched in a week's time, then I can call and tell him when to truck them over to us."

"It will be done. I'll get on it first thing tomorrow morning." He held up his bandaged arm. "I'm sure my arm is ready to go to work again, especially since the fence isn't in too bad shape." He felt the two women needed time alone, and he pushed back from the table to leave the kitchen.

"Where you goin'?" Gus demanded, scowling.

"Er . . . to my room."

"Sit back down."

Griff hesitated, halfway out of the chair. "I thought you might need some private time together."

Jabbing her index finger down at the table, Gus growled, "Sit down, young man. I'll decide when I don't want you to hear something!"

A sour grin crossed Griff's mouth as he sat back down. "Yes, ma'am."

"That's better." Gus studied him for a long moment. "Val tells me you have an accounting background. Is that true?"

Nodding, Griff told her more about the MBA he'd earned at Harvard.

"Well, don't ya think it's time you put it to work here at the ranch?"

"Yes, of course I can, Miss Gus. I can pick up accounting duties for the ranch if you want."

"I'll pay you extra to do that." And then she shot a smile over to Val. "I ain't too good at keepin' the books, like I used to be. Hate giving up things, but I need someone like you to straighten them out. The only way a ranch knows if it's belly-up or not is by its books. I'll give you the second set of books, too."

Val frowned and stared at Gus. "A second set of accounting books?"

Gus nodded. "The one with my savings account of my ranch sale money. You never saw 'em. They're the books that contain all the expenses for the ranch."

"That's a good plan," Griff told her. "The Bar H should have its own set of books. And legally, because the sale of the ranch belongs to you, it shouldn't be mixed in with this ranch's books."

"You got it," Gus crowed, delighted. She

slid Val a look. "I knew this gent was the right wrangler for this ranch of ours. And now, it's proving to be true."

Val grinned a little. "You were right, Gus." She always was, Val realized. Some people, she'd discovered, just had a very clear eye on life. Gus was one of those people who could read a person like a book — and be right. Val wasn't that good and she was grateful for her grandmother's insights.

Pleased, Gus nodded. "Now, Griff, you're carrying a double load with fence mending and book balancing."

"If it's okay with you, Miss Gus, I'll do the fence mending first. When I get back at night and after dinner, I'll sit down with the books. You'll be my go-to source to figure it all out."

"I'd be pleased to do it. Maybe, once everything is straightened out and cleaned up, you can share them with Val?"

"Of course."

"Technically, she owns the Bar H."

"Legally, though," Griff countered, "it's in your name, Miss Gus."

"That's gonna change," Gus said, giving Val a sly look. Reaching out, she gripped her granddaughter's hand. "Some day in the near future, when things are settled, you will want the Bar H back. It won't be now, but when you're ready to assume ownership, you let me know. I'll deed it back to you. Fair enough?"

"Fair enough," Val replied. In her heart of hearts, she really didn't think she'd ever want the Bar H, but there was such hope burning in Gus's eyes, Val kept that to herself. She loved her spunky grandmother with a fierceness that had always been in her heart. Gus was truly her guardian angel.

Griff tried to keep the surprise out of his face early the next morning as he entered the Horse Emporium. Clarissa Peyton, the recently divorced wife of Senator Peyton, was in the store. And next to her was Curt Downing.

"Morning, Griff," Andy called from the front counter. "How you doing? Haven't seen you here for a while."

Smiling at his former boss, Griff came up and handed Andy a list. "Doing fine, Andy. And you?"

Andy patted his protruding belly. "Dr. Jordana has me on high-blood-pressure medication," he said in a complaining voice. "Makes me feel lousy."

"Sorry to hear that, Andy." Griff glanced over at Clarissa and Downing. They were in deep, quiet conversation with each other.

Lowering his voice so only Andy could hear him, he asked, "That is Clarissa Peyton, isn't it?"

Andy leaned forward and whispered, "Did you hear? She is now going by her maiden name, Clarissa Reynard. You know that her daddy, Hank Reynard, owns the Triple R ranch over in Cheyenne? It's one of the biggest and most successful in the state. Apparently, her father disowned her and now, with her senator ex-husband, Carter Peyton, going to prison, she's out on the street."

"I heard Miss Gus say Clarissa was one of the richest women in the state. I guess her status changed?"

"Yes, in a big way," Andy said, sad. "She's a nice lady. Her son, Bradley, is now eighteen and into drugs. Hate to see all of this hit her. Clarissa has done a lot for the poor here in Jackson Hole. She was once part of a global effort to raise huge amounts of money through her favorite charities for the poor. Isn't it something that now, she's one of 'em?"

"It is." Griff knew what it felt like to lose millions and be thrown out on the street, too. "Does she live here or in Cheyenne?"

"Clarissa lives here. She just sold the senator's big house and has a nice sum, but nothing like she had before. Right now,

236

she's looking for an apartment or condo. I think that's what she and Mr. Downing are discussing right now." Andy raised his brows and said, "You did know Downing owns a string of condos here in the valley?"

Downing was just full of surprises. "No. I know he owns a very successful trucking company and has his endurance breeding facility."

"The guy has his fingers in every pie you can think of," Andy said in a grumbling tone.

Griff couldn't help wondering what other pies Downing had his fingers in, and how he could find out.

"Clarissa knows he's a bad dude," Andy continued. "It's just that she's desperate for someplace to live."

Quirking his mouth, Griff said, "Sometimes, when you're down-and-out, you don't have the choices you'd like, Andy."

"Right about that. Bradley and Zach Mason are sharing an apartment. Both of 'em, from what I've heard through gossip, are selling and moving drugs through the valley."

"That has to bother Clarissa a lot." Griff wondered if he were in her shoes, what he'd do in such a situation. There weren't any easy answers.

"Oh, it does. Right now, she has a job over at Franny's Mercantile on the main plaza. She's a working woman again."

"Coming from a ranch background, it's too bad she can't go home to her father's ranch."

Andy scratched his chin. "She had a heck of a falling-out with her father when she turned eighteen. She's the oldest in the family, but in his will Hank left the ranch to his only son, the baby of the family. She was pissed off, to say the least."

"I don't blame her," Griff said, feeling badly for the beautiful woman in her early thirties. Clarissa was dressed in jeans with a tasteful denim blazer over a pink blouse. She was all class, Griff decided, even if she didn't have the same kind of money as before.

"Well," Andy said, waving the list in the air, "it looks like you need four-by-four posts and plenty of barbed wire. Fence mending?"

"You got it."

Andy turned and called to one of his helpers. A young man in his early twenties hurried up to the counter. Handing the lad the list, Andy said, "Jacob, load all that stuff in Mr. McPherson's truck. He'll bring it around to the dock."

"Yes, sir." Jacob turned and hurried toward the rear door of the store.

"I can't say I miss working here," Griff told Andy with a smile.

"I miss you, Griff. You were a hard worker, reliable and responsible." Andy's blue eyes sparkled with mirth. "Now, if you ever need another job . . ."

Griff held up his hand. "No thanks. I'm happy at the Bar H."

"It's working out okay?"

"Better than I hoped."

"Good, good. Because Miss Gus is known to be a tough boss."

"Only if you don't do your fair amount of work." He saw Downing part from Clarissa and walk toward the counter.

"From the looks of that list, you're gonna be puttin' cattle back on the Bar H pretty soon?" Andy guessed.

"Yes, Miss Gus wants to buy twenty head of heifers."

"Heifers for the Bar H?" Downing asked, overhearing the conversation. "I didn't realize Miss Gus had the money to buy anything, much less twenty head of prime breeding cattle."

Frowning, Griff stared hard at the rancher. Downing acted like everything was his business. Griff wasn't about to let Downing

239

know anything about the ranch's financial status. "Surprises abound."

Downing's mouth cut downward at the corners. "You're feeling pretty cocky this morning, McPherson."

Griff knew he had the upper hand. He'd encountered this kind of swaggering bastard on Wall Street all the time. Money made some men power hungry, arrogant and bullies. Downing had all those stellar traits.

When McPherson wouldn't answer, Curt prodded, "Well, tell me, does Miss Gus need twenty head? I've got some fine Hereford stock over at my ranch that I'd be willing to sell her."

"The cattle have already been bought."

Brows flying upward, Curt said, "Really? Why, that's a *lot* of money."

"Yes, it is." Griff watched amazement cross Downing's face for a moment before, suddenly, the unreadable mask was once more in place.

"Well, well, that's mighty interesting, because word around town is that the Bar H is near foreclosure." Drilling McPherson with a stare, Curt said, "And if it is, Miss Gus can't afford those cattle."

Sauntering around the counter, Griff shrugged and said, "I wouldn't know, Mr. Downing. I only work for her." He moved past the scowling rancher and headed for the front door. It was time to drive his truck around to the dock to pick up the supplies. Lifting his hand at the door, Griff called, "Nice seeing you again, Andy."

"Same here, Griff. I'll just put this on Miss Gus's account with us."

"Great. Thanks." Griff smiled to himself as he saw Downing mouth a curse. Let the jerk think what he wanted. Griff climbed into the truck and drove it around to the rear dock.

He was surprised to see Clarissa Reynard standing on the dock — waiting for him. As he hopped up on the platform, he tipped his hat. "Miss Reynard?"

"Hi, Griff, I know your brother, Slade." Clarissa held out her hand and shook his. "I saw you in there and I wanted to talk to you privately."

Griff could smell the faint whiff of jasmine perfume around Clarissa as he shook her soft hand. She wore makeup, her lips ruby-red to match her carefully coiffed hair. "Yes, ma'am. What can I do for you?"

Clarissa moved a bit closer and lowered her voice. "I was wondering if Miss Gus has a house or cabin to rent out on the Bar H? I'm looking for a place to live and I really don't want to be in town."

"Miss Gus only has the main ranch house, I'm afraid." He saw the hope in Clarissa's large green eyes die. Feeling badly, he offered, "But I can ask her if she knows of another ranch around here that might?"

"No, that's okay. I know just about everyone here in the valley. I love the Bar H because it is south of town and is in truly beautiful country. I'm looking for peace and quiet and that would have been the perfect spot."

"I see," Griff said, apology in his voice. Nearby, Joe and another worker began loading the fence posts into the back of his truck. "I'm sorry."

Stepping back, Clarissa smiled a little. "That's okay. I'll find something. I'm not Wyoming bred for nothing."

Smiling a little, Griff said, "Wyoming bred and Wyoming tough."

"You should know. You're from here, too." She brightened. "I've been meaning to visit Slade and his new wife, Jordana. Would this be a good time to drop by and see them?"

Griff liked her openness and warmth. And she had sincerity to boot, unlike Downing.

"Sure. I would think they'd like to see you."

"When I held my charity events to raise money for the poor, Slade always managed to give some even if he didn't have it. Your brother is a stand-up guy. I hope you know that."

"I do," Griff said, meaning it. "And I'm sure Slade and Jordana would like to hear from you."

"Do you know if they have a house they might rent?"

Shrugging, Griff said, "I really don't know. But you can ask them."

Brightening, Clarissa said, "I'll do that." She reached out and squeezed his upper arm. "Thanks for everything, Griff. Please give Miss Gus and Val my best. Tell them I'll call one day soon and we'll share a cup of coffee with one another and catch up."

Tipping his hat, Griff murmured, "I will." He watched Clarissa walk back into the Horse Emporium. He knew she didn't want anything to do with Downing, and hoped that Slade had an extra house to rent to her.

Joe had finished loading the fence posts and spools of barbed wire into the truck. Griff thanked him and leaped off the platform, climbing into the driver's seat. Heading toward the highway, he thought about Clarissa's question as to whether the Bar H had any cabins for rent. And that gave him a great idea. He wondered what Gus and Val would think about it.

CHAPTER THIRTEEN

Curt Downing's upper lip lifted into a snarl. He watched from his truck as fashion plate Clarissa Reynard left the loading dock of the Horse Emporium. He felt his body harden with desire. Curt liked women, and it was easy enough for him to bed them, what with his money and his power. But he especially liked women that snubbed him. They were a challenge. Hands tightening on the wheel of his truck as it was loaded with feed for his horses, Downing cursed softly.

Finding Clarissa at the Horse Emporium had been good luck. When he'd gone over to talk with her, he'd found out she was looking for a condo or, better yet, an apartment. He had both for rent. And he even lowered the price for her because she would be nearby and available for his unexpected visits. But she'd said no and then sought out McPherson. Curt bet his last dollar that

Clarissa was asking if there was any room at the Bar H for her. He knew there wasn't. There was one main ranch house, a barn and several outbuildings, but nothing she could rent. Good.

Although she was newly divorced from Senator Peyton, Clarissa was still a power player. She might not have the millions the senator had provided when they were married, but she still had clout. And that was something Curt worked to get. He thought about how he could manipulate her into working with him in some way. Her son, Bradley, was now living with Zach Mason. And both were dealing drugs in the valley through his vast network. Oh, Zach didn't know Curt was a regional drug lord. No, he was too smart to be discovered. His minions were so far removed none of them could point a guilty finger at him for the cops or federal agents.

Now, how to snag Clarissa? Bradley, her teenage son from a previous marriage, had been in drugs since twelve years old. Bradley was now eighteen and a rebel. The kid was cantankerous as a wild mustang. Senator Peyton had hired a contract killer to kill Lieutenant Matt Sinclaire, a firefighter who had let Peyton's family burn to death during a snowstorm several years ago. Peyton had planned to kill anything Sinclaire loved, which included his mute daughter and his love interest, Casey Cantrell. The plan blew up on Peyton and he was turned over to law enforcement. As soon as Clarissa discovered her husband was a would-be murderer, she presented evidence in court against him. It didn't take her long to divorce him, either. The senator got even because of a pre-nup agreement and Clarissa ended up with the house in Jackson Hole and nothing else. She'd just sold it for far less than it was worth because of the ailing economy. Curt knew she was looking around to do more charity work. She worked part time at the local mercantile, but it was a menial job far below Clarissa's station.

"Mr. Downing," Joe called from the dock, "you're loaded and ready to go, sir."

Curt turned the key and the big Chevrolet purred to life. He eased away from the dock and turned onto the highway, heading back to his ranch. His mind, however, was focused on Clarissa. That bitch was, at one time, the queen of the town. She raised millions for charity and had ties to rich people around the world. She was an important player to him. And he wanted her for good reason. It didn't hurt she was curvy, beautiful, smart and a natural born hellion. How to get Clarissa to like him?

The light was bright and Curt put on his sunglasses. Warm, sunny days in Wyoming were to be celebrated. This part of the state had winter eight months out of the year, so sun was like gold to the residents. Yes . . . what could he do to pull Clarissa into his orbit? Mind ticking off possibilities, Curt decided that he had a chance to trap Clarissa in her own web. One thing about people who used to have money: they always wanted it and their station back.

As he swung onto the main highway leading out of town, he saw the empty elk-feeding center on his right. During the winter, thousands of elk came down from the mountains to eat the hay distributed by the federal government. Without it, many would starve to death. The ten-foot-tall fence paralleled the highway and red-tailed hawks and other raptors were sitting on the posts looking for a meal across the flat, grassy land.

His thoughts careened back to the Bar H. Damn. Somehow, he *had* to buy that property out from under Miss Gus! The old woman was stubborn and hated him. Curt didn't know why. He'd never done anything to her. He'd tried cajoling Miss Gus, buying her flowers and candy. He'd even sent his Realtor to visit her. He too had failed. So what was it going to take to lever Miss Gus out of that ranch and sell it to him?

Miss Gus had to be broke. She'd lived here for twelve years and the Bar H had consistently deteriorated in that time. If she had money, she'd have used it on the ranch. Or was she already in financial straits? The fact that she could buy twenty head of prime Hereford heifers told him she had *some* money squirreled away.

He had to find some way to get that ranch out from beneath Gus. Curt slowed down and turned right onto a narrow dirt road that would lead to his ranch. It was time to employ some extreme measures. Maybe he could get his minions to do some dirty work for him? He had some handlers who took care of Zach, as middlemen who made sure the boy didn't know that Curt was the brains behind the operation. Still, Downing wanted to think through his strategy. Most crucial was he couldn't be tied to the ugly deed. And if Zach was caught, he couldn't point a finger at him — only at his handlers.

"Clarissa Reynard wants you to call her," Griff told Miss Gus after he'd climbed out of the truck. Gus and Val had been in the barn cleaning out the horses' stalls.

Wiping her brow, Gus pushed the blue baseball cap back on her head. "Clarissa Peyton?"

"Yes, she's gone back to her original name of Reynard. I guess the divorce is final and she's using it instead."

Val walked up. "How's she doing?" She felt herself respond simply to Griff being present.

"Seems okay. She's looking for a place to rent."

"What in tarnation? She has that million-dollar house to live in!"

"Not anymore." Griff filled them in on what he knew. Gus looked shocked after he'd finished his explanation.

"This is terrible! Clarissa is a fine young woman! She's done nothin' but *good* for this valley. Her charities have helped millions of starving and poor people around the world."

Val managed a grimace. "Prenups by the rich aren't exactly fair, are they?"

Griff nodded. Val looked delicious in the white long-sleeved cotton blouse and jeans. "Prenups were never meant to be fair," Griff told them. "They're designed to save a man's fortune, never mind paying what is fair to the spouse."

Snorting, Gus said in a grumbling tone, "Senator Peyton is a killer. He had no *right* to take money from Clarissa because she is responsible for raising Bradley, her eighteen-year-old son by her first marriage. The woman has responsibilities!"

"I guess the senator thought he was being fair by giving her the Jackson Hole house."

"Hells bells!" Gus said, "That sidewinder has *five* homes dropped all over the US and other countries. He could sure afford to give Clarissa more than one."

Val smiled a little. When the oldster got fired up, she was something to behold. "Well, we can't help her, Griff. We don't have anything to rent to her, much as we might like to."

Griff hesitated. He'd had an idea to help the ranch get back on solid financial footing and decided to share it with them now. "Miss Gus, I have an idea. Part of my job in my uncle's firm was as an investment banker. I look for ways to increase property income. Have you ever thought of building some small cabins on Long Lake and renting them out to fishermen and tourists?"

Gus thought deeply for a moment. "Son, I like your idea. In fact, I'd talked to Cheryl about building five or six cabins along the lakeshore. We were lookin' for ways to bring money in to keep the Bar H solvent."

"Really?" Val asked her grandmother.

Gus nodded. "Your mom wanted nothing to do with it. I thought it was a *great* idea! The lake is stocked every spring by the state. We have five different types of trout in it. Fishermen would kill for this kind of setup. I figured if we built six cabins with three rooms each, we could rent them out for two hundred dollars a day during the summer. That's a lot of money when you look at it." Gus looked up at Griff. "And with your Harvard MBA, I know you can see money potential."

Grinning, Griff said, "Yes, ma'am, I do. It's a good income base."

"Six cabins would mean twelve hundred dollars a day times three months," Val said, thinking aloud. "That's a *lot* of good money coming in."

"Hmm," Gus said, peering up at her granddaughter, "maybe we need to relook at all our options? It wouldn't take much of an investment to have six cabins built. We could do it this year. And by next spring, after advertising on the internet, we could lure those fishermen in here. Those types don't blink at paying two hundred bucks a day for a cabin when they know a lake is stocked with trout. You open to it, Val?"

"I am." Val glanced over at Griff. "I think we need time to figure out what the costs and outlay are to us. After all, Gus, it's coming out of *your* savings. Technically, the Bar H can't afford it."

"Griff, do you have any construction experience?"

"Very little," he admitted. "Before Slade and I got split up, we worked with our father on building another house at the Tetons Ranch. I admit, I was five at the time, and I don't remember a lot about it."

"I don't imagine," Gus intoned with a wry smile, "that your job on Wall Street afforded you any construction knowledge?"

"Yes, in one way it did. We had a number of construction companies in our portfolio. I was the one who had to go out in the field yearly and visit them. We had two others who were developers, building condos or home packages. I learned a lot about construction from those companies."

"You have Slade for help, too," Gus reminded him, poking her index finger into his chest. "Slade is good at everything."

Mouth curving a bit, Griff liked the feisty old woman. She had fire and grit in her eyes. "Yes, he is. And I could talk with him about such a project. We could sit down and figure out what the needs would be as well as the costs."

"Good, you do that," Gus said, triumphant.

"Gus, he has a lot of other things to do, too," Val gently reminded her.

"Oh, pshaw. He'll figure out how to parcel out his time." She turned and walked slowly down the slope toward the ranch house.

With a chuckle, Griff traded a warm look with Val. "Your granny gets excited, doesn't she?"

Laughing a bit, Val nodded her head. "To say the least."

"Did you inherit the trait?" Griff wondered, feeling good about sharing a private moment with Val.

"Oh," she said, some of her smile disappearing, "I guess I did as a real young child."

Hearing pain in her voice, Griff wanted to reach out to Val. The stricken look on her face told him everything. "I'm sorry," he confessed, "I didn't mean to dredge up bad memories."

Val took a deep breath and shrugged. "No matter where I go on this ranch, Griff, it's all the same. One place isn't any better than another." She saw the care burning in his dark green eyes. For a second, Val had a wild, unchecked urge to step forward and embrace him. Somehow, she knew that he would hold her, would shield her against the oppressive weight she always carried. Warmth opened her heart and for the first time, Val realized just how much she was drawn to this tall wrangler. His face was sunburned, chiseled and becoming sculpted by Wyoming weather. It had a rugged quality gained by working in the harsh wilds of the state. And Griff wore it like a knight in shining armor. Swallowing hard, she took a step back from him instead of walking toward him like she really wanted to do. She saw care in his eyes — for her. It was a startling realization and Val was desperate to have time to feel her way through all of this. "It's not your fault, so don't worry about it," she said, slightly breathless.

Turning, Griff hooked a thumb toward the loaded truck in the driveway. "I'm going to get busy unloading the fence posts."

Val nodded. "If Gus really wants you to add building cabins to your list, you won't be able to handle it all by yourself."

"No," he agreed. "One person can only do so much."

"If I helped you dig post holes and string wire, two people could get it done in half the time."

Griff wanted nothing more than to have Val at his side. And he knew she was a consistent worker. "Stringing wire is hard work," he warned her.

"You're right, it isn't for sissies."

Grinning at her, Griff said, "You're not a sissy. Why wouldn't I want a partner?"

A partner. Val liked that concept. "I'll finish cleaning the stalls in the barn and join you." Val saw pleasure gleaming in his eyes. Excitement shimmered through her. Griff always made her feel light and happy.

"Good enough," Griff said with a slight smile. "See you soon."

By the time lunch rolled around and Gus called them in to eat, Griff had unloaded what he needed to from the truck. New fence posts were stacked in neat piles. A spool of barbed wire and ten posts remained in the vehicle. Griff would drive down the road and start the repair at the gate and lake area first. Wiping his brow, he settled his cowboy hat back on his head and joined Val as she walked up to the house.

"Good work," he said. "We're a good team." And they were.

Feeling heat in her cheeks even though she was perspiring, Val walked with enough distance between herself and this brazen wrangler so their hands couldn't accidentally touch. She pulled off her leather gloves and said, "Ranch work isn't for the lazy, is it?"

"No," Griff agreed amiably.

"Where'd you get your work ethic?" Val said over her shoulder, climbing the stairs.

"Our parents initially. Then Wall Street gave me a different kind of ethic." Griff hurried ahead and opened the screen door for Val.

He walked in behind her and sniffed the fragrant air. Spaghetti? Miss Gus had been promising for the past few days to make it from her home-canned tomatoes from last year's greenhouse garden. Inhaling the scent of garlic and butter, Griff felt his stomach growl. He quickly went to his room to wash up.

In the kitchen, Val helped Gus get the spaghetti and sauce from the stove to the table. Griff entered minutes later and set the table.

"That spaghetti smells mighty good," Griff told Miss Gus.

"It should! I used a couple jars of my stewed tomatoes, with onions and red peppers, from last year." Gus was wearing a white apron around her waist and there were red splotches from the sauce all over it. She proudly carried a large oval platter of steaming spaghetti to the table.

"I remember your spaghetti over at your

ranch in Cheyenne," Val said, placing the bowl of sauce on the table. "I always loved it, Gus."

"My recipe is the same now as then. There's another good reason for you to stay here, young lady. *My cooking!*"

Laughter filled the kitchen as they sat down. Val retrieved a basket of toasted French bread that had been slathered with butter and garlic. Picking up the wide forks, Val hefted spaghetti onto Gus's awaiting plate. Next, she piled a good amount onto Griff's plate, and then her own. Ranch work was hard, physical work and they ate hearty.

Spooning the sauce that contained small beef meatballs onto her plate, Gus said, "Dunno about you two birds, but I'm a starvin' cow brute."

Griff enjoyed the patter between the women. The kitchen smelled wonderful and the warm, toasted garlic bread melted in his mouth. There was such a familiarity to this scene. He poignantly recalled his mother making all their meals. As a family, they sat at their table in the kitchen, eating together. How badly Griff had missed those times. He hadn't realized it until arriving at the Bar H.

For many minutes, there was no chatter, just people enjoying the food on their plates.

Val saw how famished Griff had become. He had eaten enough for two of them. Still, he was tall, strong and carried absolutely no fat on his muscular body. "What did you like about Wall Street?" she asked toward the end of their meal.

Hesitating, Griff said, "Looking back on it and seeing it differently now, not much. I got caught up in my uncle and aunt's world. They were the rich and elite of the city. Charity functions, parties, cocktail events and eating at the right restaurants were important to them."

Curious, Val saw the question in his face. "And of course, they wanted you to share it with them?"

"Yes," Griff said, placing his plate aside. He picked up his cup of coffee. "My aunt and uncle had a personal cook, two maids, and I had a nanny growing up in their household."

"Musta been nice," Gus said with a growl in her voice, patting her mouth with the napkin, "to have servants do your bidding. We could use a few of them around here."

"It was a way of life."

"And you got used to it, but I dunno if you liked it or not."

"I did like it, Miss Gus. At one time I had a limousine, a driver and a penthouse."

"Quite a fall from grace," Gus said, giving him a sharpened look. "While Wall Street crumbled, the American people lost even more. All the money I'd placed in the stock market is gone. And no one's come along to pay me back for those losses. There's many people out there near retirement who have had their entire life savings wiped out. Now, they have nothing. At least," and Gus gazed fondly around the kitchen, "we have a working ranch. A place where, even without much money, we could have a garden, raise food and get by. Most others don't have that option."

Guilt ate at Griff. "I was part of the problem on Wall Street," he admitted quietly to them. "I was the head of our company at the time and I was doing business as usual. When the crash occurred, everything was pulled out from beneath me. I didn't have two hundred bucks to my name when it was all over. I came crawling home to Slade, begging for a place to live."

Val's heart twinged. She saw the humility in Griff's eyes and heard it in his deep, husky voice. "That must be very hard to live with."

Appreciating her insight, Griff rallied and managed a thin smile. "It was. Slade and I had a pretty thorny time together. But he did help me. And I did learn a lot about ranching from him. As for what Wall Street did to the American public . . . well, that's a shame I'll carry to my grave."

Gus nodded, her eyes narrowing. "You've paid a hefty price, too. But you're right, what you and Wall Street did to Americans is a guilt you'll carry forever. It can't be undone. All you can do is move forward and try to be a better person than before."

The table became very quiet and Griff could feel the heaviness of his former life weighing down on his shoulders. "I've committed a lot of wrongs," he told Miss Gus. "I promised myself I'd do what I could to be a help to this country, and not be the cancer eating away at it."

Val wanted to reach out and touch Griff's hand. His fingers had curled into a slight fist. She saw how contrite he was. Clearly, he understood and took responsibility. He was a man who admitted his mistakes and was willing to atone for them any way he could. That made him a man of integrity. Clearing her throat, she said in a whisper, "I don't think anyone at this table is lily-white, Griff. Each of us has made some terrible mistakes. And I guess the only thing we can do is learn and not repeat them."

Wanting to caress her cheek, Griff forced

his hands to remain where they were on the table. The forgiveness in Val's blue eyes was like balm to his guilt-ridden soul. "Thanks, I needed to hear that. I know there are people out there who — and rightfully so — will never forgive Wall Street for what we did to them. I understand and I accept it."

"Well," Gus said, pushing her plate away, "you're coming home, Griff. You're a Wyoming man, proud and strong. Now you're reclaiming and rediscovering your roots where you were born. And after a piece of chocolate cake, you're off to dig postholes and string wire."

"I'm helping him, Gus," Val shared.

Brows shooting up, Gus said, "You are?"

"Why not? I know how to lay a fence line. And if you're thinking of building six cabins near the lake, don't you think he needs some help? We can finish the repairs in half the time together."

"Oh," Gus murmured, patting her mouth with the napkin, "I hadn't thought that far ahead. Yes, you're right." She looked down at the watch around her wrist. "Dinner is at eight o'clock. Don't be late."

Grinning, Val stood up and said, "Not to worry. We wouldn't want to miss any meals you make, Gus."

CHAPTER FOURTEEN

Slade was walking between the barn and the house as Griff drove into the graveled parking area of the Tetons Ranch the next day. He turned off the ignition and climbed out. Settling his Stetson on his head, Griff lifted his hand in greeting to his twin.

"Hey, you got a minute, Slade?" His brother was six feet five inches, toned and sculpted by the hard weather of Wyoming.

Slade nodded. "Sure. Got time for a cup of coffee, or are you just passing through?"

"Yeah, I'm on my lunch hour." His twin wasn't the usual, cranky self he had been in the past. Since his marriage to Jordana, he'd mellowed. Maybe love tamed even the toughest of men, Griff thought as he joined Slade.

"How's things going?" he asked Slade as they stepped into the mud porch and stomped their dusty boots off on a woven rug.

262

"Couldn't be better. How about you? How's life at the Bar H?"

Griff followed Slade into the ranch house. "Okay. That's why I'm here." They went to the brightly lit kitchen. Even before Slade had been married, everything was always spit and polish. Of course, nothing had changed. "Jordana at work?"

Slade poured them coffee and brought it over to the table. "She's pulling her daily eight hours over at the hospital," Slade said, sitting down. "I like the fact she has work Monday through Friday. The weekends are ours."

Griff joined him at the table. "Getting called out at all times of the day and night isn't any fun," he agreed. His stomach was tied in knots. He was fearful that Slade, no matter how good his mood was right now, might turn irritable. Just because they'd made peace with one another earlier didn't mean the foundation was solid. By asking Slade's help, he hoped his brother would continue to mend the fence between them. "It probably makes your married life less chaotic."

Shrugging, Slade sat back in the chair. "Got that right. Jordana likes the weekends off because she can do more endurance riding and training."

Griff picked up his mug and sipped the black, hot brew. Slade was wearing a white cowboy shirt beneath the black leather vest, the shirt sleeves rolled up to just below his elbows. His jeans were dusty. "I know she wants to get more into endurance riding with you. How is Stormy coming along?" Jordana's gray mustang mare had torn a tendon some time ago.

Slade said, "The mare is tough. But all mustangs are. She's doing okay and is healing ahead of schedule."

"That's good to hear," Griff said.

"What about you? How's things at the Bar H? I know Miss Gus was having problems getting a decent wrangler to help rebuild it until you came along."

Griff was happy they were discussing the Bar H. "You're right. Val, her granddaughter, is a big help to me. We were repairing fence yesterday."

"When Gwen Garner told me about Val returning, I was really surprised. She sure went through a lot growing up here." Shaking his head, Slade said in a low growl, "I almost got into a fight on the dock of the Horse Emporium with Buck about a year before he died."

"Growing up in New York left a big hole of unknowns as to what happened around

Jackson Hole while I was gone. I'm working at catching up."

"Are you glad to be out here?"

"I am." Griff cupped his hands around the mug. "Growing up in a huge city was like growing up on a different planet."

"More like another universe."

"Can't argue that." Griff was amazed at how friendly Slade was compared to their stiff connection before. "Marriage seems to be agreeing with you?" He saw Slade's eye grow warm.

"Jordana was the missing puzzle piece in my life," Slade answered. "I didn't realize how alone I really was until after we married." His voice grew husky. "I'm the luckiest cowboy in the world, Griff. I feel like I won the national lottery."

"Well deserved," Griff said, meaning it. "Even Andy at the Horse Emporium said you've changed for the better."

Slade chuckled. "Probably true. Jordana has tamed the last cowboy in Wyoming."

Griff set his mug down in front of him and took a deep breath. "I came over here for a reason, Slade. Miss Gus wants six cabins built alongside the lake and it's on my list to start gathering information on how to construct them."

Slade brightened. "I can help you there."

He gestured out the window. "I've rebuilt the barn and added two houses to the place over the years."

"I'm going to need some handholding on this, Slade. They can afford to hire a construction crew to build, but they're looking at me to supervise the project. I'm not sure I can."

"I'll help you with the planning stage. That's a good idea. Cabins at their lake will rent out to trout fishermen and tourists coming through Jackson Hole. That's a nice, tidy sum that can be made in the long run. It will help the ranch's bottom line."

"That's what we think. I need to create a list of what's needed. She's buying the building packages over in Cheyenne and they'll be trucked out here."

"Is the company who's selling you these packages giving you everything you need to erect them?"

"They say everything we need is supplied in the price."

"That's good news. Have the company send you the blueprints ahead of time and we'll sit down and look at them. I can give you some guidance."

Happiness threaded through Griff. This was the kind of relationship he'd hoped wasn't destroyed by their past. Slade was friendly and helpful. "Sounds good. I appreciate this.

"Hey, before I leave, can I see Jordana's mare? Miss Gus knew about Stormy and she wanted an update."

Getting up, Slade said, "Come on, see for yourself."

Griff followed him out of the house to the barn. Shorty was taking Thor, the medicine-hat mustang stallion, out into a lush green paddock for the day.

"Nice seein' you, Griff," the wrangler called as they passed one another.

"Same here, Shorty," Griff called, lifting his hand. He admired the chestnut-and-white stallion who pranced and snorted at his leader's side. Turning to Slade, he said, "Thor is incredible."

Slade said, "You know, since Jordana won the Teton endurance ride on him, he's gotten so many breedings with mares that we're filled for the season."

"That's great," Griff said, following him into the large red barn. The whinny of horses greeted them. "That's another source of income for you."

"Tell me about it. It's as if marrying Jordana suddenly opened up the skies, and good fortune is raining down on me instead of crap."

267

Griff appreciated his brother's coarse description of his life. They halted at a stall in the center of the barn. Griff saw a small gray mustang inside munching contentedly on hay and recognized her as Stormy.

Slade slid the door open and clucked to the gray mare, who came willingly up to him. "You can see we have that rear leg wrapped. Jordana has a friend who is a homeopath and she came out to see her. Gave her a remedy and we're seeing an improvement in her gait already." Slade patted the mare, threading his fingers through the horse's thick, black mane.

"Do you think she'll be ready for next year's endurance circuit?" Griff asked. Jordana was hoping to get the mare prepared starting in May, after most of the snow was off the ground.

Slade rubbed Stormy's ears, the mare closing her eyes in appreciation. "If she continues at this rate, yes." He patted the mare and slid the door shut, locking it. Turning, he gestured out the other end of the barn. "Jordana and I are thinking of building an indoor riding facility."

Eyes widening, Griff said, "That's a huge endeavor." Indoor riding arenas were massive buildings with enough room to ride a horse when the weather was inclement.

"And a lot of money."

"I know." Slade placed his hands on his narrow hips. "Jordana loves dressage and without an indoor arena, she can't ride and stay in shape for way too much of the year."

Dressage was the ultimate riding training, Griff knew. And Jordana was a champion dressage rider. "You could also use the place to break and tame Thor's offspring. I know you like to get them green broke before you sell them."

"Exactly," Slade said. His dark brows fell. "But the local banker is not going to loan us one cent. He's in bed with Downing. That little bastard purposely raised my mortgage to force me into foreclosing. It was a good thing Jordana won that ten thousand dollars in the race for us. Otherwise, I'd have gone belly-up."

Frowning, Griff murmured, "Yeah, and at that time, I didn't have two nickels to rub together to help you, either."

Slade slapped him on the back. "The fact you offered any help at all was enough."

Hearing the warmth in his brother's voice, Griff felt the rest of his fear dissolve. "I like what we have now, Slade. I intend to be a good brother to you."

Slade grinned and removed his hand from Griff's shoulder. "Right now, it looks like

I'll be helping *you.*

"Call me when the blueprints arrive. I'll drop by the Bar H and go over them with the three of you. Of course, Miss Gus has to okay it."

"Oh, I think she'll be tickled pink you're involved. She thinks the world of you."

"Really? Miss Gus is such a cantankerous old gal."

Seeing the surprise in Slade's eyes, Griff laughed. "She can be, but in her world, you're cowboy number two, right behind her late husband, Pete."

"Mmm, that's a real compliment. Thanks for letting me know."

"What about this bank? Are you going to have to go outside of Jackson Hole to find one that will loan you the money?"

"Yes. Jordana is calling around to some banks in Idaho Falls."

"That's a long way to drive." Griff knew Idaho Falls, Idaho, was roughly a three-hour drive one way from Jackson Hole.

Slade shrugged. "Hey, you gotta go where the money's at."

As they walked across the gravel driveway, the sky was clear above them. A hawk called in the distance as Griff followed his brother back to his truck. Glancing over at Slade, he saw him in thought, his brows drawn down, mouth pursed.

"What are you thinking about?"

"Was I that obvious?"

"We're twins. I think we share a little better communication than most others," Griff said.

They halted at the front of the truck. "I was just thinking . . . Downing desperately wants to own the Bar H. Why is it so important to him?"

"He was always griping to Andy that he needed more land in order to enlarge his endurance-riding operation."

Slade looked up and one corner of his mouth quirked. "I don't know . . . my gut tells me, as usual, he's up to no good." And then he slid a glance to Griff. "You sure Miss Gus doesn't have oil sitting under that ranch? It would be like him to know about it and never tell anyone in order to get the ranch at a reduced price."

"There's oil in Wyoming," Griff agreed. "I haven't heard Miss Gus say anything about it under her property. She owns the mineral rights so no one can come in and mine the land. All she's wanting to do is put her half of Long Lake to work for them to earn some income."

Digging the toe of his scarred cowboy boot into the red dirt, Slade grunted.

"Maybe he wants the lake, then."

"Yeah, he'd put as many condos on it as the county would allow. And when the county said stop, he'd probably slip them money to look the other way as he continued to populate it with condos. That's how he operates. Money talks."

"Downing has a way of staining anything he touches." Again, Griff wondered just how many dirty dealings Downing had, and of what sort. That was the kind of information he needed about Downing. "At least Miss Gus is being conservative with a few cabins. She's environmentally minded and six cabins isn't going to muck up the lake." Slade pushed the brim of his hat up. "Keep me in the loop as your plans move forward?"

"I will." For a moment, Griff wanted to reach out and throw his arms around Slade. Thinking better of it, he walked around and opened the truck's door. "Thanks for everything."

Smiling a little, Slade pulled his hat down so it shaded his eyes once more. "Anytime." He lifted his hand and then turned toward the barn.

Griff could see warmth in Slade's gray eyes. Feeling hopeful, he drove the truck out of the yard and onto the road. Like Westerners in general, Griff knew that actions spoke a lot more loudly than words. Griff wanted to continue to mend the bad blood from their past. He'd have to prove himself to Slade, one day at a time. As he drove toward the highway, he felt a sudden and unexpected ache in his throat. Tears! He gulped several times, trying to swallow them back. It was impossible. The road blurred in front of him as he tried to blink them away.

For a sweet, unexpected moment, he thought of Val. He replayed the softness he'd seen in her blue eyes for that split second when he'd gently pushed a red strand of hair behind her delicate ear. It had been such a galvanizing and unexpected gesture on his part. Griff couldn't get it — or her — out of his mind and heart.

As he drove down the long, straight road toward Jackson Hole, Griff felt the ache in his throat move down to his heart. He thought about Slade falling in love with Jordana. He could see a vulnerability taking root in his brother that had never been there before. Did real love change the other person? Complete them? Make them feel safe and secure so that they didn't have to erect hard walls around them in order to survive?

His mind churned over the idea in regards to Val. In some ways, she was very similar to

Slade: both had walls and no one was allowed to move past them to get to the real person. Slade's had probably been created by the death of their parents and having to run a ranch from such a young age. Val's had been beaten into place by her alcoholic father. Griff felt lucky in comparison, for his aunt and uncle had done nothing but shower him with love. He realized the differences. And he had a confidence that neither Slade nor Val possessed. His dilemma was in figuring out how to get beyond those walls to the person who hid behind them.

Slade's guard had dissolved because of his love of Jordana. Love . . . Griff had never considered that feeling in this way before. Perhaps love could dismantle Val's guardedness, as well.

Her face shimmered before him. Griff clung to the image, her beauty and naturalness. He liked it when she took her hair out of its ponytail and wore it loose around her shoulders. The red frame around her oval face brought out the youthful freckles that covered her cheeks and clean, straight nose. At times, Griff glimpsed the child within Val. She didn't show it often and when she did, she quickly hid it from view. Griff wished he could see more of the real Val.

Glancing to his right, Griff appreciated

the Teton that rose like blue dragon's teeth out of the flat plane that surrounded them. The highway was thick with tourists from around the world driving through on their way to Yellowstone Park.

Traffic was heavy and as he began his descent down a very long hill into Jackson Hole, Griff felt marginally better. As he entered the town, Griff crawled through the main plaza. He spotted Gwen Garner's quilt store on one corner. Gwen was the heart of the town, knew all the gossip, but also treated everyone with respect. Miss Gus opined Gwen as being more of a mayor to the town than the one who was elected. She would be a good person to talk to if one had questions.

Maybe Gwen was the right person for his questions regarding Curt Downing. On a whim, Griff quickly turned into the quilt store driveway.

Griff parked his truck in back of the store. Nervousness danced through him. He'd never met Gwen Garner, but her reputation as a wise and compassionate person goaded him into asking for help.

Griff walked up to the counter where two young women were manning the cash registers. "Excuse me," he said, taking off his hat, "I'm looking for Mrs. Gwen Garner. Is she here?"

"Oh, sure," one of them said, pointing to the other side of the store. "She's over there. The lady with gray hair, wearing the calico skirt and yellow blouse."

Tipping his hat, Griff murmured, "Thanks," and turned around. There were about twenty women in the store, selecting fabric for quilts. He spotted Gwen near the window talking with a woman about her own age. Slowing down, Griff waited until she had finished speaking with the lady. Then, he moved around the end cap of one of the fabric aisles.

"Mrs. Garner?" Griff removed his hat.

Gwen turned toward the male voice. "Yes?"

"Hi, I'm Griff McPherson. Do you have a moment to spare?"

Her eyes sparkled. "For a moment, I thought you were Slade." She offered her hand. "Call me Gwen. I heard Slade's twin was in town, but this is the first I've gotten to welcome you back to your birthplace."

Taking her hand, Griff found it warm and firm. There was kindness in Gwen's eyes. "I've been told by everyone around here that you're the woman who knows everything."

Laughing a little, Gwen straightened some

of the fabric bolts in front of her. "Oh, not everything, Mr. McPherson. Just some things. How can I help you?"

"Well," he murmured with a slight smile, "start by calling me Griff."

"You got a deal, Griff."

CHAPTER FIFTEEN

"We're done!" Val crowed, throwing her hands above her head in celebration. They had just strung the last of the barbed wire. She gave Griff, who was climbing the slope of the grassy hill, a triumphant smile. There was something calming about Griff. She wasn't quite sure what it was about him, but she was grateful he possessed this quality. Val felt her heart respond to his slow, masculine smile as it broadened. His skin glistened with perspiration beneath the late-afternoon sun.

"We're finished and, yeah, it's time to celebrate." Griff dropped the tools at his feet. This week had been special for him in so many ways. Mainly because Val had worked at his side from dawn to dusk repairing the fence line with him. Her company made even the hardest work seem effortless. The sun danced across her hair and Griff could see gold and crimson threads shimmering

278

beneath the strong light.

His heart opened wide at Val's smile, her eyes shining with real joy as she dropped her hands to her sides. "Couldn't have done this without you, Val." Griff gestured down the stout, straight fence line. "I'd have been out here another week without your help."

"Good thing we got it done." Val rested her gloved hands on her hips and looked into his shadowed face. "Those twenty heifers arrive tomorrow morning."

"I know. Nothing like a little pressure."

Val watched as Griff settled the hat back on his head. Around its brim were sweat stains, a sign of hard work. She felt suddenly uplifted and swept away by the warmth dancing in his green eyes. Something was happening between them and Val couldn't define it. She had always been afraid of working in close quarters with men. The past couple of weeks she had discovered Griff was a "safe" person to be around. And magically, she responded to his friendly smile and the look gleaming in his eyes. And then, her heart started a slow beat of possibility. She wanted to kiss Griff. For a moment, her nerves jangled, raw with fear. She knew she would be vulnerable to Griff if she initiated a kiss. She tried to settle her fears. How she wanted to taste this man against her lips!

"We need to celebrate once we get back to the ranch house," she said, pulling off her worn leather gloves. Swallowing against a dry throat, Val allowed her yearning to kiss him override her fear.

Griff nodded and tucked his gloves into the waist belt of his Levi's. He saw a longing look in Val's blue eyes. She seemed suddenly more available, as if another invisible wall had dissolved between them. As the past week had worn on, she'd become more relaxed, chatting with him and sharing a laugh every now and again. What was going on? Griff wasn't sure, but he liked the desire banked in her gaze as she studied him from only a few feet away. Did she want to kiss him?

Before Griff could say or do anything, Val stepped forward, placed her hands on his chest, reached up and pressed a chaste kiss against his jaw. Eyes widening, Griff was in such shock he didn't move. He felt her hands leave his chest, his skin tightening beneath the damp fabric. Suddenly, he ached for more of her butterfly touch. He opened his mouth to speak, but no words came out. Val's expression was filled with happiness and shyness.

Lifting his hand, he touched his jaw where

she'd placed the kiss. "Thanks," he said.

Val laughed a little giddily. "I — I just wanted to thank you, Griff. I was wrong about you." Unsure of herself because it had been a long time since she had kissed a man, Val shrugged and said, "You're different from other men, Griff. I don't know why I did it, but I just wanted to say thank you." Turning, Val hurried over to her ground-tied gelding. Her heart was still pounding, but now, it pulsed with joy. Just the male scent of his skin, the roughened stubble of his cheek against her lips had thrown open the doors of her fearful heart. As she picked up Socks's reins, Val gulped, relief flowing through her. Griff invited her, rather than repelling her as most men had in the past. There was something so heady and masculine about him, and woven with his sensitivity toward her, it made Val feel safe.

Light-headed, Griff's fingers rested where her soft lips had brushed his flesh. When he'd looked into Val's eyes, he'd seen a hunger. For him? Griff wasn't sure. Smiling a little, he absorbed the unexpected event. How many nights had he awakened from overheated dreams of Val? He was sure if she knew about his dreams, she'd run away screaming from him.

He gathered up the tools and walked over

to the Appaloosa. Freckles was happily munching the lush green grass where he stood. Feeling a little more confident as he opened the saddlebags and tucked the gear into them, Griff knew, based upon Val's past, she mustn't be crowded. He'd come to understand being hurt by her father meant feeling trapped for a long time afterward. He had to remain patient and let Val come to him. Otherwise, she would run away and he'd have no chance of a relationship with her ever again.

Buckling the saddlebags, Griff looked across his horse. Val was checking and tightening Socks's cinch. The sun was hot, the breeze warm with the scent of the evergreens that surrounded them. High, graceful-looking strands of clouds patched the sky, which reminded him of a horse's mane unfurling as it galloped. Gathering up the reins, he pulled them over the horse's head and looped them around the saddle horn.

Damn, it was so hard *not* to respond to that kiss, not to walk up to Val right now, slide his arms around her waist and haul her against him. Griff wanted to taste her lips. He wanted to taste all of her in every way. But as he mounted his horse, he reminded himself that was off-limits until Val made the move.

Val mounted Socks and turned to see concern in Griff's face. For a moment, she wondered if kissing him had been the wrong thing to do. What was he thinking about her brazen show of affection? She knew she'd kissed him spontaneously because she trusted him. Fully and without reservation.

Turning Socks, she called to him, "Let's go home. . . ."

Home. The word held such nostalgic magic for Griff. This time, as they rode over the grassy slopes to reach the dirt road below, Val remained close to him. And sometimes, their boots would brush against one another as their horses plodded along. He watched as Val's freckled cheeks reddened. She was suddenly very shy. Uncertainty lurked in her blue gaze.

Griff managed a one-sided smile he hoped would ease her fears. "Thanks for the kiss. It's nice to be appreciated."

Heart squeezing with yearning, Val managed, "I don't know what came over me. I guess I got spontaneous."

"Don't be sorry. I'm not." Griff shared a tender look with her. Her brow was wrinkled and she had tucked her lower lip between her teeth.

"I used to get in such trouble with my father when I was kid because of my tendency toward spontaneity. I found out early on it wasn't a good way to be." Risking a glance over at him, Val saw care burning in Griff's eyes. It was nearly four o'clock, and although he'd shaven this morning, his beard was quickly growing back and it made his cheeks appear hollow and accentuated his high cheekbones. He looked even more desirable to Val as a result.

The horses moved at a slow, swaying gait. Griff smiled a little. "I like spontaneity. It breathes life into the world, into a relationship."

Some of the tension bled out of Val as she heard the lightness in his husky voice. "Oh . . . good. It's gotten me into so much trouble in the past."

"It won't with me," Griff promised, holding her gaze. "I like what we have, Val. I don't consider your kiss anything more than celebrating a job well done." Griff meant it and he could see that Val's face went from stress to relief. Of course, he wanted to add so much more, but he knew it would scare her off. And that's the last thing he wanted to do. She was a wonderful person. She had a wry wit that made him laugh and he liked the fact they were equals. All those ingredients conspired to make him want to know her on a deeply personal level. And patience was the key to getting her to open up and trust him.

By the time they arrived at the ranch house, it was time for dinner. Griff took the horses to the barn and Val went inside to help Gus with preparations.

His heart sang. He was tired and dirty, but he felt like he was walking above the ground. With quick efficiency, Griff unsaddled the horses, rubbed them down and turned them out in the pasture next to the barn. He'd feed the rest of the livestock before going to wash up for dinner.

Val was busy in the kitchen with Gus. "We got the fence repairs done," she told her grandmother with pride. "Griff is such a hard worker. You were right, Gus, he was the right man to hire."

"Yep," Gus said, taking a bowl of steaming turnip greens over to the table. "Griff is solid gold." She raised an eyebrow at her granddaughter. "He's the kind of man any woman would want for a husband."

Val felt heat rush up her neck and nettle in her cheeks. "He's a decent sort, Gus."

"He's single, you know." Gus took freshly baked spelt bread out of the oven and set the loaf on a trivet to cool.

"No," Val replied, drying her hands, "I

didn't." Well, that was good to know. Val had always suspected it.

"Yep, I talked to Gwen Garner about him yesterday. I was over buying two yards of calico cloth because I want to make us a couple of new aprons. I nosed around about Griff." She slathered the bread's golden-brown top with butter. "He's the real deal, Val. A good person with Wyoming blood in his veins who got a bad hand dealt to him early on in life. He's come back to make amends with Slade and to prove to every-one that he's a reliable, honest man with integrity."

"Wish I could have heard your conversation."

Gus placed a huge CorningWare casserole on the table. She could smell the tuna and noodles in the air.

Val quickly set the table and heard the front screen door open and close.

Griff peeked in. "Miss Gus, do I have ten minutes to grab a shower? I don't think you want me at the table otherwise."

"Go ahead." She chuckled and waved her hand in his direction.

Griff glanced for a moment at Val. Usually, when dinner came, her walls went up. But she continued to look relaxed. He hurried up the stairs to shed his dirty clothes and wash ten hours of sweat and dust off his body.

Emerging from the shower a few minutes later, running a comb through his damp, darkened hair, Griff hesitated a moment as he stared back at himself in the antique mirror on the dresser. Did he look happy? He couldn't remember a time when he'd felt like this. Griff dressed and pulled on his good set of cowboy boots. As he went down the wooden stairs, his stomach growled. Even more important, his heart burst open as he walked into the kitchen.

They sat at the table waiting for him. Val had released her hair from its ponytail. The red strands hung around her face emphasizing her pink cheeks and darkened freckles. Griff took his chair opposite her. "Smells good, Miss Gus. What's for dinner?"

"Tuna-and-noodle casserole," Gus said, pointing to the serving dish on the table. "And organic turnip greens steamed and sprinkled with pine nuts. That's freshly made spelt bread near your elbow."

Griff gave her a grateful smile. "My mouth is watering." Gus lifted her plate and he placed a huge spoonful of casserole on it. Val was next. She asked for two helpings. And he would give himself the same amount.

"So you two finished the fence repairs," Gus murmured between bites. "That's a cause to celebrate. You finished early."

"I have a good partner out there on the land, Gus," Val said, and she gestured with her fork toward Griff.

"You're a quality wrangler, Griff, and we're mighty appreciative of your work ethic," Gus praised.

"I think the land agrees with you. It's like coming back home and resonating with it once more," Val said. She took the dish and their fingers met. A thrilling sensation, a tingle, raced up her hand and into her arm. She saw a smoldering look in Griff's gaze. But he wasn't hunting her. He wasn't crowding her and that was good to know. It made her yearn for more of a serious connection with him. Something intangible within her heart was driving her toward him. Val didn't have the answers and didn't know why. She felt safer accepting her driving need to know him because he wasn't chasing her.

"My soul thrives here, unlike in New York City." Griff squeezed a wedge of lemon across the fragrant greens.

"I can't tell you how much I loved being outdoors with Pete," Gus said. "I always looked forward to riding with him, working the cattle and repairing fence lines. He was a man with a good sense of humor and I can't tell you how much he entertained me out there." Gus cackled fondly over the memories.

Griff wondered if he and Val were sharing something similar. "Val's been not only my teacher," he told Gus. "We've also shared a lot of stories about our lives with one another."

"That's good," Gus said, giving Val a look of praise. "When you're a team, it happens automatically."

Val wanted to move the conversation elsewhere. She was still dealing with the surprise of kissing Griff. She needed time to digest her actions. "So when are the heifers set to arrive?"

"At ten sharp, tomorrow morning. Dr. Bennett will be out here to meet the truck. Each heifer needs to be vet checked before we accept it."

Excited about getting cattle back on the Bar H, Griff asked, "You'll probably want us to take them to the round corral near the barn? It has a chute so we can get each heifer into it for examination."

"Yes. Once the vet has okayed the twenty, then I pay for them."

"Gus, you do so much for this ranch," Val

said. "Thank you. . . ."

Patting her hand, Gus said in a gravelly voice, "Honey, you deserve the world. I can't give it to you, but if I could, I would. At least, this is the start of the rebirth of the Bar H. Cattle were *always* a part of this ranch. Now, it will be so again."

Griff sat there digesting Gus's emotional reply. He saw tears in her eyes and she fought them back. Yes, Val deserved the world. And in his own way, Griff wanted to be a part of the blossoming now taking place on the ranch.

"Well," Gus said, "I don't know about the rest of you, but I'm going to bed early tonight. I'm plumb tuckered out. I'm even passing up dessert. There's lemon cream pie over there on the counter if you want a slice." She rose and placed her linen napkin on the table.

Val nodded and planted a kiss on Gus's wrinkled cheek. "Good night, Gus. We'll take care of everything from here."

"Thanks, Honey. Night, everyone."

Val sat there feeling a sudden rush of emotion after her grandmother left the kitchen. What was this all about? Surprised, she felt her way through the unexpected tears. It had to do with Griff, she realized. She saw him looking at her intently from across the table. "Don't mind me," she murmured, sniffing.

"Tears are good.

"What touched you just now?"

Giving him a searching look, Val realized Griff cared enough to ask the right question. His rugged, sunburned face, the narrowing of his green eyes all conspired to touch her aching heart. She forced out in a low voice, "I've always had a hard time trusting men, Griff."

"I can see why."

Knotting the linen napkin in her lap, Val forced herself to hold his tender gaze. "There's something different about you. I can't put my finger on it . . . but you're not like other guys."

"You're a very courageous person in my eyes, Val."

"I don't see myself as anything but a survivor, Griff." She looked around the quiet kitchen and then met his gaze. "Your care is genuine."

Griff had so much to tell her but he knew now wasn't the right time to bring those topics to light. "I do care. And so does your grandmother. She's really glad you're home."

Opening her hands, Val sighed. "I didn't want to be here, Griff. And here I am," she said, looking out the window behind where Griff sat.

"It's different now," he counseled quietly. "Your parents are gone. I know there are bad memories, but doesn't Gus offset some of them? She's creating new and positive memories for you every day."

Mouth quirking, Val said, "I'm just now realizing Gus loves me more than I love myself."

The raw admission slammed into Griff. For an anguished moment, he wanted to reach out and pull Val into his arms. It would be so easy. There was less than two feet separating them at the table. Val was vulnerable right now and would trust him. But something cautioned him to remain in his chair and instead, he reached for his mug of coffee and wrapped his hands around it. "I think Gus is trying to prove to you that your birthright is worth saving. When you love someone, you want only good things for them."

"I mean," Val said unsteadily, "Gus sold her ranch, her *home,* to come here when I was a teenager. What kind of person does that? She had a lifetime's worth of memories at their ranch in Cheyenne."

"What's really important is family, Val. If you don't have that, you have no home. My feeling is when Pete died, she had the opportunity to come here and protect you and your mother against your father."

She held his warm gaze and she found herself wanting to get up, walk into Griff's arms and be held. Her heart told her he would hold her, keep her safe and love her. Taken aback by the realization, Val felt vague panic. She'd only ever met one man she could say she'd loved. Studying Griff, his hair drying, a lock hanging precociously over his smooth brow, Val wondered if what she saw in his eyes was love for her.

"If you look at us," Griff told her wryly, his mouth lifting in one corner, "we're both strays who left the family nest for one reason or another. And like a prodigal son and daughter, we've finally come home. And it's not been easy for either of us."

"I don't understand why you gave your half of the ranch back to your brother. You *had* a home."

"He deserved my half. He's the one who's kept the Teton going all these years, no thanks to me. And anyway, I feel comfortable living anywhere in the Jackson Hole area. I like the Bar H. To me, this place is about dreams coming true."

Happiness, like a quiet and gentle shadow, stole through Val. Griff lifted the dark depression that usually surrounded her. She said in a teasing tone, "Yes, one fence post in the ground at a time."

Griff grinned back at her. "And tomorrow, we're going to get cattle for your ranch. That's another important step forward." He saw a new softness to Val's face. His heart soared with joy because they'd shared a serious and personal discussion with each other. Griff felt she had opened the hidden doors to herself and finally invited him in.

"It is," Val said, pushing away from the table. "Let's save dessert for tomorrow's lunch, clean up and turn in early. We have a very busy, long day ahead of us."

Val was asleep when suddenly she felt the entire house shake and shudder. Jerking upright in bed, momentarily disoriented, she felt the shaking stop but heard an airplane fly directly over the ranch house. What the hell? Twisting around, she looked at the clock on her nightstand. It read 3:00 a.m. Pushing strands of hair out of her face, Val quickly got to her feet.

She moved to the window and pulled the drapes aside. The window faced north, toward Long Lake. Val searched the sky but could not see anything. It was a moonless night and only the stars twinkled like pinholes poked in the fabric of the midnight sky. Off in the distance, she could hear the faint sound of a plane's engine. It seemed to be circling low somewhere nearby but she couldn't see it. There were no lights flashing on the plane's tail and wingtips to help her locate it. That was odd too.

Val knew FAA flight regulations forbade any aircraft to fly beneath one thousand feet unless it was landing. And there was no place to land around here! She wondered if it was a new pilot who was trying to find the airport, which was located near Grand Teton National Park, north of Jackson Hole. If that was the case, he was a good twenty-five miles off base. Convincing herself it was a lost pilot, she pulled the drapes closed once again and walked over to her queen-size bed. The flying-geese quilt that Gus had made for her lay across her bed. She grazed the material with her fingertips, taking comfort in its link to her beloved grandmother as she did when she was a child. Wrapping the quilt around her as she lay down was like having her grandmother always holding her, shielding her at night as she slept.

She pulled the quilt up and over her shoulders, and closed her eyes. As she began to drift off, Val heard Griff's husky words echo through her head: we're both strays that left the family nest for one reason or another. And now, like the prodigal son and daughter, we've come home.

She felt powerfully drawn to him. Every day he was proving himself. And every day, he was much more appealing to Val. She'd had one serious relationship. She knew what love felt like. And the feelings growing within her for Griff were similarly vibrant and filled with promise. For a woman who had never expected to feel happy again, his company seemed to make it a real possibility.

CHAPTER SIXTEEN

Val didn't know who was most excited when the livestock truck drove into their driveway. Griff was standing with her and Gus on the porch as the truck chugged slowly into the wide drive in front the ranch house.

"You look tired, Val," Griff said.

"Did that plane wake you up last night?" Val wondered, looking up at him. Today, Griff wore a pale green plaid cowboy shirt, the usual red bandanna around his strong neck and a pair of well-worn Levi's. He'd just shaved and his hair was still damp from a shower beneath his hat. There was nothing tame about the masculine energy that surrounded him like the sun's rays. He was all male. In a powerful but nonthreatening kind of way.

"I thought I heard something, but I was so tired I just rolled over and went back to sleep." There were faint shadows beneath Val's blue eyes but her exhaustion didn't take anything away from her looks. Griff liked the feminine pink blouse with long sleeves she wore. The color accented her glorious hair now caught up in the usual ponytail. It was impossible to ignore how the Levi's fit her shapely body and long legs. She was a beautiful woman. And he wanted her. All of her. Griff couldn't get her kiss, her full lips pressing lightly against his cheek, out of his mind. He didn't want to.

"I heard it, too," Gus grumbled, unhappy. "Danged thing roared over us like a commercial jet liner ready to land on our roof!"

"At first, when I woke up," Val told her, "I thought a plane was going to crash into the house. It scared the daylights out of me."

"Some fool of a pilot probably on his first night-flight was lost and huntin' for the Jackson Hole airport. We aren't no darned runway!"

Smiling a little, Val tucked her arm around Gus's small, proud shoulders. "I'm sure he found the airport."

"Musta," Gus said with a grin. "There's no crash I heard last night and no reports of one on the radio this morning."

"That's true." Val squeezed her grandmother's shoulders. The truck was now directly in front of them.

Gus moved slowly down the stairs with

the aid of her hated cane and called, "Why don't you two mount up and we'll get ready to release these girls?"

Griff nodded. "Will do," he called, starting down the steps with Val at his side.

Val saw Dr. Bennett, a large-animal vet, pull into the driveway in his silver Chevy truck. Val waved hello to him as she took the steps and hurried to catch up with Griff. They already had their horses saddled and ready to go. The gate to the huge, round corral was open and ready for its new additions.

She heard the bawling of the brown-and-white Herefords in the long truck. Their hooves on the thin steel floors made a lot of noise. They wanted out of there too and Val didn't blame them.

Griff untied Socks from the hitching post near the barn and handed Val the leather reins. Their gloved fingers met briefly and he secretly savored the contact. She pulled her hat down a little more tightly on her head and mounted. In no time, Griff was on Freckles and they were moving at a fast walk down the gentle slope toward the truck parked in the driveway.

The morning air was crisp and clean. Griff inhaled it deeply into his lungs. The horses were fresh and eager to work. With Val

299

riding at his side, he decided life didn't get any better than this. The sun had risen, sending out long golden rays across the grassy pastures and darkly treed mountains surrounding the ranch. These cattle, he decided, would think they'd died and gone to heaven.

At the truck, they waited on their horses while Gus signed for the shipment after the heifers were all accounted for. The vet, Dan Bennett, was standing with Gus, his equipment bag in hand. Excitement rose in the air as the wrangler who'd delivered the cattle gestured for Val and Griff to ride over to the ramp where the heifers would be released. It would be their job to move the animals into the corral.

Val took the left side of the truck and Griff was to the right of the eighteen-wheeler. When the wrangler released the huge metal gate, the first animals bolted out and clattered down the ramp. As Griff urged Freckles forward to catch the leader, the horse instantly went into action. Luckily, these were cutting horses and they knew that if the leader of the drove was bracketed between the two of them, the other cattle, by nature, would follow it. They had herd mentality and rarely left their friends. Val rode with relaxed ease as she kept the first four heifers in line to move into the corral up ahead. The cattle tossed their heads, spittle drooling from their open mouths as they anxiously charged ahead. Griff thought he could see relief in their big, brown eyes as they eagerly headed for the familiarity of the corral. Once inside, they trotted over to a long, rectangular watering trough.

Griff turned his horse around, wanting to make sure the rest of the girls were following the leaders. And indeed, they were a docile brown-and-white line, heads bobbing, following their leaders who were already in the corral. The smell of water was really the magnet as they trotted into the corral. Every one of them dunked their muzzles into the fresh, cool water. They'd been without water for the long trip from Cheyenne to their ranch.

Dismounting, Griff dropped the reins and Freckles stood still. He quickly closed the huge steel gate.

"Thirsty girls, but they all look real healthy," the vet said as he approached.

Gus stood at the fence, critically assessing the new herd. "They do look fine, Doc, but as soon as they're done drinking, I want you to examine each of them." She looked over at Griff and Val. "Get the chute ready. You'll have to cut one of 'em from their herd and drive her over to it."

Griff looked up at Val, who was still mounted. "You want to do the cutting?"

"Sure. You get to drop the door behind the heifer after I drive her up into the chute." She grinned. "I'd rather cut."

"You got it," Griff said, sharing her smile. The sense of teamwork made his heart swell in his chest. Everyone was involved. Everyone cared for those heifers who would become the foundation for the new era of the Bar H. Life was returning to this place that was once nightmarish and full of deep suffering.

Gus had opened the gate just enough to allow Val to ride in on Socks. The heifers now stood in a tight group near the water trough, warily watching the horse and rider approach. They grew even tighter as Val loosened the reins on Socks. Gus always enjoyed a good cutting horse in action, and this was one of the best in the county. The gelding lowered his head, snaked it out and cleanly separated one of the heifers away from the group. Instantly, the animal tried to return but Socks anticipated it and blocked her. Frantic, the heifer wheeled and tried to gallop around the cutter. The sorrel quarter horse sat down heavily on his rear haunches, lifted his front legs and swiftly turned.

The heifer was thwarted. She bawled, panicked now. Socks leaped forward, driving her rapidly toward the open chute entrance. All Val had to do was sit quietly in the saddle, keep the reins loose and let the horse do what he was good at. In moments, the heifer was driven up into the wooden structure.

Griff swiftly dropped the thick wooden door behind the heifer. She stood there panting and bawling, fearful to be separated from her herd. The vet stood next to Griff. He quickly got to work, sizing up the animal, looking for any injuries, cuts, bumps or anything else that might tell him she wasn't healthy. He pressed his stethoscope to the heifer's chest, listening not only to her heart, but her lungs and stomach, too, to make sure she wasn't impacted and had good digestion.

For the next three hours, the same chain of events occurred. After each of examination, Griff released the animal out the other end of the chute into a smaller corral that had hay and water in it, so she could take comfort in eating, which they loved to do. By lunchtime, they were finished.

Gus consulted with Dr. Bennett. He gave

the entire herd a clean bill of health. Gus walked over to the wrangler waiting at the truck and handed him a check. The wrangler tipped his hat to Gus and thanked her before making the eight-hour drive back to his ranch in Cheyenne. Gus then wrote a second check to the vet and he went on his way, as well.

"I'm starving!" Val called as she dismounted and tied Socks to the hitching post in front of the house. She'd already given the horse a hefty drink at the water trough. Patting the quarter horse's thick, sweaty neck, Val loosened the girth on the saddle. After lunch, they'd need to drive the heifers out to their lush green pasture. For now the horse could at least relax a little under the shade of a maple tree.

Gus moved to the porch and took off her cowboy hat. "Come on in. Chow time!" She opened the screen door and disappeared inside.

Griff trotted up on Freckles and dismounted. After tying his Appaloosa to the post, he loosened the girth on the animal and joined Val. Taking off his hat, he wiped his brow. "It got hot all of a sudden."

Val looked at the temperature gauge on the porch post. "It's eighty-five degrees. Hot for us." She laughed a little, feeling the comradeship of working with Griff like a well-oiled team.

He opened the door for Val. "I'm used to hot temperatures from New York, but when you're working like we were, it's something else." He caught a whiff of sweetness that reminded him of honeysuckle in bloom. It was the shampoo Val had used to wash her hair this morning. He wanted to lean down, press a kiss to the shining mass of red hair, but resisted. As the screen door closed, Griff simply enjoyed the womanly sway of her hips as she walked to the kitchen in front of him.

Gus had already placed a huge bowl of salad on the table. Val went over to help make the tuna sandwiches. Griff retrieved the dishes, bowls and flatware for the table. The kitchen hummed with a happy silence as they all worked together.

"I gotta say," Gus said proudly, "those are fine-lookin' heifers! Don't you think so, Val?"

"I think they're all queens, Gus. Beautiful, fat, well fed. Their coats shine."

"Yes, and Doc Bennett said they're all in estrus, which means we gotta find a bull to cover them. I don't want a bull on this property. They're too much trouble." She glanced over her shoulder toward Griff.

"What about Slade's bull, Diablo, Griff? He's an ornery son of a gun, but he drops babies with mega beef on them. Do you think Slade would be open to contracting his bull to cover our girls?"

Surprised, Griff straightened. "Why . . . I don't know. I could call him after lunch?"

"You do that. There's no question Diablo's the best bull in the area."

Griff agreed. And the breeding fees would help Slade economically. Griff would be happy to help out his brother and the Bar H in one fell swoop.

Griff stood on the front porch after lunch with his cell phone. "Slade, I need to know if Diablo is available to breed twenty heifers in the next week."

"Whose stock?" his brother asked.

"The Bar H's. The vet has given them a clean bill of health and they're all in estrus. They're ready to be bred. Gus wants Diablo, since he's the best around."

"Twenty heifers," Slade said, impressed. "Does she know Diablo's breeding fee? It's a hundred-and-fifty dollars per heifer."

Griff whistled softly. "That's a lot of money."

"For them, it might be," Slade said. "What I can do is create a payment plan. Gus can pay one-third up front and the rest can be paid over a twelve-month time frame."

"That's generous of you," Griff said, meaning it. "Let me see what they think."

After hanging up with Slade, Griff went back into the kitchen to tell the women about the conversation. Gus sat at the table enjoying her coffee and Val stood at the sink washing dishes. Her hands were dripping with water and soap. Eyes huge, she said, "That's three thousand dollars, Gus. That's a *lot* of money."

Griff heard the worry and concern in Val's voice. He thought the same but said nothing.

"You call Slade back and tell him that we'll be trucking those heifers up to him starting tomorrow morning," Gus ordered. "Thank him for being kind and letting us do payments, but I got the money. I'll cut him a check for the full amount."

He saw the sparkle in Miss Gus's blue eyes. "You're a woman of action."

With a chuckle, Gus said, "I'd rather pay the fee than deal with a damned bull that's ten times the headache of any heifer."

"I don't disagree with you," Griff said, keeping Diablo's nasty temper in mind. He remembered how much of a problem Diablo was. Even Slade, who had raised him, had been gored in the leg by the beast. A bull was contrary and never to be trusted. Yet, when he was with his herd of "girls" he was sweet to them. He seemed to only hate humans.

Val finished washing the dishes. "Then that means we have to get our stock trailer repaired pronto, Griff. It's got four flat tires that need to be replaced and the rear gate needs some repair." Stock trailers were part and parcel of a ranch operation. Val knew the one near the barn hadn't been used in at least five years, maybe longer. It needed a new coat of paint, greasing of the ball bearings and other essential inspections to make sure it could hold the weight of the heifers. "We can get seven heifers in it at a time, but we really have to make sure it's roadworthy first."

"I know." Gus looked over at Griff. "You ever repaired a trailer?"

"No," Griff replied, "but I think I can do it. I'm good with autos and trucks."

Grunting, Gus thought for a moment. "Well, we're in a hurry. I want you to grease that stock trailer up and check it out from stem to stern for any problems. It has to carry a lot of weight. You're gonna need a whole set of new tires for it. I'll give you the money to run into town and buy 'em."

Griff recalled the stock trailer sitting at the side of the barn. It was in rough shape. The white paint had been peeled off by the harsh winters, revealing the gray aluminum beneath it. All the tires were aged, cracked and flat. "Okay, first Val and I should get the heifers to that small pasture near the barn. Then, I'll check out the stock trailer. I'll make a list of things we need for it and go into town later today and buy the stuff."

"Do you think you can be ready to roll by tomorrow afternoon?"

"Unless I run into something major, like a broken axle, I can have it ready."

Griff walked out of the house to make the second call to Slade, letting him know they'd be by tomorrow. By the time he was done, Val sauntered out to the porch and settled the Stetson on her head.

"You're going to be really busy."

Shrugging, Griff tucked his cell phone into his shirt pocket and smiled over at Val. "Hey, I like ranching. This is what it's all about."

Val nodded and they walked down to the shade of the maple tree where Freckles and Socks were tied. She tightened the girth on Socks's saddle and pulled the reins over the animal's head. "We need to see what shape that stock trailer is in. It's a mess. . . ."

Griff patted Freckles, tightened the girth and mounted his horse. "Yeah, it's not very inspiring, is it?"

"The trailer should have been brought inside every winter, but it wasn't." Val turned her horse toward the barn.

"We'll find out shortly. I've been focused on fence posts and stringing barbed wire up until now."

Val met his teasing smile. She could see happiness glimmering in Griff's eyes. She was happy too. There was something magical going on between them. They were a team. And they were good at what they did. Her heart burst open with a sensation of joy.

Griff trotted ahead of her. He was slouched easily in the saddle, at one with his horse and the elements around him. His shoulders were broad, proud, and his rugged face burned dark by the sun. In that split second, Val wanted to love Griff. What would it be like to kiss this man? She finally desired a man after the loss of her fiancé. Confused and a little afraid, Val tucked all those yearnings and fears away. Right now, they had to focus on moving the heifers to a nearby pasture. And then, they had work ahead of them with the disheveled stock trailer.

■ ■ ■ ■

Griff was on his back beneath the stock trailer. The late-afternoon heat made him sweat even more as he used the flashlight Val had provided to check things out. "This axle isn't looking good," he said in a low tone. Sweat ran down in his eyes. He blinked several times as he dug the heels of his boots into the dirt to push himself a few more inches forward to inspect the entire rusted axle.

Val was down on her hands and knees, leaning over to watch his progress beneath the trailer. "I asked Gus how long it had been since this trailer was used and she said ten years." She saw Griff inching along, carefully inspecting the entire length of the axle from one side to the other. A crack would render it useless. And if Griff found a problem, it would mean having to buy another trailer this afternoon. Which would cost a lot of money.

Grunting, Griff said, "I believe it." This was a sixteen-foot aluminum trailer with a double rear axle. It took four tires and all of them had to be thrown away. Griff had already replaced the tires. Perspiration ran down his temples. His back felt every hard stone and clod of dirt digging through the fabric of his shirt and into his flesh. He wondered if there were black widow spiders among all the cobwebs he had to keep sweeping away from his face, but pushed that fear aside. Making it to the other side, he wriggled out and slowly sat up.

Val got off her knees and walked around to meet him as he brushed some of the dust off his shoulders. "Here, let me help," she said, moving around to his back. His shirt was filthy with dirt, bits of grass and dry weeds clinging to the material. As she wiped at his back, she reveled in the secret pleasure of getting to touch him. She could feel his muscles respond to her light contact. A thrill coursed through Val and she inhaled Griff's masculine scent as if it were perfume.

"There," she said, stepping away and brushing her hands on one another. "You're ready to inspect the second axle."

Griff wanted to tell Val that her touch was like heaven. Her help had been an unexpected pleasure. Her touch even more so. "It's rusty but I don't see any fractures or cracks in the first one. It could use a good wire brushing and some protective rust coating."

"Sometime in the future," Val said. "Not today."

Griff reached for the iced tea that sat on the aluminum fender of the trailer. "No," he agreed, "not today."

Val watched the sweat trickle down his gleaming neck as he drank the contents of the glass. Griff didn't mind getting dirty. That was part of being a wrangler. She watched as he set the glass down on the fender and dropped back down to his hands and knees. He turned on his back, pushing in under the trailer to begin inspecting the second axle. For a moment, Val was able to absorb the sight of his narrow hips and long, powerful legs. He had a body meant to ride a horse. Although his legs weren't bowed, as many wranglers got to be after a while, he had what it took to become a good rancher.

Her mouth went dry and she picked an ice cube out of the empty glass, popping it into her mouth to suck on it. Griff slowly disappeared beneath the trailer. Val knew it was important to remain here with him. If, for some unknown reason, the twenty-five-hundred-pound trailer unexpectedly shifted or fell off the jack, it could kill him. There was an unspoken agreement when someone worked around a trailer, a second person

313

was always there just in case.

Getting down on her knees again, Val saw how hard he concentrated as he worked under the trailer. "I wonder, do you pay this kind of attention to all the details in the rest of your life?"

Griff laughed abruptly but held his focus on the rusted axle. "Wall Street was nothing but details. I've always liked all kinds of details. If you don't pay attention to them, they'll bite you in the butt."

Laughing softly, Val saw the faint outline of his rugged face. He was smiling. "Well stated."

"In your business in the Air Force, you had to do plenty of detail work too. It can't be easy to pick things out in photos from satellite distance."

"I'm like you. I enjoy details."

"And we both like horses. Yet another thing we have in common." There was something euphoric about talking intimately with Val.

"Did you ride horses in New York City?"

"No, I just played banker and stock broker."

"No walks in Central Park?" It was a huge rectangular area in the city that had grass, water and trees, unlike the canyons of concrete, steel and glass that surrounded it.

"I walked in Central Park every chance I got. You've been there?" Griff rested for a moment. The heat was intense and there was little breeze beneath the trailer. He felt like his body had turned into a wringing wet sponge.

"Once. Too much noise and bustling activity. It overwhelmed my senses."

"A lot of country and rural people have the same reaction."

"How could you handle it?"

"I grew up with it." Pushing the heel of his boots into the soil, the top of his head emerged from beneath the trailer. His eyes narrowed as he slowly inspected the metal. "I guess I didn't know any different. But Wyoming has her own magic she sprinkles over an unsuspecting person."

Smiling a little, Val said wistfully, "I always missed Wyoming no matter where I went in the world. I can't say I liked the desert of Bahrain. I missed the lush green grass, trees and the weather."

"Not a fan of a *haboob?*" Griff teased. It was Arabic for dust storm. He rolled onto his hands and knees. Looking over, he gave her a grin and then stood up, brushing himself off once more.

Val stood. "I hated them. I had to dust everything for days afterward to get rid of the sand."

"That's probably when you missed Wyoming the most." Griff laid the flashlight down on the fender, took off his hat and used the back of his sleeve to wipe the sweat from his brow.

"You're right, I did." The look in his eyes stirred her. Val felt her breasts responding to his narrowed look. There was more in his gaze than she first realized. If she read it right, it was the look of a man appreciating his woman. The realization was like a lightning bolt through Val. She'd gone so long without a man that she'd nearly forgotten what it was like to be desired. And clearly, if she was reading Griff's look correctly, he wanted *her*. Excitement, need and fear coursed through Val.

She calmed herself enough to ask, "What do you think about the axles? Are they fit for the road or not?"

"Yes." Griff scowled and critically studied the beat-up trailer. "But I have a lot of work to do before the sun goes down."

Nodding, Val said, "I'll go get us some more iced tea."

"You must have been reading my mind." Griff laid down the flashlight, took off the bandanna from around his neck and wiped his face dry.

Val hurried down the gentle slope toward the ranch house, glasses in hand.

Griff stood in the shade of the barn and appreciated the way Val moved before walking over to the tack room where all the tools, nuts and bolts were kept. There was a cooling breeze down the center aisle and it felt good against his hot, damp skin.

Just as he had brought out a toolbox and was walking toward the trailer, he saw another pickup enter the yard. Halting, Griff realized with a scowl that it was a very unwelcome visitor. Curt Downing. What the hell did he want?

CHAPTER SEVENTEEN

Griff instantly went on internal guard. Curt Downing was dressed in a white shirt and Levi's, a black Stetson on his reddish-blond hair. There was another man whom he didn't recognize climbing awkwardly out of the truck, dressed in a dark pin-striped business suit. He looked like a banker. Griff could spot one a mile away. He watched Downing and the banker climb the stairs to the porch, where Miss Gus was sitting in her favorite rocker. Val came with two glasses of iced tea in her hands and abruptly halted. The relaxed look on her face turned to instant distrust as she spotted the two men.

Griff didn't want the women alone with these two jackals. He hurried down the slope. He rounded the ranch house to see Downing was taking off his hat and addressing a scowling Gus.

Gus squinted and glared up at the tall

cowboy. "I don't recall any phone call or appointment with you, Mr. Downing."

Crusty old bitch, Downing thought as he settled his hat back on his head. "I apologize, Miss Gus. But my banker from Cheyenne, Frank Latimer, and I just happened to be driving by." Curt smiled a little, gloat in his voice. "We're working on a land-swap deal with the forest service to buy their side of Long Lake."

Brows flying upward, Gus looked at Val, who was now standing beside her. Val was frowning, a look of anger in her eyes. As she swung her gaze back to Downing, she saw a feral look in his expression. He was smiling, but his eyes were colder than a winter blizzard. Sensing something important was afoot, Gus waved her hand toward two wooden chairs next to hers. "Have a seat, gentlemen."

Val opened her mouth to protest, but she saw Gus signal her with a slight shake of her head to remain silent.

"Val, give these two men the glasses of iced tea you're holdin'. They look parched." Gus made an effort to smile. She didn't like playing games but when she had to be a coyote, she could do it.

Val did as she was told and Downing took his glass without saying anything.

The banker thanked her. Latimer was overweight and sweaty. He pulled out a white handkerchief and blotted his small forehead. Val trained her gaze on Griff, who came up the steps with authority. She could see the set of his jaw and the flash of distrust in his eyes. She felt the same way.

Griff looked toward Miss Gus. "Can I be of help?"

"Sure, but why don't you shed those dirty clothes, catch a quick shower and come back and join us?"

"I will." Griff gave Downing a look of warning. The son of a bitch was up to no good. He could feel it. Swinging past the screen door, Griff disappeared.

"Miss Gus," Downing purred, "I have business to discuss with you and Miss Hunter. I don't think you need a hired hand to overhear our conversation, do you?"

Ah, Downing was spooked by McPherson. That told Gus a lot. "Well now, my wrangler is more than what he first appears to be, Mr. Downing. He's got an MBA from Harvard." Gus sat forward, a slight smile cracking her mouth. "Do you?"

"Er . . . no," Downing said in a huff, trying to appear unmoved by that information.

"And you, Mr. Banker?" Gus inquired sweetly, swinging her narrowed gaze to the sweaty banker.

"Why, no I don't, Miss Gus."

"I see," she murmured, rocking back and forth, smiling and looking out over the land.

Fuming inwardly, Downing said nothing. He drank the sweetened iced tea and made small talk for fifteen minutes before McPherson reappeared. The wrangler came out and took the chair next to Gus. Val sat on the other side of her grandmother. Clearly, the two visitors distrusted him, their faces openly showing hostility over his presence. Too bad.

Val appreciated Griff's strong, straight posture, his broad shoulders thrown back. He'd cleaned up, his dark hair gleaming with dampness, his darkening stubble making him look like the warrior he was. She was discovering that even though Griff was soft-spoken and thoughtful, there was a very protective knight within him. Right now, his bristling guard dog energy surrounded her and Gus. When he sat down, he pulled out his chair to directly face the two men. Resting his elbows on his knees, Griff's mouth remained thinned. He didn't like these men, either. None of them did.

"Okay, Mr. Downing," Gus said, "why don't you tell us why you've dropped by without warning?"

"Well," Curt said, setting his emptied glass on a small nearby table, "I just couldn't contain my good news and wanted to share it with you, Miss Gus."

"What? That you're tryin' a land-swap deal with the supervisor, Charley, and the forest service? What's happy about *that?*"

Val hid her smile. She saw one corner of Griff's mouth crook upward as if to silently challenge Downing, who looked unhappy over Gus's response. Val tucked her hands in her lap and sat back to enjoy the fencing between the two valley titans. Her grandmother might be small and in her mid-eighties, but she was a stalwart giant everyone respected. Except for Downing, of course, who thought he ran everything. His millions in the trucking business had turned him into a power-hungry, selfish human being.

Struggling to maintain his lightness, Curt laughed and shrugged. "Well, when it goes through, I'll be your neighbor Miss Gus. I wanted to celebrate the good news with you."

"Wait a minute," Griff interjected, straightening, hands tense on his thighs, "a land-swap deal like that can take years and even then, it's not guaranteed. There has to be public input and if there are objections, the trade can disappear off the table."

"I know that!" Downing snarled and glared over at the wrangler. "And here I was hoping you weren't anything like your brother."

"Maybe Griff's a little nicer on the outside," Gus said, "has a bit more polish than Slade, but he's still a McPherson."

Wiping his mouth, Downing glared over at the banker. "Dammit, Frank, tell them the rest!"

Latimer shot to his feet as if Downing had fired a gun at him. He nervously knotted his handkerchief. Stammering, he said, "What Mr. Downing is saying is that once the deal goes through — and we feel quite sure it will — he'll own half of Long Lake. We foresee this as a huge real estate development opportunity." He gestured toward the unseen lake to the north of the ranch. "We felt that it might be a good idea to approach you, Miss Gus, about selling the other half of the lake to us." He added a limp smile with his suggestion. And then, he abruptly sat back down, tense and expectant.

Gus sat back, drumming her fingers on the rocker arm. She cut a glance to Griff. "Well, what do you think about this?"

Nostrils flaring, Griff said in a low growl,

"This is all way too premature. There's no way they can be guaranteed the forest service will work with them on this deal. I can't speak for you, Miss Gus, but I don't think you want a high-end real estate development next door."

"Now wait a minute!" Downing said in a condescending tone, and he shifted his gaze to Miss Gus. "Frank didn't tell you the rest of it." He glared at the banker, fought for composure and lowered his voice. "Miss Gus, I'm willing to pay you two million dollars for your lakefront property." He sat up, expecting her to be impressed and awed by his generosity.

One silver eyebrow hitched upward as Gus looked at Val. "Two million dollars," she drawled to her granddaughter.

Val smiled a little. "I heard."

Gus looked at Griff. "Two million?"

Downing was frustrated. The old woman was being cagey. What the hell was going on here? "Two million dollars is a *lot* of money!" he exhorted, waving his hand to emphasize the point.

"I know the worth of my property," Gus said in a clear, steady voice as she drilled Downing with a stare. "That lake is worth a whole lot more than that."

"But," Frank said hastily, "it's very hard

to get to."

"So what, Mr. Latimer?" Griff said. "That doesn't lessen its value. You can bankroll roads being built into it."

Damn! Curt wanted to curse out loud, but he knew Miss Gus hated such talk. It would only lower her opinion of him and he was desperate to keep some footing. "The lake is worth a lot," he admitted, his voice unsteady. He forced a plastic smile toward Miss Gus. "I'll up the ante to two million, five hundred thousand dollars."

Griff's scowl increased. Curt could see the disgust in Val's eyes even though she was letting Miss Gus do all the talking and maneuvering.

"And so," Gus said, tapping her chin, "you want our side of the lake to go with your side of the lake?"

"Yes."

"And then you want to put a real estate development on it? My guess is two- or three-story condominiums all crowded shoulder to shoulder around ninety percent of it."

Frank blotted his brow. "Well, perhaps not that many, Miss Gus. We have to be aware of county bylaws and the fact that we'd have to construct our own sewage system."

"That means," Griff said, "that you're

looking at a very large development."

"We're looking at nine hundred units," Downing admitted in frustration.

"I bet," Gus said. "Stacked like egg cartons on top of one another."

It was hard for Downing to sit still, but he forced himself to continue to smile. "Well, yes, they will be three stories high."

"And we'd see them from our ranch house," Val added in an angry tone. She wasn't very good at keeping her rage at bay. Downing was slippery and frightening. He reminded her of Buck in so many ways it made her stomach roll into a painful knot.

"We'd plant trees, tall trees," Curt said. "You wouldn't see them."

"It would take a tree twenty to thirty years to reach that kind of maturity and height," Val shot back. "In the meantime, we'd see them."

"And hear them. And what about all the gas fumes from all those cars coming and going?" Gus said in a demanding voice. "Our once pristine, quiet and clean lake would be gone to hell in a handbag."

"Now, wait, wait," Curt begged, holding up his hands. "We would work with you on this. We'd do whatever you wanted to ensure your privacy."

"You can't hide from the sounds of cars

or their pollution," Griff pointed out.

Curt wanted to smash McPherson in the jaw. Miss Gus was right: he was just like Slade, damn him! "No," he choked, "I suppose that's true."

"Nine hundred units means nine hundred cars coming and going," Griff pointed out.

"That's a lot of pollution," Val said, looking fondly around the quiet, natural property.

"Not to mention people wandering around on your property, Miss Gus."

"McPherson," Curt ground out, "we'll take care of that. We'll build proper fences with No Trespassing signs. No one will come wandering onto their property."

Val moved in her chair and twisted her lip. "Oh, really? Just like you didn't wander onto our property when you rode your endurance horse along our road for the last five years without permission? I think we have a fair idea of how you'll treat this situation." Val gave Downing a steady stare. There was truth in her words and she felt them flow strongly through her. Downing looked like he wanted to strike her. That frightened her for a moment. It was the same crazy look Buck used to have in his eyes when he was going to beat her. Reflexively, her adrenaline shot up and she suddenly felt shaky inside. But she stood her ground.

Griff saw fear come to Val's eyes. Slade had said Downing was abusive to people and animals, and he quickly figured out why she looked so scared. He rose to his feet. Even though he wanted to go over and stand in front of her to shield her from Downing, he anchored himself. He watched Val fight her fear and saw it replaced with a calm. His admiration for her poise in such tense circumstances rose even more.

"I admit," Curt rasped, "I did ride my stud on your property and I was wrong. I should have come to Miss Gus and asked for permission. I told you it would never happen again and it hasn't."

"That was after you got caught," Gus reminded him stiffly. "And I wonder what you will do under the radar until you're caught by one of us after you build that snazzy condo development?"

"Everything would be listed in a contract. A contract can list whatever demands the seller wants."

"Sure it can," Griff said with a drawl. He liked to see Downing sweat. There were beads forming across his hairline. "Miss Gus would have to hire a boatload of lawyers and pay them an arm and a leg to ensure that long list was followed."

"Just what makes you think Charley is gonna support your land swap?" Gus demanded.

"I own some property near Deaver, Wyoming, near the oil fields. I have a hundred thousand acres of confirmed oil and natural gas in the ground. It's worth a fortune. The forest service could make a load of money off it," Downing bragged with confidence.

"I don't think," Griff told Miss Gus, "the forest service would want to get into mining activities. It takes millions of dollars to extrude the oil from the shale and it's just not productive for them to do so."

Nodding, Gus said, "I'm a Wyoming gal. Oil and natural gas are a big part of our state. And I know enough to agree with Griff here."

"It's not a done deal," Frank agreed amiably, trying to smile. "But it's an interesting deal where if there is a forest-service swap they'll put three-point-five million into it. The geologists have run tests on Mr. Downing's current property and speculate that the oil and natural gas extruded from the rocks would be worth well over thirty million dollars."

"Whew," Gus muttered. "Thirty million?" She swung her gaze to Curt. "Now, I might be a country gal, but I gotta tell you, Mr. Downing, that this doesn't make sense. Long Lake is *not* worth thirty million. Oh, it's expensive property, I'll give you that. But not that much." So why did he want the lake property so badly? That was the part Gus couldn't figure out.

Shaking his head, Griff said, "I'm not sure about this, but I can look into it and see if the forest service has swapped mining claims for land before."

"They haven't," Curt said, "but they will."

"I can't believe Charley would go for it." Gus snorted. "He hates land swaps."

"True, true," Frank said hastily. "But with the double-dip recession and all, even the forest service must look elsewhere for new money sources."

Val sighed. "Gus, you really aren't considering selling our half of the lake to him, are you?"

"Maybe, maybe," Gus said in a murmur, rocking and thinking. She studied Downing. Sweat was trickling down the sides of his face. Good, let him sweat. "But I'm stuck on one thing, Mr. Downing."

"What's that?" Curt asked, hopeful that the old woman would sell.

"It makes no good sense to me," Gus said slowly, "that you'd let a thirty-million-dollar property in the hand go for a much less expensive piece of land just because it has a lake on it." She drilled him with an intense look, her head tilted like a bird.

Licking his lower lip, Curt said, "I happen to like water, Miss Gus. There isn't much outside the national parks. You know that. I feel I can recoup what I lose in the swap over time. Frank has worked on the numbers and he agrees with me."

Doing quick calculations in his head, Griff said, "I highly doubt your figures. Given the millions in construction, plus the loss of the income in the shale, you won't begin getting even for forty years." He turned to Gus and added, "Now, these are rough calculations, but there's no way he can ever make ends meet on this one."

Rubbing her chin, Gus looked over at Val. "Well, what do you think?"

"I think he has other reasons for wanting the lake." Val turned and glared at Downing. "But he's not telling us what they are."

Bridling with fury, Curt said more loudly than he intended, "McPherson, you're wrong! You don't have a clue as to the money involved in construction!"

"I'm afraid I do, Downing. I worked for a financial services firm that underwrote many construction projects that went into the billions, all around the world. I have a lot of experience in construction matters." He saw Downing move into real fury, his face reddening. There was a great deal, Griff realized, that Downing didn't know about his background. Including the fact that Griff was watching, looking for any suspicious activity to report back to the FBI. And this was about as suspicious as it got. This whole drama was something he'd call and report to Special Agent Josh Gordon. Downing was up to something. But what?

Downing turned to Gus, desperate. "I'll give you *three* million for your lakefront property, Miss Gus. Now, you must agree, that's a tidy sum and I'm sure you can use it." He swept his hand around the Bar H. "Everyone knows this ranch is on its last legs. Buck drove it into the ground with his drinking. Surely, you need this kind of money if you're going to resurrect it?"

Gus gave him a feral smile. "I don't like gossip, Downing. And I especially don't like people like you thinkin' they know everything about my family finances. Buck was an alcoholic, no question. And he did drive the Bar H under." She gave Val a warm smile, the love shining in her eyes. "I don't know who your land and property experts are, but they failed to note one thing." She held up her index finger toward Curt. "I'm the matriarch of this ranch and my family. I might have spent most of my life over in Cheyenne, but I can assure you, this is where my roots are at." She jabbed her finger down toward the porch in a swift motion. "And as usual, you come bustin' in here thinkin' you're the man with all the money and power in the valley. Well, I got news for you. We ain't as hard up as you may think. I sold my husband's ranch after he died."

Curt's face fell.

"And I sold it for an awful lot of money. But you don't need to know that number," Gus whispered, anger rising in her tone. "What you do need to know is we don't need your money. I would *never* sell our half of the lake or its surrounding property to anyone. Especially to the likes of you."

Frank blustered and started to stand up for Downing until Gus wagged her finger warningly at him. He quickly sat down.

"You're a snake in the grass, Downing." Gus hardened her jaw. "You might have got your gossip wrong about the Bar H, but I can guarantee you I have resources and connections in this valley you'll never have. You've hurt a lot of people around here over the years, Downing. And we aren't going to be another injured party in your quest for power."

Griff watched Downing's face turn cherry-red to the roots of his hair. His eyes were bulging with rage, his mouth clamped shut and thinned. He realized he was watching a very smart, politically savvy old gal in action. In that moment, Griff loved the feisty elder. He looked up to see Val's face smiling, pride shining in her eyes for her warrior grandmother. There was no need for him to step in and say anything. Gus was handling Downing like a fractious, unruly colt. She'd snubbed him down to a post and he couldn't move.

"But . . . but," Curt sputtered, getting to his feet, "you aren't the *owner* of this property!" Desperate, he turned to Val. "You're the owner, Miss Hunter. Surely, you don't agree with your grandmother?"

"Oh, give it a rest, Downing!" Gus yelled, leaping to her feet. Now she was mad. "You young whippersnapper! Did you even go to the county records to see who the owner of the Bar H is? Obviously not! Well, go take a gander! In the meantime, get off *my* property!" She whipped her hand toward their truck in the driveway. Breathing hard, she added, "I don't ever want you to step foot on Bar H property again. If you do I'll call the sheriff and make sure he puts you in jail for trespassing. You got it?"

Shocked, Downing stood there staring at the short gray-haired woman. Her mouth was set, eyes blazing with anger, and her hands curled into fists jammed on her hips. He glanced over at Frank, who quickly leaped to his feet.

"Didn't you check owner of record at the county courthouse?" he snarled at the banker.

"Why . . . er . . . my assistant said she did."

Cursing under his breath, Curt strode off the porch, red-faced and fuming. He desperately needed that land. If he was going to show the Garcia drug cartel he could give them a foothold in the area, he *had* to have that entire lake! His mind churned. Well, if the old woman wouldn't sell him her half of the lake, then maybe terrorizing them until they couldn't take living on the Bar H anymore was another way to get them to sell the property. Curt promised to make life so miserable for the two women they'd come begging him to buy it off them.

Frank had barely made it into the passenger seat before Downing stomped down the accelerator, the tires screaming and spinning on the vehicle. Dust rose in huge, thick clouds as he spun the truck around. Once they were on the highway, the tires were still smoking. That was how angry Downing was.

Griff reached out and patted Miss Gus on the shoulder. "You're a sight to behold when you get your dander up."

Gus cracked a smile. "They don't call me matriarch for nothin'. You *earn* that title, young man." She scowled at the highway where Downing had disappeared. "That man is a snake. He's wantin' our property pretty badly. I just can't figure out *why.*"

Taking off his Stetson and running his fingers through his drying hair, Griff said, "I feel the same way. He's up to something."

Val hugged her grandmother. "You were incredible! I've never seen you so fired up!"

"When a snake comes crawlin' around and wanting our home, honey, I get into my defense mode. Downing wants to destroy us. I know he does."

Griff felt the dark threat of Downing, too. Slade had always warned him about the rancher, that he could never be trusted. He moved over to where Val stood. "Are you okay? You looked a little pale for a moment."

Feeling Griff's nearness, his protectiveness, Val held his worried gaze and whispered, "I'm okay."

"Downing reminded you of Buck, I could

tell," Gus said with apology. "He's an abuser just like your father was." She shook her head sadly and walked into the house.

Reaching out, Griff spontaneously touched Val's shoulder-length red hair. "I'm sorry. You didn't need this. I saw how scared you became."

His grazing touch was calming to Val. She wanted to lean forward and step into the circle of Griff's arms. The desire was so powerful it startled her. She took a deep breath, smiled hesitantly and said, "The two of you gave me the courage to shake it off."

Warming to her tremulous admittance, Griff forced himself not to touch Val again. God knew, he wanted to. When he'd grazed her hair, Griff had seen calm instantly come to her eyes. "We helped, but you're stronger than you think." He opened the screen door for her and she walked into the house ahead of him.

Looking over his shoulder, Griff saw the empty driveway. At some point, he'd have to call the FBI agent. Something was going on with Downing. It was his job as an undercover mole to report anything out of the ordinary. And this visit sure as hell had been that.

CHAPTER EIGHTEEN

"Downing is up to something," Slade told his brother after he heard the story of the visit the night before. He watched the twenty heifers stand in a group within the pipe corral. Griff and Val had delivered the final trailer load of cattle so that the group could be put into a pasture to be bred with Diablo.

Leaning against the fence, Val at his side, Griff nodded. "Miss Gus tarred and feathered him." He smiled a little. "You should have been there to see it."

Slade chuckled and hooked a boot on the lowest rung of the fence. "I'd like to have had a front-row seat to see Downing cut down to size." He looked over at Val, a lazy smile on his face. "Your grandmother totes two guns. You wouldn't imagine it just looking at how tiny and thin she is, but you take her on, and you're taking on a pissed-off wolverine."

Everyone laughed. The sun was high overhead, the day cloudless. In the distance the Teton blue slopes had little snow left on them except for near their jagged summits.

Griff enjoyed being with Slade. Since his apology, Slade had softened toward him. "Is Jordana at the hospital?"

"Yeah, but she'll be home at five." Slade lifted his head and pinned Griff with a look. "We're going to the Fourth of July dance. Are you?"

"I didn't know about a dance."

"It's one of the big events in the valley. It's a time when everyone gets together and catches up with one another. We get snowed in eight months out of the year, so any excuse for a party in the summer is a good one."

"I can see that."

Val moved between the two brothers. "We need to get this poor old stock trailer back to the ranch, Griff."

Rousing himself, Griff straightened and unhooked his boot from the corral. "Yep, we've rested enough."

Slade studied the rusted trailer. "I'm surprised it held together. It looks pretty old."

Val gave Griff a look of admiration. "He spent a lot of time inspecting it before we loaded up the heifers, Slade. I know it looks

339

beat-up, but that's pretty much what all of Bar H looks like right now."

Slade studied Val's determine face. She wore a tan Stetson, her hair drawn back in a red ponytail. "I understand," Slade said. "We're just coming out from under a dark cloud, too."

Griff walked between Val and Slade. "I'm going to wire brush the trailer in a couple of days and then paint it. By the time we pick up our heifers in two weeks, it will look pretty decent."

"Always work, isn't there?" Slade asked in a teasing tone.

"Yes," Griff agreed, "it's nonstop."

Arriving at the truck, Val climbed into the driver's seat.

Slade held out his hand to his brother. "Take care of yourself, Griff. Jordana was saying that she'd like to invite you over for dinner real soon. Are you still interested?"

Griff tried to be nonchalant about the request. His heart beat a little harder because all he wanted was a good relationship with his twin. "Yes, I'd like that. Thanks."

"Good enough. I'll be in touch." Slade walked back to the corral to take care of the heifers.

Griff lifted the ramp on the trailer. He locked it into place and visually inspected the rest of it before climbing into the truck with Val. He closed the door and brought the seat belt across his chest. "We're ready to go."

Val slowly pulled out of the circular driveway between the huge red barn and Slade's ranch home. "Hey, this is a good day," she said, driving out to the dirt road that would lead to the main highway.

"It is." Griff enjoyed every moment he was able to spend with Val. This morning they'd loaded the heifers and made three trips to get the herd to Slade's ranch. All morning there had been an unspoken happiness between them. It felt damned good. His heart started to pound. And then fear rose in Griff. Giving Val a glance, he asked, "Would you like to go with me to that Fourth of July dance?" Trying to shield himself from being turned down, he waited, unsure of what her answer would be.

Val's hands tightened on the steering wheel for a moment as she considered his request. Her heart screamed yes. Her head wasn't so sure. Yet, she'd gained such respect for Griff in the past weeks that she gave in to her desires. "It sounds like fun."

Having expected her to say no, Griff was thrilled. He released his held breath. A smile lurked at the corners of his mouth as joy coursed through his heart. "We need a break from all the work. Do you think Miss Gus would like to go with us?"

The fact that he would include her grandmother made Val glad she'd accepted his invitation. She was touched. "We can ask her. She won't dance, though."

Looking out the window, his elbow resting on the frame, Griff said, "That's okay. She needs to have a day off, too. We work like dogs."

Val stopped at the T intersection and looked both ways before driving the rig out onto the highway that would lead into Jackson Hole. "I think Gus needs people. She's always grousing she hates crowds and prefers the quiet of nature to chatty people, but I'll bet she's ready to party a little, too." Her smile faded and she added softly, "We've all been through a lot since I came home."

Griff wanted to reach out but didn't dare to. "Then this dance is a good reason to celebrate a little. You two women have worked your tails off to turn the Bar H around."

"We have. With a lot of great help from you." Val gave him a quick look of admiration. "I was so impressed yesterday with how you took on Downing and that banker."

"Oh . . . that." Griff snorted. "They're nothing compared to the business titans of Wall Street. You think those two are tough, they're marshmallows in comparison."

Shaking her head, Val said, "Gus tore them apart but you were equally effective. Can you imagine the banker didn't even bother to see who owned the Bar H? What kind of people does he have working for him? They sure aren't into the details, aren't they?"

"Happens all the time. The devil's in the details and when you get into land, property and real estate, those titles from the county are your heart and blood. That banker was being dragged around by Downing to do his dirty work. And Latimer wasn't very good at it, either."

"He was sweating the whole time."

"Did you think Miss Gus would sell that lake property?"

"No, not for a second." Val sighed and smiled fondly. "The lake was one of the places of my best childhood memories, Griff. I would escape from the house and sit for hours on the bank. I was alone and I felt safe out there. Gus knows that and she's not about to sell what few happy memories I have out from under me."

"Did she talk to you about it after

they left?"

"Yes, she did. She's bent on getting the Bar H in tiptop shape and then transferring the property into my name. Downing will never know that, however."

Shaking his head, Griff said, "Your grandmother is an exceptional human being. She's a good role model for all of us."

"Gus wants me happy." Val's voice became raspy. Tears threatened and she fought them back. "My grandmother has been the backbone of our family for two generations. She saw her daughter broken by Buck. I think she feels guilty she wasn't around to stop him from abusing us. I think she's trying to make up for it."

"She's doing the right thing," Griff agreed. They were coasting down the long, sloping hill that would bring them into Jackson Hole. Traffic was a tourist snarl as vacationers came by the millions every summer to visit the Teton and Yellowstone. At the base of the hill they began their slow crawl through the town clogged with unrelenting traffic.

"Gus wasn't sure I'd stay. We've had several talks about it."

Frowning, Griff hadn't even considered that Val wouldn't stay and grow her ranch. "And?"

"I'll stay. When I told Gus my decision, she said within the year, she'd legally turn the ranch over to me. But first, she wants to settle the cattle on the land and get those six cabins built. She's a long-range planner. Gus says ranchers have to care for their money and grow it in order to survive. She sees those cabins as insurance."

"I'm impressed with her financial sense," Griff said. "She's right. Beef prices go up and down like a yo-yo and a rancher can't count on just one source of income. That's why so many ranches in this area offer dude-ranch vacations. It's another important stream of income."

"I'm so glad you have business sense. I don't have a whole lot, but I'm learning fast from you and Gus."

That made Griff feel good. They cleared the town and were now speeding down the highway that would lead to the ranch ten miles south of town. The traffic had lightened considerably. The wind coming in the cab felt good against his hot, sweaty flesh. His heart pounded with possibilities as he thought about the dance two nights from now. Val had agreed to go with him! Of her own free will. And if he was reading Val's face right now, she seemed happier than he'd ever seen her before.

345

■ ■ ■ ■

Nervously, Val smoothed down the colorful southwest-designed skirt she wore. In the mirror, she looked calm, but inwardly, as she critically stared at her image in it, she was scared. Griff had asked her to the dance! Val had forgotten how important the summer events around Jackson Hole were for those who lived in the valley and surrounding area. By the time spring came after the long, hard winter, everyone had cabin fever. And any excuse for a dance or get-together by the locals, was enthusiastically embraced.

Touching her hair, the crimson strands gleaming beneath the light in her bedroom, Val felt pretty. Again, she smoothed the colorful skirt, her palms damp. Every time she thought of Griff holding her, his hands on her body, she felt excitement, followed by a keening ache within her. Val adjusted the small peach-colored pearl earrings for a fifth time. The pearls on the single-strand choker were each separated by an inch of gold chain. The solid-colored tee of dark purple was perfect for her complexion and red hair. She knew gossip around town had let the citizens know she was home. Now, this was a place to meet them. Val was sure they'd have questions and she wasn't looking forward to some of them. But looking at herself one last time in the mirror, she felt satisfied that she looked good enough to face the townspeople again for the first time in so long.

"Ready?" Gus called from the opened bedroom door.

Turning, Val smiled. "I am. Don't you look nice all gussied up!" Indeed, Gus had her hair primped, curled around her head and she looked elegant in the tasteful and conservative beige dress with a Peter Pan collar, long sleeves, and a thin silk ribbon around her waist. It was her favorite dance dress, she'd confided to Val earlier. Never mind it was at least twenty years old. Gus never parted with anything. Val liked the two-strand white pearl necklace she wore along with a pair of small pearl earrings of the same color. It struck her that her grandmother's genes were strong in her. Val loved pearls as much as Gus did.

Gus patted her hair and cackled, "Honey, at my age, if I look good, that's a miracle!"

Laughing with her, Val walked over and gave her grandmother a warm embrace. "You look divine, Gus!" She had put on some makeup, which she never wore, and it made her look like another person to Val.

"It's nice to have someplace to go and dress up," Gus said. She appraised Val and smiled. "And you look beautiful. Those bright colors work well with your red hair."

Val was suddenly seized with fear. "Will I stand out like a sore thumb, Gus?"

"Naw, don't fret. The other women are gonna be absolutely jealous of you!" She got a sly look on her wrinkled face. "And I'll betcha Griff will think he's the luckiest wrangler at the shindig there with you on his arm."

Heat swept into Val's cheeks until she felt like her skin was on fire. Tentatively, she touched her cheek and whispered, "Oh . . ."

Gus wagged her finger toward her. "You need to lighten up, Val. Just be yourself. Enjoy the evening. It's time you got some play into your life."

"I'm . . . just nervous, Gus. It's been so long since I've danced, or gone out with a man. . . ." Gus knew about Dan Bradley, her former fiancé, and she knew how long ago their relationship had taken place.

"I know, but things change." She smiled a little. "The only thing we can count on is change. Even I'm going to try and kick up my heels tonight. Normally, I don't dance due to my hip, but I think it's time I tried a little shuffle. Come on, Griff is waiting downstairs to drive us into town."

Val picked up her purse, hurried out of the room and followed Gus down the stairs. Her grandmother's arthritis usually prevented her from climbing stairs. Tonight, Gus hadn't let the challenge stop her. Val was grateful to her for coming up to tell her she looked fine. Love flooding her, she cupped her grandmother's elbow and steadied her as they made their way down the wooden steps together.

"You should see Griff," Gus whispered in a conspiratorial tone. "You won't recognize him!"

"Really?" Val craned her neck to look out the front door, but it was impossible.

"That gent is a handsome devil when he wants to be," Gus added with a wily smile. "You better keep hold of him tonight, Val. Some young filly who thinks he's unattached might try movin' in on you."

Her laugh was strained as she realized Gus was serious. "He *is* unattached. He's not mine."

"Hmm." Gus halted at the bottom of the stairs to catch her breath. "You can't be blind, Val. He *likes* you. Can't you see that?"

Val suddenly felt panic through her happiness. "I guess . . ."

"You should see the way he looks at you when you're not aware. He's got eyes only for you, honey."

Dragging in a ragged breath, Val confided, "I know, Gus. I've been focused on the ranch."

A pleased look came to Gus's face. "I understand. But tonight, just be yourself and enjoy Griff. I know you like him, too. I see it in your face. And you could do a lot worse."

Feeling trapped by her all-seeing grandmother, Val managed a nervous laugh. "Okay, okay, I surrender. I'll do my best to enjoy myself. Now let's go outside to where he's waiting for us." Her heart raced for a moment. What would he say when he saw her? Anxiety sped through Val because she wanted Griff to find her beautiful.

Out on the front porch, Griff waited for the two ladies. He tugged at the collar of his shirt, feeling a bit nervous. Val was going to a dance with him. It was a dream come true. Footsteps sounded and both women appeared in the doorway. Swallowing convulsively, Griff's heart thundered momentarily in his chest. Val looked exquisite, like a beautiful wildflower, bright and pretty.

"Ladies, you're both looking beautiful," Griff said, meaning it. He saw Miss Gus grin. Val colored, her eyes downcast and not meeting his.

"Why thank you, Griff. I think me and my granddaughter clean up pretty well. Don't you?"

His heart wouldn't stop pounding. He'd never seen Val looking like this. "I agree," he said with a smile. He held out his hand as Miss Gus reached out. Keeping a firm hold on the elder's hand, he looked over at Val. Seeing a tender flame in her eyes, Griff knew the look was for him alone. It made him feel strong and good.

"I'll get your purse," Val said before stepping back inside momentarily. She tried to stop from feeling giddy and happy. Griff was incredibly handsome in his suit and Stetson. There was nothing to dislike about this wrangler. And she felt her heart yearning to be closer to him. Much closer . . .

Griff heard the country band strike up a slow song, the first for the evening. Gus and Val had been sipping wine near the crowded bar when the music began. The huge armory was decorated with red, white and blue decorations hanging from the ceiling and draped across the width of it. The place was crowded with locals. The women were tastefully dressed, the ranchers in their best suits, their good boots and cowboy hats.

Griff's heart skittered between fear and desire as he walked up to Val. "Would you like to dance?" He held out his hand toward her.

Val felt panic mingle with yearning. Griff was wearing a clean white shirt, a gray cowboy suit coat, a black ribbon tie at his throat and gray trousers. "Sure," she murmured, taking his hand.

Gus patted Griff's arm. "You two go out there and have some fun!"

Grinning, Griff nodded and gently led Val to the center of the crowded dance floor. There were at least fifty other couples for the first dance of the evening. He saw the panic in Val's eyes as he gathered her into his arms. Being respectful, he kept distance between them. Griff tried to monitor Val's expression so she would relax in his arms. Just getting to hold her this close thrilled him. Her hand felt damp within his.

"It's all right," he teased, giving her a tender smile. "You aren't going to an execution."

Rolling her eyes, Val swayed in time with the music. Griff was an excellent lead. "Am I that obvious?"

Griff said, "Just to me." He lifted his head as the dancers moved slowly around them.

"I think everyone else just sees a young and beautiful woman on the dance floor. Most of the men probably wish they were standing where I am."

The sparkle in Griff's green eyes sent warmth through Val. He was being sincere. She was realizing more than ever that although he was a man of few words, when he spoke, he meant what he said. "Thanks," she said in a soft tone. His hand felt firm and dry against hers. "I'm just nervous."

"I know. There are a lot of people here who remember you. You've been surrounded by well-wishers and greeters from the moment we walked into the armory."

She inhaled his special masculine scent that made him the man he was. Griff had taken a shower with the lime soap he used. "They've all been so kind. They're glad to see me."

"Why so surprised?" Griff gazed into her mystified-looking eyes. Val had put on some pale blue eye shadow, a bit of mascara and pink lipstick. It simply enhanced her natural beauty. He was glad she didn't try to hide her freckles.

"I've just been gone so long, is all. I thought they'd forget. I wanted to." Her mouth quirked. Sighing, she felt Griff's hand monitor the pressure against the small of her back. Her skin prickled with delight where his lean fingers rested tentatively against her body. Val found herself wondering what it would feel like if his fingers trailed a path up and down her spine. As she drowned in his intense gaze, every cell in her body wanted to respond to him as the man he was. And when her gaze dropped to his mouth, her entire lower body exploded with raw need. What would it be like to really kiss Griff? What kind of kiss would he give her in return?

"Gone, yes, but I can't imagine you were ever forgotten," Griff said. He saw Slade and Jordana on the edge of the dance floor. They were deep within each other's arms, dancing a very intimate dance. Griff wanted to hold Val in the same way. But if he tried that, he'd break the trust he was building with her. Patience, he cautioned himself. Patience.

Maybe it was Griff. Maybe it was her. Val didn't care and ignored her fear. She stepped closer to Griff, her breasts grazing his powerful chest. He didn't look surprised. Instead, she saw his eyes narrow upon her, his hand tighten around hers. For a moment, Val wanted to ignore her distrust of men. She simply wanted to fall into Griff's arms and surrender to him. Resting her brow against his shoulder, she felt him hold her gently. The movements of their bodies began to automatically move in sync with one another.

Val could feel the muscles beneath his suit move as her fingers grazed the material. She allowed the music to lull her and within moments, she melted against his tall frame. Feeling her breasts tighten as she danced, Val felt an intense hunger to be with Griff in every possible way. When his hand curled and entwined around hers and he brought it gently against his chest, Val closed her eyes and dissolved. There was such quiet strength about Griff. Intuitively, she realized as she pressed her body against his, he would protect her from the storms of life. He was that kind of man. And she'd never run into anyone like him until now.

The end of the song neared but Val didn't want it to end. Looking up at Griff, she could tell he wanted to kiss her. Should she? Feeling his hand slide slowly up her spine and then cup her shoulder, she felt Griff silently asking her the same thing. Did she want to be kissed by him or not? The chatter of people's voices dimmed as Val focused on Griff's lips. Something rebellious swept through her as she realized Buck's abuse had kept her from freedom. Freedom to be herself and not worry what others thought. Freedom to love.

In that moment as the music drifted to a close, Val leaned forward, her hand upon Griff's chest and she placed her mouth against his. For once, she didn't care what anyone thought. This time Val wanted to satisfy her longing and share how she felt about this wrangler who had walked into her life. As her lips met his, she felt him tense. Griff's fingers tightened on her shoulder and he drew her near. Their bodies were pressed tightly against one another. His mouth opened and he took hers gently, testing and tasting her.

Her lips gliding across his, Val closed her eyes and absorbed Griff into her entire being. She felt his moist, ragged breath against her cheek, felt his shaven skin rub against her softer flesh, felt the power of his mouth as he molded and shaped her to him. The lime fragrance of his soap swirled with his aphrodisiac masculine scent. They combined and Val opened her mouth to eagerly explore him. The world around Val withdrew. She no longer heard the music or the chatting dancers still on the floor around them. Her entire being was anchored around Griff. As his lips moved and he invited her to respond, Val felt bold. There was a part of her that had cried for this moment for years. Now, he was kissing her, holding her, their bodies melting against each other. The world swirled and Val enjoyed the slow exploration between them.

Gradually she eased away from Griff. She lifted her lashes to see his eyes burning with need — for her. Startled and yet pleased by the realization, she managed a shy smile as she pulled away. Griff shared an intimate look with her and Val felt her knees go soft. She felt feminine and desirable beneath his hungry look. He wanted to make love with her.

Searching her face, Griff saw desire burning hot in Val's blue eyes. They were wide with wonder, like a young woman who had just discovered a hidden treasure. He felt his lower body hardening with painful need. Releasing his hand from her back, he allowed her to step out of the circle of his arms. Her cheeks were flushed a soft pink. More than anything, Griff liked the fact Val had initiated the kiss, not him. He understood the importance of her gesture more than ever. Val trusted him enough to kiss him. What kind of courage had it taken for her to step outside the box Buck had imprisoned her within? Letting go of her hand, he said in a low tone, "Would you like to get a drink from the bar?"

As they separated, Val felt bereft. For those stolen moments, she'd felt safe, protected and, most of all, loved. The feelings she had were so new to her, she felt overwhelmed. "No . . ." she said, her voice unsteady. "I need to get some fresh air."

Nodding, Griff slipped his hand beneath Val's elbow. He led her toward the doors of the armory. "All right?"

"I'm . . . not sure." The light from above accentuated the rugged features of Griff's face. His gaze was banked with desire. Val swallowed hard. In her tumbling mind and senses, she saw them in the barn, lying in the straw, making wild, unfettered love. And suddenly, the last place she wanted to be was here.

CHAPTER NINETEEN

As they walked through the crowds toward the opened doors of the armory, Val was still wrapped in the sensual heat of Griff's kiss. He had rocked her world. Pushing some strands of hair off her brow, she realized a number of people had been watching them. They'd seen her kiss him. Her earlier boldness began to disintegrate as chagrin and then embarrassment flowed through her. She needed to escape. To think through what had just happened. Griff walked at her side, his hand resting lightly on her back, guiding her through the last group of people near the door.

The stars twinkled and danced in the black velvet of the night as Val walked away from the entrance of the armory. She wrapped her arms around herself and continued to move to the edge of the parking lot. There were a number of couples outside, some smoking cigarettes and others chatting in small parties. She knew from growing up here that the armory served as the center for most social gatherings.

Val halted at the edge of the asphalt and turned toward Griff. He stood a respectful distance from her. Beneath the low lights sprinkled throughout the massive parking lot, his face was carved by the light and dark. Val saw smoldering desire banked in his narrowed eyes. Trembling inwardly, she absorbed his predatory look with anticipation. Griff halted about four feet in front of her, his thumbs hooked into the pockets of his trousers. She saw so much in the expression of his deeply tanned face.

Her voice came out low and unsteady. "I owe you an explanation." Glancing around, Val made sure no one was within earshot.

"Why?" Griff studied her and he saw angst in her eyes. *This has to do with the past. Had his kiss unlocked her fears?* That would explain why she was slowly shifting from one foot to another like a wild horse that had been cornered.

She uncrossed her arms. "I haven't had a stellar track record with relationships, Griff."

An understanding smile crossed his face. "Makes two of us."

Brows raising slightly, Val studied him.

There was mirth in his eyes and a wry quality to his low voice. "Really?"

"I never could settle down. I had a lot of relationships in New York, but they all fell through for one reason or another." Then he added softly, "I figured one day I'd meet the woman I was really looking for." In his heart, Griff knew Val was that woman. He didn't say anything because it wasn't the right time or place. Seeing Val's brows fall, her gaze avoiding his as she absorbed his admission, Griff tried to remain relaxed. It was impossible, of course, because they'd now kissed. He'd tasted her soft lips against his own. Griff knew they could never go back to the way things were before. What did it mean? Was Val angry or upset because he'd kissed her? Was she going to tell him he was fired because he'd overstepped his bounds as a wrangler who worked on her ranch? Inwardly, he sighed and realized this talk was going to be edgy and tense.

"What I've been through, the abuse has stained me . . . or has done something to make me terrified of *all* men. Oh, I know that only one man did this to me. But men have always triggered an irrational fear in me even though I consciously know it isn't their fault." Val rested her fingers over her heart. "I like men, don't get me wrong. It's just that . . ." Her voice trailed off as she searched for the right words.

Griff provided the words for her. "You can't trust us?"

"Yes, that's it. I've always had trouble with trust because of my past. Lord knows, I struggle with it all the time. Any man I met in my life, it was the same story. I constantly told myself these men had not hurt me." Val's mouth moved into a pained slash for a moment. Looking away, her voice trembled. "I've fought this fear my entire life, Griff. I've made strides, but I'm not there yet."

Griff gave her a tender look. "You're trying, Val. That's as good as it gets." He saw anguish in her darkened eyes and in her expression. Wanting to reach out and touch her hair, Griff stopped himself. The kiss they'd shared had opened a wound he couldn't have guessed lived within her. Now, he saw her shame, her hopelessness and need of him all wrapped up in her struggles.

Just being near Griff made Val want to step back into his arms. She wanted to explore his masculinity, savor the hardness of his muscled frame against hers once more. He made her feel safe, wanted, cherished and protected all at once. Never having experienced this particular response to any man shook her to the roots of her being. "Our kiss . . ."

"I liked sharing it with you, Val."

"I . . . liked it too, but it opened up a can of worms that's always inside me, Griff." Val stared up at him. "I'm such an ambivalent mixture of emotions right now."

"It's okay, Val. I'm not going to force myself on you. I've been wanting this to happen for a long time. I see you as a strong, beautiful, Wyoming-bred woman. You have spirit, moxie and you're not afraid to throw yourself at hard work."

The warmth in his rasping tone sent fluttering tremors along every inch of her flesh. Melting beneath his tender gaze, Val felt like a thief stealing his heart energy. "I — I guess I'm just realizing how much I've missed in my life. I've denied myself most relationships with men. When I did get involved, it always ended in a mess because of my own fears. I was afraid that the guy would turn out to be just like my father. In all but one relationship, I would break it up and run away."

"It would be easy to project that onto any man," he quietly agreed.

With a raw sigh, Val opened her hands. "My head knows I'm wrong for always running away from a possible relationship,

Griff. My emotions aren't at the point yet to help me stay the course. No matter how much I tell myself you aren't a threat to me, I've only climbed that hurdle once before."

Nodding, Griff held her tearful gaze. He ached to sweep Val into his arms and embrace her. He knew he could give Val solace, the sense of protection that she clearly wanted but didn't know how to get. "I've always thought your name was short for valiant, not Valerie. You are a valiant warrior whether you know it or not. You are trying to change. Don't stress on this, Val. We have all the time in the world."

"Thanks for understanding. I like the idea of being valiant. It's something to aspire to become. In some ways, I see myself like a wild mustang that runs free. I see most men trying to rope and imprison me in a corral and then force me into a saddle and bridle."

"Good analogy. No mustang likes to be alone in her or his life. They are herd animals and they're happiest when they're running with their own kind."

Some of the tension dissolved in Val. Griff was willing to talk and share with her. He wasn't going to grab and try to kiss her again as other men had, pushing her beyond her comfort zone. That made him different. A sense of safety surrounded her for the first time. Hungry for understanding, she said, "You're right. I think all humans are herd animals of a sort. We can't go through life alone."

"We need one another. I need my brother, Slade. Even though we were separated at birth, my need for him was always there even though I was on the other coast. And, all things being equal, I'm glad my life fell apart in New York City and I was forced to come home and ask him for help."

"Now, you're in a positive relationship with him."

"I am, but the important thing is it didn't happen overnight. There was a lot of work on both our parts to make it happen. I'm still integrating with him. We still have rough spots to work through."

"Slade is giving you a chance to do that, though." Val saw Griff's eyes go soft. "You're fraternal twins. You share an invisible bond that can't be broken no matter how far apart you live."

Griff stubbed the toe of his cowboy boot against the green grass. "Yes, it's true." Lifting his head, he met and held Val's warm gaze. "The same concept applies to men and women, too. Not that I'm a great spokesman for it." He managed a derisive laugh. "Our nature is to be together, to form a relationship, later a bond where trust and respect can grow. And then, who knows? Maybe live together and later, get married when it looks like it's going to work out."

"I guess we're all wild mustangs in a way." Val studied the stars high above them, her eyes settling on the Milky Way. The billions of stars looked like a glittering river of spilled milk across the sky. Tearing herself from the nighttime beauty, she met Griff's interested gaze. "Why haven't you married? I would have thought you would be seen as a very eligible bachelor back in New York."

Lifting his hands, Griff draped them across his hips. "Well, there's a hidden dilemma with that observation." He gave her a sour smile. "I found out very quickly, and I was also warned by my uncle and aunt, a lot of women would want to marry me precisely because I was rich. I grew up with those warnings in my ears. And they were right. I had my pick of just about any woman I wanted." His brows fell. "They loved my money but they didn't love me."

"How could you tell?"

"If I talked about Wyoming or about my twin, I could see their eyes glaze over with boredom. But if I talked about going to a five-star restaurant or to a Broadway show, they perked back up. It's a subtle thing, Val, but I saw it so many times it became glaring to me."

"How sad," she murmured. Without thinking, she reached out and briefly touched his arm. "I'm sorry. I guess in the military, we didn't see women of that caliber very often. They're patriots, they have a job they're proud of. Their focus is on their career, not finding a man who is rich."

Griff tried to ignore how his skin grew hot where she'd briefly touched him. "Yeah, the sincerity wasn't there, that's for sure. And you're right, women in the military are a different breed from these other women I encountered. It had nothing to do with the fact they were in New York City. You can find gold diggers anywhere in the world."

"Has that jaded you toward women in general? That you can't trust any woman's motives?"

"A little. I'm always wary when a woman approaches me. The first thing I wonder is why she's interested in me. My money? Or me?"

"Well," Val laughed, "you don't have to ask that question anymore, do you?"

Griff joined her laughter. He knew Val wasn't making fun of him or deriding him for his fall from grace. "Touché."

She absorbed his mirthful expression.

"You have a good sense of humor, Griff. And you're humble. I like that about you. You see a lot, but you don't normally share it with others."

"You know how men are," Griff teased, his mouth widening into a full smile. "We don't communicate very well. I'm trying to improve."

It was impossible to not melt beneath Griff's genuine smile and his low, deep voice. Val's shoulders relaxed. "I think we're all struggling with our different wounds and trying to heal ourselves."

"Absolutely. We're in the same kettle of stew when it comes to wounds. I'm trying to work through mine and get well. It's a slow, tedious process but one I feel is worth it."

"You have that Wyoming cowboy honor and integrity. You'll do it."

"Those things were bred into me. And I'm glad of it. A man's word is his bond out here. The biggest lesson I've learned of late is I can't get through life without others."

"I see it the same way. Everyone is struggling to survive. And we do need our family and friends to help us get there."

"You're trying to change your perceptions about men and I feel over time, you will." Griff glanced over his shoulder at the armory. The music was floating out of the opened doors. Turning, he said, "Would you like to go back in? Or would you like me to take you home?"

"Gus is having such fun in there, I couldn't leave."

Silently applauding Val's unselfish decision, Griff walked with her back toward the armory. He made no move to place his hand at the small of her back even though he wanted to. Instead, he walked at her side. Trust. Yes, that was the answer to his quandary. Griff knew he had to give Val the time she needed in order to trust him. And from the sound of it, Val had had at least one positive relationship with a man. It wasn't as if she was a lost cause. He wanted to ask more about it but had to leave it to her to broach the subject. Would Val eventually allow herself to like him as much as he liked her? She was worth the wait. He remembered a favorite saying of his mother's: Good things take time.

Inside the armory, there was a fast-paced-square-dance caller singing. Gus was on the floor with a gent her age. They were dancing, smiling and laughing. Val didn't know who the bald-headed elder was. He wore a dark charcoal business suit that hung on his skinny frame and flapped around him like a set of crow's wings.

"Come this way," Griff murmured near her ear.

Val followed him. Near the punch table, they stood and watched Gus out on the dance floor. The violins were twanging, the accordion bleating and drums thundering as the square dance caller, a cowboy in his late sixties, bellowed out the next move. Val took comfort in having Griff near her. She could feel the heat from his body. Maybe it was her imagination. It didn't matter, Griff made her feel safe and secure. Someday, Val wanted to tell him that.

The square dance ended and the crowd broke into wild clapping for the perspiring dancers and the band. Gus was being led off the floor by the older man.

"Who is that?" she asked Griff, pointing toward Gus.

"I don't know. But it looks like Miss Gus is having the time of her life," Griff said, grinning.

"This is what she needs," Val told him. "She's had such a rough time with my mother and then having to take over the Bar H afterward. I'm so glad to see her happy."

The band struck up a nice, slow tune once more.

"May I have this dance, Miss Hunter?"

Val felt the hair on the back of her neck stand up. The man's voice was close but it wasn't Griff's. Her nostrils flared as she inhaled his faintly onion-laced breath. Turning, she stared up into the cold eyes of Curt Downing. He was holding out his hand, dressed in an expensive black cowboy suit. His blond-red hair was slicked down. He was looking at her the way a predator studied his next meal. Without thinking, Val automatically took a step away and moved against Griff. "No, thank you, Mr. Downing."

Curt smiled genially and left his hand outstretched. "I saw you two on the dance floor earlier and became jealous. Come on, let me take you for a twirl."

Val was about to open her mouth when Griff stepped forward. There was no mistaking the snarl in his low voice.

"She said no, Downing. Time to leave."

Glaring at Griff, Curt allowed his hand to fall to his side. "I believe Ms. Hunter can speak for herself. You're only her wrangler."

Unconsciously, Griff's hand moved into a fist. The smug look on Downing's face reminded him of so many arrogant rich men who assumed their money was a lure for any woman. "I might only be a wrangler,

Downing, but I believe I speak for her. She's not interested in dancing with you. Go find someone else."

Griff stood tall, bristling, his gaze narrowed like a raptor on Downing. His entire frame was tense and Val saw his hands curve into fists. Alarmed, Val stepped forward. "He's right. I'm not interested, Mr. Downing."

"Pity," Curt murmured, bowing and giving her a smile. "You look more gorgeous than ever tonight."

Val could feel the anger radiating off Griff. His mouth moved into a slash, his gaze turning into a glare. "Sweet-talking me won't do a bit of good. I'm here with Griff." Stunned that the words had flown out of her mouth, Val stood her ground and stared back at Downing. The cowboy simply smiled and looked at her.

"Don't you know? McPhersons are nothing but trouble," he said in a conspiratorial tone. "But it's your business, Ms. Hunter. Good evening."

Griff watched Downing move away, head high and his gaze roving around looking for the next woman to target. He forced himself to unclench his hands. Looking over at Val, he saw she was clearly distressed. "A snake is a snake, no matter how well dressed he is."

Val felt a tremble move through her. It was a clear warning. She had seen rage in Downing's eyes. He clearly hated Griff. And he didn't want him standing in the way. Reaching out, she touched his upper arm. "He's a rattler for sure. Thanks." Her voice sounded breathy and uneven to her.

Without thinking, he placed his hand at the small of her back. "Would you like to join Miss Gus over at the table in the corner?"

Relieved and feeling the reassuring warmth of his hand on her back, Val closed her eyes for a moment. "Yes, yes I would." Opening them, she allowed Griff to guide her effortlessly through the merry crowd. By the time they reached the table, Gus was back on the dance floor. Griff pulled out a chair and Val sat down.

"Would you like something to drink?" he asked, leaning down so she could hear him.

"A stiff shot of whiskey?"

He liked her black humor. "Makes two of us. I wanted to hit him."

"I know you did. Bring me some fruit punch?"

Nodding, Griff eased to his full height,

turned and walked toward the refreshment stand.

Releasing a shaky breath, Val was glad to be sitting in a far corner, her back to the wall. Downing scared her a lot. There was something sinister about him. Val could tell by her father's body language alone when he was ready to explode into a rage. Downing was just like him, only a smoother, more dangerous version. Val wanted to relax. She'd been so happy earlier when Griff had kissed her. And their quiet talk in the parking lot showed her another facet of him. He was considerate of her boundaries. He hadn't tried to kiss or pull her into his arms again. In all but one of the relationships she'd had, the men had been aggressive, expecting her to do their bidding. Aggressive men like Downing triggered her deeply entrenched terror.

Looking up, she saw Griff with two cups of red fruit punch in his large hands. The glasses looked delicate against his brawn. For as powerful as he outwardly appeared, Val was lured by his inner quiet and contemplative nature. When he spoke, she knew he had fully thought out what he was going to say. Yes, Griff was like a diamond among the rocks of the other men she usually encountered. And Downing was completely wrong: McPherson men had honor, integrity and, in her eyes, they were anachronistic knights from the far past.

The music ended just as Griff brought the cups to their table. Val gave him a soft smile, her eyes shining with warmth and thanks. He felt jittery and tense from the confrontation with Downing earlier. He wanted to plant his fist into the braggart's leering face. He had seen no respect in Downing's demeanor toward Val. More than likely, Curt had seen them kiss on the dance floor and wanted to kiss Val himself. That thought made Griff's stomach tighten and rage flitted through him. Curt would never lay a hand on Val if he had anything to say about it.

"Well, well," Gus crowed, coming over smiling. "Good to see you two! You disappeared for a while." The balding man pulled out a chair and Gus sat down. She smoothed her dress and said, "Val and Griff, I want you to meet another old friend of mine. This is Mortimer Pressman. Mort, meet my granddaughter Val and our wrangler and friend, Griff McPherson."

Mort leaned over and gently shook Val's hand and then pressed a stronger, firmer shake in Griff's hand. "Mighty glad to meet you." He sat down, blotted his perspiring brow with a white handkerchief.

"You were having a good time out there," Val told the smiling couple.

"Well, of course we were!" Gus beamed at her partner, who beamed back. "I've got a great dance partner. What more could I ask for?"

Laughing, Val felt suddenly happy. "Another dance?" She saw Gus and Mort laugh over her response to Gus's rhetorical question.

Griff looked at the older couple. "Can I get you two anything to drink or eat from the refreshment table?"

Mort nodded. "A glass of fruit punch is what we need. Right, Augusta?"

"Right as rain. Thank you, Griff."

"My pleasure." Griff stood. "I'll be right back."

Gus reached out and patted Val's hand. "I saw you two lovebirds kiss out there!"

Heat raced up from her neck into her face. Val lowered her gaze as Gus grinned. "Well . . . I . . ."

"Goodness, we thought it was wonderful!" And then, she peered deeply into Val's eyes. "Didn't you think it was wonderful?"

Squeezing her grandmother's hand, Val smiled. "It was a wonderful surprise."

"I'll bet." Gus touched her curly hair and

primed it back into place. "I figured it would happen tonight. Dances are for more than just dancing!"

Val saw coyness in her expression. "Am I the last to know all of this?"

Leaning over, Gus cupped her hand close to Val's ear. "Griff is sweet on you. I told you that earlier. Surely you see it clearly now?"

Val's cheeks prickled. She straightened and stared at Gus. "I do see it."

Rolling her eyes, Gus gave her a warm smile. "Honey, I'm so glad you've finally taken off your blinders!"

Val laughed over her grandmother's teasing. "What else did you see that I missed?"

Gus gave her a very satisfied smile, like a cat who had just licked all the cream from the bowl. "The look in his eyes. That wrangler is falling in love with you. . . ."

CHAPTER TWENTY

"Well, what do you think of our progress?" Gus asked Val. "Griff already has all six cabins under construction."

Val was sharing a midafternoon break with her grandmother on the front porch. The swing moved back and forth and dispelled some of the summer heat. "I can't believe he's done so much in such a small amount of time." She smiled a little as she sipped her iced tea. "It was smart to buy the log cabin packages from the company over in Cheyenne." Val knew they could be erected within a week with a good crew.

"Griff hired four good men to help him, too." Gus was pleased. "That young man has a lot on the ball. He's a good manager. Funny how you don't know a person until they get put to the test and then you find out what they're made of."

"We owe a lot to Slade coming out to help get things started. Those two twins worked like a well-oiled machine."

"And it was very nice of Jordana to drop by to have coffee with us while the guys worked," Gus said. "Slade is a lucky man to have married the lady doctor. She's one smart cookie, like you."

Val didn't think she was as smart as Jordana, but they had all gotten along famously over coffee and cookies that muggy afternoon. "I hope she comes back often for visits. I love her dressage stories."

"The McPhersons are back! I remember when their parents died, it was as if a light went out in this valley. Now, both brothers are home and they're renewing their ties with each other. Nothing but good is going to come of it."

From where they sat on the porch, Val couldn't see the six cabins. Gus had decided to build them near their property line to parallel the banks of Long Lake. It was a perfect place to fish. "I have to admit, Griff is surprising me." It was more than that but Val remained silent about the rest. Since that kiss the night of the Fourth of July dance at the armory, her dreams had turned torrid and provocative. Daily, Val wondered what kind of lover Griff would be.

"Griff is a pleasant surprise." Gus pulled the wedge of lemon off the tall glass, squeezed the juice out of it and plunked the rind into her iced tea. Giving her granddaughter a steady look, she said, "I know you're liking him more and more."

Val grew uncomfortable under her grandmother's intent stare. "Yes. Yes, I am."

"But?"

"I don't have a great track record in relationships, Gus. As you know, only one worked."

"Most folks fail a number of times before the right gent comes along."

"I'm afraid to get involved again, if you want the truth."

Giving her a wry look, Gus smiled a little. "Well, I'd rather have you cautious than jumping into a relationship every other week."

A lopsided grin pulled at Val's mouth. "You're right, I'm very cautious. I just need time, I guess."

"There's a lot going on around here." Gus held up her fingers. "We've got cabins goin' up, our heifers are back and all are pregnant by Diablo. We're remodeling the barn and installing new horse stalls. I think that's enough for one summer's work, don't you?"

"I do." Gus usually slept in until about seven in the morning. By that time, Val and Griff were working out in the field. They came in for lunch and only when darkness forced them indoors in the evening hours did they get dinner. Gus made sure there was always a substantial, nutritious meal waiting for them, too. Val fiercely loved her grandmother for her unflagging support. "I'm feeling hopeful. This place was so broken down. Now, months later, it's like the mythical phoenix bird rising from the ashes and reinventing itself. I've enjoyed working on the brochure for our cabins. The web designer in Jackson Hole has the website up and running. We're getting a lot of reservations coming in already." Val couldn't help but be impressed. "It's like a dream, Gus. I'd never have thought of fishing cabins as an income source."

"Honey, that's why many minds are better than one. Griff has brought a lot of new and innovative ideas to the Bar H. He's more than a wrangler. And you can see his business background is really helping us thrive."

"It is." Val sat rocking and thinking about Griff. There was nothing to dislike about him. Oh, he had his moments, but who didn't? He was a patient person with inborn sensitivity. And yet, when it came to strength and endurance, he bested most of the workers hired to construct the cabins.

He was honest, sometimes painfully so, and Val found that refreshing. So many men had lied to her in the past and told her what she wanted to hear in order to get her into their bed. Reminding herself that Griff wasn't like them, Val felt a keen need to continue discovering him as a person.

"Tomorrow, all the appliances and furniture are going to be delivered," Gus said.

"They start arriving at ten," Val agreed. "I'm really excited about it. The painting is done, the electric and plumbing fixtures are in. They're really beautiful cabins, Gus."

Hearing the pride and excitement in her voice, Gus smiled fondly over at her. "I want to leave this life with the peace of knowing the Bar H is not only going to live, but prosper with you at its helm."

Touching her grandmother's wrinkled hand, Val patted it gently. "Thanks, Gus. You've done so much for me . . . for this ranch." She knew the sacrifices Gus had made to ensure she'd have a birthright that would continue.

"I'm excited too, Val. It's all coming together."

Zach Mason was at Curt Downing's ranch mucking out horse stalls when someone he didn't know walked into the airy barn.

Horses nickered back and forth at the huge endurance-racing facility. Straightening, Zach pushed his straight brown hair off his sweaty brow. Who was this dude? Not recognizing him, Zach called out, "Can I help you?"

"Yeah, you Mason?"

Zach looked at the thin, sharp-faced man who wore a red baseball cap, a short-sleeved shirt, jeans and biker's boots. It was the look on his face that made Zach suspicious. But then, he'd seen this type of dude around here off and on. "Yeah, I am. Who are you?" he hurled back, disliking the man's unblinking stare.

"I got a job for you and you don't need to know any more than that," he said in a low, growling voice. "It pays well. You always need cash, don't you?"

Frowning, Zach sized up the man. It was true, he spent every nickel he had on drugs. He'd been arrested three times for possession by the sheriff's department. Such was his need for the drug. And right now, if he didn't have this job, he'd be penniless. His sister Regan refused to loan him any more money because he never paid her back. "Yeah, I can use some cash. What's up?"

Looking down the aisle to make sure no one was around, the man said, "No names.

I got five thousand dollars here." He patted his pocket. "If you want to do something for me . . ."

That was a lot of money. Zach frowned. "Then . . . how did you find me?"

There was frustration dripping from his voice. "Because word's around town you do things on the side when they need to get done."

"Yeah, that's right. I don't care if it's legal or not." The dude probably was aware he had a rap sheet. Everyone in town knew about his drug habit.

"I need someone to set fire to some cabins. It's easy and out of the way. I'll supply the gasoline. All you have to do is take the fuel to the cabins, light the fire and get the hell out of there. I'll give you half the money up front." He pulled the wad of bills out of his pocket. "And the other half after you're done. Only, we won't meet here at Downing's place. He has no idea I'm here and I don't want him to know. I'll give you a piece of paper with a map of the road and the time we'll meet."

"Sounds good." Zach didn't want his boss to know about his illegal activities. He needed to keep this job. Five thousand dollars would keep him in marijuana for some time. He could also pay the rent on his room in town. Regan had kicked him out of her apartment, disgusted with his need to stay high on grass all the time.

Grunting, the man shoved half the hundred-dollar bills into Zach's hand. He then pulled two pieces of paper from his pocket. "The first is where the cabins are located. I want you to drive in on the forest service road. They're located across from a locked fence. Drive up to the gate tonight at three a.m. There will be a pair of wire cutters to cut the barbed wire and you'll see the six cans of gas nearby. Start with the cabin at the other end of the line and work your way toward the gate. Once they're all on fire, get out of there. I doubt anyone will see them go up, but just in case they do, don't get caught hanging around."

Zach shoved the money into his pocket. He studied the map. "This is the Bar H. I heard they were building cabins out there in town the other day."

"There's six of 'em. They aren't locked, either. They're wide open. I went out there the other night and checked. Walk into each cabin with a can of gas, spread it around, then light it. Close the door and go to the next one. Got it?" He drilled Zach with a steely glare.

"Yeah, sure, I got it." He wrapped the pa-

385

per up and shoved it into one pocket.

"Here's where you meet me for the rest of the money."

Reading the paper, Zach recognized a forest service road out in the middle of nowhere, south of town. "I know where this is at. I'll be there at six the morning after the cabins are torched."

Grunting, the man turned around and left.

Zach stood there, his heart pounding with happiness. Maybe word was getting out that he'd do jobs like this for good money. The wad of bills felt good in his bulging pocket. Understanding the man wasn't about to give his name, he saw him disappear around the corner of the barn. He heard the growl of a diesel truck engine start up. Hurrying down the aisle, Zach saw a black Chevy pickup heading quickly out of Downing's main gate. He'd memorize the vehicle so he could recognize it next time he saw it. Smiling excitedly, his mind spun with possibilities of having enough marijuana on hand to last a long time.

As he went back to mucking out the stalls, Zach wished he knew the man's name. Maybe, if he did this torch job right, he'd have more for him later on? Then, he could have a steady job doing things like this, and making good money. Using the pitchfork, he scooped a bunch of cedar shavings into the wheelbarrow outside the stall he was working in. The snort of horses soothed Zach's nerves. His heart pumped with excitement. He'd never torched anything before, so this was a new kind of gig for him. It seemed easy enough. Knowing his older sister wouldn't approve, nor would his grandmother, he had no one to celebrate his good fortune with. Tonight couldn't come soon enough!

Val tossed and turned in bed. Frustrated, she finally flopped onto her back and opened her eyes. Why couldn't she sleep? Was it a full moon tonight? She always experienced broken sleep during the full moon. Whatever the energy, it affected her adversely. But no, it was actually the new moon and the sky outside looked like spilled black ink. Lying there, Val stared over at the nightstand to her right. The clock read 3:20 a.m. Maybe it was the excitement of the appliances and furnishings for the cabins arriving this morning? Or was this all about Griff? Closing her eyes, Val sighed in defeat. She sat up, facing the large window with ruffled white curtains around it. She drank from the half-filled water glass next to her bed. Rubbing her eyes, she felt wired. Why?

Frowning, she looked toward the window. Things seemed unusually bright outside, considering there was no moon. Val pushed off the bed, landing on bare feet, and padded across the cool polished wooden floor. She smoothed out her rumpled pink cotton nightgown that fell to her knees. Approaching the window, she pulled back the drapes.

A cry tore from her lips. "Oh, my God!" There, on the horizon, were tongues of red and orange flames leaping into the sky. The cabins! Val couldn't see them, but she could see the fire above the top of the evergreen grove. Panicked, she turned on her heel and raced for the door. She tore it open, ran across the hall and jerked open Griff's bedroom door.

"Griff!" Val's voice cracked as she ran into his room. He was sleeping on top of the covers, on his belly, wearing only a pair of pajama bottoms. He didn't move. She gripped his shoulder and shook him hard. "Griff! Wake up! The cabins are on fire! Get up!"

Disoriented, Griff jerked out of his deep, heavy sleep. He'd heard Val's cry, the panic in her voice. He leaped out of bed, saw her turn and run down the stairs. Sleep was torn from him as he raced across the hall to the window in Val's room. His eyes widened, a breath of disbelief exploding from his lips.

The cabins were on fire! Wheeling around, he ran back to his room, threw on some clothes, socks and boots as swiftly as he could. Thunking quickly down the stairs, he saw Val on the landline phone, talking with the Jackson Hole fire department. He raced past her and threw open the main door. The screen door slammed behind him as he rushed out onto the porch. The air was thick with smoke drifting their way. He could see the orange glow near the lake hidden by large stands of forest trees between the cabins and the ranch.

He hurried to the pickup truck parked at the bottom of the porch and in moments was spinning and racing toward the fire. His mind was wild with unanswered questions. There was no way he could fight a fire. How many cabins were involved? Griff gripped the wheel hard as he pushed the truck to maximum speed, bumping heavily along the rutted dirt road. Skidding around the large curve, he gasped.

All six cabins were on fire! My God! Slamming on the brakes, Griff stopped within a hundred feet of the first cabin and leaped out. It was fully engulfed in flames. The light they caused made it easy to see as he rapidly worked his way up the line of blazing structures. The last cabin was barely burning. Running to the front door, Griff saw it was ajar. Looking around for just a moment, he saw no one. He smelled the heavy odor of gasoline when he stepped inside. The fumes hung in the air, choking him. The fire had just started and was racing along one wall of the cabin.

Griff knew there were huge canvas drop cloths left on the porch by the workman who had finished painting yesterday. Grabbing one, he quickly worked to snuff out the flames. Coughing from the smoke, his eyes watering from the heavy fumes, Griff worked nonstop to halt the spread of the voracious flames. The canvas was thick and heavy. When he slapped it against the wall, the flames were instantly doused. Hurriedly, he moved to catch the rest of the fire. Flames licked upward, burning the backs of his hands and his lower arm. Griff didn't care. This cabin *had* to be saved!

Just as he smothered the last of the flames and staggered out onto the porch, dizzied by the smoke and fumes, Griff heard the wail of sirens in the distance. Good, the fire department was almost here! Turning, he leaped off the porch with another canvas drop cloth in hand, heading for the next cabin. There, too, the door was wide open. He jumped up on the porch. The fire was eating into two walls. Could he stop it? Unsure, Griff dived into the cabin, the smoke instantly enveloping him. Choking, coughing, his eyes watering, he started at the worst end of the west wall, throwing the canvas against the flames.

Dizzied and disoriented, Griff worked his way from the first wall to the other, which was barely starting to burn. Over and over, he used the stout canvas to smother the flames. By the time he'd snuffed it out, the wail of sirens surrounded him. Collapsing on the floor, Griff coughed violently. Crawling toward the door, canvas in hand, Griff managed to drag himself out onto the front porch. It was there that he met two of the firefighters, a hose in hand and wearing breathing equipment. Yelling at them, he said, "It's out. Get to the others!"

They nodded and quickly went to the cabin next door. Griff couldn't take a deep breath. He lay down, gasping and trying to fight the anxiety racing through him.

"Griff!"

Val's voice broke through his panic. Looking up, he saw her in jeans and a T-shirt, her uncombed hair falling around her face, eyes wild with anxiety. Griff sat up just as she fell on her knees at his side. He felt her hand grip his shoulder, her face close to his.

He could see her pupils were large and black. Her breath was ragged, her lips parted as she rapidly assessed him.

Val wrapped her hands firmly around his shoulders and asked, "Are you all right?" Griff's eyes were dazed-looking. Tears were running down his drawn face. He was having trouble breathing. Oh, God, no! The cabins could burn, but he couldn't die! Val tried to think clearly. "Are you having trouble breathing?" Her voice turned demanding as she shook him. His eyes finally focused on her.

"Y-yes . . . smoke . . . inhalation." Griff sagged forward, coughing hard, gripping his chest with his hands.

"Stay here!" Val ordered. "I'll get help."

Griff felt Val leave his side. He struggled to breathe, his whole world focused on getting air into his lungs. In the distance, he could hear orders and shouts of men above the roaring flames. There were firefighters with hoses running for the fully involved structures like silhouettes against the roaring flames. Finally, he got a breath, sat up and saw the firefighters valiantly working to stop the cabins from being burned. It was no use. Three were completely enveloped by flames and Griff knew none of them would be saved. He watched as two firefighters were ordered to start pouring water on the side and roof of the cabin where he sat. The water would prevent any sparks from setting it or the roof on fire.

Griff felt slightly better when Val returned shortly with a paramedic. He lifted his hand in greeting to the woman paramedic. Val crouched near him, her eyes anxious as she placed her arm around his shoulders.

"I'm Cat," the paramedic said as she squatted down in front of him. "How are you doing?"

"Smoke inhalation . . . I think. . . ."

Cat set the oxygen tank aside and pressed the stethoscope to his heart and listened. "Can you take a deep breath, Mr. McPherson?"

"No, I can't."

"We'll get you on oxygen," Cat said, quickly fitting a cannula around his head and nose so he could breathe in pure oxygen from the nearby tank.

Val tried to steady her shaken voice. "Is he going to be all right?"

"We need to transport him to the hospital to get checked out by a doctor," Cat told her. She took Griff's pulse and wrote the info down on a piece of paper she'd retrieved from the pocket of her dark blue uniform.

The oxygen was like life to Griff. He was able to breathe deeply and instantly his fear and anxiety dissolved. Val at his side, her hand on his shoulder to steady him, was all he needed. Looking over at the burning cabins, his heart broke. Val's stricken face mirrored how he felt. She was crying. Griff reached over and gripped her hand to try and soothe her. He knew Gus had spent her personal money to buy the cabin packages. Now, three of them were gone. Griff knew this wasn't an accident. Anger warred with grief. Who had done this?

Griff's hand was steadying to Val. She gripped his, dividing her attention between him and the cabins that were being quickly tamped down by the firefighters. Searching his face, she asked, "Are you feeling better?" The noises were loud and she could barely hear herself think. Between the roar and crackling of the fire, the water hissing from the hoses onto the flames and the growl of the pumpers sending the water through the hoses, it was controlled chaos.

Griff turned and said, "Better. Much better."

Cat put her hand on his other shoulder. "Looks like you have some second-degree burns on your hands, too. I'll be right back. We need to get you on a gurney and to the hospital."

Griff grimaced. "I can walk and I feel fine." He lifted his hand and saw it was reddened with some blisters across it. "I'll be okay, Cat. I want to stay here."

Val said, "No way. You are going to the hospital, Griff."

"She's right," Cat said. "I need a doctor to check your throat and lungs. You may not feel it now but smoke can burn them. An hour from now, your throat tissue could swell and shut off your breathing. You could suffocate to death. I don't think you want that, do you?"

Griff scowled. "I guess I'll go." Turning, he said to Val, "I'll be back as soon as I can. Does Miss Gus know what's happened?"

"Yes, she heard me on the phone calling the fire department."

Griff sighed. "Damn. I'm sorry, Val. Someone did this on purpose."

"Yes." Her voice shook. "I called the sheriff's department right after I called the fire department. Deputy Sheriff Cade Garner is here on scene. He's already beginning his investigation."

"Good." Griff struggled to his feet with Val and Cat's help. The paramedic carried the portable oxygen bottle for him. He continued to hold Val's icy hand. There was devastation in her eyes. Leaning down, he tenderly kissed Val's cheek. Her skin was damp from the tears. Griff promised her, "We'll get through this. You stay here and take care of Gus. I worry what this will do to her. Okay?"

Skin softly tingling in the wake of his kiss, Val jerkily nodded her head. "You just get well, Griff. If you have to stay at the hospital, call me. I'll come and see you as soon as we get this fire taken care of and Cade has completed his investigation."

His mouth pulled into a grimace. "I'm *not* staying that long in the hospital. I'll be back." Reluctantly, Griff released Val's hand. How badly he wanted to kiss her parted, tear-stained lips. Every cell of his being wanted to protect her, hold her and keep her safe from a world suddenly gone insane. But he couldn't. Hospital first, and then he'd get home as soon as possible.

Griff was in the hospital bed wearing a blue gown when Val came to visit him late the same morning. Dr. Jordana Lawton had been the emergency room physician on duty when they'd brought him in. At least he knew her and when she told him he had to stay twenty-four hours under observation, he didn't argue with her.

"Hey, how you doing?" Val called, gently closing the door. She saw the unhappy look on Griff's face. He hadn't shaved and the stubble accentuated his grim expression. Her heart beat hard remembering how brave he had been. Val walked to his bedside and slid her fingers gently across his gowned shoulder. Both his hands and his right forearm were wrapped in dressings. "It's good to see you, Griff." Her voice quavered, but she didn't care. Leaning over, Val kissed his wrinkled brow. His hair was mussed and uncombed and it gave him a rebellious look.

Straightening, she watched his green eyes flare with pleasure after her kiss. Val wanted to kiss his mouth, but this was the wrong time and place.

"Better now." Griff reveled in the warmth of her breath as she'd kissed his forehead. The intimacy was real and genuine. "How many cabins were lost?"

"We lost three. You and the firefighters saved the other three." Her hand tightened briefly on his shoulder. "You could have died."

"I didn't, though."

"No, but the fire chief said what you did to save those cabins was beyond courageous."

Griff saw the gleam of pride in her eyes

and the soft tremble of her lower lip. Her voice was unsteady. But who wouldn't be shaken up under a circumstance like this? Rallying beneath her glowing look, he managed a slight shrug. "Anyone would have done it."

Val gave him a look of tenderness. "You're a hero in our eyes, Griff. You were so brave."

Feeling heat nettle his cheeks, Griff drowned in Val's blue gaze. An overwhelming emotion, something he'd never felt before, tunneled through him and opened his swiftly beating heart. "How is Miss Gus? I've been worried about her."

"She's spitting angry but all right."

"I think we all are."

"I'm worried, Griff. Cade said it was arson. He's got samples of the accelerant and is taking all his findings to the lab. After Cade came to talk to us once he'd completed his investigation, Gus got even more upset."

"Does Cade have any idea who would do this?" Griff demanded, feeling his own anger surge.

"No. But he said there were boot prints around the cut barbed wire where the guy got onto our property. He's taken moldings of the prints. And there were tire tracks nearby. He made moldings of them, too."

"I'm sure they don't have boot prints in their computer system," he said, trying to hide the bitterness in his tone.

"Gus thinks the fire is Curt Downing's doing. When she told Cade, he said that there's no evidence pointing in that direction. At least, not yet."

Griff had a feeling Downing was involved, too. The guy had caused way too much drama over the property to be completely innocent in this event. Reaching out with his bandaged hand, Griff held Val's fingers. He searched her dark blue eyes. "How are you doing?"

Haltingly, Val said, "I'm in utter shock." She curved her fingers around his. "I'm more worried for you. Jordana said there were no burns in your throat, thank goodness."

"I'll be okay." He held up his other arm. "First- and second-degree burns. Nothing that won't heal fast."

"Slade called," Val said. "Jordana had let him know that you were going to be here overnight for observation. He's coming over to visit you in a little bit."

Warmed by that knowledge, Griff said, "That's good. Maybe he'll have some ideas of who could have done this to you and Miss Gus.

"He's lived here all his life. My brother knows the bad guys around here."

Val sighed. "That's what Jordana said. Slade knows where all the rats hide."

Lifting Val's hand, Griff boldly pressed a kiss to the back of it. He could smell a slight lemony scent. Val had showered before visiting him. "Seeing you is all I really needed, Val. Thanks for coming."

As Griff released her hand, Val swayed forward. Catching herself, she drowned in Griff's uplifted gaze. His eyes were narrowed upon her. She could feel his need for her. All of her. In that moment, Val realized she wasn't erecting the barrier of fear that always came up when a man looked at her in that way. Had trust finally taken root between them? Shattered her past? Shaken by the possibility, Val eased her hand from his shoulder. "I'll be back tomorrow at this time to pick you up and bring you home."

"That sounds good." Griff appreciated the sway of her hips as she walked to the door. "Tell Miss Gus to take it easy," he called after her. "We'll rebuild starting tomorrow."

CHAPTER TWENTY-ONE

A droning sound awoke Val the next night. Her bedroom window was open to allow the cool night air in as a sort of natural air-conditioning. She had been sleeping lightly because of the arson fire last night. As well, Griff wasn't here and, feeling unprotected, Val had not slept well. Plus, Gus was looking pale and sad.

The sound continued to come closer and closer. Throwing off her sheet, Val quietly left her bedroom, padded down the wooden stairs on bare feet and hurried to the door. As stepped out on the porch, the sound of the approaching airplane was very close. Moving away from the ranch house, Val looked up. She definitely saw a plane, but there were no red and green blinking lights on its wings to indicate its position. It was so strange!

The phantom airplane passed overhead. Val could see it even in the darkness as the stars were quickly blotted out where it flew. It was very low and Val could swear she saw floats on the plane instead of landing gear. She heard it heading toward Long Lake. Was it going to try landing there? She looked down at her watch, saw it was three in the morning. The plane disappeared over the stand of high firs that stood in a thick grove between her and the lake a mile away. Listening closely, she heard the engine sputter and then stop.

Chilled, Val wrapped her arms around herself as she stared toward the lake. What was going on? Had she really seen a float plane? It was so hard to see in nearly total darkness on a moonless night. Tension thrummed through Val. Was this plane involved in last night's fires? Or was it a pilot coming in to fish on the Lake in the morning? Val had never seen a floatplane on this lake. It seemed out of place. But what did she know? Half the lake was owned by the forest service and they may have opened it up to such planes. Still . . . she was disgruntled about the unexpected air activity and its tendency to steal sleep from her.

Val turned on her bare feet and hurried back into the house. Making a mental note to call Charley, the Teton forest-service supervisor, to find out if he knew anything,

Val quietly closed the door. She didn't want to disturb Gus, who slept on the first floor. Back in her bed, Val snuggled beneath her sheet and pulled up Gus's light quilt. Nestling her head into the goose-down pillow, Val closed her eyes. When she did, she saw Griff's face hovering before her.

Her heart pined for him, pure and simple. Val felt a vast difference between him being in the house and not being here. She didn't realize until just now how much she relied on him being around. Griff represented safety and security to her. It was more than that, however. Val sighed softly and felt sleep tugging at her. The last image in her mind before drifting off to sleep was the memory of their dance at the armory, and his mouth gliding across hers.

Val was surprised the next morning when Griff walked into the ranch house unannounced. It was barely five-thirty and she was preparing to make herself some breakfast. When Griff appeared at the entrance and removed his Stetson, he grinned a little self-consciously.

"I got a lift from Slade," he explained, hanging his hat on a nearby hook.

"Are you feeling all right?" Val asked. He was wearing the fresh set of Levi's and pale blue cowboy shirt she'd brought him yesterday. He was clean shaven, his hair recently washed. She rallied as she saw the warmth dancing in his eyes. Her body responded powerfully to him.

He walked over to the counter where she stood. "I'm fine. Jordana let me go early. She said I have a clean bill of health and my burns aren't bad." He smiled down into her widening eyes. "I'll live."

"That's good news," she said, taking eggs out of the nearby carton. "I was going to fix myself some scrambled eggs, ham and toast. Are you hungry?"

"Starved. Hospital food is terrible." They fell into their normal morning routine. As he placed plates on the table, he said, "How's Miss Gus?" Normally, she did not join them for their early breakfast.

"I'm worried, Griff," Val confided, cracking the eggs into a green ceramic bowl. "Ever since she saw the burned cabins it's as if something vital got knocked out of her."

"It was her money that went up in flames."

"I know," Val said, biting her lower lip. "The insurance adjuster was out here yesterday afternoon and said the three destroyed cabins were a complete loss. She said the other three are salvageable, thanks to you and the firefighters."

404

"We'll rebuild," he promised. Griff leaned against the counter, absorbing the quiet morning with Val. This kind of companionship was what he lived for. He never knew what he missed until he didn't have it. Maybe that's why living in New York City had left a hole in his heart he couldn't explain. It was home and family that really mattered. His heart was focused on what he shared with Val and her grandmother. Giving Val a tender look, Griff added in a husky tone, "This experience has taught me a lot. I had plenty of time sitting in the hospital to think." Looking around the kitchen, he could hear a robin singing melodically outside the partially opened window. It only underscored the happiness bubbling up within him. "I was thinking how, when I lived on the East Coast, I felt something was missing here." He touched his heart. "I never could define or understand it. Now, I do." His mouth quirked. "It's about home, family and what is really important."

Stirring the eggs briskly and dropping in the cubes of ham she'd cut up earlier, Val said, "Yes, it looks like we both did a lot of soul-searching after the fire. When I was in the Air Force, I felt the same way. Something was missing but I didn't know what it was." She walked to the stove and poured the mixture into a heated iron skillet. "Being home with Gus, reconnecting with my roots hasn't always been fun, but now . . ."

Griff heard the softness in Val's voice as she busily stirred the mixture in the skillet. He walked to the counter and dropped two slices of bread into the toaster. "We were wanderers looking for something. And we found it by coming home."

"Yes, exactly." Her heart ballooned with a fierce need for him. She wanted to kiss him until she lost herself within his arms and body. "The old saying that home is where the heart is . . ."

"It's true," Griff agreed, absorbing the tender look on Val's face. She had yet to pull her hair up into its usual ponytail and, while he wanted so badly to explore the silky strands, he kept his hands on the counter. The pink blouse she wore matched the flush across her cheeks. She never wore lipstick, but she didn't have to. His gaze settled on her lush mouth. He'd tasted those lips and wanted to explore them much, much more. The toast popped up and he busied himself with buttering the slices and dropping in two more.

As they sat and ate at each other's elbows, Val told him about the plane that had flown over the ranch house during the night. She saw Griff's brow furrow with consternation. "I'm calling Charley over at the Teton head-quarters this morning. I want to see if they are allowing floatplanes to land on Long Lake."

"Good idea," Griff said. He wiped his mouth with the linen napkin and set it aside. "I'm going to drive down to the cab-ins. I need to mend the barbed-wire fence and then I'm going to see what I can do to clean up those three cabins. I'll look to see if there's a floatplane on the national forest side."

"You've got your work cut out for you," Val said. She finished her breakfast and stood up. "I've got a lot of calls to make this morning. Gus and I are going to reor-der three cabin packages and get them shipped out here immediately. Can they be rebuilt in a week's time?"

Nodding, Griff pushed back his chair and took the plates over to the sink. "Yes, if the manufacturer can rush us the order. Find out what time they'll arrive. Call the four men who were working with me. I'll need them out here as soon as possible. We've got a lot of cleanup ahead of us. And I need to survey the concrete slabs we had built those cabins on to ensure they're not cracked from the heat of the fire and have to be replaced."

"I'll also get a dump truck out here to take away the debris. When I have some answers, I'll drive out and see you."

Griff headed for the entrance and settled his hat on his head. He stuck his thick elk-skin work gloves into his belt. He smiled over at her. "It's nice to be home."

She met and held his green gaze. "Last night, when the plane woke me up, I really missed having you here." Val took a deep breath and added in a softer tone, "You make me feel safe, Griff. I just want you to know how I feel."

It took everything Griff had in the way of control not to walk over to Val, slide his arms around her, press her tightly against him and kiss her until they melted into one person. The need ate at him like a wolf starved for food. Only, he was starved for Val. "That's good to know," he said, and gave her a tender look. "It's good to be back."

Val watched his male mouth widen into a smile. It sent her heart into a skitter of pleasure. The pressures upon them returned and Val became more businesslike. "Stay in touch by cell phone. Let me know if that floatplane is on the lake."

"You'll be the first to know," he promised,

leaving the kitchen and heading outdoors to the truck. There was a lot to do to clean up after the arson fire. And no one wanted those cabins rebuilt more than Griff.

Deputy sheriff Cade Garner dropped by at lunchtime. Griff was taking a short break from directing his four-man team who were piling burn debris into a dump truck. The deputy's black Tahoe cruiser pulled up and Griff saw Val emerge from the law-enforcement vehicle along with the deputy. His upper body was naked and he turned and grabbed his shirt, shrugging it over his shoulders as he moved from the shade to meet them. He saw the seriousness of Cade's expression. And Val didn't look happy either. What was up?

Val saw him pull on his white long-sleeved shirt as they approached. Before Griff was clothed, she couldn't help but admire his powerful chest covered with dark hair, the breadth of his shoulders and the way his gleaming muscles moved. Gulping, she felt her heart race as he walked toward them, snapping the buttons shut on his shirt. Griff called to the four men to break for lunch under the cover in the shade of the trees along the lake front.

"You're making a fast cleanup," Cade said

as he shook Griff's hand.

"That's our goal. It's a hot day. Let's get in the shade," he suggested as he nodded hello to Val. Griff saw warmth come to her blue eyes and he felt his heart surge with joy.

In the shade of a very old cottonwood tree, Cade said, "We've got more info about this arson. Our lab has created a plastic replica of the boot and tire tracks and we've identified the source of the gas. Whoever did this got it from Bob's Gas Plaza in town."

"Good to know." Griff added in a teasing tone, "Now, you have to go around town like Cinderella's prince and try to fit that boot tread to everyone's foot until you find the culprit?"

Cade smiled. "We have to keep it with the evidence we're collecting. We know the brand of the boot. There are two stores in town that sell this boot. I'm going to try and hunt it down and identify any buyers of the boot. Probably won't get lucky, but you never know. We will do the same with the tire track imprint. See if it's a local tire or not and then go through the records to see who bought this type. A lot of gumshoe work ahead for me."

Val pulled her hat off and ruffled her hair.

"I was telling Cade about this plane we hear flying over the ranch house twice a week, Griff. I called Charley over at the Teton headquarters and he said he knows nothing about it. He said there are floatplanes in the area because of all the lakes, but that's it."

"None for Long Lake?" Griff asked, wiping his sweaty brow.

She shook her head. A slight breeze made the eighty-five-degree temperature feel less daunting. "None that he knows about. Technically, a floatplane can land on any lake so long as it's not on private property. They don't need any permission from the forest service."

Cade grimaced. "You know, one of the many drug fronts we're fighting grows marijuana in national forests in warmer climes. There are mules, people who transport the drugs for money, coming in by car or by plane into specific areas."

Griff's stomach clenched. "Anyone in this area you know of?"

Shrugging, Cade lowered his tone so that his voice wouldn't carry. "We're looking at Curt Downing. He owns a regional trucking company and he's richer than hell. We think he's involved, but we can't prove it. Yet."

Griff nodded and considered the information. He wondered if Josh knew about this. "What about this plane that has starting flying over the ranch? What do you make of that?"

"All I can say is the next time it happens, drive to the lake and check it out. But you need to be careful, Griff. Nowadays, it's not smart to approach a stranger in the forest or lake. If you do see something, call me."

Val sighed. "It happens at three in the morning. I have a hard time believing it's a fisherman flying in to fish for trout."

"So do I," Cade agreed as he tucked his notebook into his upper left pocket. "It's impossible to grow marijuana up here because there isn't enough of a growing season for it to mature. But we are aware of mules moving through this area and we have our eye on a number of them. The drug trade is never static. It's always shifting and changing because they're opportunists."

Griff nodded, rubbing his chin. He needed to call Josh at the FBI office. He'd been in monthly contact with nothing to report but annoying behavior on Downing's part. And he wasn't sure this info would mean anything to the agent, either. Still, Downing's name had come up. And Josh would want to know. "This stuff about Downing . . . Have you let any other law-enforcement

412

agencies know about it?"

"No, we're keeping it within the sheriff's department at this point. We have no proof. We can't contact DEA or ATF or FBI without legitimate proof. It would be a waste of their time."

Griff heard the frustration in the deputy's voice. "A waiting game?"

"It always is," Cade said. "We wait, watch and hope that someday Downing will slip up. Until then, it's an ongoing cat-and-mouse game."

"Gus already knows what we've talked about," Val told Griff.

"How's she doing?"

"She's depressed. She didn't eat much for breakfast. I'm going back to make her lunch."

Cade surveyed the charred area. Three blackened concrete slabs were all that was left of the cabins. "Someone has it in for the Bar H."

Griff said nothing. His mind was on the phone call he'd be making shortly after they left.

"What do you think about this information?" Griff asked FBI Special Agent Josh Gordon.

"A lot of strings, Griff."

413

"Deputy Garner focused on Downing. Doesn't that mean something to you?" Griff stood beneath a tree, away from where his crew was making progress on the piles of debris from the charred remains of the cabins. He wanted this call to remain private.

"It certainly gives us a badly needed hint that Downing is being looked at. And I agree the sheriff shouldn't be saying anything to us at this point because without real proof, it's just a possibility. Still, it's good to know."

"What about this plane I told you about?"

"That's where you can help us," Gordon said. "The next time you get awakened by it, drive to the lake and check it out. But don't be obvious. You're going to have to drive that road without your lights on. If they are drug dealers and they see lights, you'll spook them. They could shoot first and ask questions later."

"I'll be careful," Griff said.

"We need to get someone close to Downing."

Griff smiled sourly. "Well, it won't be me. Downing hates me both because of my connection to the Bar H and because I'm a McPherson. There's too much bad blood spilled between the two families."

"I understand. But Downing is still interested in buying the Bar H, so we need to hold that card for later."

"Let's focus on this mysterious three a.m. flyover. See what you can get?"

"I will," Griff promised, ending the conversation. He flipped his cell phone shut and tucked it into his back pocket. The hot afternoon sun was beating down. The cleanup was nearly completed. The rental truck would haul the remains of the burned cabins to a dump. By four o'clock, they would be finished. Rolling up his sleeves and pulling on his leather gloves, Griff left the coolness of the shade and went to help his crew. In the back of his mind, we wondered whether or not the plane would fly over that night.

Griff Jerked awake as a plane rumbled overhead. He instantly got up. The wood was cool against the soles of his feet. He was on the wrong side of the house to verify if it was a plane, but it sounded like the same one. Rapidly throwing on clothes and boots, he hurried down the stairs. Everything was quiet in the house. Even Val slept through it. Griff hurried outside with the truck's keys in hand. The cool night air hit him. He halted, listening and searching the dark sky.

In the distance, he could hear a plane's

sputtering engine. It had landed and sounded like it was taxiing. He climbed into the truck and, without turning on the lights, drove slowly down the darkened dirt road toward the lake.

After easing the truck into a stand of cottonwoods near the bank of Long Lake, he turned off the engine. As he silently climbed out of the cab, Griff's heart began to pound like a sledgehammer in his chest. Gripping a pair of binoculars he'd put in the truck the night before, he slowly moved behind the tall bushes that crowded the shore. It was dark, a thin slice of moon very low on the horizon. He heard nothing and couldn't see anything on the lake with the forest surrounding it. The water appeared like a smooth ebony mirror.

Griff stood near the huge trunk of a tree to hopefully remain invisible. Holding his breath, he slowly scanned the lake through the binoculars. Nothing but the lap of water against the shore could be heard. Wait! Breath released, Griff tried to keep the specs steady. Yes . . . there!

He barely saw the outline of the nose and wing of a floatplane. The moonlight was poor but as his eyes adjusted to the darkness, Griff could make out a bit of the aircraft. He saw movement, but the blackness

416

of the surrounding trees made it impossible to actually see the people passing something from one person to another. What were they doing? Griff thought he saw a boat next to the plane. Dark figures were moving what appeared to be boxes or bales from the plane to the boat.

"Damn," he muttered softly. The plane was situated on the forest-service side of the lake. It was well camouflaged by the shadow of the mountains looming on the horizon. He was too far away to see anything conclusive. Josh had warned him not to get too close, and he was unarmed to boot.

Lifting his binoculars, Griff strained to see through the night. Josh had told him to try and get the plane's tail or fuselage number. Every plane in the USA had to have them. That way, law enforcement could look up the number, find the owner and track it down. The floatplane had shifted so only its nose and propeller were now vaguely visible. Frustrated, Griff grimaced. He'd have to wait. When it took off, maybe he would see more. But the sky was completely black. What he needed was a set of night goggles to cut through the darkness and see better.

For the next twenty minutes, Griff waited. At one point, he briefly saw a boat leave the plane and head for shore. After the boat left, the plane's engine started up with a cough and sputter. Moving down to the shore and making sure he was hidden by the brush, Griff crouched and lifted the binoculars to his eyes. The plane's engine fired up, loud and noisy this time, echoing across the lake. Coming out of the shadows, Griff saw the floatplane for the first time. The plane was gray colored and blended in beautifully with the night. The thin, milky moonlight barely outlined it. Excited, he rapidly scanned the fuselage for the numbers. There were none! He hurriedly swept the fuselage and tail once again, thinking he'd missed them, but again saw nothing. The plane sped up, heading south along the vertical lake's smooth surface. In moments, it was airborne, water dripping off the floats as it gained altitude. Griff followed it until he could no longer see it in the night sky.

Turning, he searched for the people in the boat. They were nowhere he could detect. Hunting the shoreline in hopes of seeing movement, Griff found nothing. He squatted and waited, hoping to hear the sound of a car engine. Nothing. The night had swallowed up the activity. He waited another fifteen minutes before pushing to his feet and walking quietly to the hidden truck. He would call Josh in the morning with his findings.

"No numbers on a fuselage is a dead give-away it's a drug plane," Josh told Griff the next morning.

Griff had made the call from his bedroom at five in the morning, not wanting Gus or Val to overhear the conversation. "And the gray color?"

"Another sign it's a drug flight. Gray blends in and isn't easy to spot from the air or the ground."

"I need a pair of night goggles," Griff told him. "I could see shapes, but not faces. I couldn't identify any of the people."

"I'll send you some equipment," Josh said. "Right now, this is secret to everyone, including the sheriff's department. If you are able to get more info, some photos, then we'll bring the sheriff in on it. What I want to know is who is behind it."

"Downing?"

"That's what I'm hoping, but we don't know. Downing is very, very careful. He hires men by phone, never letting them know who he is. He sends money and instructions by mail and courier, not by email. We can't indict him because he's not given them his name. He uses throwaway cell

419

phones by the dozen so he can't be tracked. No, he's wily and he's careful."

"But if you're thinking he's involved then in all likelihood, his trucking company is the transporter of these drugs."

"That's what I'm thinking, but thinking doesn't make it so. This may have nothing to do with him. It could be another drug dealer moving into the territory, testing it out and seeing if the floatplane deliveries are a good way to get the drugs into this region of Wyoming."

Rubbing his jaw, Griff said, "The more we know, the less we know."

Josh laughed bitterly. "Welcome to my world."

"I'll stick to ranching, thank you. I can get my hands around it and I see what I'm dealing with."

Josh became serious. "The FBI is appreciative of your help, Griff. Trying to pin down Downing is a long-term mission. Like I said, he's careful. We've had some of his trucks pulled over for inspections and never found drugs. And we can't do this too often or he'll get suspicious. So far, he's clean, but we know he's dirty."

"I know he is too," Griff said, "but it comes from being around him and knowing his family's rotten history."

"Right, which is why we're glad you're there sitting in the catbird seat. You'll get the night-vision equipment in two days," Josh promised.

Slipping the cell phone in his back pocket, Griff stood immobile for a moment. His mind churned with worry. If this was a drug plane, it placed Val and Miss Gus at risk. Should he tell them? No, Josh wanted it kept a secret. Still, he felt anxious as he opened the door to go downstairs and join Val for breakfast. Literally, the Bar H could suddenly be the center of a drug cartel trading arena. Griff knew from the FBI agent's warning, those who were in the trade would kill to protect their secrets.

CHAPTER TWENTY-TWO

Hiding behind the brush, Griff adjusted the night-seeing goggles. The floatplane had just landed and no longer cast a shadow on Long Lake. His heart beat fast to underscore the threat of danger. With a camera that Josh had sent along, Griff could see a grainy green outline of the floatplane. There was a pilot who climbed out on the float and two men in a boat who docked next to it. Griff was just inside Bar H property as he clicked the camera. The plane was a good half mile away and he had no idea if the digital images would reveal what the FBI agent wanted to see.

He couldn't pick up any conversation. The three men hustled quickly and were offloading bale after bale of what was probably marijuana. Within ten minutes, the plane was on its way, heading into the darkened sky once more. A sound caught his attention: a truck. Who was it? His heart rate soared. Turning, he saw it was Val in the other pickup, the lights off. Taking off the goggles, Griff stuffed them into the back pocket of his Levi's and slipped the camera into his shirt pocket. Emerging out of the brush, he heard her gasp.

"It's okay," Griff called softly. "It's just me."

Val pressed her hand across her hammering heart. She came around the front of the truck to where Griff stood. "I heard the plane. When I saw the truck, I knew you were around here somewhere." She peered through the brush at the quiet lake. "Something's going on," she said in a low voice, coming to a halt beside Griff. "What did you see?"

Val's hair was mussed and Griff could still see drowsiness in her eyes. Josh had warned him not to divulge what he was doing. But he just couldn't lie to Val anymore, not when things were getting serious with this plane situation. This was her property and Griff knew she was concerned about the mysterious plane. He wanted to reach out and smooth the rebellious strands from her cheek. She was in a pair of Levi's, white blouse and a long-sleeved denim jacket. Plus, she already had trust issues without him adding to them by keeping such important things from her. He pulled out the night goggles. "I need to confide in you, Val," he said. "Can we go to my truck and talk?"

Confused, she gazed up into his darkened face. The seriousness of his low voice sent fear through her. "Sure . . ."

In the truck, Griff handed her the night goggles. He told her he was working as a mole to try and apprehend Downing. The plane was a twist, he confided, and the FBI agent wasn't sure if Curt was connected to it or not.

Studying the goggles, Val frowned. "You're more than meets the eye."

"I'm sorry I couldn't tell you before," Griff said, holding her stare. Above all, he didn't want Val to distrust him. And yet, he couldn't blame her if she did. Griff knew this event could break the fragile bonds that had just recently been built between them. He felt his stomach tie into a knot. Would Val retreat from him? Torn, Griff knew he had to tell her the truth whether the FBI agent wanted him to or not. "I understand your concern."

Nodding, she handed the goggles back to him. "You're basically operating as an undercover agent." Her heart twisted. "Did you get the job here on our ranch just to follow Downing?"

Griff was alarmed. He didn't want her to think that, not for a second. "No. Not at all. I'm not being paid to do this, Val, and I needed a job. The FBI agent felt since I was coming home and they already had Downing on their radar, I could do this as a favor to them." He told her how he'd met Josh during the Wall Street crash and had helped them behind the scenes. He shrugged and said, "The FBI is shorthanded and they can't put an agent out here to watch this guy. I was sort of a civilian intermediary, is all."

"I see . . . so you aren't taking money for this?"

"None." He searched her face and saw she was deep in thought. Griff wanted to reach out and hold her hand but he didn't dare. He could understand if she was unsure of him being the man she'd thought he was. "It was a favor, nothing more."

"You had no idea this plane was involved in drug smuggling?"

"Not at first, no." Griff pulled out the small camera and showed it to her. "The agent wants me to email him these photos I took. Based upon them he said that if it proves there are drugs involved, he's sending an agent out here to investigate. That's

425

the end of my work with them on this."

"What about Downing?"

"That's an ongoing investigation on their part."

Val looked toward the lake. "And no one knows if this drug smuggling is connected with him?"

"That's right." Griff tucked the camera away. "I'm hoping the FBI can identify these men." He managed a grimace. "I've never been taught to investigate."

Mouth quirking, Val said in a whisper, "This all has to be tied to the burning of our cabins, Griff. Did the FBI say anything to you about the arson?"

"I told them about it, but there are no proven ties as yet."

Shaking her head, Val stared at him. "I worry about Gus. She's not herself, Griff. You aren't going to tell her about this, are you?"

"I won't say anything unless you want me to, Val. I can see she's been shaken to the core by the cabins being torched."

"She's in her mid-eighties. Older people don't roll well with the shocks of life like us younger ones." She studied Griff, his face dark and almost predatory looking. "If I hadn't come out here tonight, would you have told me about all of this?"

Griff had been told not to say a thing but over the course of the night, even before Val had shown up, he'd been thinking about it. "Yes, I would have. It's your land, your home and you have a right to know what's going on. I don't want you to come out here alone again under any circumstances, Val. I'm not going to leave you or Miss Gus open to danger." God knew it was the last thing he wanted for them. Griff saw the confusion and hurt in her eyes. To hell with it. He reached out, his hand covering hers. "I know how this looks. That you can't trust me. I'm sorry if I hurt you, Val. It was the *last* thing I ever wanted to do."

Griff desperately wanted Val to believe him. Panic unwound deep within him. What if she didn't? Suddenly, as never before, Griff realized this one incident could kill whatever hope he had of being with her. His desperation deepened as he saw Val begin to waver. His fingers tightened around hers, a silent plea for her to continue to trust him despite the revelations.

Val felt the warm strength of Griff's hand coupled with the anxiety in his shadowed green eyes. She curved her fingers around his. "I . . ." she choked out in a strangled voice, "believe you."

Griff turned to her. He released her hand

and gently cupped her shoulders. "Val, I promise your trust in me is not in vain. I know we've never spoken about it, but ever since that kiss on the dance floor . . ." He gulped and forced himself to go on. "More than anything, I don't want you to *not* trust me. I know it's hard for you." His hands tightened briefly on her shoulders. "I know how this looks. It's as if I've gone behind your back to do an investigation, to keep secrets from you. But it's not true." Griff saw hesitation and another emotion he couldn't define in Val's gaze. Releasing her, he sat back as she digested his hoarse plea. Never had he wanted anything more than for Val to continue to open up and share her life with him. Griff realized all the money in the world could never buy what she was slowly starting to share with him. It made the situation even more delicate.

Opening her hands, Val said, "I understand what you did, Griff. And why. Until tonight, you didn't know anything more than I did. I suspected drug running, to tell you the truth." She saw his brows move up in surprise. Giving him a sour grin, she said, "Hey, I was an intel officer in the military. I also went out on undercover drug missions."

"I never thought of it, but that makes

complete sense." He rallied beneath her slight smile. "When did you suspect drugs?"

"A week ago," Val admitted, and she gestured toward the lake. "It had all the earmarks of a drug drop. We dealt with this in the Middle East, too. People are pretty creative in how they transport drugs. And drug drops from planes were one of the many ways they did it. Only there weren't many lakes around where I was. They'd just drop the goods out among the sand dunes."

He sighed, seeing he had met his match in Val. She was his complete equal. He was afraid to ask the question but it had to be done. "So where does this leave us?" He was even more afraid of her answer.

"No harm, no foul, Griff. You leveled with me when I asked you about it." Val hesitated and then added, "I trust you, Griff. You're like a dream come true to me. I just need time . . . and you're giving me that. It's more than anyone could ask."

Griff swallowed hard as Val lifted her chin and looked directly at him. He saw tears shimmering in her eyes. Reaching out, he threaded his fingers through her soft, mussed hair. "Thank you. I never want to break the trust we've built, Val. Ever." Griff wanted to kiss her. But that had to be her choice. He'd done enough tonight to jeopardize the fragile connection strung between their hearts. He wanted to do nothing to break it.

"We need to get back to the ranch house. I'm tired and I'm sure you are too."

"I've got to send these photos to the FBI agent first," Griff said. "I'll use the desktop computer in your office if that's all right?"

Nodding, Val slid off the seat after opening the passenger door. "Yes, that would be fine." She stood there, hand on the door. "Will you let me know what the agent says?"

"You'll know everything," Griff promised, his voice deep with conviction. He saw Val's expression lighten. The confusion left her eyes. His heart pounded with renewed hope.

"Great . . . I'll see you at breakfast then."

Griff invited Val out to the porch that evening. Miss Gus had gone to bed and they'd just finished washing and drying the dishes. He handed her a cup of coffee and they walked to the darkened porch. Sitting in the swing with her, he said in a low tone, "Josh Gordon called me before dinner."

Val sat a few feet away from Griff as the swing rocked gently back and forth. She held a mug of coffee between her hands. "And?"

"They've identified the plane. It's from

Juarez, Mexico. And it's a known drug aircraft. Josh said it was part of the Garcia cartel."

"Phew," Val whispered, meeting his worried gaze. "Bingo. I was right."

"You were," he said, proud of her. "They identified one man. The other two aren't in the FBI system."

"Who? A local?"

"Yes. Zach Mason."

"What?" Val sat up, startled by the answer. "But he's Iris Mason's grandson! Are you sure?"

"Yes," Griff said with apology. "Apparently Zach was in the Teton sheriff's photo array. He's been picked up three times for possession of marijuana. The FBI's facial recognition technology identified him from a mug shot they had as one of the two men in the boat off-loading the drugs." He saw Val's face crumple.

"This is awful, Griff. I know Iris. She's tough, honest and a bulwark to everyone in this valley. She even helped Gus a couple of times. I just can't believe this." Val stood, paced the porch with her coffee in hand, upset.

Griff stood and walked over to her. "I'm sorry, I really am."

"Damn," Val whispered, stopping and resting her mug on the rail. She stared out into the night, wrestling with a lot of feelings. Griff's nearness gave her a sense of stability in her suddenly out-of-control world. "Okay, what does this have to do with Downing? Is he implicated in this, Griff?"

"No. There's no connection, but Josh has ordered further investigation up the chain within the FBI. Sometimes there are over-lapping investigations that are ongoing and not everyone knows about them. That's the lead he's checking on right now. I told Josh it's well-known around town that Zach works for Downing. He mucks out stalls for him every day of the week. Josh said Down-ing is very careful. He doesn't think Zach would be able to legally swear that he was given orders by Downing to assist in this drug drop."

"Okay," Val said, thinking out loud, "so we have a known drug dropper working for a suspected regional drug lord?"

"Yes."

"I just wonder *where* these bales of mari-juana are being stored. That plane is com-ing in twice a week. That's a lot of bales to hide."

"Josh said two things could be happening. First, this is a new drug cartel coming into the area. They're just starting to establish a supply point near Jackson Hole. Secondly, Downing owns a trucking operation in town. Josh feels Downing is probably using it as a way to transport the incoming bales to various dealers in probably a five- to eight-state area. He said that Downing is probably not keeping the drugs anywhere near his trucking depot."

"Most likely," Val said, rubbing her brow, "at his ranch. It's a big spread with a lot of buildings on it."

Griff felt pride for Val's insight. "That's exactly what the FBI agent said."

"Being an intel officer with field experience gives me some advantage, Griff. From our headquarters we ran plenty of missions to locate illegal drug drops." She tapped her fingers against her cup, thinking about the situation. "This FBI agent must be getting his act together to do something about this. You said someone is coming out here?"

"Yes, Josh is arriving tomorrow," Griff told her. "He's flying into Jackson Hole, renting a car and going straight to the sheriff's office. They've already alerted the sheriff and they're going to work together. Josh wants us to meet him at ten in the morning at the sheriff's office. He's okay with you being on this mission because of your security background with the military. After the meeting, he's coming out here to look at Long Lake and then do some further investigation."

Relieved, Val said, "That's good, though it doesn't guarantee him Downing."

"No, but it's a strong lead. Josh doesn't know where this investigation will go."

Frowning, Val rested her hips against the rail. She searched Griff's face. "None of us do. Gus can't know about this just yet. She's still reeling from the fire. I'm afraid her health will deteriorate."

"Agreed," Griff said, worried. "This is getting dangerous. I'm not educated about being a spy. It leaves me worried for the two of you."

Reaching out, she touched Griff's arm. "Don't worry," Val said, feeling the leap of muscles beneath his shirt, "this was my bread and butter when I was in the military. I know the dance. And yes, it can be dangerous but I was trained to know how to handle myself, Griff. For an ex-Wall Street guy I think you're doing pretty good, despite having no background for this type of undercover work." She removed her hand from his arm. "One thing you have to know — these drug dealers play for keeps. They've got weapons on them at all times and they won't hesitate to shoot anyone, whether they're innocent or not. When a drug lord is moving into an area, his men are territorial, too."

Disgruntled, Griff leaned against the rail with her, inches separating them. "I've read in too many papers about innocent hikers in the mountains who get injured or killed by drug dealers who are growing marijuana in a forest."

"Right," Val said, finishing off her coffee. "And this is a similar kind of situation. You wouldn't want to go over there and ask these dudes as they row back to shore what's going on. They'd kill you, Griff." She sought out his narrowed gaze. He looked determined and yes, when Val met his gaze, she felt heat flare through her. Even though their lives were suddenly turned upside down by the sudden appearance of the drug cartel, Val wanted him. Would their lives ever quiet down so they could have time to explore one another?

"Josh said the same thing," Griff admitted, unhappy. "He said to not go out there anymore. If they ever spot us, we'd be shot."

"It's not a pretty situation," Val glumly agreed.

Shaking his head, Griff said, "We're going to have to wait and see what Josh says." He looked at his watch. "We need to get some sleep to be ready for tomorrow."

Giving him a quirked smile, Val said, "I'm whipped, too. I don't want those jerks on our lake. We're building cabins for fishermen. We can't put people's lives in jeopardy. They have to be caught so the message is sent to the Garcia cartel the lake is off-limits to them."

Easing off the rail, Griff said, "It's going to be interesting for me to see what the plan will be."

Nodding, Val followed him back into the house. "I'm curious too."

"Here's the plan," Josh Gordon told the small group assembled in the sheriff's office — the sheriff, Deputy Cade Garner, Val and Griff. "Based upon everyone's information, we need a decoy."

"What kind of a decoy?" the sheriff asked.

Josh stood at the front of the oval table. He had a number of files spread out before him. "I want to see if we can find the stash of drugs at Downing's ranch. This should be done before we try to apprehend the drug flight. It's the only way to implicate him with the Garcia cartel. We have an undercover agent in the cartel, but he's down in Mexico. He's hearing chatter about a rancher in this area being involved, but has no names. I'm sure Downing is involved, but we need proof."

"Well," Cade said, sitting up, "no judge will give you a search warrant to march into Downing's ranch to hunt for bales without absolute proof. We have no connections yet to prove he's implicated one way or another."

"That's correct," the agent said. "It's all circumstantial. But if someone he trusts goes in, they *might* find something."

"You mean, like a wiretap on an agent?" Griff said.

"Oh, no," Josh said, holding up his hand, "nothing like that. We can't afford to raise suspicions in Downing." His gaze moved to Val, who sat next to Griff. "Miss Hunter, you're the perfect cover. You have six years of military intel experience, you've performed drug busts and we know Downing wants to buy your ranch. Would you be willing to go over there and see what you can find out? Maybe use the excuse that you want to talk about possibly selling the Bar H to him?"

"Wait a minute!" Griff said in a low growl. "That's dangerous."

Reaching out, Val put her hand on his. Griff had sat up, bristling at the FBI agent. "It's a good plan, Griff. And don't worry, Downing won't suspect anything. He thinks so little of women in general that there's no way he'd suspect me of having ulterior motives." She looked across the table at the sheriff and Cade. "I have a track record in the military of going undercover for drug-smuggling operations and getting intel. This will be easy in comparison to what I did in the Middle East."

Griff tasted panic and fear. "This is too dangerous, Val. I don't want you to do it." He shot a look over at Gordon. "Why can't I do it instead?"

"Because," Cade said with a deadpan expression, "Downing hates you. You won't get a chance to do anything except to be told to get off his property. Val is the perfect foil."

"But you're sending her into an unknown situation. What if the drugs are there? What if she finds them? What if Downing sees her snooping around?"

Gripping his hand, Val lowered her voice to a soothing level. "Griff, nothing like that will happen. I won't be carrying a wire or a weapon. I can say I'm interested in buying an endurance horse. It's a solid story. Downing will never suspect me."

Struggling with his fear, he saw a new side to Val. This was the woman officer who had been in the military. She was calm and unperturbed. The opposite of how he felt. This meeting had brought up the truth: he was falling in love with this courageous woman. And the last thing he wanted was to lose her because of a bastard like Downing.

"Griff," Gordon said in a persuasive tone, "Val is right. She's trained for this. You aren't. Anyway, Downing wouldn't give you the time of day. She's the right person. This is a covert operation and she knows how to handle someone like Downing, who is a well-known womanizer."

"Look at it this way," Garner added drily. "Downing always thinks between his legs when a woman is around. I seriously doubt he'll realize Val is any threat whatsoever."

Sitting back, Griff held on to Val's hand. His was sweaty. Hers was dry and warm. "I'm worried," he said.

"Of course, we all are," Gordon said. "But this is a very straightforward operation."

"I may find nothing, Griff," Val told him, holding his anxious gaze. "Marijuana has a very distinct sickly-sweet odor. I need to walk around the buildings and see if I smell it. If I do, then that's more proof that Downing is part of the drug ring."

"And then you'll leave his place?"

Val nodded. "I'll have to get proof. I'll carry a camera and my cell phone on me.

And I'm sure we'll all be meeting back here afterward?" She saw the grave-looking men nod their heads. Releasing Griff's hand, she smiled and said, "This is a piece of cake, as Gus would say. It's going to be a painless mission for all of us, including me."

Griff desperately wanted to believe Val. His gut churned with warning and dread. He swallowed a barrage of arguments he wanted to throw out to halt the plan. But it was clear by looking at the three law-enforcement officers that they approved it. Cade's wife had just had a baby. Would she want him going to spy on Downing? No. Cade had lost too much in his life already and Griff was sure the deputy sheriff would never put his wife in jeopardy for such a plan. Frustration made his mouth taste bitter.

"Come on," Val urged, standing. "Let's get this show on the road."

Glancing at his watch, Griff saw it was one o'clock. "Already?" Alarm was in his deep tone.

Gordon rose, collected the files and stuffed them into his briefcase. "We'll wait here for your return, Val."

"But," Griff protested as he stood, "doesn't Val get anyone to watch over her? Protect her if something goes wrong?"

"No," Val said. She gripped Griff's arm gently, trying to reassure him. "Downing would suspect something if he saw a cruiser or a strange car following me into his ranch. I'll be all right, Griff. I promise. . . ."

CHAPTER TWENTY-THREE

Curt Downing was in his ranch's main training arena with a student when he saw Val Hunter drive in. Curiosity piqued, he told the student to halt and walked out to meet her. The afternoon sunlight burned overhead across the valley, the temperature in the low eighties.

"Ms. Hunter," Curt said, the riding crop in his left hand as he stopped at the door to her truck. "What brings you to my neck of the woods?" Curt liked her red hair that shined around her shoulders. Women with red hair were fiery lovers, which made him more than a little interested in her as a woman. And he knew from earlier meetings with her, she was a challenge.

Val shut the door and shouldered her purse. "Hi, Curt. Sorry I didn't call first, but this was the only day I had some free time to drop over."

He smiled down at her. "You never need

to call ahead to see me."

Keeping her own smile fixed, Val kept her disgust well hidden. Curt's smug features dripped with obvious innuendo. "Thanks, I appreciate your flexibility."

"Have you changed your mind?"

"About what?"

"Aren't you here to talk about selling the Bar H to me?"

Laughing lightly, Val shook her head. "Oh, no. I came because I'm interested in buying a good endurance horse. And everyone knows you have the best stock." Val saw him preen. Actually, Slade McPherson had the best breeding stallion in America, Thor. But if she was going to do some snooping around, better to flatter Curt's overinflated ego.

"Ah . . . well, you've come to the right place." Curt was disappointed. He was hoping she had reconsidered his offer on the property. But if he could make a sale to her, he would. Although there were things here he didn't want anyone to see, her being a woman made her no threat at all. She was innately stupid and he had no worries about her uncovering any of his illegal activities by wandering around the area. He pointed at the male student in his training arena. "I'm going to be busy for the next twenty minutes. The horses for sale are in the box stalls." He pointed to the large barn. "And there's six more in a corral behind it. Why don't you take a look around and I'll find you when I'm done giving my student his lesson?"

"Sounds good to me," Val said. She turned and walked toward the barn, her elation barely under wraps. She had hoped to find Downing distracted by something else, and twenty minutes was a good amount of time to look for the marijuana bales if they were housed here at Downing's sprawling ranch. She quickly moved inside the barn. Once there, she turned to check on Downing. He was back in the arena teaching the student.

Val pulled the long strap of her purse, which held a small camera inside it, across her body. Climbing the wooden ladder to the second floor of the barn, she wanted to swiftly check out the area. Her nostrils flared as she sniffed the air but she could find no telltale scent of marijuana.

The upper loft was neatly stacked with over a hundred bales of alfalfa and grass hay. Its sweet odor was fragrant. Val knew that a front of hay could hide bales of marijuana behind it. She moved a couple of bales here and there. Nothing. Disappointed, she descended the ladder. Next, the tack room. Val opened the door and closed it behind her, excitement thrumming through her as she flipped on the light switch to look around.

To the unobservant eye, the place was nothing but saddles and bridles hanging on the walls. She inhaled but only the scent of leather hung in the room. Looking down, Val saw cracks across the wooden floor. She spotted a very large trap-door. She knelt and felt around for a latch or handle. There! It was artfully camouflaged so that no one would easily spot it. Looking up toward the main door, Val waited a moment. She heard no voices or footsteps outside in the aisle-way. She carefully checked for an alarm system that could go off if she opened it, but found nothing. Taking a deep breath, she hauled the camouflaged door upward. It creaked loudly on rusty hinges. Fear drenched her. Had anyone heard it? She froze and waited, heart pounding.

Val heard nothing and pushed the large trapdoor fully open. The sickeningly sweet odor of marijuana drifted upward. Wooden steps led down into the darkness. She saw the door was thickly insulated around the edges. It would halt the odor from escaping. That was why she hadn't smelled it in the tack room. Grabbing her purse, she pulled out a small flashlight. Hurrying down the stairs, she flashed the light around. The underground area was huge! Almost the size of the barn itself. Hands trembling, Val pulled the small camera out of her purse. She turned it on. Nothing happened.

"Damn," she whispered. The camera wouldn't work! Heart sinking, Val knew without photos, they couldn't get a judge to sign a search warrant. She removed the battery and reinserted it. Nothing. It had to be a dead battery. And yet, it was a brand-new one! Frustration mixed with the fear of being discovered. Val didn't dare waste time trying to fix it.

She pushed it back into her purse and quickly rummaged around for her cell phone. It had a camera and could be used instead. Her fear turned to raw anxiety. Where *was* her cell phone? Her heart rate skyrocketed as she stood in the darkness frantically searching for it. Mind churning with panic, Val realized with a sinking feeling it wasn't in her purse. By some freak accident, had it fallen out on the seat of her truck when she'd grabbed the purse? She closed her eyes and tried to steady the panic surging through her. A dead camera. And no cell phone. Disappointment flowed through her, sharp and raw. What to do now? If she went out to her truck to hunt for the cell phone, Curt would become suspicious. She couldn't risk it.

Turning on her heel, Val climbed the stairs, pulled the trapdoor closed and moved silently to the tack room door. Taking in several deep breaths, she slid her hand around the wrought-iron handle. She pressed her ear to the door, trying to hear any voices or the echo of boots or horse hooves on the concrete floor outside. Hearing nothing, Val opened it and slipped through. No one was in the long, airy aisle. Heart thudding, she quickly shut the door behind her. She forced herself to stop and look at each horse in the box stalls before leaving the barn. If any of Downing's wranglers happened into the area, they would see her studying the horses.

There were other outbuildings near the corral behind the barn. Val managed to slip briefly into each one. She couldn't find any more drugs. Watching the clock closely on her wrist, she positioned herself at the corral where sale horses were munching on alfalfa hay. Any minute now, Downing would appear. She'd pretend to be possibly interested in buying one of the horses. Mouth dry, she tried to keep her heart from pounding so hard. Had anyone seen her in the barn? She knew if Downing figured out she'd found his drug stash, she was as good as dead. Right now, Val wanted to keep her cover intact and then drive to the sheriff's department and let her waiting team know what had happened. She knew Agent Gordon would be severely disappointed.

Griff could barely contain himself as Val walked into the sheriff's office two hours later. The whole team, including Josh Gordon and Cade Garner, anxiously awaited her arrival in the conference room. Griff opened the glass door for her to enter.

Without hesitating, Val walked into Griff's arms. He crushed her against him. "I'm okay," she said in a reassuring tone, kissing his cheek.

Griff pressed a kiss to her hair before releasing her. He wanted to kiss Val more, but it wasn't the right time or place. "You're sure?" he insisted, walking her to the table and pulling out a chair for her.

"Positive." Griff seemed to intuitively know she needed his embrace. He sat next to her. It gave her the security she needed. She pulled out the camera from her purse and placed it on the table, facing the two officials across the table.

"There are hundreds of bales of marijuana

beneath a well-insulated trapdoor in the tack room of Downing's barn." Her mouth turned into a slash. "The problem is this camera did not work. It had a dead battery."

Josh groaned. "You've got to be kidding me!"

"No, I'm not. It's weird because I put a brand-new battery in it before I left here."

"Did you test it before you left?" Cade asked, his brow wrinkling with concern.

"I did. And it worked when I was here. Once I got there, the damn thing was dead. I couldn't get the photos we needed."

Cade scowled. "But you had a cell phone on you. Couldn't you use it instead?"

"It fell out of my purse when I got out of the truck. I didn't see it fall on the seat. When I was in the basement beneath the barn I found out I didn't have it on me. If I'd gone back to my truck to look for it, Downing would have become suspicious." She gave them an apologetic look as she saw the disappointment cross their faces. "I'm sorry, it was a screwup. I found my cell phone lying on the seat when I was leaving his ranch."

Gordon closed his eyes, frustration in his expression. He opened his eyes, pushed his fingers through his dark hair. "Then we're back to square one. No judge will order a search warrant based upon no photos. It's a 'he said, she said' and a judge will refuse our request."

Scratching his head, Cade said, "At least we know."

"The info Val gathered is worth nothing," Gordon said tersely, pushing his notes around in front of him.

Val felt badly. "I can go back there tomorrow? I'll make damn sure the camera is working. And I'll check to make sure I have my cell phone on me. It won't take much to get back in that tack room and take the photos."

"No," Griff growled, glaring at the two law enforcement men. "You're not asking Val to go back over there." He turned toward her. "I know Downing would become very suspicious of your return."

"I did talk with him at length about a couple of horses," she argued, holding Griff's gaze. He was upset, his mouth thinned and eyes narrowed. She could feel his protectiveness. Val realized suddenly he loved her. For a moment, the shock of realization left her speechless. She saw the love burning in his eyes and worry for her safety. Reaching out, she gripped his hand for a moment. "I told him I'd be back shortly with some more questions and possibly to purchase of one of his endurance horses. Downing is expecting me back."

Shaking his head, Griff held on to her hand. "My gut tells me Downing already suspects you. It's too dangerous for you to go back there, Val." He swung his gaze to the men across the table. "Isn't there some other way to do this?"

Gordon rubbed his chin in thought. "Downing isn't going to keep those bales at his ranch along very long. It's too dangerous for him. Chances are, even if Val goes back over there tomorrow, they'll be gone. We have to figure from a different angle."

Cade looked through his file. "Val has kept a record of that floatplane flying over the ranch," he said. "If it follows the same pattern as it has been, it'll show up again two days from now. Why not set up a trap for them? We can at least apprehend the plane, the pilot and the men in the boat. One of them may talk and implicate Downing."

Gordon sighed. "It's our only course of action. It won't guarantee us Downing, though."

Sad, Val said, "I'm really sorry, Josh."

Gordon shook his head. "You did everything right, Val. And you did a good job. Equipment fails out in the field all the time, we know that. Go home and resume your normal life. I'll be in touch with you and Griff as soon as Cade and I can devise a strategy for that next plane landing on Long Lake."

Upon arriving home, Val pretended nothing was wrong as she spotted Gus in the kitchen. She walked over to her grandmother and placed a kiss on her brow. Val critically searched her wrinkled face. "Are you feeling any better?"

Gus snorted. "I'm fine, honey. You get your shopping done in town?"

Val had lied and said she and Griff were going to the Horse Emporium for some items. "Yep, we did. I'm going to check emails and see if we have some more people wanting to reserve our cabins next year." She saw Gus perk up and smile.

"Do that. And I'm going to go out this afternoon and look at the work Griff has done to get ready for those cabin packages coming in tomorrow."

"He's got it all ready," Val said. She left the kitchen and walked down to her office. Relieved that Gus didn't suspect anything, Val turned on her Apple computer. She frowned when she saw her inbox. There, among the new items, was an email from Zach Mason. How did he get her address?

452

Then she remembered she'd listed it on the new website they'd put up for cabin reservations. What did he want? Clicking on it, Val rapidly scanned the short message.

Can you meet me at Long Lake at midnight tonight? Near the boat landing on the forest service side? I have something I need to share with you.

Val reread it several times, stymied. Zach was known to be linked to the drug drops at the lake. Why was he contacting her? Val sat back in her chair and thought about the message. She had not seen Zach at Downing's ranch although she knew he worked for him. And she was positive no one saw her go into the tack room or had discovered her down in the basement where the bales of marijuana were hidden. Did the kid want to tell her about the drug drops? And why? Was it a trap? Val got up, shut the computer down and went hunting for Griff.

She found him at the barn putting building supplies into the truck. Approaching him, Val told him about the email. "What do you think?" she asked him.

Pushing the tip of his hat off his brow, he said, "I don't know. Zach wasn't around when you were there. Why would he contact you after you'd been at Downing's ranch?"

Val shrugged. "Got me. I've met Zach a couple of times in town. Ran into him and his sister, Regan, at Mo's Café where I was getting some lattes to go. I know him casually, but that's all."

"I think we should tell Gordon and Cade."

"No," Val said. "Let's not jump the gun. What if Zach wants to turn evidence over on Downing? If I show up with a SWAT team, he'll run. We're already on thin ice after my visit to Downing's ranch. We can't risk having people lurking around nearby as I meet him. If he suspects anything at all, he's liable to do something rash."

"Why contact you, though? Why a stealth meeting at midnight at the boat ramp? Why couldn't he meet you at Mo's Café or somewhere else during daylight hours?"

"Maybe he's afraid he'll be spotted by Downing and his men?"

Rubbing his jaw, Griff said, "This doesn't feel right to me, Val. We need to take this to Cade and show him the email."

"No. For all we know, Griff, this could be a very innocent request. Can you imagine what Zach will feel like if he finds out I showed up with law enforcement in tow? What kind of message does that send him?

Do you think he'll ever reveal whatever it is he has to say? I've worked with snitches before and this is typical behavior. They don't want to be seen but they have valuable information to pass on." Usually for an amount of money.

"I see your point," he said. Pulling the hat off his head, Griff wiped the sweat from his temples. The sun had climbed toward zenith and it was already eighty degrees. "Still . . ."

Reaching out, Val touched his darkly sunburned arm. Running her fingers lightly across his damp flesh, she said, "It will be all right. I'll be fine. I've met operatives in the field before and I won't be dumb about it."

"I want to go with you."

"You can hide nearby. One person should be fine. But if Zach sees you, he might run. Trust me on this, Griff." Val searched his grim features. She saw stubbornness burning in his eyes. She perked up and smiled a little. "Who knows? This just might be the break we need to crack the case on Downing. Isn't that worth the gamble?"

Griff grumbled to himself as he watched her walk back to the house to answer Zach's email. The last thing he wanted was Val in danger. Wiping his mouth, he glared out over the lush landscape.

He loved Val. There, he'd admitted it. Realizing that he'd been falling in love with her ever since he'd met her, Griff felt his gut churn. Something wasn't right about this meeting. He sensed it. What to do? Break her trust and go to Gordon and Cade? Could their fragile relationship stand such a decision? Griff knew it could destroy what he'd been patiently building over time with Val.

"Stay alert," Griff warned Val as they pulled up to the darkened boat ramp on Long Lake. He reached out, gripping her hand for a moment.

Val turned and looked into his eyes. "I will," she promised. "Zach is there."

Lifting his chin, Griff saw the spindly dark outline of the kid waiting on the dock. "Yeah, and he's nervous." He pulled a holster from the glove box. It was his .45 pistol. He'd stashed it there before they headed out to the dock. This was a weapon that would stop an attacker with a single shot. And it was one of the small arms that had won him the pistol championship last year, so he was familiar with using it.

Picking up the night goggles, he said in a low voice, "I'm putting these on now. You can't see into the night, but I can. Let me look around before you leave the truck, to make sure there are no traps."

Val waited. She felt fearful and on guard. She knew Griff was an expert marksman. He'd shared that detail with her during one of their many conversations, and she was relieved to see the .45 sitting on the dash-board, in case he needed to use it in her defense. She tried to peer into the darkness. "Anything?" she asked in a hushed tone.

"No, not that I can see," he said. Maybe Val was right. Maybe Zach Mason was alone and just wanted to tell her something. He took off the goggles. "Go ahead. But be *careful.*"

Leaning over, Val cupped his face and placed a warm kiss on his mouth. It was a swift kiss, one meant to tell him she loved him. Withdrawing enough to look up into his surprised gaze, she whispered, "I have you, Griff. You've given me new life by just being yourself. I'm not throwing you or us away." She left the truck.

Griff's mouth tingled hotly in the wake of Val's unexpected kiss. He'd nearly said I love you, but at the last second he'd with-held the admission. Putting the goggles back on, he continued to peruse the brushy area around the boat landing. His heart pounded with fear for her as she walked confidently around the bank of the lake to where Mason stood on the end of the boat ramp.

As Val approached Zach she saw his hand trembling as he smoked a cigarette. When he looked up and stared hard at her, she saw how pale he looked beneath the watery moonlight. His pupils were huge and she realized he was on drugs. Moving within six feet of him, she could smell the marijuana he was smoking. The joint moved restlessly between his fingers.

"Zach?"

"Yeah, it's me." His eyes became squinty and his voice petulant. "You didn't come alone. I told you to come by yourself."

Val halted. This was exactly why she hadn't wanted anyone with her. Why she'd insisted they not tell Cade and Gordon, since they might make their presence known and they couldn't risk that. But she couldn't go back in time now. Griff was here and all she could do was hope Zach didn't run as a result. "Griff is with me. He wasn't about to let me come out here by myself. I hope you understand." She made a point of not turning her back to the thick brush nearby. Instead, she positioned herself between the bank and the ramp, her back to where Griff was parked in the truck. "Don't you think it's a little unusual to meet someone at midnight out in the middle of nowhere?" she asked.

Zach looked at her, the truck and then at the brush. Shuffling his feet, he didn't answer her and refused to meet her gaze. Perspiration dotted his upper lip, which hadn't been shaved in several days. He took another jerky drag off the joint.

Val waited. She keyed her hearing. Oddly, there were no frogs croaking as they would be on a normal night. Why? Had Zach's appearance frightened them into silence? "What is it you wanted to tell me, Zach?"

Before Zach could say anything, the brush to Val's left suddenly exploded with violent activity. Val heard the movement and spun toward it. Her eyes widened enormously. Two large, heavy men in camo gear, rifles in hand, charged her. Their faces were blackened, their heads wrapped in black bandannas so they wouldn't be easily seen.

Zach leaped off the wooden platform, racing the other way, as fast as he could go.

Val gasped as the first man, his eyes filled with anger, lunged at her. At the same moment, she heard the door to Griff's truck open. Leaping to one side, Val lifted her foot and jammed it into the man's chest. She heard him gasp, his eyes suddenly wide with surprise.

The second man had turned toward the truck. He lifted his rifle and fired.

Val heard the windshield on the truck shatter. Glass exploded in all directions beneath the splatter of several bullets. Griff! She had no time to do anything except evade her attacker, who had landed in a heap on the dock after her kick. Val lunged forward. Grabbing the rifle, she jerked it out of his hand and turned toward the second shooter. All her military training came online. She saw the man running toward the truck. Lifting the rifle, Val sighted on the goon.

Before Val could get off a shot, she saw Griff fire a shot from the .45. The man attacking him screamed. The rifle flew out of his hands, the bullet jerking him backward off his feet.

A hand grabbed at Val's ankle. The fingers dug deep into her flesh, bruising her skin. Gasping, she felt herself thrown off her feet. The rifle flew out of her hands and she landed hard on her back, face inches from the water.

Her assailant, clearly recovered from the kick, leaped to his feet and went for the rifle that had landed near her head. Val kicked out wildly, her boot landing in the man's groin. With a scream, the man grabbed his crotch and crumpled onto the sandy beach.

Shoving herself to her feet, Val reached for the rifle. Jerking a look to her left, she saw Griff leaning over the man he'd wounded in the leg. He took the rifle from him, his pistol trained all the while at his head. Turning, her breath coming in explosive gasps, Val aimed the rifle down at the moaning soldier who was huddled in a fetal position. She called out in an unsteady voice, "Griff! Are you all right?"

"I'm fine. You?" he shouted.

"Okay . . . I'm okay. Call the sheriff's department. Nine-one-one on your cell. Now!" Val backed off enough to have both attackers well within the sights of the rifle she held. She quickly looked around for Zach Mason but he was nowhere to be found. Had he run away? Or was he waiting to attack them? Not feeling safe, Val moved backward until she was at Griff's side, keeping her rifle trained on the crumpled goon. Griff called in the attack and gave the dispatcher details of where they were located. Val's gaze moved restlessly around the area.

"Put on those night goggles," she told Griff. "Zach Mason is around here somewhere. He could be armed."

Griff nodded and placed the rifle on the

hood of the truck. Pulling the goggles in place, he looked around, though careful to keep an eye on the guy lying on the ground before them. "I don't see anything."

Val felt as if her heart was going to burst out of her chest. "Keep looking. I don't trust him."

Glancing toward her, he asked, "You're really okay?"

"Yes," she answered, her voice hoarse, her gaze never leaving the two men.

It seemed like hours before the sheriff arrived. Griff was relieved when Cade Garner, Josh Gordon and two other deputies arrived to take the men into custody. Neither man was very happy that they hadn't told them about this plan in the first place. Val explained her reasoning, and rationalized that with her drug enforcement background and the fact Griff was an expert marksman, they felt they could handle the situation. It seemed to appease them somewhat, but they weren't out of the woods.

The ambulance arrived, its lights flashing yellow and red. The man that Griff had shot in the leg was taken care of by two paramedics. The other attacker was handcuffed while Deputy Garner read him his rights and shoved him toward the awaiting sheriff's cruiser.

Val breathed a sigh of relief as she and Griff handed the rifles to another deputy after the two attackers were in custody. Instantly, Griff's now-empty arms went around her. Closing her eyes, she rested her head against his chest, felt his strong, male protectiveness. He pressed his lips to her hair, placing small kisses across the strands. "We did it," she whispered, hugging him tightly. "And you were right, Griff. It was a setup."

Inhaling her sweet, feminine scent, Griff released Val just enough to look down into her eyes. He saw fear in them. "Thank God, you're okay."

"You two all right?" Gordon demanded as he walked over.

Griff released Val but kept his arm around her shoulders. "Yes, we're shaken up, but fine."

Gordon frowned. "Tell me what happened."

When Val finished with the story, the FBI agent scowled. "Mason was the decoy and he's still on the loose. We need to apprehend him."

"He's a scared rabbit," Val said. "Someone made him do this. It was an ambush."

"Who ordered this hit?" Gordon asked. "That's the real question."

"I'll bet it was Downing," Griff said. "Did he somehow figure out Val discovered those bales of marijuana yesterday?"

"We don't know." Gordon glanced at the cruiser pulling out to head back to the sheriff's department. "We'll start interrogation on these two right away. I'll ask Deputy Garner to send someone over to Zach Mason's apartment to arrest him."

"Better idea is to send a cruiser down this dirt road," Val said, pointing toward it. "We don't know if he's got wheels or not. If he doesn't, then he's walking and this is the only road leading to the highway."

"We found car keys on one of the assailants," Gordon told them. "I'll get someone to scour the area for a vehicle. We don't know if Mason is still hanging around or if he has a second set of keys."

Val shivered in the cool night air. "Gus was in bed before we left. I wonder if the ambulance siren woke her up."

"There were no lights on in the house as we drove by," Gordon told her. "And we didn't use the siren. She's probably still asleep."

Nodding, Val said, "I want to drive back to the house to make sure. Griff and I can come into town after that and fill out the police reports."

"Sounds good," Gordon said. "I'll have hot coffee waiting for you."

CHAPTER TWENTY-FOUR

"Why can't the law indict Downing?" Gus asked at the breakfast table after hearing of last night's escapades.

Griff glanced across the table at Val. They'd been at the sheriff's department until three in the morning, then grabbed a few hours' sleep just in time to wake up and tell Miss Gus everything. She sat there, her silver hair brushed, wearing her usual Levi's, boots and a long-sleeved red blouse. Because the mornings were cool, she wore her favorite cream-colored cardigan over the blouse. Griff thought she was taking the information with amazing calm. "The deputies picked up Zach Mason at his apartment," he said. "According to Cade, the two men apprehended at the boat ramp are telling the same story independent from each other."

"What?" Gus snorted, salting and peppering the eggs Val had just scrambled for her.

"That some mysterious, unnamed gent paid them to kidnap Val?"

"That's the story they're sticking to. The plan was to kidnap me," Val said, not really feeling like eating.

"Makes no sense to me!" Gus gave a shake of her head. "Why kidnap you?"

Val shrugged. "There's conjecture it was the Garcia cartel. They kidnap a lot of people for money. But Cade and the FBI agent think Downing's behind it, even though there's no proof."

"Cade had a photo array of known felons in the area," Griff added. "And when he showed them the photos, they fingered the same man. A dude named Earl Henderson."

"Never heard of him," Gus said with a frown.

"He's a freelance criminal who contracts other criminals," Val said. She pushed the eggs around on her plate. The seriousness of what had happened last night was really taking hold of her. Val knew that if Griff hadn't been with her last night, she'd have been kidnapped. And then, probably killed. She'd seen enough such crimes in her days as an intel officer. She gave Griff a warm glance and the tender look Griff returned halted her terrible thoughts. She loved him and couldn't wait to tell him. She had to find the right time and place to talk to him.

"I still think," Gus said, "that Downing's the puppeteer behind it. Val, you said there was a trapdoor to the basement below the tack room. What if Downing had it rigged with an alarm? That could tip him off you were in there, right?"

"Yes, that's entirely possible. I looked for any wires or an alarm device before I opened it." She shrugged. "That doesn't mean, with today's advances in technology, that there wasn't some sort of silent alarm I didn't discover. And yes, if that's the case, Downing would know. And he would come after me."

"And it would explain why he assembled those goons and Zach to set you up," Gus said.

A shiver flowed through Val. She didn't want to upset Gus and yet she knew her grandmother was probably right. "Well, thanks to Griff, I was safe and sound." Val reached out and patted her grandmother's hand to reassure her.

"Unless one of those three guys in custody can identify Downing," Griff said, slathering strawberry jam across his toast, "he's off the hook."

"Val, what about those bales you found in his tack room?" Gus asked, frustration evident in her voice.

"The FBI agent can't search Downing's ranch without proof. The judge needs to see a photo, or a law enforcement officer has to have seen it before a search warrant can be issued. I'm not in law enforcement, so it doesn't matter what I saw. Right now, everyone's hands are tied. It confirms Downing *is* involved in drug smuggling, however. And because of what I saw, Agent Gordon has received authorization from FBI headquarters to bring an agent into Jackson Hole to try and prove Downing is a regional drug kingpin." Val shared a look of relief with Griff. The new FBI agent would take over. Josh Gordon had officially released Griff from his duties as a spy.

Buttering the toast, Gus asked, "Do you think Downing still has the bales at his ranch?" Gus asked. "If he's behind this, don't you think he'd have gotten rid of them by now?"

"Absolutely," Val confirmed. "If he had a warning device, he knows law enforcement would come down on him in a heartbeat. He didn't know my camera didn't work or that I didn't take photos with my cell phone. Downing is smart enough to realize if I had photos, a search warrant would have already been issued by the sheriff and they'd be coming to find those bales. My experience as an undercover operator tells me those bales are gone and that basement is not only cleared out, but he's gotten rid of the odor of the marijuana. I did see some huge fans against one wall, probably for that very purpose."

"I wonder if Downing has some kind of infrared camera in place down in that basement," Griff pondered.

"It's possible but I didn't see it. My sense tells me he knew I went down there and wanted me kidnapped so I couldn't testify against him in court."

"You would be the only witness to the marijuana stashed there," Griff agreed, giving her a grim look.

Gus shook her head. "This is all conjecture, though." She gave Val a concerned glance. "Do you think Downing will try to get to you again?"

Val wanted to dispel her grandmother's uneasiness. "No, I don't think so. Like most drug lords, he doesn't want to keep things stirred up. My gut tells me Downing hired Zach and the other two men. And chances are none of them even know he was behind the orders. A guy like Downing would have others do the dirty work so no one can point a finger at him."

"You think he'll stop using his ranch as a place to stash those bales until they're ready to be transported?" Griff asked.

"Yes. More than likely he'll shift to another storage area but it won't be anywhere near his ranch."

"Like Gordon said, drug lords are forever creative and flexible."

She nodded at him. "Far more mobile and inventive than law enforcement. In the Middle East, I was continually amazed at their ability to shift and move drugs. We were always playing catch-up and so is the FBI on this case."

"Sounds like the FBI is gonna have to wait until another time to try and nab Downing."

Val gave Gus a sad look. "I'm afraid you're right."

"But you think he'll leave us alone?"

"I think so. People who have something to hide don't want to stir up a hornet's nest where they live. They want it quiet. He's smart enough to let it go and focus on where to put his incoming drugs. He'll see soon enough law enforcement isn't coming knocking, so he'll realize they can't touch him."

"And," Gus said, "this kidnapping attempt might have failed, but Downing is probably hoping you got the message and will keep your mouth shut."

"Right. Downing, I'm sure, doesn't realize I found the bales on purpose. He probably figures I was just wandering around and stumbled onto them by accident. He'll just chalk it up to a stupid woman being nosy and that's all." Val tried to give them a slight smile. "He'll make changes at his ranch and he'll figure the kidnapping attempt will scare me enough so I'll never say anything to anyone." And shortly after things calmed down, Val would call Downing to tell him she'd changed her mind about buying an endurance horse right now because her cash flow wasn't what it needed to be. That way, she closed all the loops with him.

"You think Downing will just let this blow over?" Griff asked.

"If these three guys can't point a finger at him, yes, he will."

"Hold on a second," Gus protested. "Is that consarned plane gonna keep landing at our lake?"

"Agent Gordon doesn't think so," Griff said. "*If* Downing is connected with the Garcia cartel, they won't use the lake anymore because their cover is blown."

"And if it ain't, then that plane is gonna land twice a week."

"If it does," Val said in a soothing tone, "all we have to do is call the sheriff and they will capture the group and that will be the end of it."

"Good," Gus said in a huffy tone, "because I want my peace and quiet back!"

"Oh, I think calm will descend on the Bar H once more, Gus." She shared a tender look with Griff. "And you're no longer expected to be an undercover spy."

"Good, because I was never comfortable about being an untrained mole, anyway," Griff said, feeling enormous respect for her courage under the harrowing circumstances that had erupted last night. She was cool under fire, there was no doubt.

Gus gave him a look of pride. "You're a McPherson. Your daddy was a brave man in the Vietnam War. And your grandfather was a hero in World War II. Both earned a bunch of medals. You've got the blood of heroes in your veins, Griff. And you sure showed your stuff last night by saving Val's life." Reaching out, she patted his hand. "The world needs more heroes like you."

Embarrassed by the elder's high opinion of him, Griff said, "I had a lot to pay back in some ways, Miss Gus." He glanced up at Val. "And I've found a home here and I'm grateful."

Val heard the quaver in his deep voice and understood it. "Well," she said with a slight smile, "despite all the stuff going on around Long Lake, we still have fence to repair today."

The phone rang and Griff excused himself to answer it. It was Cade Garner.

Val watched with curiosity, as did Gus. Griff's voice went low with surprise. He twisted around and stared at them. There was a stunned look in his eyes. He finished the conversation and hung up. "Zach Mason just admitted that he was hired by Earl Henderson to torch your cabins," he told them, walking to the table and sitting down. "He found out the guy's name when he picked up the money afterward."

"What?" Gus said, incredulous. "Iris Mason's boy doing this to *us?* I can't believe that!" and she slapped her hand down on the table.

"Seriously?" Val said. "He admitted doing it?"

"Yes, Cade said one of their detectives got Zach to trust him and the kid spilled the rest of his involvement in the arson."

Gus pressed her hand to her mouth, her eyes wide with shock. "Oh, my God, this is going to hurt Iris and her family so much. That kid's goin' to prison, for sure. Zach's mother is already there serving time." She shook her head. "We need to visit Iris, Rudd and the rest of the Mason family. This is just going to be so hard on 'em."

Reaching out, Val took her grandmother's hand. "We'll all go over to see how we might be able to help."

"I'm sorry, Miss Gus," Griff said. "I know this isn't what you wanted to hear."

"I wanted the culprit caught, for sure. But, Lord Almighty, I *never* thought for an instant one of our ranch kids would ever stoop so low as to do something like this! Especially Zach! I know he's been through a lot with that mother of his, but the Elk Horn is the richest and most successful ranch in the valley. Iris dotes on Zach and Regan. This is just too much for that poor family to bear."

"Cade drove out this morning and talked to the family," Griff said. "Zach is in jail and the judge denied him bail because he's a flight risk. He'll stay there until his trial. We've got an appointment with the prosecutor today at —" he glanced at his watch "— two o'clock. Do you feel like making the appointment, Val? We're both hurting for sleep."

"Yes, I'll go in with you. We can get a good night's sleep tonight." Val envisioned not

475

only being in Griff's bed, but finally being able to love him.

Curt Downing hissed a curse. He walked the long aisle of his main barn where his students' endurance horses were kept. His attorney had just called. The sheriff wanted to talk to him about Zach. Rubbing his jaw, Curt knew there was no link law enforcement could make to him. He'd roll over and play dumb about Henderson coming onto his ranch to hire Zach to burn down the cabins. One of his cronies in Idaho had hired Henderson, given him the money and orders to hire Zach. And it had been Henderson who had hired the kid to move marijuana bales from the float plane. Zach was never taken to his property to know the bales were being stored there. No one knew his tangled web of connection around North America, nor would they find out.

Curt felt angry he'd been thwarted from showing the Garcia drug cartel he could make things happen. Long Lake, his primary plan, was off the table. The feds and the sheriff were on to the drops. And the burning of the cabins hadn't scared Gus or Val at all. They were tough, stubborn women. Plus they had that McPherson there to help them out. Halting, he crossed his arms over his chest, the late-afternoon breeze warm. The snort of horses soothed his fractious state. Horses always calmed him.

The Bar H would be off-limits to him. He couldn't continue to terrorize the women to force them to sell. Most of all, he was going to walk a long circle around Val Hunter. After running the videotape and finding her in his marijuana stash, his plan to have her kidnapped and murdered had failed too. No, he had to release his plans for the Bar H. There would be no retribution because Downing knew the feds were probably bringing in an agent to watch for drug cartel activity. That meant he had to really be careful using his trucking company to move drugs from now on.

Feeling defeated, Curt ran his fingers through his short sandy-red hair. He'd lost this battle. And it had been two women and a wrangler who had stalemated him. They'd ridden roughshod on him. His hatred of Griff McPherson rivaled the feelings he had for his twin, Slade. These were people he could no longer tangle with or try to manipulate. He'd have to find new players who he could move around on his chessboard plan for this valley.

■ ■ ■ ■

Griff and Val silently entered the ranch house close to midnight. Val quietly closed the main door and locked it. Other than the hall light that had been left on, the house was still. Gus was asleep.

Val reached out at the base of the stairs, her fingers wrapping around Griff's hand. He pulled to a halt, turned and looked down at her. "I don't want to sleep alone tonight," she said in a whisper near his ear. Val felt his roughened fingers squeeze hers.

"I don't either." He moved close, his hand sliding across her jaw. Looking deeply into her eyes, Griff asked, "Are you sure?" He searched her shadowed blue eyes intently because this had to be mutual. Was Val's trust in him strong enough to take this next serious step? His heart pounded with anxiety as he waited to hear her answer.

"I've never been more sure of anything in my life, Griff."

With a nod, he removed his hand from the soft line of her jaw. He led her quietly up the stairs and, at the top, pulled her against him. A softened sigh issued from Val's parted lips as she stepped into his embrace. They stood absorbing one another in the calm of the ranch home. Kissing her ear, the strands of her hair tickling his nose and cheek, Griff said in a low tone, "One last chance to say no?"

She eased back just enough to see his darkened gaze, and said in a teasing voice, "It's too late to ask, wrangler."

"What made the decision for you?" he asked, his fingers trailing across her freckled cheek. Her flesh was soft and firm. A flush moved across her face as he continued to stroke her cheek.

"Last night and today." Her voice thickened with emotion. "Getting grilled by the prosecutor for three hours, and then being pitched around to different attorneys and law-enforcement officials wore me out. I realized through it all, I just wanted you at my side." She shared a tender smile with him. "You've earned my trust, Griff. You've done so much for Gus, for our ranch."

Holding her sultry look, he said, "That's no reason to love someone, Val."

"No, but it says something about a person's character." She trailed her fingers lingeringly along the hallow of his stubbled cheek. His eyes narrowed and she saw the fire leap within them. "It's you, Griff. You're a man with a past who proved that he could rise from the ashes and become a true hero."

"I'm not a hero," Griff uttered in protest, leaning down and kissing her brow. Inhaling Val's scent only made him more hungry for her. "I'm a man who has fallen in love with you, Val." He pressed his mouth gently against hers. He wasn't disappointed as she leaned forward, her breasts pressing insistently against his chest, her breath warm and punctuated as she hungrily drank from his mouth.

Val's world began to dissolve as Griff's mouth explored hers. In moments, he lifted her off her feet and cradled her against his chest. It seemed so natural to slide her arms around his broad shoulders as he carried her to the door of his room. Resting her head against his neck and jaw, Val closed her eyes as Griff pushed the door open with the toe of his boot. Once inside, he nudged it shut.

Moonlight filtered through the lacy white curtains and moved silently across the colorful quilt that Gus had made decades earlier. Everything seemed so right to Val as Griff gently deposited her on the bed. She sat there as he knelt down and took off her first boot and then her second one.

Looking up as she sat relaxed, her hands resting on the quilt, he said in a whisper, "I've always dreamed of undressing you like this," he whispered, "starting with your boots, and then your socks." Griff trailed his fingers down her ankles and slid them beneath the tops of her white cotton socks.

Flesh tingly wildly in the wake of his grazing touch, Val said softly, "Let's dream together, then."

With the socks dropped to his side, Griff gently explored each of her fine, delicate feet. Her skin was soft as he curved his fingers around each of her heels and then focused on her toes, giving each feathery attention. He heard Val sigh as he slowly moved his hands from her feet up to her exposed ankles. Without a word, he slowly eased the buttons open on her blouse. He began with the top one, his fingers grazing her flesh. A soft gasp from Val made him smile and told him she liked his slow seduction.

"I want to discover you like a flower opening her petals to me," he said in a thick tone as he guided his hands beneath the blouse and opened it. Val wore a lacy white cotton bra. Removing the blouse from her shoulders, he allowed it to drop beside the bed. Sliding his hands around the bra band, Griff leaned forward to unhook it. Moving his fingers up across her strong, supple back, he slid the straps off her shoulders and the lingerie fell to the floor.

"This is a two-way street," Val said, her voice husky, and she began to snap open the pearl buttons on his shirt. "If you think I'm just going to sit here . . ." She laughed breathily as she saw Griff's very male smile in response. "I'm not."

In moments, Griff's shirt had joined the other clothes on the floor. Val playfully moved her fingers through the dark hair across his chest. She felt her breasts contract as his gaze settled them. His masculinity screamed at her and Val continued to explore his taut, hard chest, thick collarbone and heavily muscled shoulders. The sensation of finally getting to touch Griff was utter joy for Val. She closed her eyes as he leaned forward, a predatory look in his green gaze.

The moment his roughened hands curved around her breasts, Val moaned. His mouth took hers. She lost herself within his strength and the scent of Griff as a man. His thumbs moved tantalizingly around her hardening nipples. Arching breathlessly into his hands, Val clung to him. His mouth was commanding and Val moaned with pleasure, lost in the escalating heat bolting downward like lightning and turning into a molten river within her womanly core.

Wanting to love her fully, Griff reluctantly eased from her lips. He stood up and pulled off his boots and jeans. Val caught his hands before they reached his dark blue boxer shorts.

"My turn," she said, sliding her fingers within the elastic band. His need of her was obvious and she took delight in pulling the fabric off his narrow hips and down his long, well-muscled legs. Griff stood naked before her. Her gaze moved upward and appreciated every inch of his taut, hardened body. She saw his mouth curve sinuously and he took a step forward and in moments, he'd maneuvered her onto the bed, her back pressed into the quilt.

"It's my turn," he said, looking deep into her smoldering blue eyes. In moments, he'd unbuttoned her Levi's and slid his hands beneath the fabric as he explored her waist. She arched into his hands, hunger burning in her gaze. His fingers met silky lingerie and he lingered for a moment, the slick material heightening his need of her. Giving Val a heated look as she moaned and lifted her hips, Griff pulled off her pants. Depositing them beside the bed, he leaned over and placed a series of slow, warm kisses along the low band of her pink lingerie. He heard Val give a little cry, her hands opening and closing frantically against his shoulders. Her breathing was ragged as he purposely and slowly slid the silky material off her hips and down her shapely legs. She was perfect to him as he removed them. Her hips were wide and her curved thighs flowed into an apex that drew his full attention.

Val surprised him as she sat up and gripped him by the shoulders.

Her mouth whispered across his. "My turn . . ." She guided him to lie on the bed and pushed him down on his back. In one smooth, unbroken motion, Val mounted him. As her strong thighs bracketed his hips, he gave her a fierce look mixed with pleasure. Lifting his hands, he captured her shoulders and pulled her down until their lips met and molded together. Heat exploded throughout Griff as she deliberately dragged her breasts against his chest. She moved suggestively against him and felt heat and moisture explode where they slid hotly against one another.

A groan rumbled through his chest, the vibration heightening her need for him. As his hands caught and captured her breasts, she released the wild, untamed woman inside. In seconds, he gently teethed first one nipple and then the other. Concentric waves of heat and tingling riddled Val and she gasped. Her fingers dug reflexively into his thick, bunched shoulder muscles as he tasted and suckled her. Everything disappeared except Griff's roughened breathing, his moist breath ragged against her flesh, his hands and mouth worshipping her.

Moving her hips suggestively across him, Val pulled him within her confines. Capturing him brought heat and pressure deep within her core and she gave a cry of raw gratification. She felt him tense, stiffen and an animal-like sound vibrated through his entire body. The primal sound goaded her on, her cheek sliding against his stubbled one, breath exploding in gasps, hips emulating a powerful ride on a stallion. Her mass of her silky hair swept across his face as she seized his mouth with wanton fierceness. Heat roared through her slick body riding rhythmically in sync with his.

She was a full partner with him, giving, taking, loving and pleasuring. Lifting his hips, Griff drove even more deeply into her. For a moment, she tensed, and then she lifted away from his chest and placed her hands on either side of his head. Griff saw an incredible glow of satisfaction wreathing her face. Her lips were parted and wet as he slid his hands from her shoulders down her long torso to settle around her hips. He trapped and moved her even faster and deeper than before. Like a volcano holding red-hot lava deep within them, the orgasm simultaneously erupted between them. Griff felt himself spinning off into space, nearly losing consciousness as they bathed one another with their love. He heard Val utter a sharpened cry and then tense like a bow that had been pulled too tight. Her fingers dug convulsively into his taut chest.

For moments out of time, that still point where nothing existed for Val except Griff, his scent, his male body locked within hers and his teasing mouth, orbited her blown senses. She floated out of body and yet felt the vibrant, white-hot lava exploding again and again throughout her lower body. Seconds reeled into golden colors exploding behind her tightly shut lids. Breath coming in sobs, Val dug her fingers frantically into his thick, hardened chest muscles. For a moment they were fused in the molten luminosity of their frantic love. Her heart blossomed fiercely as the heat lessened within her. Val felt a pleasant exhaustion stealing through her body. She relaxed against Griff's damp flesh, his chest heaving with exertion as Val nuzzled her cheek against his jaw. Instantly, his strong arms slid around her naked body, holding her tightly, holding her forever.

Val lost track of how long she slept. When she first awoke, she realized her naked form was pressed against the hard lines of Griff's body beneath the covers. Dawn was creeping up on the horizon, the first hints of light seeping in beneath the closed bedroom door. Griff stirred. Val smiled, nuzzled his stubbled jaw and kissed his cheek. His eyes slowly opened and a tender smile pulled at her mouth as she eased up on her elbow, her hand falling across his uncombed hair. Griff's beard was dark and it gave him the look of the warrior she knew he really was. Meeting his unfocused green eyes, she leaned down and cherished his mouth with her lips.

Val wasn't disappointed as his arm came up and his fingers moved across her naked back, trailing up her spine and cupping her shoulder. Licking his lower lip with her tongue, she whispered, "I love you, Griff McPherson. I've never been happier than this moment."

Val's husky words aroused his waking state. Her body was warm against his, her smile soft and tremulous. Reaching up, Griff framed her face and looked deeply into her glistening eyes. "I love you . . . I should have

487

told you there at the lake when you kissed me." He slid his hand across her jaw, worshipping her natural beauty and trusting expression. "I want to wake up every morning just like this, Val. With you." Leaning upward, he pressed his mouth lightly against hers. He said in a whisper, "Marry me? Be my wife? My partner? My best friend?"

Heart pounding with unparalleled joy, Val closed her eyes and glided her mouth against his. "Yes, to all your questions. With you, Griff . . . only with you."

Gus was busy in the kitchen making breakfast when they came down the stairs together. She was leaning over the stove scrambling a bunch of eggs with bacon bits and cheddar cheese in the huge iron skillet. Looking up, Gus grinned wickedly.

"You two youngsters got something to share with me, I hope?"

Val grinned and looked over at Griff. "We do. How did you know?"

Gus cackled. "I might be old, but I ain't blind, deaf or dumb. You two are probably hungrier than two bobcats this morning."

Griff felt heat in his cheeks as he released Val. She went over to the stove, hugged her grandmother and then proceeded to help her with the cooking. The elder's eyes glittered with humor and he saw the smile widen across her mouth. "We wouldn't want to hide good news from you, Miss Gus," he said, stepping into the kitchen.

Gus emptied the hefty amount of scrambled eggs into a bright red ceramic bowl. "I 'spect that's so, Griff. Go sit down, son."

Griff waited until Gus washed her hands at the sink and then wiped them dry on the green-and-white-checked apron she wore. Pulling out the chair, he helped her sit down at the head of the table. In the meantime, Val poured coffee into three mugs and brought them over. Griff pulled out Val's chair and then sat down opposite her.

"Well," Gus murmured, a very pleased look on her wrinkled face. "This is a celebration breakfast?"

Val laughed a little. "It is, Gus." She shared a warm look with Griff.

"Miss Gus, we would like your blessing," Griff began. His voice went off-key. "I've loved Val, I think, from the first time I ever saw her. And over the months, I've realized she's the woman I want to go through my life with." He reached over and gripped Gus's hand. "Will you bless our marriage?"

Tears glimmered in the elder's eyes. She wiped them away, gave Val a glowing look of love, and then squeezed Griff's hand. "I was hopin' this would happen. From the moment I ever saw you two together, I knew."

"Knew what?" Val asked, tilting her head.

"Knew that you were right for one another." Gus waved her hand. "Oh, I knew it could take you two some time to figure it out, but eventually, I felt you would."

Griff felt relief. He passed the bowl of scrambled eggs to Gus. "You knew all along?"

Gus spooned some eggs onto her plate. "Yep, I surely did!" She eyed them fiercely and said, "I was beside myself! When I met my husband, I knew the instant I laid eyes on him, he was the right man for me. You two sure took your sweet time. I just had to be patient and wait until you two figured it out."

Sipping his coffee, Griff felt giddy. The warmth at the table, the joy in the women's eyes, served only to make him happier. Setting the cup down, he said, "Then, we want you to know that we'd like to get wed near Christmas time. I'd like my brother, Slade, to be my best man."

"And I hope Jordana will be my matron of honor," Val added. "And more than anything, I want you to give me away, Gus. We

490

want this to be a family affair. What do you think?" Val saw her grandmother's face go tender and her eyes fill with tears. Reaching out, she touched her small shoulder. For as tough and strong as Gus had been all her life, in this moment she was like putty. Gus nodded, sniffed and wiped her eyes.

"It sounds perfect to me. But I warn you, the whole town will show up!" She shook her finger at them. "And if you're wise, you'll rent the armory in town because, trust me, half of the population will want to cheer you two on in marriage."

Griff grinned as he looked across the table at Val. Her cheeks were pink, flushed from the love they had made before rising to join Gus for breakfast. The gleam in Val's eyes, the love she had for him, made him feel as if he could do anything in life with her at his side. "Okay, can we entrust the ceremony and details to you, Miss Gus?"

"Really? You'd like me to handle that?" Gus asked, surprised by the offer.

"Why not?" Val said. "Griff and I have a *lot* to finish out here at the ranch before the snow starts flying by mid-September. We need someone like you, Gus. We trust you and know you'll make great choices."

Gus beamed. "I won't let you down, honey." She patted Val's hand. She turned to Griff. "I'll make sure your wedding is one you'll never forget. I know the people who really want to be there to see you get hitched. It will be a beautiful ceremony."

"But," Griff cautioned gently, "there will be a budget."

Gus gave an indulgent chuckle. "I'm good at budgets, not to worry."

They all shared a laugh. If it hadn't been for Gus and her budgeting and business savvy, the Bar H would no longer exist. And for the first time, Val was glad it did. This was her home. This was where her family was. The teasing between Gus and the man she was going to marry made her heart swell. Val knew her grandmother loved Griff. Not only that, Gus respected him because he was a hard worker, a man of his word and he was a Wyoming wrangler. Gus had admiration in her gaze as she smiled over at Griff. It was important to Val that Gus like the man she fell in love with. Clearly, she did. And now, Griff had a grandmother and Val knew how important getting his family back together was to him. Despite all the ups and downs, their love had taken root and grown. There would be hard, tough days ahead, but Val knew Griff had Wyoming grit and would see it through with her. They were a team. And they would love one another — forever.